BRIDAL
Blessings

BRIDAL
Blessings

Two Historical Romances of
Challenging the Barriers to Love

TRACIE PETERSON

BARBOUR
PUBLISHING

© 1997 *Logan's Lady* by Barbour Publishing, Inc.
© 1997 *My Valentine* by Tracie Peterson

Print ISBN 978-1-61626-955-5

eBook Editions:
Adobe Digital Edition (.epub) 978-1-62029-420-8
Kindle and MobiPocket Edition (.prc) 978-1-62029-419-2

All scriptures quotations are taken from the King James Version of the Bible.

This book is a work of fiction. Names, characters, places, and incidents are either products of the author's imagination or used fictitiously. Any similarity to actual people, organizations, and/or events is purely coincidental.

Cover image: Image Source

Published by Barbour Publishing, Inc., P.O. Box 719, Uhrichsville, Ohio 44683, www.barbourbooks.com

Our mission is to publish and distribute inspirational products offering exceptional value and biblical encouragement to the masses.

ecpa Member of the
Evangelical Christian
Publishers Association

Printed in the United States of America.

LOGAN'S LADY

Dedication

To Rebecca Germany, one of my favorite editors.
Your friendship means a great deal to me and I
thank God upon my every remembrance of you.

Chapter 1

A melia grimaced as she heard her father and Sir Jeffery Chamberlain break into yet another discussion on the implementation of fertilizer to boost agricultural yields. *It was this dreadful country that did it,* she thought. *America! A country filled with barbaric men, ill-mannered women and positively rotten children.*

Shifting uncomfortably in the seat of their stage, Amelia wished fervently that if there were a God, He would reach down and smite the lot of them in order that she might be allowed to return home to England. But of course that wasn't going to happen because Amelia had firmly decided for herself that there was no God.

"I say, Chamberlain," her father stated with a marginal note of enthusiasm. "I believe we're slowing down."

"Yes, quite right," the younger man responded and peered out the window. "We've made an excellent way thanks to our time spent on the railroad. American railroads are quite the thing. Good money here, what?"

"Indeed, the stage coaches are just as abominable as those back home, but I believe their railway system to be quite superior," came the reply and the conversation erupted into a spirited discussion of the American rail system. Amelia sighed, adjusted her lace collar and waited for the announcement that they had arrived in some small, forsaken Colorado town.

She hadn't wanted to come on this trip to America. America had been the furthest thing from her mind, in fact, but her father was insistent and clearly closed the matter to discussion. Amelia's sisters Penelope and Margaret were just as loath to travel, but they were quite interested in Sir Jeffery Chamberlain.

Amelia held a small wish that she could share their enthusiasm. After all, he was to become her husband. At least that was the plan as her father saw it, but Amelia had no intention of marrying the pompous man. Jeffery Chamberlain was a long-time crony of her father's. He wasted his days doing as little as possible, furthering his already-sound reputation of being a spoiled dandy. He had been knighted, but only because his mother held a tender place in the queen's heart. And he owned vast estates with wondrous woods that beckoned the visitor to take a turn about, but those were his only redeeming qualities as far as Amelia was concerned.

Her father viewed him in a different light, however. Sir Jeffery Chamberlain was rich and popular with Queen Victoria's court. He had a sound education and a quick wit that had managed to keep him out of trouble on more than one occasion, and he was worth an enormous sum of money, which not only could keep his own lands well-kept but also would surely flow over to his future father-in-law, Lord Reginald Amhurst, the sixth earl of Donneswick—should that need arise.

Staring hard at the man, Amelia noted all of his flaws. His nose was too long, his forehead too shiny. He had perfect white teeth, which seemed to be constantly bared for all the world behind unflattering smiles and his beady eyes were placed too close together. Added to this, the man was an unmitigated bore.

Amelia shook her head uncomfortably and tried against the rocking and bouncing of the stage to look at the magazine she'd bought in Cheyenne. Flipping through pages of ladies' fashions, Amelia tried to rationalize her thoughts. *I cannot blame Father for setting out to arrange a marriage. It is done all the time in my circle of friends. Why, I don't even remember the last time one of my companions managed to marry for love, and not because the union was of financial benefit to one family or the other.* Some of her friends had grown to genuinely love their intended mates. Others had not. Her dear friend and confidant, Sarah Greene, had managed to find herself engaged to a charming man of wit and gentlemanly breeding and had quickly lost her heart. But that was not to be the case for Amelia. She could not find it in her heart to love Sir Jeffery, as he insisted they call him, nor did she think love would grow there for this man.

Amidst a roar of "whoa's" and a cloud of dust, Amelia realized that they had come to a stop. Ignoring her father's window description of the town, Amelia tucked the magazine into her bag. Immediately Penelope and Margaret began fussing and going on about the wilds of America.

"I suppose we might very well be scalped by Indians," Penelope said with a fearful expression. She allowed Sir Jeffery to assist her from the stage before adding, "We're so very glad to have your company, Sir Jeffery." She oozed congeniality and interlaced her arm with his. At seventeen she was more than a little bit aware of the power a young woman's simpering could have over the male gender.

"It is my pleasure, Miss Penelope," he assured her.

Margaret, a year Penelope's junior, secured her place on the opposite arm of Sir Jeffery as soon as her father had helped her from the stage. "Yes, it would be quite frightful to have come all this way into the heart of the American wilderness with only Father and Mattersley to offer protection. Why, whatever would three women and two old men do should the heathens truly choose to attack us?" Mattersley, the other *old man* she referred to, was the earl's manservant and constant companion.

Amelia watched all this through the open door of the stage. She rolled her eyes and sighed. *Indeed, what would Sir Jeffery, pompous dandy that he was, do in such a situation? Bore the poor Indians to death with questions of what fertilizer they were using on the Colorado plains?* She couldn't abide the simpering of her sisters and chose instead to remain in her seat on the stage until her father beckoned her forward.

"Amelia, allow me to help you down. Why, you've scarcely said two words since we left Cheyenne. You aren't ill, are you? Taken with vapors, what?"

Amelia's pale-blue eyes met those of her father's. "No, Father, I'm not at all indisposed. I simply have had my mind consumed with a variety of subjects."

Sir Jeffery untangled himself from Amelia's sisters and came to offer his hand. "May I accompany you to the hotel, Lady Amhurst?" he questioned with a slight bow. Amelia noticed her father's frown as if he could read the curt reply she was thinking. Containing her thoughts with absolute ladylike control, she nodded. "Of course. Thank you," she murmured, putting her gloved fingers into Jeffery's palm.

"I have arranged for us to have rooms at a boarding house here in Greeley," the earl began. "It's a temperance colony so there will be no wine with dinner, nor any after-dinner brandy, I'm afraid." Amelia, knowing her father's distaste for alcohol, realized that he said the latter for Jeffery's sake.

"Ah, the barbarians." Jeffery sighed and Amelia knew he meant it. To Jeffery, any measure of discomfort represented a less-than-acceptable social standing. And for Jeffery to be without his brandy was definitely a discomfort.

For a reason beyond her understanding, Amelia was put out at Jeffery's attitude. Not because of the alcohol—although she herself couldn't abide the stuff—no, it was more than simple issues of food and drink. Jeffery's entire demeanor put her at odds. Maybe it was just that she wanted to conflict with his ideals. Maybe it was the fact that she was completely disgusted with his companionship and still hadn't been able to get it across to either her father or Jeffrey that she had no desire to marry.

Glancing upward, Amelia instantly felt the noon sun bear down on her. Grimacing, she opened her white parasol and lifted it overhead to ward off the harsh rays.

"Oh, Father," Penelope began to whine, "it's ever so hot here. Must we stand about as though we were hired help?" She looked for all the world as though she might faint dead away at any moment.

They were all quite used to Penelope and Margaret's displays of weakness, and for several moments no one said anything. Finally the earl motioned for his loyal valet, Mattersley, and gave him several coins. "See if you can't arrange for our things to be brought up." The man, close in age to his employer, gave a regal bow and set out on his mission. "There," the earl said, turning to the party, "I'd say that settled itself rather nicely. Let's make our way up, what?"

"Indeed," Jeffrey answered as though his were the only opinion to be had. "This harsh American sun is quite hard on fair English skin." He said the words looking at Amelia, but she had the distinct impression they were given more in consideration of his own situation than of hers.

The dry, dusty streets of Greeley did nothing to encourage the entourage. The boarding house was a far cry from the regal estate they'd left behind in England. It wasn't even as nice as the furnishings they'd acquired in New York City or Chicago. In fact, Amelia knew it was by far the worst accommodations they'd know yet, and her opinion of America slipped even lower. Why, even when they'd toured India, they'd resided on lovely estates.

From the moment they walked into the questionable place, arguments ensued and miseries were heightened. The owners of the atrocious little house actually expected Amelia and her sisters to share one bed. The very thought of it caused Penelope to cry and Margaret to fan herself feverishly as though she might actually faint from the very suggestion.

"I believe we'd arranged to have all five of your rooms," the earl protested, combating a roving horde of black flies.

"Kain't hep it a bit, mister," the slovenly dressed proprietor announced. "I hed a man come in last night what needed a place to stay."

"This is Reginald Amhurst, the sixth earl of Donneswick," Chamberlain interjected angrily. "Lord Amhurst, to you."

The proprietor looked over the rim of his dirty spectacles. "Ferenors, eh? We gets 'em all kinds here. You sound to be them thar British gents. I guess the missus said you was comin'."

Amelia grew tired with the exchange and glanced around the room to where a crude painting hung at the base of the stairs. She studied it intently, wishing she could forget the heat. The picture fascinated her from afar, as it seemed to almost move with life. Stepping closer, Amelia found it half covered with pesky black flies. It was only then that she really noticed most everything suffered from such a fate.

"Excuse me," a stranger's voice sounded over her head. "This isn't an art gallery. Besides, I don't think old Farley's painting is all that interesting."

Amelia was so lost in thought that she hadn't realized she was blocking the stairway. She looked up with a surprised expression and found herself noticing the broad, muscular frame that accompanied the voice. The mustached mouth seemed to twitch a bit as though it might break into a laugh.

Without so much as a smile, Amelia backed away. "My pardon, sir." Her voice was haughty and her look froze the man in his place. She still found it disconcerting to be openly addressed by men without a proper introduction. Childhood teachings were hard to lay aside, even for a holiday to America.

With a grin, he gave a broad sweep. "You are quite pardoned, ma'am."

Amelia raised her handkerchief and turned away to keep from muttering something most unladylike. *Rude. That's what all Americans are.*

"Hey thar, Logan," the boarding house proprietor called as the man passed to the front door.

"Afternoon, Ted."

Amelia tried to watch the scene without letting the man called Logan see she was at all interested in the conversation.

"Logan, didn't ya tell me you was gonna be leadin' a group of ferenors up the mountains?"

"I did."

"Well, I think this here party be yer folks."

Logan eyed the group suspiciously as though he'd just been told that they were responsible for having robbed the local bank.

"You're Earl Donneswick?" Logan questioned Amelia's father.

"I am, indeed," Lord Amhurst replied, before Jeffery could speak. Amelia turned to watch the introduction. "This is Sir Jeffery Chamberlain, my man Mattersley, and my daughters."

Logan let his gaze travel around the room to each of the women before settling on Amelia. He smiled slightly when his blatant stare caused her to blush, then turned his attention to the matter at hand.

"I'm Logan Reed, your guide to Estes Park."

"Mr. Reed, we are quite anxious to be started on our journey. Can you advise us as to when we might expect to begin? The heat is positively wilting our ladies." Jeffery commented before the earl could do the same.

Logan looked again at the women. "Are you proposing to take your womenfolk along?"

"Indeed we are," the earl replied.

Amelia watched as Logan cast a skeptical glace at her. "There are places where we'll scarcely have a trail to follow. Packing into the Rockies isn't a Sunday school picnic."

"My daughters have climbed in the Alps, my good man. I assure you they are quite up to the challenge."

Logan's smile broadened. "If you say so. I just wouldn't want the ladies to get hurt." His gaze returned to Amelia, who stuck her chin in the air defiantly and turned toward the fly-covered window.

"Lady Amhurst and her sisters are quite capable," Jeffery interjected irritably.

"Lady Amhurst? I thought you said your name was Donneswick."

The earl smiled tolerantly. "I am Reginald Amhurst, the sixth earl of Donneswick, I am called Lord Amhurst, but it is common when I travel abroad to have my title mistaken for my name. My daughters, of course, are called by the family name of Amhurst. A bit confusing for you Yanks, but nevertheless, easy enough to remember."

"With that matter resolved," Chamberlain stated in a cool, even voice, "when can we expect to begin? You surely can't expect us to remain in this poor excuse for a town for much longer."

"Whoa, now. Just hold on for a minute," Logan said raising his hand. Amelia glanced back over her shoulder, fascinated in spite of herself at the way Logan Reed seemed to naturally take charge. "We've got some ground rules to cover first and I don't think standing around the front door of Ted's is the place for it. Ted, can we use the dining room?"

"Sure enuf, Logan. Ya go right ahead." Ted seemed to be happy to rid himself of the commotion. "Ya want I should have the missus bring somethin' to drink?"

He addressed Logan, but it was Lord Amhurst who answered. "Yes, please have tea and cakes sent 'round."

Ted stared at the man for a moment, then turned to Logan. "It's okay, Ted. Why don't you bring whatever's at hand." This the man understood and nodded agreement before taking himself off to the kitchen.

The party stared collectively at Logan, barely tolerating his breach of etiquette, but Amelia was certain that for Mr. Logan Reed, breaching etiquette was probably a daily routine.

"Come on this way," Logan ordered and led the way without even waiting to hear an approval from the earl or Jeffrey. The entourage followed, murmuring among themselves as to the character and manners of the tall man.

"Everybody might as well sit down," Logan said, giving his well-worn hat a toss to the sideboard.

Amelia watched in complete amazement. At home, in England, her father would never have been addressed in such a manner. At home he commanded respect and held a position of complete authority. Here in America, however, he was just a man and it didn't matter in the least that he was titled.

While Amelia stood in motionless study, Logan pulled out a chair and offered it to her. Her blue eyes met the rich warmth of his green ones. She studied his face for a moment longer, noting the trimmed mustache and square, but newly shaven jaw.

"Thank you," she murmured and slipped into her chair without taking her gaze from his face.

"Now, we need to discuss this matter in some detail," Logan announced. He stood at the head of the table looking as though he were some famed orator about to impart great knowledge up on the masses.

"Mr. Reed," Amelia's father interrupted. "I have an understanding with the owner of several cabins in the Estes Park valley. He assured me that he would send a guide to bring our party to Estes. Furthermore, there is to be another family accompanying us: Lord and Lady Gambett and their two daughters."

Logan nodded. "I know about the Gambetts and was headed up to speak to them when you arrived. According to Ted, they're staying on the other end of town at Widow Compton's place. I suppose they're planning to bring their womenfolk along as well?"

"Indeed, they are. What, may I ask, is the difficulty here?"

Logan ran a hand through his brown hair and sighed. "The problem is this: I wasn't expecting to have to pack women into the mountains. No one mentioned women at all, in fact. I was told I'd be taking a hunting party to Estes. A hunting party seemed to lend itself to the idea of men."

Amelia suppressed a laugh and received the stunned glances of her traveling companions.

"You have something to say here, Miss. . ." Logan paused as if trying to remember which name she was to be addressed by.

"I am Lady Amhurst. Lady Amelia Amhurst. And while we're to discuss this trip, then yes, I suppose I do have a few things to say. She ignored the frown on her father's face and the "darling, please be silent" glare of Jeffery. "In England, women quite often ride to the hunt. We enjoy sporting as much as our menfolk. Furthermore, I assure you, we are quite capable of handling a gun, a mount, and any other hardship that might present itself on the trip."

"I'm glad to hear that you are so capable, Lady Amhurst. You won't be offended then when I state my rules. We will begin at sunrise. That doesn't mean we'll get up at sunrise, have a leisurely tea, and be on the road by nine. It means things packed, on your horse, ready to ride at sunrise. We'll head into Longmont first, which will give you a last chance at a night's rest in bed before a week of sleeping on the ground. If you're short on supplies you can pick them up there."

No one said a word and even Amelia decided against protesting, at least until she'd heard the full speech.

Logan continued. "It gets cold at night. We'll eventually be 7,000 feet up and the air will be thinner. Every morning you'll find hoarfrost on the ground so staying dry and warm will be your biggest priority. Each of you will pack at least three blankets and a canteen. Again, if you don't have them, pick them up here in Greeley or get them in Longmont. If you don't have them, you don't go. Also, there will be no sidesaddles available. You women will be required to ride astride, so dress accordingly. Oh, and everyone wears a good, sturdy pair of boots. This is important both for riding and for walking if your horse should go lame."

"Mr. Reed!" Lord Amhurst began to protest. "You cannot expect my daughters to ride astride these American horses. First of all it is most unacceptable and second, it—"

"If they don't ride astride, they don't go," Logan replied flatly. "Having them riding sidesaddle is more danger than I'm willing to take on. If you want them to come out of this alive, they need to have every possible chance at staying that way."

"Perhaps, Amhurst," Jeffery addressed him less formally, "we could arrange to employ another guide."

Logan laughed and crossed his arms against his chest. "I challenge you to find one. I'm one of only two in the area who will even bother with you people."

"And what, pray tell, is that supposed to mean?" Amelia interjected.

Logan met her eyes. "It means, I resent European tourists and rich socialites who come to take the air in my mountains. They don't care for the real beauty at hand and they never stay longer than it takes to abuse what they will before going off to boast of their conquests. I made a promise, however, to pack you folds into Estes, but you," he pointed a finger at each of the women, "are completely unsuited for the challenge. There are far too many things to consider when it comes to women. Your physical constitution is weaker, not to mention that by nature being a woman lends itself to certain other types of physical complications and private needs."

"See here! You have no right to talk that way in front of these ladies," Chamberlain protested.

"That is exactly the kind of coddling I'm talking about. It has no place on a mountain ridge. I am not trying to make this unpleasant, but we must establish some rules here in order to keep you folks from dying on the way." Logan's voice lowered to a near whisper. "I won't have their blood on my hands, just because they are too proud and arrogant to take direction from someone who's had more experience." He said "they," but his steely gaze was firmly fixed on Amelia.

"What other rules would you have us abide by, Mr. Reed?" the earl finally asked.

"No alcohol of any kind. No shooting animals on the way to Estes. No stopping for tea four times a day and no special treatment of anyone in the party. If you can't cut it, you go back." Logan took a deep breath. "Finally, my word is law. I know this land and what it's capable of. When I tell you that something needs to be done a certain way, I expect it to be done without question. Even if it pertains to something that shocks your genteel constitutions. I'm not a hard man to get along with," he said pausing again, "but I find the institutions of nobility a bit trying. If I should call you by something other than by your privileged titles, I'll expect you to overlook it. During a rock slide it could be difficult to remember if I'm to address you by earl, lady, or your majesty. My main objective is to get your party to Estes in as close to one piece as possible. That's all."

"I suppose we can live with these rules of yours," Lord Amhurst replied. "Ladies, can you manage?" Penelope and Margaret looked to Amelia and back to their father before nodding their heads.

"Well, Amelia?" her father questioned and all eyes turned to her.

Facing Logan with a confident glare, she replied, "I can certainly meet any challenge that Mr. Reed is capable of delivering."

Logan laughed. "Well, I'm capable of delivering quite a bit, believe me."

Chapter 2

Amelia spent the remainder of the afternoon listening to her sisters alternate between their praises of Sir Jeffery and their concerns about the trip.

"You are such a bore, Amelia," Penelope said with little concern for the harshness of her tone. "Why, Jeffery has simply devoted himself to you on this trip and you've done nothing but act as though you could not care less."

"I *couldn't* care less," Amelia assured her sister.

"But the man is to be your husband. Father arranged this entire trip just to bring you two closer. I think it was rather sporting of Jeffery to endure the open way you stared at that Reed fellow."

Amelia gasped. "I did not stare at Mr. Reed!"

"You did," Margaret confirmed. "I saw you."

Amelia shook her head. "I can't be bothered with you two twittering ninnies. Besides, I never said I approved of Father's arrangement for Sir Jeffery to become my husband. I have no intentions of getting closer to the man and certainly none of marrying him."

"I think Sir Jeffery is wonderful. You're just being mean and spiteful," Penelope stated with a stamp of her foot. A little cloud of dust rose from the floor along with several flies.

"If you think he's so wonderful, Penelope, why don't you marry him?" Amelia snapped. The heat was making her grumpy and her sister's interrogation was making her angry.

"I'd love to marry him," Margaret said in a daft and dreamy way that Amelia thought epitomized the typical addle-brained girl.

"I shall speak to Father about it immediately," Amelia said sarcastically. "Perhaps he will see the sense in it." *If only he would.*

Margaret stared after her with open mouth, while Penelope took the whole thing with an air of indifference. "You know it doesn't matter what you want, Amelia. Father must marry you off before you turn twenty-one this autumn, or lose mother's money. Her fortune means a great deal to him. Surely you wouldn't begrudge your own father his mainstay."

Amelia looked at her younger sisters for a moment. As fair-haired as she, yet more finely featured and petite, Amelia had no doubt that they saw her as some sort of ogre who though only of herself. Their mother's fortune, a trust set in place by their grandmother, was specifically held for the purpose that none of her daughters need feel pressured to marry for money. The money would, in fact, pass to each daughter on her twenty-first birthday, if she were still unmarried. If the girls married before that time, the money reverted to the family coffers and could be used by their father, for the benefit of all he saw fit. Amelia knew it was this that drove her father forward to see her married to Sir Jeffery.

"I have no desire for Father to concern himself with his financial well-being. However, there are things that matter deeply to me, and Jeffery Chamberlain is not one of them." With that Amelia left the room, taking up her parasol. By the time she'd reached the bottom step she'd decided that a walk to consider the rest of Greeley was in order.

Parasol high, Amelia passed from the house in a soft, almost-silent swishing of her pale-pink afternoon dress. She was nearly to the corner of the boarding house when she caught the sound of voices and immediately recognized one of them to be Logan Reed's.

"You sure asked for it this time, Logan. Hauling those prissy misses all the way over the mountain to Estes ain't gonna be an easy ride," an unidentified man was stating.

"No, it won't," Logan said, sounding very disturbed. "Women are always trouble. I guess next time Evans sends me over, I'll be sure and ask who all is supposed to come back with me."

"It might save you some grief at that. Still," the man said with a pause, "they sure are purty girls. They look as fine as old Bart's spittoon after a Sunday shining."

Amelia paled at the comparison, while Logan laughed. How she wished she could face him and tell him just what she thought of Americans and their spittoons. It seemed every man in this wretched country had taken up that particularly nasty habit of chewing and spitting. *No doubt Mr. Reed will be no exception.*

"I don't think I'd compliment any of them in exactly those words, Ross. These are refined British women." Amelia straightened her shoulders a bit and thought perhaps she'd misjudged Logan Reed. Logan's next few words, however, completely destroyed any further doubt. "They are the most uppity creatures God ever put on the face of the earth. They have a queen for a monarch and it makes them feel mighty important."

Amelia seethed. *How dare he even mention the queen. He isn't fit to...* The though faded as Logan continued.

"The Brits are the hardest of all to work with. The Swedes come and they're just a bunch of land-loving, life-loving primitives. The Germans are much the same and always bring a lot of life to a party. But the Brits think everything goes from their mouth to God's ear. They are rude and insensitive to other people and expect to stop on a ledge two feet wide, or any other dangerous or unseemly place, if it dares to be time for tea. In fact, I'd wager good money that before I even get this party packed halfway through the foothills, one of those 'purty' women, as you call them, will expect to have tea and biscuits on a silver tray."

At this, Amelia could take no more. She whipped around the corner in a fury. Angered beyond reason and filled with rage, she took her stand. "How dare you insult my family and friends in such a manner. I have never been so enraged in all of my twenty years!" She barely paused to take a breath. "I have traveled all across Europe and India and never in my life have I met more rude and insensitive people than here in America. If you want to see difficulty and stubbornness, Mr. Reed, I'm certain you have no further to go than the mirror in your room." At this she stormed off, feeling quite vindicated.

⟨⟩

Logan stared after her with a mocking grin on his lips. He'd known full well she was eavesdropping and intended to take her to task for it quite solidly. The man beside him, uncomfortable with the display of temper, quickly excused himself and ran with long strides toward the busier part of town. When Logan began to chuckle out loud, Amelia turned back indignantly.

"Whatever are you snickering about?" Amelia questioned, her cheeks flushed from the sun and the encounter. Apparently remembering her parasol, she raised it to shield her skin.

"I'm amused," Logan said in a snooty tone, mocking her.

"I see nothing at all funny here. You have insulted good people, Mr. Reed. Gentlefolk, from the lineage of nobility, with more grace and manners than you could ever hope to attain. People, I might add, who are paying you a handsome wage to do a job."

She was breathing heavily. Beads of perspiration were forming on her brow. Her blue eyes were framed by long blond lashes that curled away from her eyes like rays of sunshine through a storm cloud. She reminded Logan of a china doll with her bulk of blond hair piled high on her head, complete with fashionable hat. Logan thought he'd never seen a more beautiful woman, but he still desired to put her into her place once and for all.

"And does your family consider eavesdropping to be one of those gracious manners of which you speak so highly?" he questioned, taking long easy strides to where she stood. Amelia recoiled as though she had been slapped.

"I see you find my words disconcerting," Logan said, his face now serious. Amelia, speechless, only returned his blatant stare. "People with manners, Miss," he paused, then shook his head. "No, make that Lady Amhurst. Anyway, people of true refinement have no need to advertise it or crow it from the rooftops. They show it in action. And they need not make others feel less important by using flashy titles and snobbery. I don't believe eavesdropping would be considered a substantial way to prove one's merit in any society."

Amelia found her tongue at last. "I never intended to eavesdrop, Mr. Reed," she said emphasizing the title. "I was simply taking in a bit of air, a very little bit I might add. Is it my fault that your voice carries above the sounds of normal activity?"

Logan laughed. "I could excuse a simple wandering-in, but you stood there a full five minutes before making your presence known. I said what I said knowing full well you were there. I wanted to see just how much you would take before jumping me."

Amelia's expression tightened. "You couldn't possibly have known I was there. I had just come from the front of the house and I was making no noise."

Logan's amusement was obviously stated in his eyes. He stepped back to the house, pulling Amelia with him. Leaving Amelia to stand in stunned silence at his bold touch, he went around the corner. "What do you see, Lady Amhurst?"

Amelia looked to the corner of the house. "I see nothing. Whatever are you talking about?"

"Look again. You're going to have to have a sharper sense of the obvious if you're to survive in the wilds of Colorado."

From around the corner Logan waited a long moment before deciding he wasn't being quite fair. He reached up and adjusted his hat, hoping his shadow's movement on the ground would catch her eye.

"Very well, Mr. Reed." Amelia sounded humbled. "I see your point, but it could have just as easily been one of my sisters. You couldn't possibly have known it was me and not one of them."

Logan looked around the corner with a self-satisfied expression on his face. "You're a little more robust, shall we say; than your sisters." His gaze trailed the length of her body before coming again to rest on her face.

Amelia turned scarlet and for a moment Logan wondered if she might give him a good whack with the parasol she was twisting in her hands. She did nothing, said nothing, but returned his stare with such umbrage that Logan was very nearly taken aback.

"Good day, Mr. Reed. I no longer wish to listen to anything you have to say," Amelia said and turned to leave, but Logan reached out to halt her.

She fixed him with a stony stare that would have crumbled a less stalwart foe.

"Unhand me, sir!"

"You sure run hot and cold, lady." Logan's voice was husky and his eyes were narrowed ever so slightly. "But either way, one thing you'd better learn quickly—and I'm not saying this to put you off again," he said, pausing to tighten his grip in open defiance of her demand, "listening to me may very well save your life."

"When you say something that seems life-saving," she murmured, "I will listen with the utmost regard." She pulled her arm away and gathered her skirts in hand. "Good day, Mr. Reed."

Logan watched her walk away in her facade of fire and ice. She was unlike any women he'd ever met in his life—and he'd certainly met many a fine lady in his day. She was strong and self-assured and Logan knew that if the entire party perished in the face of their mountain challenge, Amelia would survive and probably thrive.

He liked her, he decided. He liked her a great deal. For all her snooty ways and uppity suggestions, she was growing more interesting by the minute and Logan intended to take advantage of the long summer months to come in which he'd be a part of her Estes Park stay.

Logan stood in a kind of stupor for a few more minutes, until the voice of Lord Amhurst sounded from behind him.

"Mr. Reed," he began, "I should like to inquire as to our accommodations. The proprietor here tells me that you have taken one of the rooms intended for our use. I would like to have it back."

"Sorry," Logan said without feeling the least bit apologetic. "I'm gonna need a good night's rest if I'm to lead you all to Longmont. It isn't anything personal and I'm sorry Ted parceled out your evening comforts, but I need the room."

The earl looked taken back for a moment, apparently unaccustomed to his requests being refused, but nodded as he acquiesced to the circumstances.

Logan took off before the man could say another word. He could have given up the room easily, but his pride made him rigid. "Oh Lord," he whispered, "I should have been kinder. When I settle down a bit, I'll go back to the earl of Donneswick and give him the room." Logan rounded the corner of the house and found Penelope, Margaret, and Chamberlain sitting beneath the community shade tree. It was the only shade tree on this side of town. He couldn't help but wonder where Amelia had gone, then chided himself for even thinking of her. There'd be time enough on the trip, not to mention when they reached Estes, to learn more about her. He could take his time, he reasoned, remembering that Evans had told him the party would stay until first snow.

Whistling a tune, Logan made his way past Amelia's simpering sisters, tipped his had ever so slightly, and headed for the livery. Lady Amelia Amhurst, he thought with a sudden revelation. "There's no reason she can't be my lady," Logan stated aloud to no one in particular. "No reason at all."

Chapter 3

The following day brought the hunting party together. Lord and Lady Gambett arrived with their whiny daughters, Henrietta and Josephine. Both of the girls were long-time companions of Penelope and Margaret, and their reunion was one of excited giggles and squeals of delight. Amelia stood beneath the shade of the community tree and waited for the party to move out to Longmont. She studied the landscape around her and decided she was very glad not to live in this dusty community of flies and harsh prairie winds. To the west she noted the Rocky Mountains and though they were beautiful, she would have happily passed up the chance to further explore them—if her father would have given her the option to return home.

Lady Gambett fussed over her daughters like a mother hen, voicing her concern quite loudly that they should have to wear such a monstrous apparatus as what the store clerk had called a "lady's mountain dress." The outfit appeared for all intents and purposes to be no different from any other riding habit. A long serviceable skirt of blue serge fell to the boot tops of each young lady, while underneath, a fuller, billowing version of a petticoat allowed the freedom to ride astride.

Amelia knew her own attire to be quite comfortable and didn't really mind the idea of trading in her dainty sidesaddle for the fuller and more masculine McClellan cavalry saddle. She'd heard Lady Bird speak of these at one of her lectures on the Rockies and just remembering the older woman made Amelia smile. Lady Isabella Bird was a remarkable woman. Traveling all over the world to the wildest reaches was nothing to this adventuresome lady. She had come to the Rockies only two years earlier on her way back from the Sandwich Islands. By sheer grit and force of will, Lady Bird had placed herself in the hands of strangers and eventually into the hands of no one at all when she took a rugged Indian pony and traveled throughout the Rocky Mountains all alone. Amelia admired that kind of gumption. She'd never dreamed of doing something so incredible herself, but she thought Lady Bird's accounts of the solitude sounded refreshing. Watching the stars fade into the dawn, Amelia wondered to herself what it might be like to lay out on a mountain top, under the stars and trees, with no other human being around for miles and miles.

"You look pretty tolerable when you smile like that," Logan's voice sounded in her ear.

Startled, Amelia instantly drew back and lost the joy of her self-reflection. "Haven't you better things to do, Mr. Reed? As I recall, we were to be on our way by now. What seems to be keeping us?"

Logan smiled. "Loose shoe on one of the horses. Should have it fixed in a quick minute."

Amelia hoped this would end their conversation, but it didn't.

"You gonna ride in that?" Logan asked seriously, pointing to her wind-blown navy-blue skirt, which blew just high enough to reveal matching bloomers beneath.

Amelia felt her face grown hot. "I assure you I will be quite able to ride. This outfit is especially designed to allow a woman to ride astride. Just as you demanded."

"Good. I don't want any of you dainty ladies to be pitched over the side."

Amelia jutted her chin out defiantly and said nothing. Logan Reed was clearly the most incorrigible man she'd ever met in her life and she wasn't about to let him get the best of her.

"Logan!" A man hollered and waved from where the others were gathered. "Horse is ready."

"Well, Lady Amhurst, I believe we are about to get underway," Logan said with a low sweeping bow.

⁂

Amelia was hot and dirty and very unhappy when the party at last rode into Longmont, Colorado. The day had not been a pleasant one for Amelia. Her sisters had squabbled almost half the way about who was going to wear the blue-veiled straw riding bonnet. Penelope had latched on to it in Greeley, but Margaret had soon learned the benefits of her sister's veil and insisted she trade her. Margaret had protested that as the youngest, at sixteen, she was also the more delicate of the trio. Josephine, Margaret's bosom companion, heartily agreed. Pushing up tiny round spectacles, Josephine was only coming to realize the protection her glasses offered from the dust. While the others were delicately blotting their eyes with lace handkerchiefs, Josephine's eyes had remained a little more sheltered.

This argument over the bonnet, along with Logan's sneering grins and her father's constant manipulation to see her and Jeffery riding together, made Amelia want to run screaming in the direction of the nearest railroad station. But of course, convention denied her the possibility of such display.

Glancing around at the small town of Longmont, Amelia was amused to see the townsfolk apparently could not even decide on the town's spelling. Some signs read *Longmount,* while others gave the title *Longmont.* The name St. Vrain seemed to be quite popular. There was the St. Vrain Café, the St. Vrain Saloon, and the St. Vrain Hotel, which looked to her to be an oasis in the desert. Brilliantly white against the sun's light, the two story hotel beckoned the weary travelers forward and Amelia couldn't wait to sink into a hot bath.

Upon alighting from her horse, it was instantly apparent that Longmont suffered the same plague of black flies that had held Greeley under siege. The flies instantly clung to her riding habit and bonnet, leaving Amelia felling as though her skin were crawling. The Gambett girls and her sisters were already whining about the intolerable conditions and although Amelia whole-heartedly agreed with their analysis that this town was completely forgotten by any kind of superior being, she refused to raise her voice in complaint.

"I assure you ladies," Logan said with a hint of amusement in his tired voice, "this place is neither forsaken by God, nor condemned. The people here are friendly and helpful, if you treat them with respect. There's a well-stocked hardware store down Main Street, and if you ladies wish to purchase another veiled bonnet, you can try the mercantile just over there."

The words were meant to embarrass her sisters, but as far as Amelia could tell, neither Penelope nor Margaret were aware of Logan's intent.

"Remember, this is one of those trips where you'll have to do for yourself," Logan said, motioning to the pack mules. "You might just as well get used to the fact here and now. No one is going to care for you, or handle your things, but you. You'll be responsible for your bags and any personal items you choose to bring on this trip. Although, for the sake of your horses, the mules, and even yourselves, I suggest you greatly limit what you bring along."

Jeffery immediately appeared at Amelia's side. "Never fear, Lady Amhurst, I am your faithful servant. You find a comfortable place to rest and I will retrieve your things."

Amelia watched Logan's lips curl into a self-satisfied smile. Obviously he had pegged her for one of those who would choose to be waited on hand and foot. What further irritated her was that if Logan had not been there, she would have taken Chamberlain up on his offer.

"Never mind that," she said firmly. "I can manage, just as Mr. Reed has made clear I must." She pulled down her bedroll and bags without another glance at Logan.

"Surely there is no reason you cannot accept my help," Jeffery spoke from her side. He reached out to take hold of her bedroll. "I mean to say, you are a gentlewoman—a lady. It is hardly something Mr. Reed would understand, but certainly it does not escape my breeding to intercede on your behalf."

Amelia wearied of his nonsensical speech. She glared up at Jeffery harshly and pulled her bags away from his hands. "I am of sturdy stock, I assure you. I have climbed in the Alps without assistance from you." She couldn't help remembering the bevy of servants who had assisted her. "I have also barged the Nile, lived through an Indian monsoon, and endured the tedium of life at court. I surely can carry baggage into a hotel for myself." The chin went a notch higher in the air and Amelia fixed her gaze on Logan's amused expression. "Perhaps Mr. Reed needs assistance with *his* things."

Jeffery looked from Amelia's stern expression to Logan's near-laughing one. Appearing confused, he neither offered his assistance to Logan, nor did he protest when Amelia went off in the direction of the hotel, bags in hand.

The St. Vrain Hotel was no cooler inside than it had been outside. If anything it was even more stifling because there was no breeze and the flies were thicker here than in the streets. She turned at the front desk to await her father and struggled to contain a smile when he and Mattersley appeared, each with his own bags, and her sisters struggling dramatically behind them.

"Oh, Papa," Margaret moaned loudly, "you simply cannot expect me to carry all of this!" The earl rolled his eyes, bringing a broad smile from Amelia. The clerk at the desk also seemed amused, but said nothing. Amelia was thankful Logan Reed was still outside with the horses.

Jeffery strode in, trying hard to look completely at ease with his new task. He put his things down in one corner and announced he would go with Mr. Reed to stable the horses. Amelia was stunned by this. So far as she knew, Jeffery had done nothing more than had his horse over for stabling since his privileged childhood. How she would love to watch him in the livery with Mr. Reed!

Amelia gave it no more thought, however, as the clerk led them upstairs to their rooms. She would share a room with her sisters again, but this time there were two beds. One was a rustic-looking, double-sized bed. It looked roughly hewn from pine, yet a colorful handmade quilt made it appear beautiful. The other, a single bed, looked to be even more crudely assembled. It, too, was covered with a multi-colored quilt, and to the exhausted Amelia, looked quite satisfactory. Other than the beds, the room was rather empty. There was a single night table with a bowl and pitcher of water and a tiny closet that was hardly big enough to hang a single dress within.

"Oh, such misery!" Penelope exclaimed and Margaret quickly agreed.

"How could Papa make us stay in a horrible place like this?" Margaret added.

"I think it will seem a great deal more appealing after you've spent two or three nights on the trail," Amelia said without asking her sisters' permission to take the single bed. She tossed her things to the floor and stretched out on top of the quilt, still dressed in her dusty clothes.

The bed isn't half bad, Amelia thought. *It beats being on the back of that temperamental mount Mr. Reed had insisted she ride.* Twice the beast had tried to take his own head and leave the processional, but Amelia, seasoned rider that she was, gave the gelding beneath her a firm understanding that she was to decide the way, not he. No doubt Mr. Reed had intentionally given her the spirited horse. *He probably hoped to find me sprawled out on the prairie ground,* she mused. *I guess I showed him that I can handle my own affairs.* It was the last conscious thought Amelia had for some time.

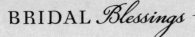

She had no idea how long she'd laid upon the bed. Her sisters had begun arguing about who would sleep on the right side of the bed and who would go to search out another veiled bonnet. The noise was something she was used to—it was the silence that seemed to awaken her. Staring at the ceiling for a moment, Amelia tried to remember where she was and what she was to do next. She had not time for further contemplation, however, when a knock sounded at her door.

"Yes?" she questioned, barely cracking the door open.

A young woman wearing a starched white apron stood before her bearing a towel and bar of soap. "We've a bath ready for you, Lady Amhurst."

No announcement could have met with her approval more. Amelia opened the door wide and grimaced at the stiffness that was already setting into her bones. It had been a while since she'd been riding, what with the boat ride to America and the constant use of trains and stages thereafter.

"Thank you. Will you direct me?"

The woman, hardly old enough to be called that, motioned Amelia to the room at the end of the hall. "I can get you settled in and take your clothes to have the dust beaten out. I'll bring you something else to wear if you tell me what you want."

Amelia stepped into the room and thought the steaming tub of water too good to be true. She immediately began unfastening the buttons of her half jacket. "You are very kind to arrange all of this for me. I must say the service here is quite good."

"Oh, it's my job," the girl replied. "'Sides, Logan told me you'd probably want to clean up and he gave me an extra coin to make sure you were taken care of personally."

Amelia's fingers ceased at their task. "I beg your pardon? Mr. Reed paid for this bath?"

"Yes, ma'am."

Amelia hesitated, looked at the tub and considered her pride in the matter. The steaming water beckoned her and her tired limbs pleaded for the refreshment. She could always settle things with Logan Reed later.

"Very well." She slipped out of the jacket and unbuttoned her skirt. "If you'll bring me my black skirt and a clean shirtwaist, I'll wash out these other things." She would show Mr. Reed just how self-sufficient she could be.

"Oh no, ma'am. I can take care of everything for you. My mother does the laundry and she can have these things ready by morning. Pressed fresh and smelling sweet. You'll see."

Amelia reluctantly gave in. "Very well." She sent the girl off with her riding clothes, keeping only her camisole and bloomers. These she washed out by hand and hung to dry before stepping into the tub. With the window open to allow the breeze, the items would dry by the time she finished with the bath. That was one of the nice things about the drier air of Colorado. Things took forever to dry back home in England. The dampness was nearly always with them and it was better to press clothes dry with an iron than wait for them to dry on their own. But here the air was crisp and dry and even in the heat of the day it was completely tolerable compared to what she'd endured when they visited a very humid New Orleans.

Sinking into the hot water, Amelia sighed aloud. How good it felt! Her dry skin seemed to literally drink in the offered moisture. Lathering the soap down one arm and then the other, Amelia wanted to cry with relief. The bath was pure pleasure and she felt like the spoiled aristocrat Logan Reed thought her to be. After washing thoroughly, she eased back on the rim of the tub and let the water come up to her neck, soothing and easing all the pain in her shoulders. It mattered very little that Logan Reed had arranged this luxury. At that moment, the only thing that mattered was the comfort at hand.

When the knock on the door sounded, Amelia realized she'd dozed off again. The water was tepid now and her muscles were no longer sore and tense.

"It's me, Lady Amhurst," the voice of the young woman called. "I've brought your clothes."

"Come ahead," Amelia called, stepping from the tub to wrap the rough towel around her body.

The girl appeared bringing not only the requested shirt and shirtwaist but also Amelia's comb and brush. "I thought you might be needin' these too.

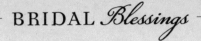

I can help with your hair, if you like."

Amelia smiled. What a friendly little thing. She'd make a good chambermaid if she were a little less familiar. But that was the way of these Americans and Amelia found herself growing more accepting of it as the days wore on. To be friendly and openly honest was not a thing one could count on in the finer classes of people. Women of high society were taught to keep their opinions to themselves, and in fact were encouraged to have no opinion at all. From the moment she was born, Amelia was strictly lectured that her father, and later her husband, would clearly do her thinking for her. Amelia had other ideas, however, and often she came off appearing smug and superior in her attitudes. People misjudged her confidence and believed her to think herself better than her peers. But it wasn't true.

Logan Reed came to mind. He, too, had misjudged her and her kind. Americans seemed more than happy to lend their opinion to a situation. Even this young woman gave her opinion at every turn. But, where Logan had made her feel quite the snob, this young woman made her feel like royalty. Then a thought crossed her mind and she frowned. "Did Mr. Reed pay for you to assist me with my hair as well?"

"Oh, no, ma'am. I was just thinking you might want some help what with it coming down in back and all. I can't do it up fancy like you had it, but I can help pin it up."

Amelia nodded. "Yes, I'd like that very much." The girl turned away while Amelia stepped into her underthings. There were a little damp and this seemed to make them cooler. Light was fading outside and Amelia knew it must nearly be dinner time. These Americans had the barbaric custom of eating a full meal not long after the time when she was more accustomed to tea and cakes. Supper at home was always an affair to dress for and always served late into the evening—sometimes even after nine. *Alas, yet another American custom to adapt to.*

The girl instructed Amelia to sit on a stool while she combed out the thick, waist-length tresses. Amelia prided herself on her hair. It was a light, golden blond that most all of her peers envied. To be both blond-headed and blue-eyed in her society, was to be the picture of perfection. Added to this was her, *how did Mr. Reed say it?* robust figure. Amelia smiled to herself. Many a glance had come to her by gentlemen too well-bred to say what Logan Reed had issued without the slightest embarrassment. She was robust, or voluptuous as her dear friend Sarah would say. When corseted tightly, she had a perfect hour glass figure, well nearly perfect. Maybe time ran a little heavier on the top half than the bottom.

"There, how's that?"

Amelia took the offered mirror and smiled. The young woman had done a fine job of replicating her earlier coiffure. "It's exactly right, Miss..."

"Oh, just call me Emma."

"Well, thank you very much Emma." Amelia got to her feet and allowed Emma to help her dress. "Are the others going to bathe?"

"Oh, the menfolk went down to the steambath at the barbershop. The other womenfolk didn't seem to take kindly to my trying to offer up help, so I pretty much left them alone."

Amelia nodded and smiled. She could well imagine her sisters' snobbery keeping them from accepting the assistance of this young woman. And no doubt, Lady Gambett and her pouty brood had taken themselves off to a private wash basin. With a final pat to her hair, Amelia gathered up her things and followed Emma from the room. "You should see my father, Lord Amhurst, for the cost of this bath and my clothing being cleaned. Mr. Reed is no more than a hunting guide to our party and certainly has no call to be arranging my affairs."

Emma smiled. "Oh, that just Logan's way. He's friendly like that."

"Well, I assure you that I am not in the habit of allowing strangers, especially men, to be friendly like that with me. Please see my father with the bill."

∞

Supper that evening was a surprisingly pleasant fare of roasted chicken, sage dressing, a veritable banquet of vegetables—mostly canned, but very tasty, and peach cobbler. Amelia had to admit it was more than she'd expected and only the thick swarm of hovering black flies kept her from completely enjoying her evening. That and Logan Reed's rude appraisal of her throughout the meal. He seemed to watch her as though she might steal the silver at any given moment. Amelia grew increasingly uncomfortable under his scrutiny until she actually found herself listening to Sir Jeffery's soliloquy on the founding of the London Medical School for Women and the obsurdity of anyone believing women would make acceptable physicians.

"Why the very thought of exposing the gentler sex to such grotesqueries is quite abominable," Jeffery stated as though that would be the collective reasoning of the entire party.

Normally Amelia would have commented loud and clear on such outdated thoughts, but with Logan apparently anticipating such a scene, she chose instead to finish her meal and quietly excuse herself. This was accomplished without much ado, mainly because Lady Gambett opened the matter and excused herself first, pleading an intolerable headache.

Amelia soon followed suit and very nearly spilled over a water glass when she got to her feet. Her hands were shaking as she righted the glass. Looking up, she found Logan smiling. She had to get away from him quickly or make a complete fool of herself, of this she was certain.

Unfortunately, she was barely out the front door when Jeffery popped up at her side.

"Ah, Sir Jeffery," she said stiffly.

"Good evening, Lady Amhurst," he said, pausing with a smile, "Amelia."

She stiffened even more. Eyeing him with complete contempt, she said nothing. There was no need. She'd often heard it said that with a single look she could freeze the heart right out of a man and Jeffery Chamberlain was certainly no match for her.

"Forgive me, Lady Amhurst," he said bowing low before her. "I sought only to escort you to wherever it is you might be going. The familiarity is born only out of my fondness for you and your good father's desire that we wed."

Amelia nodded. "You may be assured that those desires reside with my father alone. Good evening." She hurried away before Jeffery could respond. She hadn't the strength to discuss the matter further.

The evening had grown quite chilly and Amelia was instantly sorry she'd not stopped to retrieve a shawl. She was grateful for the short-waisted jacket she'd donned for dinner and quickly did up the remaining two buttons to insure as much warmth as possible. After two blocks, however, she was more than happy to head back to the hotel and remain within its thin walls until morning sent them ever upward.

Upward.

She glanced to the now-blacked images of the mountain range before her. The shadows seemed foreboding, as if some great hulking monster waited to devour her. Shuddering from the thought, she walked back to the St. Vrain Hotel and considered it no more.

Chapter 4

It was the wind that woke Amelia in the morning. The great wailing gusts bore down from the mountains causing the very timbers around her to shake and tremble. *Was it a storm?* She contemplated this for a moment, hoping that if it were, it would rain and drown out each and every pesky fly in Longmont. All through the night, her sleep had been disturbed by the constant assault of flies at her face, in her hair, and at her ears. It was enough to make her consider agreeing to marry Jeffery if her father would pledge to return immediately to England.

A light rapping sounded upon her door. Amelia pulled the blanket tight around her shoulders and went to answer it.

"Yes?" she called, stumbling in the dark.

"It's me, Emma."

Amelia opened the door with a sleepy nod. "Are we about to blow away?"

Emma laughed softly and pushed past Amelia to light the lamp on her night table. "Oh, no, ma'am. The wind blows like this from time to time. It'll probably be done by breakfast. Mr. Reed sent me to wake you and the other ladies. Said to tell you it was an hour before dawn and you'd know exactly what that meant."

Amelia frowned. "Yes, indeed. Thank you, Emma."

"Will you be needin' help with your hair and getting dressed?"

"No, thank you anyway. Mr. Reed made it quite clear that simplicity is the means for success on this excursion. I intend only to braid my hair and pin it tight. From the sound of the wind, I suppose I should pin it very tight." Emma giggled and Amelia smiled in spite of herself. *Perhaps some of these Americans aren't so bad.*

"Lady Gambett was near to tears last night because Logan told her that she and those youngun's of hers needed to get rid of their corsets before they rode another ten feet."

It was Amelia's turn to giggle. Something she'd not done in years. "Surely you jest."

"Jest?" Emma looked puzzled.

"Joke. I merely implied that you were surely joking."

"Oh, no! He said it. I heard him."

31

"Well, I've never been one to abide gossip," Amelia began rather soberly, "but I can well imagine the look in Lady Gambett's face when he mentioned the unmentionable items."

"She plumb turned red and called for her smelling salts."

"Yes, she would."

Glancing to where Penelope and Margaret continued to slumber soundly, Emma questioned, "Will you need me to wake your sisters?"

Amelia glanced at the bed. "No, it would take more than your light touch. I'll see to them." Emma smiled and took her leave.

"Wake up sleepyheads," Amelia said, pulling the quilt to the foot of the bed. Penelope shrieked a protest and pulled it back up, while Margaret stared up in disbelief.

"I believe you're becoming as ill-mannered as these Americans," she said to Amelia.

"It's still dark outside," Penelope added, snuggling down. "Mr. Reed said we start at dawn."

"Mr. Reed said we leave at dawn," she reminded them. "I for one intend to have enough time to dress properly and eat before climbing back on that ill-tempered horse."

Margaret whined. "We are too tired to bother with eating. Just go away, Amelia."

"Have it your way," Amelia said with a shrug. And with that she left her sisters to worry about themselves, and hurried to dress for the day. Pulling on black cotton stockings, pantaloons and camisole, Amelia smiled privately, knowing that she was quite glad for the excuse to be rid of her corset. She packed the corset away, all the while feeling quite smug. She wasn't about to give Logan Reed a chance to speak so forwardly to her about things that didn't concern him. Pulling on her riding outfit, now clean and pressed, she secured her toiletries in her saddlebags and hurried to meet the others at breakfast.

Much to her embarrassment she arrived to find herself alone with Logan. The rest of her party was slow to rise and even slower to ready themselves for the day ahead. Logan nodded approvingly at her and called for the meal to be served. He bowed ever so slightly and held out a chair for Amelia.

"We must wait for the others, Mr. Reed," she said, taking the offered seat.

"I'm afraid we can't," Logan announced. "You forget I'm experienced at this. Most folks refuse to take me seriously until they miss at least one breakfast. Ahhh, here's Emma." The young girl entered bringing a mound of biscuits—complete with hovering flies—and a platter of fried sausages swimming in grease and heavily peppered. It was only after taking one of the offered links that Amelia realized it wasn't pepper at all, but still more flies.

Frowning at the food on her plate, it was as if Logan read her mind when he said, "Just try to think of 'em as extra meat."

Amelia almost smiled, but refused to. "Maybe I'll just eat a biscuit."

"You'd best eat up and eat well. The mountain air will make you feel starved and after all the hard work you'll be doing, you'll wish you'd had more than biscuits."

"Hard work?"

Logan waited to speak until Emma brought two more platters, one with eggs, another with fried potatoes, and a bowl with thick white gravy. He thanked the girl and turned to Amelia. "Shall we say grace?"

"I hardly think so, Mr. Reed. To whom should we offer thanks, except to those whose hands have provided and prepared the food?"

For the first time since she'd met the smug, self-confident Logan Reed, he stared at her speechless and dumbstruck. *Good,* she thought. *Let him consider that matter for a time and leave me to eat in silence.* She put eggs on her plate and added a heavy amount of cream to the horrible black coffee Emma had poured into her cup. She longed to plead with the girl for tea, but wouldn't think of allowing Mr. Reed to see her in a weakened moment.

"Do you mean to tell me," Logan began, "that you don't believe in God?"

Amelia didn't even look up. "Indeed, that is precisely what I mean to say."

"How can a person who seems to be of at least average intelligence," at this Amelia's head snapped up and Logan chuckled and continued, "I thought that might get your attention. How can you look around you or wake up in the morning to breathe the air of a new day and believe there is no God?"

Amelia scowled at the black flies hovering around her fork. "Should there have been a God, surely He would not have allowed such imperfect creatures to mar His universe."

"You don't believe in God because flies are sharing your breakfast table?" Logan's expression was one of complete confusion. He hadn't even started to eat his own food.

"Mr. Reed, I believe this trip will go a great deal better for both of us if you will merely mind your own business and leave me to do the same. I fail to see where my disbelief in a supreme being is of any concern to you, and therefore, I see no reason to discuss the matter further."

Logan hesitated for a moment, bowed his head to what Amelia presumed were his prayers of grace, and ate in silence for several minutes. For some reason, even though it was exactly what Amelia had hoped for, she felt uncomfortable and found herself wishing he would say something even if it was to insult her.

When he continued in silence, she played at eating the breakfast. She'd hoped the wind would send the flies further down the prairie, but it only seemed to have driven them indoors for shelter. As the gales died down outside, she could only hope they'd seek new territory.

"I guess I see it as my business to concern myself with the eternal souls of mankind," Logan said without warning. "See the Bible, that's the word of God. . ."

"I know what the Bible is perceived to be, Mr. Reed. I wasn't born without a brain, simply without the need for an all-interfering, all-powerful being."

Logan seemed to shake this off before continuing. His green eyes seemed to darken. "The Bible says we are to concern ourselves with our fellow man and spread the good news."

She put her fork down and matched his look of determination. "And pray tell, Mr. Reed, what would that good news be? Spread it quickly and leave me to my meal." Amelia knew she was being unreasonably harsh, but she tired of religious rhetoric and nonsensical sermons. She'd long given up the farce of accompanying her sisters and father to church, knowing that they no more held the idea of worshipping as a holy matter than did she.

"The good news is that folks like you and I don't have to burn in the pits of hell for all eternity, because Jesus Christ, God's only son, came to live and die for our sins. He rose again, to show that death cannot hold the Christian from eternal life."

Amelia picked up her thick white mug and sipped the steaming contents. The coffee scalded her all the way down, but she'd just as soon admit to the pain as to admit Logan's words were having any affect on her whatsoever. *The pits of hell, indeed,* she thought.

She tried to compose herself before picking the fork up again. "I believe religion to be man's way of comforting himself in the face of death. Mankind can simply not bear to imagine that there is only so much time allotted to each person so mankind has created religion to support the idea of there being something more. The Hindu believe we are reincarnated. Incarnate is from the Latin *incarnates,* meaning made flesh. So they believe much as you Christians do that they will rise up to live a gain."

�

"I know what reincarnation means, and I am even familiar with the Hindu religion. But you're completely wrong when you say they believe as Christians

34

do. They don't hold faith in what Jesus did to save us. They don't believe in the need for salvation through Him in order to have that eternal life."

Amelia shrugged. "To each religion and culture comes a theory that will comfort them the most. In light of that, Mr. Reed, and considering the hundreds of different religions in the world, even the varied philosophies within your own Christian faith, how can you possibly ascertain that you and you alone have the one true faith?"

"Are you saying that there is no need for faith *and* that there is no such thing as God?" Logan countered.

"I am a woman of intellect and reason, Mr. Reed. Intellectually and reasonably, I assure you that faith and religion have no physical basis for belief."

"Faith in God is just that, Lady Amhurst. Faith." Logan slammed down his coffee mug. "I am a man of intellect and reason, but it only makes it that much clearer to me that there is a need for God and something more than the contrivances of mankind."

Amelia looked at him for a moment. *Yes, I could believe this barbaric American might have some understanding of books and philosophies. But he is still of that mindset that uses religion as a crutch to ease his conscience and concerns.* Before Amelia could comment further, Logan got to his feet and stuffed two more biscuits into the pocket of his brown flannel shirt. Amelia appraised him silently as he thanked Emma for a great meal and pulled on his drifters coat.

"We leave in ten minutes. I'll bring the horses around to the front." He stalked out of the room like a man with a great deal on his mind, leaving Amelia feeling as though she'd had a bit of a comeuppance, but for the life of her she couldn't quite figure out just how he'd done it.

Emma cleared Logan's plate and mug from the table and returned to find Amelia staring silently at the void left by their guide.

"I hate to be a busybody, Lady Amhurst," Emma began, "but your family ain't a bit concerned about Mr. Reed's timetable and I can tell you from experience, Logan won't wait."

This brought Amelia's attention instantly. "I'll tend to them. Are there more of these biscuits?"

"Yes, ma'am."

"Good. Please pack whatever of this breakfast you can for us and we'll take it along. As I recall, Mr. Reed said there would be a good six miles of prairie to cross to the canyon."

"I can wrap the biscuits and sausage into a cloth, but the rest of this won't pack very good."

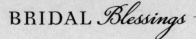

Amelia blotted her lips with a coarse napkin and got to her feet. "Do what you can, Emma, and I'll retrieve my wayward family."

Ten minutes later, Amelia had managed to see her family to the front of the hotel. Penelope and Margaret were whining, still struggling to do something with their hair. Upon Amelia's threat to shear them both, they grew instantly silent. Lady Gambett cried softly into a lace-edged handkerchief and bemoaned the fact that her nerves would never stand the jostling on horseback. Her daughters were awkward and consciously concerned about their lack of corseting, and Amelia had to laugh when she overheard Margaret tell Josephine that Mr. Reed was no doubt some kind of devious man who would do them all in once they were far enough away from the protection of town. A part of Amelia was beginning to understand Logan Reed's misgivings about her people.

Logan repacked the mules with the baggage and items brought to him by the party, but Amelia noticed he was unusually tight-lipped. Light was just streaking the eastern skies when he hauled up onto the back of his horse and instructed them to do the same.

Amelia allowed Jeffery to help her onto her horse and winced noticeably when the softer parts of her body protested from the abuse she'd inflicted the day before. She said nothing, noting Logan's smirk of recognition, but her sisters and the Gambetts were well into moans and protests of discomfort. Logan ignored them all, however, and urged his horse and the mules forward.

❧

It wasn't yet ten o'clock when Logan first heard Amelia's sisters suggesting they stop. He couldn't help but cast a smug look of satisfaction toward Amelia when Penelope suggested they should imbibe in a time of tea and cakes.

He watched Amelia's face grow flush with embarrassment, but she said nothing, choosing instead to let her mount lag behind the others until she was nearly bringing up the rear of the party. Chuckling to himself, Logan led them on another two hours before finally drawing his horse to a stop.

Dismounting, he called over his shoulder, "We'll take lunch here."

It was as if the entire party sighed in unison.

Logan quickly set up everything they would need. He drew cold water from the mountain river that they'd followed through the canyon, then dug around in the saddle-bags to produce jerked beef and additional biscuits.

"You surely don't mean this to be our luncheon fare," Jeffery Chamberlain complained in complete disgust.

The earl looked down his nose at the pitiful offering. "Yes, Mr. Reed, surely there is something better than this."

Logan pushed his hat back on his head. "We'll have a hot meal for dinner this evening. If we're to push ahead and reach our first camping point before dark, we'll only have time to rest here about ten, maybe fifteen minutes. It'll give the horses a well-deserved break and allow them to water up. The higher we go the more water you'll need to drink. Remember that and you won't find yourself succumbing to sorche."

"I beg your pardon?" Lord Amhurst questioned.

"Mountain sickness," Reed stated flatly. "The air is much thinner up here, but since you've traipsed all over the Alps, you should already know all about that. You need to take it slower and allow yourselves time to get used to the altitude. Otherwise, you'll be losing what little lunch you get and dealing with eye-splitting headaches that won't let you go for weeks. It's one more reason I insisted the ladies dismiss the idea of corsets." Shudders and gasps of indignant shock echoed from the now-gathered Gambett and Amhurst women. With the exception of Amelia. She stood to one side admiring a collection of wildflowers, but Logan knew she was listening by the amused expression on her face.

Logan continued, trying hard to ignore the graceful blond as she moved about the riverbank studying the ground. "As inappropriate as you might think my addressing the subject of women's undergarments might be, it is a matter of life and death. Up here beauty is counted in the scenery, not the flesh. The air is thinner and you need more of it to account for what you're used to breathing down below. Losing those corsets just might save your life. I wouldn't even suggest putting them back on after we arrive in Estes. The altitude there is even higher than it is here and I'd sure hate to have to run around all day picking up women in dead faints. Now I've wasted enough time. Eat or don't, the choice is yours. I'll water the horses and mules while you decide." He started to walk away then turned back. "I hate to approach another delicate subject, but should you take yourself off into the trees for privacy, keep your eyes open. I'd also hate to have to deal with an agitated mother bear just because you startled her while she was feeding her cubs."

With that said, he walked away grumbling to himself. These prim and proper Brits were more trouble to deal with than they were worth. This was the last time he'd ever act as a guide for anyone of English nobility.

He tethered his horse at the riverbank and pretended to adjust the saddle while he watched Amelia picking flowers and studying them with an almost scientific eye. From time to time, she drew out a small book and pressed one of these samples between the pages before moving on to the next point of interest. He found himself admiring the way she lithely climbed over the rocks and couldn't help but notice her lack of fear as she neared the rushing river for a closer look.

As she held a leaf up to catch the sunlight, Logan was reminded of her atheistic views. *How could anyone behold the beauty of this canyon and question the existence of God?* It was one thing not to want to deal with God, or even question whether He truly cared to deal with mankind, but to openly declare there to be no God—that was something he couldn't even fathom. Even the Indians he'd dealt with believed in God. Maybe they didn't believe the same way he did, but they didn't question that someone or something greater than man held the universe in order and sustained life.

Logan tried not to stare at Amelia, but he found himself rather helpless to ignore her. The other women were huddled together relaying their misfortunes, hoping for better times ahead and assuring each other that such torture could be endured for the sake of their menfolk. The men were gingerly sampling the lunch fare and after deciding it was better than nothing, they managed to eat a good portion before convincing the women to partake.

Logan wondered if Amelia would partake, but then he saw her draw a biscuit from the deep pocket of her skirt and nibble at it absentmindedly as she bent to pick up a piece of granite. *She is an industrious woman,* he thought, watching her turn the stone in her hand. *Who else, could have gotten that sour-faced brood of travelers together in such a short time? Who else too, would have thought to get Emma to pack food for them to take, rather than whine and beg him to allow them a bit more time for breakfast?*

As if sensing his gaze upon her, Amelia looked up and met his stare. Neither one did anything for a moment and when Amelia returned her attention to the rock, Logan tried to focus on the mules. His stomach did a bit of a flip-flop and he smiled in spite of himself at the affect this woman was having on him. Stealing a sidelong glance, he watched her cup water from the river's edge and drink. *Yes, Lady Amhurst is quite a woman.*

∞

"We'll be leaving in a few minutes," Logan announced to the weary band. "Take care of your needs before that." He walked to where Amelia sat quietly contemplating the scenery. "It's impressive, don't you think?" he asked, wondering if she'd take offense.

"Yes, it is," she admitted.

"Those are cottonwood trees," he said pointing out tall green-leaved trees. "Those with the lighter bark are aspen." He reached down and picked up a leaf. "This is an aspen leaf." Amelia seemed interested enough and so he continued. "I noticed you were saving flowers and if you need any help in identifying them later, I'd be happy to be of service. I'm pretty knowledgeable about the vegetation and wildlife in these parts." He tried to sound nonchalant for fear he'd frighten her away or anger her.

"I especially like those blue flowers," Amelia replied.

"Those are columbine. 'Tis said that absence conquers love! But, O, believe it not; I've tried alas! its power to prove, But thou art not forgot.' A fellow named F. W. Thomas wrote that. It's from a poem called 'The Columbine.'"

"How interesting." She said nothing more for a moment, then added, "What of those white ones with the short hairy stems?"

"Pasqueflowers. So named because they usually start flowering around Easter time. Comes from the Latin word *pascha* or the Hebrew *pesah* meaning 'a passing over', thus the Jewish feast of Passover and the Christian celebration of Easter, the death and resurrection of Christ." He really hadn't intended it as a mocking to Amelia's earlier lessons on *incarnate,* but even as the words left his mouth, he knew that was what they'd sound like.

Amelia stiffened, picked up her things and walked back to the horse without another word. Logan wanted to kick himself for breaking the brief civil respite from the tension between them. *Sometimes, Reed,* he thought, *you can sure put your foot in your mouth.*

Chapter 5

Amelia tried not to remember the way Logan Reed had stared at her. Or how green his eyes were. Or how his mustached twitched whenever he was trying not to smile. She found herself unwillingly drawn to him and the very thought disturbed her to the bone. He was refreshingly different from English gentlemen and far better mannered than she'd given him credit for. His gruff exterior was mostly show, she'd decided while watching him help Lady Gambett onto her horse. He had tipped his had and said something that had caused Lady Gambett to actually smile. Keeping these thoughts to herself, Amelia concentrated on the scenery around her.

"You are particularly quiet," Jeffery spoke, riding up alongside her. It was one of those rare places along the path that allowed for riders to go two abreast.

"I'm considering the countryside," she replied rather tightly.

"Ah, yes. America and her rough-hewn beauty."

Amelia frowned. "And what, pray tell, is that supposed to mean?"

Jeffery smiled tolerantly. "Simply that I'll be happy to return home to England. I'll be even happier when you reconcile yourself to our union and allow me to properly court you."

"I do not wish to discuss the matter."

"I know that very well, but I also know it is your father's intentions that we do so."

He lifted his face to catch a bit of the sun's warmth and Amelia was reminded of a turkey stretching his neck. *Perhaps he might let out a gobble at any moment.* She chuckled in spite of her resolve to be firm.

Jeffery lowered his head and stared at her soberly. "Have I somehow amused you?"

Amelia shook her head. "No, not really. I'm just a bit giddy from the thin air. I'm sure you will understand if I wish to save my breath and discontinue our conversation." She urged her horse ahead and was relieved when Jeffery chose to leave her alone.

∞

Their stop for the evening came early. The sun was just disappearing behind the snow-capped peaks in front of them when Lord Amhurst's pocket watch read 3:35. Amelia slid down from the horse and stretched in a rather unladylike display. Margaret gasped and Penelope laughed, while the Gambett women were too intent on their own miseries to notice. Amelia shrugged off her sisters' questioning stares and began pulling her bedroll free from behind the saddle.

"Get your horses cared for first," Logan called out. "Take down your things and I'll come around and take care of the saddles and staking the animals out."

Moans arose from the crowd and Amelia wasn't sure but what even Mattersley was echoing the sentiment of the group. The older man looked quite worn and Amelia felt concern for him. He would die before leaving her father's side, and thus, he accompanied them whenever they traveled. But this time the trip was so much rougher. Amelia wondered if he would be able to meet the demands of the American wilderness.

"You did good today," Logan said, taking the reins of her mount. "If you think you're up to it, I could use some help putting up the tents and getting dinner started."

Amelia nodded and for some reason she felt honored that he'd asked for her assistance. While Logan removed saddles, Amelia went to Mattersley and helped him remove his bedroll. She didn't know why she acted in such a manner but felt amply rewarded when Mattersley gave her a brief, rare smile. She took his mount and led it to where Logan was staking out Lady Gambett's mount.

"I see you're getting into the spirit of things," Logan said, quickly uncinching the horse.

"I'm worried about Mattersley. He doesn't seem to be adapting well to the altitude." Amelia looked beyond the horses to where Mattersley was trying to assist her father. "He won't be parted from my father," she added, as though Logan had asked her why the old man was along. "He is completely devoted to him."

"I can't imagine what it'd be like to have someone devoted to you like that," Logan replied softly.

Amelia looked into his eyes and found him completely serious. "Me either," she murmured. He made her feel suddenly very vulnerable, even lonely.

Logan's green eyes seemed to break through the thinly placed wall of English aristocracy, to gaze inside to where Amelia knew her empty heart beat a little faster. *Could he really see through her and find the void within that kept her so distant and uncomfortable?*

"My mother was devoted to my pa that way," he added in a barely audible voice.

Amelia nodded. "Mine, too. When she died, I think of a part of him died as well. There is a great deal of pain in realizing that you've lost something forever."

"It doesn't have to be forever," Logan said, refusing to break his stare.

Amelia licked her dry lips nervously. "No?"

"No. That's one of the nice things about God and it isn't just a theory to give you comfort when somebody dies. If you and your loved ones belong to Him, then you will see them again."

Amelia swallowed hard. For the first time in many years, in fact since her mother's death, she felt an aching urge to cry for her loss. "My mother believed that way," she murmured.

Logan's face brightened. "Then half the problem is solved. She's in heaven just waiting for you to figure out that she knew what she was talking about. You can see her again."

Amelia's sorrow faded into prideful scorn. "My mother is entombed in the family mausoleum and I have no desire to see her again." She walked away quickly, feeling Logan's gaze on her. *How dare he intrude into my life like that? How dare he trespass in the privacy of my soul?*

❧

"Come on," Logan said several minutes later. He tossed a small mallet at Amelia's feet and motioned her to follow him.

Picking up the mallet, Amelia did as she was told. She wasn't surprised when she found Logan quite serious about her helping him assemble tents. He laid out the canvas structures and showed her where to drive the stakes into the ground. Pounding the wooden stakes caused her teeth to rattle, but Amelia found herself attacking the job with a fury.

Logan secured the tent poles and pulled the structure tight. To Amelia's surprise and pleasure, an instant shelter was born. Two more structures went up without a single mishap, or word spoken between them. Amelia was panting by the time they'd finished, but she didn't care.

Logan had sent the others to gather wood, but their production was minimal at best. When he and Amelia had finished with the tents, he then instructed the weary entourage to take their things into the tents. "The ladies will have two tents and the men can use the other. It'll be a close fit, but by morning you'll be glad to rug up with the other occupants."

No one said a word.

Amelia took her things to the tent and started to unroll her bedding.

"Leave it rolled," Logan instructed from behind her.

"I beg your pardon?" She pushed back an errant strand of hair and straightened up.

"Unrolled, it will draw moisture or critters. Wait until you're ready to sleep."

Amelia nodded. "Very well. What would you like me to do now?"

"We're going to get dinner going. Hungry?"

She smiled weakly. "Famished." In truth, she was not only hungry but also light-headed.

"Come along then," he said in a rather fatherly tone. "I'll show you how to make camp stew."

"Camp stew?" she said, concentrating on his words against the pulsating beat of her heart in her ears.

He grinned. "Camp stew is going to be our primary feast while en route to your summer home. It's just a fancy way of saying beans and dried beef. Sometimes I throw in a few potatoes just to break the monotony."

Amelia allowed herself to smile. "At this point it sounds like a feast."

"You can take this to the river and get some water," he said, handing her a coffee pot. "I'll unpack the pot for the beans. You'll need to fill it with water first; then bring the coffee pot back full and we'll make some coffee."

She nodded wearily and made her way to the water's edge. Her head was beginning to ache and a voice from within reminded her of Mr. Reed's warning to drink plenty of water. Scooping a handful to her lips, Amelia thought she'd never tasted anything as good. The water was cold and clear and instantly refreshed her. With each return trip Amelia forced herself to drink a little water. On her last trip she dipped her handkerchief in the icy river and wiped some of the grime away from her face. She drew in gasping breaths of chilled mountain air, trying hard to compensate for the lack of oxygen. For a moment the world seemed to spin.

Lowering her gaze, Amelia panicked at the sensation of dizziness. It seemed to come in waves, leaving her unable to focus. She took a step and stumbled. Took another and nearly fell over backward. *What's happening to me?* she worried.

"Amelia?" Logan was calling from somewhere. "You got that coffee water yet?"

The river was situated far enough away that the trees and rocks kept her from view of the camp. She opened her mouth to call out, then clamped it shut, determined not to ask Mr. Reed for help. Sliding down to sit on a small boulder, Amelia steadied the pot. *I'll feel better in a minute,* she thought. *If I just sit for a moment, everything will clear and I'll have my breath back.*

"Amelia?" Logan stood not three feet away. "Are you all right?"

Getting to her feet quickly, Amelia instantly realized her mistake. The coffee pot fell with a clatter against the rocks and Amelia felt her knees buckle.

"Whoa, there," Logan said, reaching out to catch her before she hit the ground. "I was afraid you were doing too much. You are the most prideful, stubborn woman I've ever met."

Amelia tried to push him away and stand on her own, but her head and legs refused to work together and her hands only seemed to flail at the air. "I just got up too fast," she protested.

"You just managed to get yourself overworked. You're going to lay down for the rest of the night. I'll bring you some chow when it's ready, but tillthen, you aren't to lift a finger." In one fluid motion he swung her up into his arms.

"I assure you, Mr. Reed—"

"Logan. My name is Logan. Just as you are Lady Amhurst, I am Logan. Understand?" he sounded gruff, but he was smiling and Amelia could only laugh. She'd brought this on herself by trying to outdo the others and keep up with any task he'd suggested.

"Well?" His eyes seemed to twinkle.

"I understand!" she declared and tried not to notice the feel of his muscular arms around her.

His expression sobered and Amelia couldn't help but notice that there was no twitching of that magnificent mustache. Sometimes, just sometimes, she wondered what it would be like to touch that mustache. *Is it coarse and prickly, or smooth and soft like the pet rabbit Margaret had played with as a child?*

He was looking at her as though trying to say something that couldn't be formed into words and for once, Amelia didn't think him so barbaric. These new considerations of a man she'd once thought hopelessly crude were disturbing to her. Her mind began to race. *What should I say to him? What should I do? I could demand he release me, but I seriously doubt that he would. And what if he did? Did she really want that?*

This is ridiculous, she chided herself. Forcing her gaze to the path, she nodded and said, "Shouldn't we get back? Maybe you could just put me down now. I'm feeling much better."

Logan gave her a little toss upward to get a better hold. She let out an audible gasp and tightly gripped her arms around Logan's neck.

"Don't!" she squealed with the abandonment of a child. Logan looked at her strangely and Amelia tried to calm her nerves. "I—I've always been afraid of falling," she offered lamely. "Please put me down."

"Nope," he said and started for camp. When he came to the edge of the clearing it was evident that everyone else was still collecting firewood. Logan stopped and asked, "Why are you afraid of falling?"

Amelia's mind went back in time. "When I was very young someone held me out over the edge of the balcony and threatened to spill me. I was absolutely terrified and engaged myself in quite a spell until Mother reprimanded me for being so loud."

∽

"No reprimand for the one doing the teasing, eh?" Logan's voice was soft and sympathetic.

"No, she knew Jeffery didn't mean anything by it." Amelia could have laughed at the stunned expression on Logan's face.

"Not Sir Jeffery?" he asked in mock horror.

"None other. I think it amused him to see me weak and helpless."

"Then he's a twit."

Amelia's grin broadened into a smile. "Yes, he is."

"Amelia! What's wrong?"

"Speaking of the twit," Logan growled low against her ear and Amelia giggled. His warm breath against her ear, not to mention the mustache, tickled. "Amelia's fine, she just overdid it a bit. I'm putting her down for a rest."

"I can take her," Jeffery said, dropping the wood he'd brought. He brushed at his coat and pulled off his gloves as he crossed the clearing.

"Well, Lady Amhurst, it's twits or barbarians. Which do you prefer?" he questioned low enough that only Amelia could hear.

Amelia felt her breath quicken at the look Logan gave her. *What is happening to me? I'm acting like a schoolgirl. This must stop*, she thought and determined to feel nothing but polite gratitude toward Mr. Logan Reed. When she looked at each man and said nothing, Logan deposited her in Jeffery's waiting arms.

"Guess your feelings are pretty clear," he said and turned to leave.

"But I didn't say a thing, Mr. Reed," Amelia said, unconcerned with Jeffery's questioning look.

Logan turned. "Oh, but you did." As he walked away he called back to Jeffery, "Put her in her tent and help her with her bedroll. I'll have some food brought to her when it's ready."

"He's an extremely rude man, what?"

Amelia watched Logan walk away. She felt in some way she had insulted him, but surely he hadn't really expected her to choose him over Jeffery. He was only a simple American guide and Jeffery, well, Jeffery was much more than that. If only he were much more of something Amelia could find appealing.

"Put me down, Jeffery. I am very capable of walking and this familiarity is making me most uncomfortable," she demanded and Jeffery quickly complied. She knew deep in her heart that Logan would never be bullied in such a way.

"Mr. Reed said to have you lie down."

"I heard him and I'm quite capable of taking care of myself. Now shouldn't you help get the firewood? Mr. Reed also said we were to expect a cold night." Jeffery nodded and Amelia took herself to the tent, stopping only long enough to give Logan a defiant look before throwing back the flaps and secluding herself within.

"Men, like religion, are a nuisance," she muttered as she untied the strings on her bedroll.

Chapter 6

Morning came with bone-numbing cold and Amelia was instantly grateful for her sisters. Snuggling closer to Penelope, Amelia warmed and drifted back to sleep. It seemed only moments later when someone was shouting her into consciousness and a loud clanging refused to allow her to ease back into her dreams.

"Breakfast in ten minutes!" Logan was shouting. "Roll up your gear and have it ready to go before you eat. Chamberlain, you will assist in taking down the tents."

Amelia rolled over and moaned at the soreness in her legs and backside. *Surely we aren't going to ride as hard today as yesterday.* Pushing back her covers, Amelia began to shiver from the cold of the mountain morning. *Could it have only been yesterday that the heat seemed so unbearable?* Stretching, Amelia decided that nothing could be worse than the days she'd spent on the Colorado prairie. *At least here, the black flies seem to have thinned out. Maybe the higher altitude and cold keeps them at bay.* Amelia squared her shoulders. *Maybe things are getting better.*

But it proved to be much worse. A half-day into the ride, Amelia was fervently wishing she could be swallowed up in one of the craggy ravines that threatened to eat away the narrow path on which she rode. The horse was cantankerous, her sisters were impossible, and Mattersley looked as though he might succumb to exhaustion before they paused for the night.

When a rock slide prevented them from taking the route Logan had planned on, he reminded the party again of the altitude and the necessity of taking it easy. "We could spend the next day or two trying to clear that path or we can spend an extra day or two on an alternate road into Estes. Since none of you are used to the thinner air, I think taking the other road makes more sense."

Logan's announcement made Amelia instantly self-conscious. *Was he making fun of me because of the attack I suffered last night? Why else would he make such an exaggerated point of the altitude?*

"I do hope the other road is easier," Lady Gambett said with a questioning glace at her husband.

"I'm afraid not," Logan replied. "It climbs higher, in fact, than this one and isn't traveled nearly as often. For all I know that trail could be in just as bad of shape as this one."

"Oh dear," Lady Gambett moaned.

"But Mama," Josephine protested, pushing her small spectacles up on the bridge of her nose, "I cannot possibly breathe air any thinner than this. I will simply perish."

Logan suppressed a snort of laughter and Amelia caught his eye in the process. His expression seemed to say "See, I told you so" and Amelia couldn't bear it. She turned quickly to Lady Gambett.

"Perhaps Josephine would be better off back in Longmont," Amelia suggested.

"Oh, gracious, perhaps we all would be," Lady Gambett replied.

"But I want to go on, Mama," the plumper Henrietta whined. "I'm having a capital time of it."

"We're all going ahead." Lord Gambett spoke firmly with a tone that told his women that he would brook no more nonsense.

"Are we settled and agreed then?" Logan asked from atop his horse.

"We are, sir," Gambett replied with a harsh look of reprimand in Josephine's direction.

Amelia tried to fade into the scenery behind Margaret's robust, but lethargic, palomino. The last thing in the world she wanted to do was to have to face Logan. She was determined to avoid him at any cost. Something inside her seemed to come apart whenever he was near. It would never do to have him believing her incapable of handling her emotions and to respond with anything but cool reservation would surely give him the wrong idea.

Logan was pushing them forward again. He was a harsh taskmaster and no one dared to question his choices—except for the times when Jeffery would occasionally put in a doubtful appraisal. Logan usually quieted him with a scowl or a raised eyebrow and always it caught Amelia's attention.

But she didn't want Logan Reed to capture her attention. She tried to focus on the beauty around her. Ragged rock walls surrounded them on one side, while what seemed to be the entire world spread out in glorious splendor on the other side. The sheer drop made Amelia a bit light-headed, but the richness of the countryside was well worth the risk of traveling the narrow granite ledge. Tall pines were still in abundance, as were the quaint mountain flowers and vegetation Amelia had come to appreciate. Whenever they stopped to rest the horses she would gather a sample of each new flower and press it into her book, remembering in the back of her mind that Logan Reed would probably be the one to identify it later.

Soon enough the path widened a bit and Amelia kept close to Lady

Gambett, hoping that both Jeffery and Logan would keep their distance. Her father was drawn into conversation with Lord Gambett, and Lady Gambett seemed more than happy for Amelia's company.

"The roses shouldn't be planted too deep, however," Lady Gambett was saying, and Amelia suddenly realized she hadn't a clue what the woman was talking about. "Now the roses at Havershire are some of the most beautiful in the world, but of course there are fourteen gardeners who devote themselves only to the roses."

Amelia nodded sedately and Lady Gambett continued rambling on about the possibility of creating a blue rose. Amelia's mind wandered to the rugged Logan Reed and when he allowed his horse to fall back a bit, she feared he might try to start up a conversation. Feeling her stomach do a flip and her breathing quicken, Amelia gripped the reins tighter and refused to look up.

"Are you ill, my dear?" Lady Gambett asked suddenly.

Amelia was startled by the question, but even more startled by the fact that Logan was looking right at her as if awaiting her answer. "I. . .uh. . .I'm just a bit tired." *It wasn't a lie*, she reasoned.

"Oh, I quite agree. Mr. Reed, shouldn't we have a bit of respite?" Lady Gambett inquired. "Poor Mattersley looks to be about to fall off his mount all together."

Logan nodded and held up his hand. "We'll stop here for a spell. See to your horses first."

Amelia tried not to smile at the thought of dismounting and stretching her weary limbs. She didn't want to give Logan a false impression and have him believe her pleasure was in him rather than his actions. Without regard to the rest of the party, Amelia urged her horse to a scraggly patch of grass and slid down without assistance. Her feet nearly buckled beneath her when her boots hit the ground. Her legs were so sore and stiff and her backside sorely abused. Rubbing the small of her back, she jumped in fear when Logan whispered her name.

"I didn't mean to scare you," he apologized, "I hope you're feeling better."

Amelia's mind raced with thoughts. She wanted desperately to keep the conversation light-hearted. "I'm quite well, thank you. Although I might say I've found a new way to extract a pound of flesh."

Logan laughed. "Ah, the dilemma of exacting a pound of flesh without spilling a drop of blood. The Merchant of Venice, right? I've read it several times and very much enjoyed it."

Amelia tried not to sound surprised. "You are familiar with Shakespeare?"

He put one hand to his chest and the other into the air. "'My only love sprung from my only hate! Too early seen unknown, and known too late!'" He grinned. "'Romeo and Juliet.'"

Yes, I know," she replied, still amazed at this new revelation.

"'Hatred stirreth up strifes: but love covereth all sins.'"

Amelia tried to remember what play these words were from, but nothing came to mind. "I suppose I don't know Shakespeare quite as well as you do, Mr. Reed."

"Logan," he said softly and smiled. "And it isn't Shakespeare's works, it's the Bible. Proverbs ten, twelve to be exact."

"Oh," she said and turned to give the horse her full attention.

"I thought we'd worked out a bit of a truce between us," Logan said, refusing to leave her to herself.

"There is no need for anything to be between us," Amelia said, trying hard to keep her voice steady. *How could this one man affect my entire being? She couldn't understand the surge of emotions, nor was she sure she wanted to.*

"It's a little late to take that stand, isn't it?" Logan asked in a whisper.

Amelia reeled on her heel as though the words had been hot coals placed upon her head. "I'm sure I don't understand your meaning, Mr. Reed," she said emphasizing his name. "Now if you'll excuse me, I have other matters to consider."

"Like planting English roses?" he teased.

Her mouth dropped open only slightly before she composed her expression. "Have we lent ourselves to that most repulsive habit of eavesdropping, Mr. Reed?"

Logan laughed. "Who could help but overhear Lady Gambett and her suggestions? It hardly seemed possible to not hear the woman."

Amelia tried to suppress her smile but couldn't. *Oh, but this man made her blood run hot and cold. Hot and cold.* She remembered Logan stating just that analysis of her back in Greeley. Just when she was determined to be unaffected by him, he would say or do something that made the goal impossible. She started to reply when Lady Gambett began to raise her voice in whining reprimand to Henrietta.

"It would seem," Amelia said, slowing allowing her gaze to meet his, "the woman speaks for herself."

Logan chuckled. "At every possible opportunity."

Lady Gambett was soon joined by Josephine, as well as Margaret and Penelope, and Amelia could only shake her head. "I'm glad they have each other."

"But who do you have?" Logan asked Amelia quite unexpectedly.

"I beg your pardon?"

"You heard me. You don't seem to have a great deal of affection for your sisters or your father. Sir Jeffery hardly seems your kind, although I have noticed he gives you a great deal of attention. You seem the odd man out, so to speak."

Amelia brushed bits of dirt from her riding jacket and fortified her reserve. "I need no one, Mr. Reed."

"No one?"

His question caused a ripple to quake through her resolve. She glanced to where the other members of the party were engaged in various degrees of conversation as they saw to their tasks. How ill-fitted they seemed in her life. She was tired of pretense and noble games, and yet it was the very life she had secured herself within. Didn't she long to return to England and the quiet of her father's estate? Didn't she yearn for a cup of tea in fine English china? Somehow the Donneswick estates seemed a foggy memory.

"Why are you here, Amelia?"

She looked up, thought to reprimand him for using her name, then decided it wasn't so bad after all. She rather liked the way it sounded on his lips. "Why?" she finally questioned, not truly expecting an answer.

"I just wondered why you and your family decided to come to America."

"Oh," she said, frowning at the thought of her father and Sir Jeffery's plans. There was no way she wanted to explain this to Logan Reed. He had already perceived her life to be one of frivolity and ornamentation. She'd nearly killed herself trying to work at his side in order to prove otherwise, but if she told him the truth it would defeat everything she'd done thus far. "We'd not yet toured the country and Lady Bird, an acquaintance of the family who compiled a book about her travels here, suggested we come immediately to Estes."

"I remember Lady Bird," Logan said softly. "She was a most unpretentious woman. A lady in true regard."

Amelia felt the challenge in Logan's words but let it go unanswered. Instead, she turned the conversation to his personal life. "You are different from most Americans, Mr. Reed. You appear to have some of the benefits of a proper upbringing. You appear educated and well-read and you have better manners than most. You can speak quite eloquently when you desire to do so, or just as easily slip into that lazy American style that one finds so evident here in the West."

Logan grinned and gave his horse a nudge. "And I though she didn't notice me."

Amelia frowned. "How is it that you are this way?"

Logan shrugged. "I had folks who saw the importance of an education

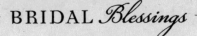

but held absolutely no regard for snobbery and uppity society ways. I went to college back east and learned a great deal, but not just in books. I learned about people."

"Is that where you also took up religion?" she questioned.

"No, not at all. I learned about God and the Bible from my mother and father first, and then from our local preacher. The things they taught me made a great deal of sense. Certainly more sense than anything the world was offering. It kept me going in the right direction."

Amelia nodded politely, but in the back of her mind she couldn't help but wonder about his statement. Most of her life she had felt herself running toward something, but it was impossible to know what that something was. Her mother had tried to encourage her to believe in God, but Amelia thought it a mindless game. Religion required you to believe in things you couldn't see or prove. Her very logical mind found it difficult to see reason in this. *If God existed, couldn't He make Himself known without requiring people to give in to superstitious nonsense and outrageous stories of miraculous wonders? And if God existed, why did tragedy and injustice abound? Why did He not, instead, create a perfect world without pain or sorrow?*

"I've answered your questions, now how about answering some of mine?" Logan's voice broke through her thoughts.

"Such as?" Amelia dared to ask.

"Such as, why are you really here? I have a good idea that Lady Bird has very little to do with your traveling to America."

Amelia saw her sisters move to where Jeffery stood and smiled. "My father wanted me to come, so I did. It pleased him and little else seemed to offer the same appeal."

"Is he still mourning your mother's passing?"

"I suppose in a sense, although it's been six years. They were very much a love match, which was quite rare among their friends."

"Rare? Why is that?"

Amelia smiled tolerantly. "Marriages are most generally arranged to be advantageous to the families involved. My father married beneath his social standing." She said the words without really meaning to.

"If he married for love it shouldn't have mattered. Seems like he did well enough for himself anyway," Logan replied. He nodded in the direction of her father in conversation with Mattersley. "He is an earl, after all, and surely that holds esteem in your social circles."

"Yes, but the title dies with him. He has no sons and his estates, well—" she found herself unwilling to answer Logan's soft-spoken questions. "His estates aren't very productive. My mother had a low social standing, but she brought a small fortune and land into the family, which bolstered my father's position."

"So it *was* advantageous to both families, despite her lack of standing?"

"Yes, but you don't understand. It made my father somewhat of an outcast. He's quite determined that his daughters do not make the same mistake. It's taken him years to rebuild friendships and such. People still speak badly of him if the moment presents itself in an advantageous way. Were we to marry poorly it would reflect directly on him and no doubt add to his sufferings."

"But what if you fall in love with someone your father deems beneath you?" Logan asked moving in a step. "Say you fall in love with a barbarian instead of a twit?" His raised brow implied what his words failed to say.

Amelia felt her face grow hot. *He is really asking what would happen if I fell in love with him.* His face was close enough to reach out and touch and as always that pesky mustache drew her attention. *What if?* She had to distance herself. She had to get away from his piercing green eyes and probing questions. "It could never happen, Mr. Reed," she finally said, then added with a hard stare of her own, "Never."

Chapter 7

Estes Park was like nothing Amelia had ever seen. Completely surrounded by mountains, the valley looked as though someone had placed it there to hide it away from the world. Ponderosa pine, spruce, and aspen dotted the area and Lord Amhurst was delighted to find the shrub-styled junipers whose berries were especially popular with the grouse and pheasants. She knew her father was becoming eager for the hunt. She had seen him eyeing the fowl while Jeffery had been watching the larger game.

They made their way slowly through the crisp morning air, horses panting lightly and blowing puffs of warm air out to meet the cold. To Amelia it seemed that the valley wrapped itself around them as they descended. Birds of varying kind began their songs, and from time to time a deer or elk would cross their path, pausing to stare for a moment at the intruders before darting off into the thicket.

Gone was the oppressive prairie with its blasting winds, insufferable heat, and swarming insects. Gone were the dusty streets and spittoons. The place was a complete contrast to the prairie towns she'd seen. Even the air was different. The air here, though thinner, was also so very dry and Amelia marveled at the difference between it and that of her native land. Already her skin felt tough and coarse and she vowed to rub scented oils and lotions on herself every night until they departed. But departing was the furthest thing from her mind. What had started out as an unpleasant obligation to her was now becoming rather appealing. She found herself increasingly drawn to this strange land, and to the man who had brought them here.

She silently studied Logan's back as he rode. He was telling them bits and pieces of information about the area, but her mind wouldn't focus on the words.

What if she did fall in love with a barbarian? What if she already had?

∽

The lodge where they'd made arrangements to stay was a two-story log building surrounded by smaller log cabins. Lord Amhurst had arranged to take three cabins for his party, while Lord and Lady Gambett had decided to stay in the lodge itself. Lady Gambett had declared it necessary to see properly to the delicate constitutions of her daughters. This thought made Amelia want to laugh, but she remained stoically silent. Delicate constitutions had no place here and it would provide only one more weapon for Logan Reed to use against them. She was bound and determined to show Logan that English women could be strong and capable without need of anyone's assistance. Amelia chose to forget that Lady Bird had already proven her case to Logan Reed two years ago.

"This place looks awful," Margaret was whining as Mattersley helped to bring in their bags.

Amelia looked around the crude cabin and for once she didn't feel at all repulsed by the simplicity. It was one room with two beds, a small table with a single oil lamp, and a washstand with a pitcher and bowl of chipped blue porcelain that at one time might have been considered pretty. A stone fireplace dominated one wall. Red gingham curtains hung in the single window and several rag rugs had been strategically placed in stepping stone fashion upon the thin plank floor.

"It's quite serviceable, Margaret," Amelia stated firmly, "so stop being such a ninny. Perhaps you'd like to sleep in a tent again."

∞

"I think this place is hideous," Penelope chimed in before Margaret could reply. "Papa was cruel to bring us here, and all because of you."

This statement came just as Logan appeared with one of several trunks containing the girls' clothes. He eyed Amelia suspiciously and placed the trunk on the floor. "I think you'll find this cabin a sight warmer than the tent and the bed more comfortable than the ground," he said before walking back out the door.

Amelia turned on her sisters with a fury. "Keep our private affairs to yourselves. I won't have the entire countryside knowing our business. Mother raised you to be ladies of quality and refinement. Ladies of that nature do not spout off about the family's personal concerns."

Margaret and Penelope were taken aback for only a moment. It mattered little to them that Logan Reed had overheard their conversation. Amelia knew that to them he was hired help, no different than Mattersley. They were quite used to a house filled with servants who overheard their conversations on a daily basis and knew better than to speak of the matters, even amongst themselves. Logan Reed was quite a different sort, however, and Amelia knew he'd feel completely within his rights to inquire about their statement at the first possible moment.

"I suggest we unpack our things and see if we can get the wrinkles out of our gowns. I'm sure you will want a bath and the chance to be rid of these riding costumes," Amelia said, taking a sure route she knew her sisters would follow.

"Oh, I do so hope to sink into a tub of hot water," Penelope moaned. At seventeen she was used to spending her days changing from one gown to another, sometimes wearing as many as six in the same day. "I'm positively sick of this mountain skirt or whatever they call it."

"I rather enjoy the freedom they afford," Amelia said. Satisfied with having distracted her sisters, she unfastened the latches on the trunk. "But I would find a bath quite favorable."

They spent the rest of the day securing their belongings and laying out their claims on the various parts of the room. By standing their trunks on end they managed to create a separate table for each of them and it was here they placed their brushes, combs and perfumes. Helping Penelope to string a rope on which they could hang their dresses, Amelia realized they'd brought entirely too many formal gowns and not nearly enough simple outfits. *Where had they thought they were traveling? It wasn't as if they'd have anyone to dress up for.*

Logan came to mind and Amelia immediately vanquished his image from her thoughts. She would not concern herself with looking nice for him. Her father expected her to look the lovely English rose for Sir Jeffery. That was why the clothes were packed as they were. Her desires were immaterial compared to her father's.

ℂℂ

"Amelia has twice as many gowns as we have," Penelope complained at dinner that evening.

Lord Amhurst gave her a look of reprimand, but it was Lady Gambett who spoke. "Your sister is the eldest, and by being the eldest, she is to have certain privileges afforded her. You mustn't complain about it for once she's married and keeping house for herself, you shall be the eldest."

This placated the petite blond, but Amelia felt her face grow hot. She was grateful that Logan was nowhere to be seen.

"I suggest we make an early evening of it," the earl said with an eye to his daughters. "There is to be an early morning hunt and I'm certain you won't want to lag behind."

Margaret and Penelope began conversing immediately with Henrietta and Josephine about what they would wear and how they would arrange their hair. Amelia could only think on the fact that she would be forced to spend still another day in Logan Reed's company.

"Papa," she said without giving the matter another thought, "I'd like to rest and walk about the grounds. Please forgive me if I decline the hunt."

The earl nodded, appraising her for a moment then dismissing the matter when Lady Gambett spoke up. "I will stay behind as well. I can't possibly bear the idea of another ride."

With the matter settled, the party dispersed and went to their various beds. Amelia faded to sleep quickly, relishing the comfort of a bed and the warmth of their fire. In her dreams she kept company with a green-eyed Logan, and because it was only a dream, Amelia found herself enjoying every single moment.

Logan was glad to be home. The valley offered him familiar comfort that he had never been able to replicate elsewhere. His cabin, located just up the mountain, wasn't all that far from the lodge where he'd deposited the earl and his traveling companions. But it was far enough. It afforded him some much-needed privacy and the peace of mind to consider the matters at hand.

Kicking off his boots, Logan built a hearty fire and glanced around at his home. Three rooms comprised the first floor. The bedroom at the back of the cabin was small but served its purpose. A kitchen with a cookstove and several crude cupboards extended into the dining area, where a table and chairs stood beneath one window. This area, in turn, blended into the main room, where the fireplace mantel was lined with small tin-type photos and books. A comfortable sofa, which Logan had made himself, invited company, which seldom came, and two idle chairs stood as sentinels beside a crude book shelf. The tall shelf of books seemed out of place for the rustic cabin, but it was Logan's private library and he cherished it more than any of his other possessions. Whenever he went out from the valley to the towns nearby, he always brought back new books to add to his collection. This time he'd picked up an order in Greeley and had five new books with which to pass the time. Two were works by Jules Verne that promised to be quite entertaining. Of the remaining three, one was a study of science, one a collection of poetry, and the final book promised an exploration of Italy.

With a sigh, Logan dropped down onto the sofa and glanced upward. Shadows from the dancing fire made images against the darkened loft. The house was silent except for the occasional popping of the fire, and Logan found his mind wandering to the fair-haired Lady Amelia. He knew he'd lost his heart to her, and furthermore he was certain that she felt something for him. He wanted to chide himself for his love-at-first-sight reaction to the delicate beauty, but there was no need. His heart wouldn't have heeded the warning or reprimand. Lost in his daydreams, Logan fell asleep on the sofa. He'd see her tomorrow before the party went out on the hunt, but how would he manage the rest of the day without her at his side?

∞

Amelia hung back in her cabin until well after her family had left for the hunting expedition. She was determined to keep from facing Logan Reed and having to deal with his comments or suggestions. She couldn't understand why he bothered her so much. *It isn't as if he has any say in my life. It isn't as if he could change my life, so why give him the slightest consideration?*

Making her way to the lodge, Amelia guessed it to be nearly eight o'clock. She could smell the lingering scents of breakfast on the air and knew that Logan had been right about one thing. Mountain air gave you a decidedly larger appetite.

"Morning," a heavyset woman Amelia knew to be the owner's wife called out. "You must be Lady Amhurst. Jonas told me you were staying behind this morning." Amelia nodded and the woman continued. "I'm just making bread, but you're welcome to keep me company."

Amelia smiled. "I thought to tour around the woods nearby, but I'd be happy to sit with you for a time, Mrs. Lewis." She barely remembered her father saying the place was owned by a family named Lewis.

The woman wiped her floury hands on her apron and reached for a bowl. "Just call me Mary. Mrs. Lewis is far too formal for the likes of me and this place."

Amelia sensed a genuine openness to the woman. "You must call me Amelia," she said, surprising herself by the declaration. The mountain air and simplicity of the setting made her forget old formalities. "What is that you are doing just now?" she asked, feeling suddenly very interested.

Mary looked at her in disbelief. "Don't tell me you've never seen bread made before?"

"Never," Amelia said with a laugh. "I'm afraid I've never ventured much into the kitchen at all."

"But who does the cooking for your family?"

"Oh, we've a bevy of servants who see to our needs. Father believes that young women of noble upbringing have no place in a kitchen."

Mary laughed. "I guess I'm far from noble in upbringing. I was practically birthed in the kitchen." She kneaded the dough and sprinkled in a handful of flour. "Would you like to learn how to make bread?"

Surprised by an unfamiliar desire to do just that, Amelia responded, "I'd love to."

Mary wiped her hands again and went to a drawer where she pulled out another apron. "Put this on over your pretty dress so that it doesn't get all messy. And take off those gloves. It doesn't pay to wear Sunday best when you're working in the kitchen."

She turned back to the dough while Amelia secured the apron over what she had considered one of her dowdier gowns. The peach and green print was far from being her Sunday best. Amelia tucked her white kid gloves into the pocket of the apron and rolled up her sleeves like Mary's.

"I'm ready," she said confidently, anxious to embark on this new project. Lady Bird had told her that only in experiencing things first hand could a person truly have a working knowledge of them. One might read books about crossing the ocean or riding an elephant, but until you actually participated in those activities, you were only touching the memories of another.

"Here you go," Mary said, putting a large hunk of dough in front of her. "Work it just like this." She pushed the palms of her hands deep into the mass. "Then pull it back like this." Amelia watched, catching the rhythm as Mary's massive hands worked the dough. "Now you do it." Mary tossed a bit of flour atop the bread dough and smiled.

Amelia grinned. "You make it look simple enough." But it was harder than it looked. Amelia felt the sticky dough ooze through her fingers and laughed out loud at the sensation. *Father would positively expire if he saw me like this.*

"That's it," Mary said from beside her own pile. "You can work out a great many problems while kneading bread."

"I can imagine why," Amelia replied. Already her thoughts of Logan were fading.

She worked through two more piles of dough with Mary's lively chatter keeping her company. When all of the dough had been prepared Mary showed her how to divide the mass into loaves. Placing the last of her dough into one of the pans, Amelia wiped a stray strand of hair from her face and smiled. It was satisfying work. Twenty-two loaves lay rising before her and some of them had been formed by her own hands.

"There are so many," she commented, noting some of the dough had been placed in pans before her arrival. Already they were rising high, while still others filled the lodge with a delicious scent as they baked.

"I've been collecting bread pans for most of my life. Working this lodge takes a heap of bread for the folks who stay, as well as those who help out. I alternate the loaves so that some are always baking or rising or getting kneaded down. Bread is pretty much alike the country over, so travelers take right to it when they won't eat another thing on the table. And I sell a few loaves on the side. Menfolk around here don't always want to bake their own bread, so they come here to buy it from me." As if on cue the door opened and Logan Reed strode in.

Amelia stared at him in stunned silence, while Logan did much the same. A lazy smile spread itself under the bushy mustache, making Amelia instantly uncomfortable. "You don't mean to tell me that Lady Amhurst is taking lessons in bread baking?"

"She sure is," Mary said, before Amelia could protest the conversation. "Amelia here is a right quick learner."

"Amelia, eh?" Logan raised a questioning brow to keep company with his lopsided smile.

"Sure," Mary said, betraying a bit of German heritage in her voice. "She's a charming young woman, this one."

"That she is," he replied then turned his question on Amelia. "Why aren't you on the hunt?"

Amelia couldn't tell him that she'd purposefully avoided the hunt because of him. She tossed around several ideas and finally decided on the closest thing to the truth. "I wanted to tour about the grounds. I've had enough horsebacking for a while."

"I see."

For a moment Amelia was certain he really did see. His expression told her that he knew very well she'd made her decision based on something entirely apart from the discomfort of the old cavalry saddle.

"Why are you here? I thought you'd be off with the others." Amelia knew that if he had doubted the reason for her decision, she had just confirmed those doubts.

Mary looked rather puzzled. "He comes for the bread. One of those menfolk I told you about." She nudged Amelia playfully. "He's needs a good wife to keep him company and make his bread for him."

"Mary's right. That's probably just what I need." Logan said with a knowing look at Amelia.

"If you'll excuse me, Mary, I'm going to go clean up and take my walk. I appreciate your lessons this morning." Amelia untied the apron and put it across the back of a nearby chair, her kid gloves forgotten in the pocket.

"Come back tomorrow morning and we'll make cinnamon rolls," the heavyset woman said with a smile.

"Now there's something every good wife should know," Logan piped up. "Mary's cinnamon rolls are the best in the country. Why, I'd walk from Denver to Estes to get a pan of those."

"If time permits, I'd be happy to work with you," Amelia said and then hurried from the room.

Images of Logan Reed followed her back to the cabin, where Amelia hurriedly grabbed her journal and pencil, as well as a straw walking-out hat. Balancing the journal while tying on the bonnet, Amelia quickened her pace and determined to put as much distance as possible between her and the smug-faced Mr. Reed. *Why couldn't he have just taken her party on the hunt and left her to herself? Why did he have to show up and see her wearing an apron and acting like the hired help?* But she'd enjoyed her time with Mary, and she never once felt like hired help. Instead she felt. . .well, she felt useful, as though she'd actually accomplished something very important.

Making her way along a tiny path behind the cluster of cabins, Amelia tried to grasp those feelings of accomplishment and consider what they meant. Her life in England seemed trite when she thought of Mary's long hours of work. She was idle in comparison, but then again, she had been schooled in the graceful arts of being idle. She could, of course, stitch lovely tea towels and dresser scarves. She could paint fairly well and intended to sketch out some pastoral scenes from her hike and later redo them in watercolors. But none of these things were all that useful. Mary's work was relied upon by those around her. She baked their bread and kept them fed. She braided rugs and sewed clothes to ward of the mountain chill. She knew all of this because Mary had told her so in their chatty conversation. *Mary's is not an idle life of appearances. Mary's life has purpose and meaning.*

Before she realized it, Amelia was halfway up the incline that butted against the Lewis property. She turned to look back down and drew her breath in at the view. The sun gave everything the appearance of having been freshly washed. The brilliance of the colors stood out boldly against the dark green background of the snow-capped, tree-covered mountains. The rushing river on the opposite side of the property shimmered and gurgled in glorious shades of violet and blue. But it was always lighting which appealed to her painter's eyes. The light here was unlike any she'd ever seen before. It was impossible to explain, but for a moment she felt compelled to try. She sat down abruptly and took up her journal.

"There is a quality to the light which cannot be explained. It is, I suppose, due to the high mountain altitude and the thinner quality of oxygen," she spoke aloud while writing. "The colors are more vivid, yet, if possible, they are also more subtle. The lighting highlights every detail, while creating the illusion of something draped in a translucent veil. I know this doesn't make sense, yet it is most certainly so." She paused and looked down upon the tiny village. She would very much like to paint this scene, but how in the world could she ever capture the light?

Beside her were several tiny white flowers bobbing up and down in the gentle breeze. She leaned over on her elbow, mindless of her gown, and watched them for a moment. She considered the contrast of their whiteness against the green of their leaves and wondered at their name. Plucking one stem, she pressed it between the pages of her book, jotted a note of its location and got to her feet.

The higher she climbed, the rougher the path. Finally it became quite steep and altogether impassable. It was here she decided to turn away from the path and make her own way. The little incline to her left seemed most appealing even though it was strewn with rocks. The way to her right was much too threatening with its jagged boulders and sheer drops. Hiking up her skirt, with her journal tucked under her arm, Amelia faced the challenging mountainside with a determined spirit. She was feeling quite bold and was nearly to the top when the loose gravel gave way beneath her feet and sent her tumbling backward. Sliding on her backside and rolling the rest of the way, Amelia finally landed in a heap at the foot of the incline. Six feet away stood Logan Reed with an expression on his face that seemed to contort from amusement to concern and back to amusement.

Amelia's pride and backside were sorely bruised, but she'd not admit defeat to Logan. She straightened her hat and frowned. "Are you spying on me, Mr. Reed?" she asked indignantly from where she sat.

Logan laughed. "I'd say you could use some looking after given the scene I just witnessed. But, no, I didn't mean to spy. I live just over the ridge so when I saw you walking up this way, I thought I'd come and offer my services."

Amelia quickly got to her feet and brushed the gravel from her gown. Seeing her book on the ground, she retrieved it and winced at the way it hurt her to bend down. "Your services for what?" she asked, hoping Logan hadn't seen her misery as well.

"To be your hiking guide," he replied coming forward. "It would sure save on your wardrobe." He pointed to a long tear in the skirt of her gown. "Why in the world did you hike out here dressed like that?"

"I beg your pardon?"

"At least that riding skirt would have been a little more serviceable. You need to have sturdy clothes to hike these hills," he chided.

"I will hike in whatever is most comfortable to me, Mr. Reed."

"And you think corsets and muslin prints are most comfortable?"

Amelia huffed. "I don't think it is any of your concern. I'm quite capable of taking care of myself."

Logan rolled his eyes and laughed all the harder. "Yes, I can see that." He shook his head and turned to walk back to the lodge, leaving Amelia to nurse her wounded pride.

Chapter 8

Amelia spent the rest of the morning making notes in her journal and contemplating Logan Reed. As much as she tried to forget him, she couldn't help thinking of his offer to be her hiking guide. *Logan knows every flower and tree in the area. He would certainly be the most knowledgeable man around when it came to identifying the vegetation and landmarks. If I am going to put together a book on the area it seems sensible to utilize the knowledge of the most intelligent man.*

The book idea wasn't really new to her. She'd been considering it since speaking with Lady Bird long before departing for America. Lady Bird told Amelia she should do something memorable with her time abroad. *Writing a book and painting dainty watercolor flowers seems very reasonable. Falling in love with a barbaric, American guide does not.*

Closing her book with a loud snap, Amelia got to her feet. "I'm not in love," she murmured to the empty room. "I will not fall in love with Logan Reed." But even as she said the words, a part of Amelia knew that it was too late for such a declaration.

⁂

At noon, she made her way to the lodge house, where the hunting party had returned to gather for a large midday meal. Amelia saw the hunt was successful, but for the first time she wondered about the business of cleaning the kill and how the skins of the animals were to be used afterward. She'd never given such matters much though in the past. There was always someone else to do the dirty work.

"I say, Amelia, you missed quite a hunt. Sir Jeffery bagged a buck first thing out."

Amelia glanced at Jeffery and then back to her father. "How nice." She pulled out a chair and found Jeffery quickly at her side to seat her.

"It was a clean and easy shot, nothing so very spectacular," he said in false humility. "I could name a dozen animals that present a greater challenge to hunt."

"Perhaps the challenge comes in bagging a wife, what?" Lord Amhurst heartily laughed much to Amelia's embarrassment and the stunned expressions of the others.

"Indeed true love is the hardest thing on earth to secure," Lady Gambett said in a tone that suggested a long story was forthcoming. She was fresh from a day of napping and eager to be companionable.

"Papa had a good morning as well," Penelope declared quickly and Margaret joined in so fast that both girls were talking at once. This seemed to be a cue to Josephine and Henrietta, who began a garbled rendition of the hunt for their mother's benefit.

Jeffery took a chair at Amelia's right and engaged her immediately in conversation. "I missed your company on the hunt. Do say you'll be present tomorrow."

"I'm afraid I didn't come to America to hunt. Not for animals of any kind," she stated, clearly hoping the implied meaning would not be lost on Jeffery. The sooner he understood her distaste for their proposed matrimony, the better.

"What will you do with your time?"

Amelia folded her hands in her lap. "I plan to write a book on the flowers and vegetation of Estes Park." The words came out at just the exact moment that her sisters and the Gambetts had chosen to take a collective breath. Her words seemed to echo in the silence for several moments. Stunned faces from all around the table looked up to make certain they had heard correctly.

"You plan to do what?" Margaret asked before anyone else could give voice to their thoughts.

"You heard me correctly," Amelia said, taking up a thick slice of bread she'd helped to make that morning. "The flowers here are beautiful and quite extraordinary. Nothing like what we have at home. Lady Bird told me I should use my time abroad to do something meaningful and memorable. I believe a book of this nature would certainly fit that suggestion."

The earl nodded. "If Lady Bird believes it to be of value, then I heartily agree." With Mattersley nowhere in sight, he filled his plate with potatoes and laughed when they dribbled over the rim. "Waiting on yourself takes some practice." The dinner party chuckled politely and the mood seemed to lighten considerably.

As everyone seemed intent on eating, Amelia's declaration passed from importance and escaped further discussion. With a sigh of relief, Amelia helped herself to a thick slice of ham and a hearty portion of potatoes. Jeffery would think her a glutton, but let him. She was tired of worrying about what other people thought. She found it suddenly quite enjoyable to be a bit more barbaric herself. Almost guilty for her thoughts, Amelia's head snapped up and she searched the room for Logan. She knew he wouldn't be there, but for some reason her conscience forced her to prove it.

"So how will you get about the place?" the earl was suddenly asking and all eyes turned to Amelia.

"I beg your pardon, Papa?"

"How will you travel about to gather your flowers and such? Will you have a guide?"

Amelia felt the ham stick in her throat as she tried to swallow. She took a long drink of her tea before replying. "Mr. Reed has offered to act as guide, but I told him it wasn't necessary."

"Nonsense," her father answered. "If you are to undertake this project, do it in a correct manner. There is a great deal to know about this area and you should have a guide, what?"

"I suppose you are fair in assuming that," Amelia replied. "But I hardly think Mr. Reed would be an appropriate teacher on flowers."

Mary Lewis had entered the room to deposit two large pies on the table. "Logan's an excellent teacher," she said, unmindful of her eavesdropping. "Logan led an expedition of government people out here last summer. He's got a good education—a sight more than most of the folks around these parts, anyway."

Everyone stared at Mary for a moment as though stunned by her boldness. "It seems reasonable," the earl said, nodding to Mary as if to dismiss her, "that Mr. Reed should direct you in your studies. I'll speak to him this afternoon and make certain he is reasonably recompensed for his efforts. Perhaps this evening at dinner we can finalize the arrangements.

Amelia said nothing. In truth, she had already decided to speak to Logan about helping her. She knew herself to be a prideful woman and what had once seemed like an admirable quality now made her feel even more of a snob. Lady Bird had lowered herself to even help harvest the crops of local residents. How could she resist the help of Logan Reed and possibly hope to justify herself? But just as her feelings were starting to mellow toward the man, he ruined it by joining them.

"Looks like you did pretty good for yourself, Amhurst," Logan said, taking a seat at the table.

Mary Lewis entered, bringing him a huge platter of food. "I saved this for you, Logan."

"Much thanks, Mary." He bowed his head for a moment before digging into the steaming food.

Everyone at the table looked on in silent accusation at Logan Reed. Even Mattersley would not presume to take his meals at the same table with the more noble classes. Logan Reed seemed to have no inclination that he was doing anything out of line, but when he glanced up he immediately caught the meaning of their silence. Rather than give in to their misplaced sense of propriety, however, Logan just smiled and complimented Mary on the food as she poured him a hot cup of coffee.

"Will Jonas be taking you out again tomorrow?" Logan asked as if nothing was amiss.

Amelia saw her father exchange a glance with Lord Gambett before answering. "Yes, I suppose he will. I understand you have offered to assist my daughter in gathering information for her book. I would like to discuss the terms of your employment after we finish with the meal."

Logan shook his head. "I didn't offer to be employed. I suggested to Lady Amhurst that I act as a hiking guide and she refused." He looked hard at Amelia, but there was a hint of amusement in his eyes and his mustached twitched in its usual betraying fashion.

"It seemed improper to accept your suggestion," Amelia said rather stiffly.

"Nonsense, child. The man is fully qualified to assist you," Lord Amhurst stated. "I'll make all the arrangements after dinner."

Amelia felt Logan's eyes on her and blushed from head to toe. The discomfort she felt was nothing compared to what she knew would come if she didn't leave immediately. Surprising her family, she got up rather quickly.

"I beg your forgiveness, but I must be excused." Without waiting for her father's approval, Amelia left the room.

Much to her frustration, Jeffery Chamberlain was upon her heels in a matter of seconds. "Are you ill, Amelia?" His voice oozed concern.

"I am quite well," she replied, keeping a steady pace to her walk. "I simply needed to take the air."

"I understand perfectly," he replied and took hold of her elbow as if to assist her.

Amelia jerked away and once they had rounded the front of the lodge, she turned to speak her mind. "Sir Jeffery, there are some issues we must have settled between us."

"I quite agree, but surely you wouldn't seek to speak of them here. Perhaps we can steal away to a quiet corner of the lodge," he suggested.

Amelia shook her head. "I am sure what I desire to speak of will not be in keeping with what you desire to speak of."

"But Amelia—"

"Please give me a moment," she interrupted. Amelia saw his expression of concern change to one of puzzlement. She almost felt sorry for him. Almost, but not quite.

"You must come to understand," she began, "that I have no desire to follow my father's wishes and marry you." She raised a hand to silence his protests. "Please hear me out. My father might find you a wonderful candidate for a son-in-law, but I will not marry a man I do not love. And, Sir Jeffery Chamberlain, I do not now, nor will I ever, love you."

The man's expression suggested anger and hurt, and for a moment Amelia thought to soften the blow. "However, my sisters find you quite acceptable as a prospective husband, so I would encourage you to court one of them."

At this Jeffery seemed insulted and puffed out his chest with a jerk of his chin. "I have no intentions of marrying your sisters," he said firmly. "I have an agreement with your father to acquire your hand in matrimony."

"But you have no such agreement with me, Sir Jeffery."

"It matters little. The men in our country arrange such affairs, not addle-brained women."

"Addle-brained?" Amelia was barely holding her anger in check. "You think me addle-brained?"

"When you act irresponsibly such as you are now, then yes, I do," he replied.

"I see. And what part of my actions implies being addle-brained?" she questioned. "Is it that I see no sense in joining in a marriage of convenience to a man I cannot possibly hope to love?"

"It is addle-brained and whimsical to imagine that such things as love are of weighted importance in this arrangement. Your father is seeing to the arrangement as he would any other business proposition. He is benefiting the family name, the family holdings, and the family coffers. Only a selfish and greedy young woman would see it as otherwise."

"So now I am addle-brained, whimsical, selfish, and greedy," Amelia said with haughty air. "Why in the world would you seek such a wife, Sir Chamberlain?"

Jeffery seemed to wilt a bit under her scrutiny. "I didn't mean to imply you were truly those things. But the air that you take in regards to our union would suggest you have given little consideration to the needs of others."

"So now I am inconsiderate as well!" Amelia turned on her heel and headed in the direction of the cabin.

Jeffery hurried after her. "You must understand, Amelia, these things are done for the betterment of all concerned."

She turned at this, completely unable to control her anger. "Jeffery, these things are done in order to keep my father in control of my mother's fortune. There hasn't been any consideration given to my desires or needs, and therefore I find it impossible to believe it has anything to do with my welfare or betterment."

"I can give you a good life," Jeffery replied barely keeping his temper in check. "I have several estates to where we might spend out our days and you will bring your own estate into the arrangement as well. You've a fine piece of Scottish land, or so your father tells me."

"But I have no desire to spend out my days with you. Not on the properties you already own, nor the properties that I might bring into a marriage. Please understand, so that we might spend our days here in America as amicably as possible," she said with determined conviction, "I will not agree to marry you."

Jeffery's face contorted and to Amelia's surprise he spoke out in a manner close to rage. "You will do what you are told and it matters little what you agree to. Your father and I have important matters riding on this circumstance and that alone is what will gain consideration. You will marry me, Amelia, and furthermore," he paused with a suggestive leer on his face, "you will find it surprisingly enjoyable."

"I would sooner marry Logan Reed as to join myself in union to a boorish snob such as yourself." Silently she wished for something to throw at the smug-faced Jeffery, but instead she calmed herself and fixed him with a harsh glare. "I pray you understand, and understand well. I will never marry you and I will take whatever measures are necessary to ensure that I win out in this unpleasant situation."

She stormed off to her cabin, seething from the confrontation, but also a bit frightened by Jeffery's strange nature. She'd never seen him more out of character and it gave her cause to wonder. She knew there had always been a mischievous, almost devious side to his personality. The memory of hanging over the banister in fear of plunging to her death on the floor below affirmed Amelia's consideration. Jeffery had always leaned a bit on the cruel side of practical jokes and teasing play. Still, she couldn't imagine that he was all that dangerous. He wanted something very badly from her father and no doubt he could just as easily obtain it by marrying one of her sisters. After all, they adored him.

Reaching her cabin, Amelia reasoned away her fears. Her father's insistence that she marry Jeffery was in order to preserve the inheritance. Perhaps there was some other legal means by which Amelia could waive rights to her portion of the estate. It was worth questioning her father. If he saw the sincerity of her desire to remain single, even to the point of giving up what her mother had planned to be rightfully hers, Amelia knew she'd have no qualms about doing exactly that.

"I would sooner marry Logan Reed." The words suddenly came back to haunt her. At first she laughed at this prospect while unfastening the back buttons of her gown. *What would married life be like with the likes of Logan Reed?* She could see herself in a cold cabin, kneading bread and scrubbing clothes on a washboard. She didn't even know how to cook and the thought of Logan laboring to choke down a meal prepared with her own two hands made Amelia laugh all the harder.

The gown slid down from her shoulders and fell in a heap on the floor. Absentmindedly Amelia ran her hands down her slender white arms. Laughter died in her throat as an image of Logan doing the same thing came to mind. She imagined staring deep into his green eyes and finding everything she'd ever searched for. Answers to all her questions would be revealed in his soul-searching gaze, including the truths of life that seemed to elude her. Shuddering in a sudden wake of emotion, Amelia quickly pulled on the mountain skirt.

"He means nothing to me," she murmured defensively. "Logan Reed means nothing to me."

⌒

Having dismissed himself from the dinner table on the excuse of bringing in wood for Mary, Logan had overheard most of the exchange between Jeffery and Amelia. At first he thought he might need to intercede on Amelia's behalf when Jeffery seemed to get his nose a bit out of joint, but the declaration of Amelia preferring to marry Logan over Jeffery had stopped him in his tracks.

At first he was mildly amused. He admired the young woman's spirit of defense and her ability to put the uppity Englishman in his place. He imagined with great pleasure the shock to Sir Chamberlain's noble esteem when Amelia declared her thoughts on the matter of marriage. At least it gave him a better understanding of what was going on between the members of the party. He'd felt an underlying current of tension from the first time he'd met them, especially between the trio of Lord Amhurst, Jeffery, and Amelia. Now, it was clearly understood that the earl planned to see his daughter married to Jeffery, and it was even clearer that Amelia had no desire to comply with her father's wishes. *But why?* Logan wondered. *Why would it be so important for the earl to pass his daughter off to Chamberlain?*

"I would sooner marry Logan Reed." He remembered the words and felt a bit smug. He knew she'd intended it as an insult to Jeffery, but it didn't matter. For reasons beyond his understanding, Logan felt as though he'd come one step closer to making Amelia his lady.

Chapter 9

In spite of her father's desire to have Amelia seek out Logan's assistance as her hiking guide, Amelia chose instead to hike alone. She was often up before any of the others and usually found herself in the kitchen of the lodge, learning the various culinary skills that Mary performed.

"You're doing a fine job, Amelia," Mary told her.

Amelia stared down at the dough rings as they floated and sizzled in a pool of lard. "And you call these doughnuts?" she questioned, careful to turn them before they burned on one side.

"Sure. Sure. Some folks call them oly koeks. The menfolk love 'em though. I could fix six dozen of these a day and have them gone by noon. Once the men learn doughnuts are on the table, I can't get rid of them till they get rid of the doughnuts."

Amelia laughed. They didn't seem all that hard to make and she rather enjoyed the way they bobbed up and down in the fat. It reminded her of the life preservers on board the ship they'd use to cross the Atlantic. "I'll remember that."

"Sure, you'll make a lot of friends if you fix these for your folks back in England," Mary replied.

Amelia couldn't begin to imagine the reaction of her "folks back in England" should they see her bent over a stove, laboring to bring doughnuts to the table. "I'm afraid," she began, "that it would never be considered appropriate for me to do such a thing at home."

"No?" Mary seemed surprised. "I betcha they'd get eaten."

"Yes, I'd imagine after everyone recovered from the fits of apoplexy, they just might eat the doughnuts." She pulled the rings from the grease and sprinkled them with sugar just as Mary had shown her to do. It was while she was engrossed in this task that Logan popped his head through the open doorway.

"Ummm, I don't have to ask what you're doing today, Mary."

"Ain't me, Logan. It's Amelia. She's turning into right handy kitchen help."

Logan raised a brow of question in Amelia's direction. "I don't believe it. Let me taste one of those doughnuts." He reached out before Amelia could stop him and popped half of the ring into his mouth. His expression changed as though he were considering a very weighty question. Without breaking his stoic expression he finished the doughnut and reached for another. "I'd better try again." He ate this one in three bites instead of two and again the expression on his face remained rigidly set. "Mary, better pour me a cup of coffee. I'm going to have to try another one in order to figure out if they're as good as yours or maybe, just maybe, a tiny sight better."

Amelia flushed crimson and turned quickly to put more rings into the grease before Logan spoke again. "Now I know we'll have to keep this one around."

Mary laughed and brought him the coffee. "That's what I keep tellin' her. I don't know when I've enjoyed a summer visitor more. Most young ladies of her upbringin' are a bit more uppity. They never want to learn kitchen work, that's for sure."

Amelia tried not to feel pride in the statement. She knew full well that Logan had once considered her one of those more uppity types and rightly so. For the past few weeks even Amelia couldn't explain the change in her attitude and spirit. She found the countryside inspiring and provoking, and with each passing day she felt more and more a part of this land.

Not realizing it, she shook her head. *I'm English,* she thought and turned the doughnuts. *I cannot possibly belong to this place.* She looked up feeling a sense of guilt and found Logan's gaze fixed on her. A surge of emotion raced through her. *I cannot possibly belong to this man.*

Swallowing hard, she took a nervous glance at her pocket watch. "Oh, my," she declared, brushing off imaginary bits of flour and crumbs, "I must go. I promised I'd wake Margaret by seven."

Mary nodded. "You go on now. I've had a good long rest."

"Hardly that," Amelia said and took off her apron. "I have been here three weeks and I have yet to see you rest at any time."

"I saw it once," Logan said conspiratorially, "but it was six years ago and Mary was down sick with a fever. She sat down for about ten minutes that day, but that was it."

Amelia smiled in spite of herself. "I thought so. Thanks for the lesson, Mary. I'll see you later." She hurried from the room with a smile still brightening her face.

"Don't forget," Mary reminded, "you wanted to start quilting and this afternoon will be just fine for me."

"All right. I should be free," she replied over her shoulder.

"Hey, wait up a minute," Logan called and joined her as she crossed from the lodge to the grassy cabin area.

Looking up, Amelia felt her pulse quicken. "What is it?"

"I was hoping you'd be interested in a hike with me. I thought you'd like to go on a real adventure."

Amelia's curiosity was piqued. "What did you have in mind?"

"Long's Peak."

"The mountain?"

Logan grinned. "The same. There's quite a challenging climb up to the top. If you think you're up to it, I could approach your father on the matter."

"He'd never agree to such a thing."

Logan's smile faded. "He wouldn't agree, or you don't agree?"

Amelia felt a twinge of defensiveness but ignored it. She found herself honestly wishing she could hike up Long's Peak with Logan Reed and to argue now wouldn't help her case one bit. "Without an appropriate chaperone, Logan," she said his name hoping to prove her willingness, "it would never be allowed."

Logan cheered at this. "So what does it take to have an appropriate chaperone?"

"Someone like Mary or Lady Gambett."

Logan nodded. "I guess I can understand that. I'll work on it and let you know."

Amelia saw him turn to go and found a feeling of deep dissatisfaction engulfing her. "Logan, wait."

He turned back and eyed her questioningly. "Yes?"

"I've collected quite a variety of vegetation and flower samples and I thought, well actually I hoped—" she paused seeing that she held his interest. "I was too hasty in rejecting your offer of help. My father wanted me to accept and so now I'm asking if you would assist me in identifying my samples."

"What made you change your mind?" he asked softly coming to stand only inches away. His eyes were dark and imploring and Amelia felt totally swallowed up in their depths.

"I'm not sure," Amelia said, feeling very small and very vulnerable.

Logan's lopsided grin made his entire face light up. "It doesn't matter. I'd be happy to help you. When do you want to start?"

"How would this morning work out for you? Say, after the others have gone about their business?"

"That sounds good to me. I'll meet you at the lodge."

Amelia smiled and gave a little nod. It had been a very agreeable conclusion to their conversation. She watched Logan go off in the direction of the lodge and thought her heart would burst from the happiness she felt. *What was it? Why did she suddenly feel so light?* For weeks she had fought against her nature and her better judgment regarding Logan Reed. Now, giving in and accepting Logan's help seemed to free rather than burden her.

She approached the cabin she'd been sharing with her sisters and grew wary at the sound of voices inside.

"Amelia is simply *awful*. She gives no consideration to family, or to poor Papa's social standing." It was Penelope, and Margaret quickly picked up the challenge.

"Amelia has never cared for anyone but Amelia. I think she's hateful and selfish. Just look at the gowns she has to choose from and you and I must suffer through with only five apiece. I'm quite beside myself."

"And all because Papa is trying to see her married to poor Jeffery. Why he doesn't even love Amelia, and she certainly doesn't love him. I overheard Papa tell him that he would give him not only a substantial dowry, but one of the Scottish estates, if only Jeffery could convince Amelia to marry him before we returned to England."

"She'll never agree to it," Margaret replied haughtily. "She doesn't care one whit what happens to the rest of us. She never bothers to consider what might make others happy. If she hurts Papa this way and ruins my season in London, I'll simply die."

Amelia listened to the bitter words of her sisters and felt more alone than she'd ever felt before. Her entire family saw her only as an obligation and a threat to their happiness. *Surely there is some way to convince them that I don't care about the money. All I really want is a chance to fall in love and settle down with the right man.* Instantly Logan Reed's image filled her mind and Amelia had to smile. She would truly scandalize her family if she suggested marriage to Mr. Reed.

The conversation inside the cabin once again drew her attention when Penelope's whining voice seemed to raise an octave in despair. "I hate her! I truly do. She's forced us to live as barbarians and traipse about this horrid country, and for what? So that she can scorn Sir Jeffery, a man in good standing with the queen herself?"

Amelia felt the bite of her sister's words. She'd never considered her siblings to be close and dear friends, but now it was apparent that even a pretense of affection was out of the question. Hot tears came unbidden to her eyes and suddenly years of pent up emotion would no longer be denied.

"Oh, Mama," she whispered, wiping desperately at her cheeks, "why did you leave me without love?" Gathering up her skirt, Amelia waited to hear no more. She ran for the coverage of the pines and aspens. She ran for the solitude of the mountainous haven that she'd grown to love.

Blinded by her own tears, Amelia fought her way through the underbrush of the landscape. She felt the biting sting of the branches as they slapped at her arms and face, but the pain they delivered was mild compared to the emptiness within her heart. Panting for air, Amelia collapsed beside a fallen spruce. Surrendering to her pain, she buried her face in her hands and sobbed long and hard.

It isn't fair. It wasn't right that she should have to bear such a thing alone. Her mother had been the only person to truly care about her and now she was forever beyond her reach. A thought came to Amelia. *Perhaps a spiritualist could put her in touch with her mother's spirit.* Then just as quickly as the thought came, Amelia banished it. In spite of the fact that spiritualists were all the rage in Europe and America, she didn't believe in such things. *Life ended at the grave—didn't it?*

"I don't know what to believe in anymore," she muttered.

She was suddenly ashamed of herself and her life. She wasn't really a snob, as Logan had presumed her to be. Her upbringing had demanded certain things of her, however. She didn't have the same freedoms as women of lower classes. She wasn't allowed to frolic about and laugh in public. She wasn't allowed to speak her mind in mixed company, or to have her opinion considered with any real concern once it was spoken. Amelia found herself envying Mary and her simple but hard life here in the Rocky Mountains. The men around Mary genuinely revered and cared for her. Her husband had no reason to fear when he took a party out hunting, because everyone looked out for Mary.

I wish I could be more like her, Amelia thought, tears pouring anew from her eyes. She'd not cried this much since her mother's passing. Mother was like Mary. Amelia could still see her mother working with her flowers in the garden wearing a large straw bonnet cocked to one side to shield her from the sun, and snug, mud-stained gloves kept her hands in ladylike fashion. Amelia traced the fingers of her own hands, realizing that she'd forgotten her gloves. *Oh, Mama, what am I to do?*

Looking up, Amelia was startled to find Logan sitting on a log not ten feet away. "What are you doing here?" she asked, dabbing at her eyes with the edge of her skirt.

"I saw you run up here and got worried that something was wrong. Generally, folks around here don't run like their house is on fire—unless it is." He gave her only a hint of a smile.

Amelia offered him no explanation. It was too humiliating even to remember her sister's words, much less bring them into being again by relating them to Logan.

Seeming to sense her distress, Logan leaned back and put his hands behind his head. He looked for all the world as though he'd simply come out for a quiet moment in the woods. "There's an old Ute Indian saying that starts out, 'I go to the mountain where I take myself to heal, the earthly wounds that people give to me.' I guess you aren't the first person to come seeking solace, eh?"

"I'm not seeking anything," Amelia replied, feeling very vulnerable knowing that Logan had easily pegged her emotions.

"We're all seeking something, Amelia," Logan said without a hint of reprimand. "We're all looking to find things to put inside to fill up the empty places. Some people look for it in a place, others in things, some in people." His eyes pierced her soul and Amelia looked away as he continued. "Funny thing is, there's only so much you can fill up with earthly things. There's an empty place and a void inside that only God can fill and some folks never figure that out."

"You forget, Mr. Reed," she said in protected haughtiness, "I don't believe in the existence of God." The words sounded hollow even to Amelia.

Logan shrugged. "You're sitting in the middle of all this beauty and you still question the existence of God?"

"I've been among many wonders of the world, Mr. Reed. I've traveled the Alps, as well as your Rockies, and found them to be extraordinarily beautiful as well. What I did not find was God. I find no proof of an almighty being in the wonders of the earth. They are simple, scientifically explained circumstances. They are nothing more than the visual representation of the geological forces at work in this universe. It certainly doesn't prove the existence of God." She paused to look at him quite seriously. "If it did, then I would have to counter with a question of my own."

"Such as?"

"Such as, if the beauty of the earth proclaims the existence of God, then why doesn't the savagery and horrors of the world do as much to denounce His existence? This God you are so fond of quoting and believing in must not amount to much if He stands idly by to watch the suffering of His supposed creation. I've seen the beauty of the world, Mr. Reed, but so, too, have I seen many of its tragedies and injustices. I've been in places where mothers murder their children rather than watch them starve to death slowly. I've seen old people put to death because they are no longer useful to their culture. I've beheld squalor and waste just as surely as I've seen tranquility and loveliness, and none of it rises up to assure me of God's existence."

"Granted, there's a lot wrong in this world, but what about the forces of evil? Don't you think evil can work against good and interfere with God's perfect plan? When people stray from the truth, the devil has the perfect

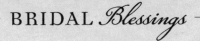

opportunity to step in and stir up all kinds of chaos."

"Then your God isn't very strong, is He?" She lifted her chin a little higher. "As I recall, the devil you believe exists is a fallen angel named Lucifer. Is not your God more powerful than a fallen angel? Don't you see, Mr. Reed, these are nothing more than stories designed to make mankind feel better about itself and the world. The poor man trudges through life believing that even though he has nothing on earth, he will have a celestial mansion when he dies. A rather convenient way of bolstering spirits and keeping one's nose to the grindstone, don't you think?"

Logan shook his head. "You're talking about something you obviously know very little about. An eternal home in heaven isn't all the repentant sinner has to look forward to."

"No?" She looked away as though studying the trees around them. "I suppose you will tell me that he can pray and have his desires magically met by a benevolent God who wants His children to live in abundance and earthly wealth."

"Not at all. God isn't in charge of some heavenly mercantile where you step in and order up whatever your little heart wants. No, Amelia, I'm talking about living in truth. Knowing that you are following the path God would have you travel, and in knowing that, you will find the satisfaction of truth, faithfulness, peace, and love."

"Oh, please," Amelia said meeting his eyes. "This is all religious rhetoric and you know it. The fact of the matter is that truth is completely in the heart and mind of the person or persons involved. I see the truth as one thing and you obviously see it as another. Do not believe I'm any less satisfied for the things I believe in, because I assure you I am not." She bit her lip and looked away. She could hardly bear to meet his expression, knowing that deep inside, the things she believed in were not the least bit satisfying.

As if reading her mind, Logan sat up and said, "I feel sorry for you Amelia. You are afraid to consider the possibility that there is a God, because considering it might force you to reckon with yourself."

"I don't know what you mean." She got to her feet and brushed off the dirt and leaves that clung to her skirt.

Logan jumped to his feet. "That's it. It's really a matter of you being afraid."

Amelia bit at her lower lip again and looked at the ground. "I need to get back. They'll have missed me at breakfast."

Logan crossed the distance to stop her. Putting his hand out, he took hold of her arm and gently turned her back to face him. "God can fill that void inside, Amelia. He can wrap you in comfort and ease your burden. He can be all that human folks fail to be."

Amelia pushed him away. She was, for the first time in a long, long time, frightened. Not of Logan Reed, but of what he represented. "I have to go."

"In a minute," Logan said softly. "First tell me why you were crying."

Amelia shook her head. "It was nothing. Nothing of importance."

Logan reached out and before Amelia could move, he smoothed back a bit of hair from her face and stroked her cheek with his fingers. "It's important to me." His voice was barely a whisper.

Amelia stared up at him and found herself washed in the flood of compassion that seemed to emanate from his eyes. Her mouth went dry and her heart pounded so hard that she was sure Logan could hear it. She struggled with her emotions for a full minute before steadying her nerves to reply. "I don't want to be important to you."

Logan laughed. "Too late. You already are."

Amelia balled her hands into fists and struck them against her side. "Just leave me alone, Logan. I can't do this."

Logan looked at her in surprise. "Do what?"

Amelia opened her mouth as if to speak, then quickly shut it again. She had nearly said, "Love you." Now, standing here in the crisp freshness of morning, Amelia knew beyond doubt, that Logan understood exactly what she'd nearly said. "I can't do this," was all she could say.

Logan backed away. "I have an idea. Why don't you come on a hike with me tomorrow? Your family and friends will be on an overnight hunt; I heard Jonas telling Mary all about it after you left the kitchen. We could spend the whole day gathering your samples and I could spend all evening telling you what they are."

"I don't think—"

"Don't think," Logan said with such longing in his voice that Amelia couldn't ignore his plea.

"All right," she said quickly, hoping that if she agreed to his suggestion he'd leave her alone. There'd be plenty of time to back out of the invitation later. Later, when she was calmer and could think more clearly. Later when the warmth of Logan's green eyes didn't melt the icy wall she'd built between them.

Logan's mustache twitched as it always did before his lips broke into a full smile. "I'm holding you to it."

Amelia nodded and headed back down the mountain. Two things deeply troubled her. One was Logan's words about God. The other was Logan, himself.

Chapter 10

Logan had spent a restless day and night thinking of what his hike with Amelia might accomplish. He saw the desperation in her eyes. He knew she longed to understand what was missing in her life. But how could he lead her to the truth about God when she didn't believe in the validity of God? Usually, whenever he witnessed to someone, Logan knew he could rely on the Scriptures to give them something solid that they could put their hands on—the written word of God. That seemed to be important to folks. With Amelia's disbelief in God and her position that the Bible was nothing more than the collective works of men from the past, Logan felt at a loss as to how he could proceed without it. His mother and other Christians he'd known had assured him that all he needed was a faith in God and in His word. And even now, Logan believed that was still true. But what he couldn't figure out was how to apply it all and show Amelia the way to God. Somehow, he felt, he must be failing as a Christian if this simple mission eluded him. *How can I defend my faith in God and show Amelia the truth, when it is that very truth that makes her run in the opposite direction?*

Logan took up his Bible and sat down to a self-prepared breakfast of smoked ham and scrambled eggs. He opened the book and bowed his head in prayer. "Father, there's a great deal of hurt inside Amelia Amhurst. I know You already see her and love her. I know You understand how to reach her. But I don't know how to help and I seek Your guidance and direction. I want to help her find her way home to You. Give me the right words and open her heart to Your Spirit's calling. In Jesus' name I pray, Amen."

Logan opened his eyes and found comfort in the Scripture before him. "The Spirit itself beareth witness with our spirit, that we are the children of God," he read aloud from the eighth chapter of Romans. A peace came over him and he smiled. God's Spirit would speak for him. It wasn't Logan Reed's inspirational words or evidence that would save Amelia; it was God's Holy Spirit. The Holy Spirit would also show her the validity of the Bible. He needn't compromise his beliefs and put the Bible aside. Neither did he need to go out of his way to defend God. God could fully take care of all the details.

He almost laughed out loud the way he'd taken it all on his own shoulders.

It was typical of him to rush in and try to arrange things on his own. But now he didn't have to and God had made that quite clear. Amelia Amhurst was here for a reason. Not for her father's matrimonial desires or Chamberlain's financial benefits in joining with her. Amelia was here because God knew it was time for her to come to the truth. The Holy Spirit would bear witness to Amelia that not only was God real but also she had a way to reconcile herself with Him. With a lighter heart, Logan dug into his breakfast and prepared for the day.

⌒

Logan whistled a tune as he came into the lodge through the kitchen. He found Amelia bent over a sink-full of dishes and paused to consider her there. Her blond hair was braided in a simple fashion to hang down her back and the clothes she wore were more austere than usual. She no longer appeared the refined English rose, but rather looked to be the descendant of hearty pioneer stock.

"I see you dressed appropriately," he said from behind her.

⌒

Amelia whirled around with soapy hands raised as though Logan had threatened a robbery. In a rather breathless voice she addressed him. "I borrowed some clothes from Mary." Gone was any trace of her agitation with him the day before.

"Good thinking." Logan felt unable to tear his gaze away from her wide blue eyes.

"She gave me some sturdy boots as well." Amelia's voice was a nervous whisper as soap suds dripped down her arms and puddle onto the wood floor.

"You gonna be much longer with those?" Logan asked, nodding toward the sink, but still refusing to release her gaze.

"No. I'm nearly finished."

"I can help," he offered.

"No. Why don't you have a cup of coffee instead? I can see to this."

Amelia was the one who finally turned away. Logan thought her cheeks looked particularly flushed, but he gave the cookstove and fireplace credit for this and took a cup. Pouring rich, black coffee, Logan nearly burned himself as his glances traveled back and forth between Amelia and the coffee.

"How'd the quilting lesson go yesterday?" he asked.

"My stitches were as big as horses," Amelia admitted, "but Mary told me not to worry about it. She said it was better to work at consistency and spacing."

"Mary should know. She does beautiful work."

"Yes, she does." Amelia finished with her task and dried her hands on her apron. "I don't suppose I'll ever do such nice work."

"You don't give yourself enough credit. Look how quick you took to making doughnuts. When you reach Mary's age you'll be every bit as good at making quilts as she is."

"I seriously doubt that," she replied and Logan thought she sounded rather sad. "You see, once we return to England, I know it will hardly be acceptable for me to sit about making quilts and frying doughnuts."

"Maybe you shouldn't go back."

The words fell between them as if a boulder had dropped into the room. Sensing Amelia's inability to speak on the matter, Logan changed the subject. "Well, I have a knapsack full of food, so if you're ready—"

Amelia nodded and untied her apron. "Let me get my coat." She hurried over to a nearby chair and pulled on a serviceable broadcloth coat. The jacket was several sizes too big, obviously another loan from Mary, but Logan thought she looked just right.

Smiling, he nodded. "You look perfect."

"Hardly that, Mr. Reed, but I am. . .well—" she glanced down at her mismatched attire and raised her face with a grin, "I am prepared."

He laughed. "Well, out here that suggests perfection. A person ought to always be prepared. You never know when a storm will blow up or an early snow will keep you held up in your house. Preparation is everything."

❦

The sun was high overhead before Logan suggested they break for lunch. Amelia was secretly relieved and plopped down on the ground in the most unladylike manner. The scenery around her was hard to ignore. The rocky granite walls were imposing and gave her a powerful reminder of how little she knew of taking care of herself. *What if something happened to Logan? How would I ever return to Estes without his assistance?*

"You up to one more thing before I break out the chow?"

Amelia looked up and hoped that the weariness she felt was hidden from her expression. "I suppose so." She made a motion to get up, but before she could move Logan reached down and lifted her easily.

"You look pretty robust," he said, dropping his hold, "but you weigh next to nothing. I've had dogs that weighed more than you."

Amelia thought it was a strange sort of observation, but then remembered back in Greeley when her beauty had been compared to a polished spittoon. "And I've had horses more mannerly than you," she finally replied, "but I don't hold that against you and I pray you won't hold my weight against me."

"You pray?" he said, acting surprised.

"It's a mere expression, I assure you. Now please show me what you had in mind and then feed me before I perish."

Logan took hold of her hand and pulled her along as though they traveled in this manner all of the time. He walked only a matter of ten or twelve steps, however, before drawing Amelia up to a frightening precipice.

"Oh, my!" she gasped, gazing over the edge of the sheer drop. She clung to Logan's hand without giving thought to what he might think. "How beautiful," she finally added, gazing out beyond the chasm. A tiny ledge of rock stuck out some six or seven feet below them, but after that there was nothing but the seemingly endless open spaces below. Beyond them, the Rocky Mountain panorama stretched out and Amelia actually felt a lump form in her throat. There were no words for what she was feeling. Such a rush of emotions simply had no words. It was almost as if this country beckoned to her inner soul. She felt something here that she'd never known anywhere else. Not in the Alps with all of their grandeur. Not amongst the spicy, exotic streets of Egypt. Not even on her father's estate in England.

Her eyes scanned the scene and her mind raced with one pounding sensation. When her eyes settled on Logan's face, that sensation was realized in a single word. *Home. I feel,* she thought, *as though I've come home.*

For a moment she thought Logan might kiss her, and for as long a moment, she wished he would. She longed for his embrace. The warmth of his hand on hers drew her further away from thoughts of her family and England. *Is this true love? Are this man and this place to forever be a part of my destiny? Yet how could it be? How could I even imagine it possible?* She was a refined English lady—the daughter of an earl. She had been presented to Queen Victoria and had even made the acquaintances of the princesses.

Logan's voice interrupted the awe-inspired moment. "Come on, let's eat."

He pulled her back to the place where she'd rested earlier, and without ceremony, plopped himself down on the ground and began wrestling with the knapsack. Amelia was very nearly devastated. *Didn't he feel it, too? Didn't he feel the compelling, overwhelming attraction to her that she felt to him?*

Chiding herself for such unthinkable emotions, Amelia sat down and took the canteen Logan offered her. She drank slowly, the icy liquid quenching her thirst, but not her desire to know more. *But what is it that I want to know?* She refused to be absorbed with questions of immortality and religious nonsense, and yet there were so many questions already coming to mind.

Logan slapped a piece of ham between two thick slices of Mary's bread and handed the sandwich over to Amelia. "It's not fancy, but I promise you it will taste like the finest banquet food you've ever had."

Amelia nodded and nibbled on the edge of the crust. She was famished and yet, when Logan bowed his head in prayer, she paused in respectful silence, not really knowing why. When he finished, he pulled out a napkin and revealed two pieces of applesauce cake.

"Mary had these left over from last night and I thought they'd make a great dessert."

"Indeed they will," Amelia agreed and continued eating the sandwich.

In between bites of his own food, Logan began sharing a story about the area. "This is called Crying Rock," he explained.

"Why Crying Rock?" Amelia asked, looking around her to see if some rock formation looked like eyes with water flowing from it.

"Legend holds that an Indian warrior fell to his death from that very spot where we stood just minutes ago. He had come to settle a dispute with another warrior and in the course of the fight, he lost his life."

"How tragic. What were they fighting about?" Amelia asked, genuinely interested.

"A young woman," he said with a grin. "What else?"

Amelia jutted out her chin feeling rather defensive. "How foolish of them both."

"Not at all. You see the warrior was in love with a woman who was already pledged to marry the other man. It was arranged by her father, but her heart wasn't in it. She was in love with the other warrior."

Amelia felt the intensity of his stare and knew that he understood her plight in full. She felt more vulnerable in that moment than she'd ever felt in her life. It was almost as if her entire heart was laid bare before Logan Reed. She wished she could rise up with dignity and walk back to the lodge, but she hadn't the remotest idea how she could accomplish such a feat. Instead, she finished her sandwich and drank from the canteen before saying, "Obviously, she lost out in this situation and had to marry the man she didn't love."

Logan shook his head. "Not exactly. After the death of her true love, she was to marry the victor in five days and so she brought herself up here and sat down to a period of mourning. As legend tells it, she cried for four straight days. The people could hear her, clear down in the village below, and folks around here say at night when the wind blows it can still sound just like a woman crying."

"What happened after that?" Amelia asked, almost against her will.

"On the fifth day she stopped crying. She washed, dressed in her wedding clothes and offered up a final prayer in honor of her lost warrior." Logan paused and it seemed to Amelia that he'd just as soon not continue with the story.

"And?" she pressed.

"And, she threw herself off the rock and took her own life."

"Oh." It was all Amelia could say. She let her gaze go to the edge of the rock and thought of the devastated young woman who died. She could understand the woman's misery. Facing a life with Jeffery Chamberlain was akin to a type of death in and of itself. And then, for the first time, the realization that she would most likely be forced to marry Jeffery truly sunk in. The tightness in her chest made her feel suddenly hemmed in. Her father would never allow her to walk out of this arrangement. There was no way he would care for her concerns or her desires to marry for love. The matter was already settled and it would hardly be affected by Amelia's stubborn refusal.

"You okay?" Logan asked softly.

She looked back to him and realized he'd been watching her the whole time. "I'm well—" she fell silent and tried to reorganize her thoughts. "The story was fascinating and I was just thinking that perhaps a book on Indian lore would be more beneficial than one on wild flowers."

Logan seemed to consider this a moment. "Why not combine them? You could have your flowers and identification information and weave in stories of the area. After all, the summer is coming quickly to an end and you've already done a great deal of work on the area vegetation."

"Would you teach me more about the lore from this area?" she asked, swallowing down the depression that threatened to engulf her.

"Sure," he said, so nonchalant that Amelia knew he didn't understand her dilemma.

No one understands, she thought as a heavy sigh escaped her lips. *No one would ever understand.*

Chapter 11

A week and a half later, Amelia watched as Mary finished packing a saddlebag with food. "Mary, are you sure that you and Jonas want to do this?" she questioned quite seriously. "I mean, Long's Peak looks to be a very serious climb."

"Oh, it's serious enough," she said with a smile. "I've made it four times before, and I figure number five ain't gonna kill me."

"You've climbed up Long's Peak four times?" Amelia questioned in disbelief.

Logan laughed at her doubtful expression. "Mary's a great old gal and she can outdo the lot of us, I'm telling you."

Mary beamed him a smile. "He only says that 'cause he knows I'll cook for him on the trail."

Amelia was amazed. Long's Peak stood some 14,700 feet high and butted itself in grand majesty against one end of Estes Park. It was once heralded as one of the noblest of the Rocky Mountains and Lady Bird had highly recommended taking the opportunity to ascend it, if time and health permitted one to do so. Amelia was still amazed that her father had taken to the idea without so much as a single objection. He and Sir Jeffery had found a guide to take them hunting outside the village area. They would be gone for over a week and during that time he was quite unconcerned with how his daughters and manservant entertained themselves. After all, he mused, they were quite well-chaperoned, everyone in the village clearly knowing what everyone else was about, and the isolation did not afford for undue notice of their activities by the outside world. Logan had immediately approached him on the subject of Amelia ascending Long's Peak, with a formal invitation to include her sisters and the Gambett family. Lady Gambett looked as though just thinking of such a thing made her faint and the girls were clearly uninterested in anything so barbaric. After a brief series of questions, in which Mary assured the earl that she would look after Amelia as if she were her own, Lord Amhurst gave his consent and went off to clean his rifle. And that was that. The matter was settled almost before Amelia had known the question had been posed.

"You've got enough grub here to last three weeks," Jonas chided his wife.

"Sure, sure," his Mary answered with a knowing nod, "and you and Logan can eat three weeks worth of food in a matter of days. I intend that Amelia not starve." They all laughed at this and within the hour they were mounting their horses and heading out.

"Some folks call it 'the American Matterhorn,'" Logan told Amelia.

"I've seen the Matterhorn and this is more magnificent," she replied, rather lost in thought.

The valley was a riot of colors and sights. The rich green of the grass contrasted with wildflowers too numerous to count. But thanks to Logan, Amelia could identify almost every one of them and smiled proudly at this inner knowledge. She would have quite a collection to show off when she returned to England. For reasons beyond her understanding, the thought of leaving for England didn't seem quite as appealing as it always had before. She pushed aside this thought and concentrated instead on the grandeur of a blue mountain lake that seemed to be nestled in a bed of green pine.

The Lewises' dogs, a collie mix and a mutt of unknown parentage, ran circles around the party, barking at everything that crossed their path, often giving chase when the subject in question looked too small to retaliate. Amelia laughed at the way they seemed to never tire of chasing the mountain ground squirrels or nipping after the heels of the mule-eared deer.

As the sun seemed to fall from the sky in an afterglow of evening colors, Amelia felt a sadness that she couldn't explain. The emptiness within her was almost more than she could bear. She thought of her mother and wondered if she were watching from some celestial home somewhere, then shook off the thought and chided herself for such imaginings. No doubt they'd been placed there by the irritating conversations of one Logan Reed. His beliefs seemed to saturate everything he said and did, and Amelia was quite disturbed by the way he lived this faith of his.

"We'd best make camp for the night," Logan called and pointed. "Over there looks to be our best choice."

Later, Amelia could see why he was so highly regarded as a competent guide. The area he'd chosen was well-sheltered from the canyon winds and had an ample supply of water. Added to this were feathery pine boughs, so surprisingly soft that when Amelia lay down atop her blanketed pine mattress, she sighed in unexpected delight. Staring up at the starry sky, Amelia uncomfortably remembered Bible verses from the thirty-eighth chapter of Job. Her mother had been particularly fond of these and had often quoted them when Amelia had questioned the hows and whys of God's workings.

"Where wast thou when I laid the foundations of the earth? declare, if thou hast understanding. Who hath laid the measures thereof, if thou knowest? or who

hath stretched the line upon it? Whereupon are the foundations thereof fastened? or who laid the corner stone thereof; When the morning stars sang together, and all the sons of God shouted for joy?"

Her mother's explanation had always been that Amelia had no right to question God, and Amelia remembered countering that if God's position wasn't secure enough to be put to the test, then He wasn't as omnipotent and omniscient as people said. Suddenly, she felt very sorry for those words. Not because she believed in God's existence, but for the sorrow she remembered seeing in her mother's eyes. Sitting up, she hugged her knees to her chest and watched the flames of their campfire for a while.

You wouldn't be very pleased with me now, Mother, she thought. The flames danced and licked at the cold night air and when a log popped and shifted, Amelia jumped from the suddenness of it.

"I'm surprised you're still awake," Logan said from where he lay watching her.

Amelia felt suddenly very self-conscious and shrugged her shoulders. "Just thinking."

Logan leaned up on his elbow. "Care to share it?"

Amelia smiled and the reassuring sounds of Mary and Jonas's snoring made her relax a bit. "I was thinking about my mother."

"I bet you miss her a lot," Logan offered.

"Yes, I do. It seems like she's been gone forever and it's only been six years. She was sick quite awhile before she died." Then as if Logan had vocalized the question, Amelia added, "Consumption."

"And she was a Christian?"

Amelia rocked back and forth a bit and looked up to the heavens. "Yes."

"So how is it that you came to believe there was no God?"

"He never listened when I prayed," she replied flatly.

"How do you know?"

"Because my mother died."

Logan said nothing for several moments, then sat up and added a few more pieces of wood to the fire. "Did your mother ever deny you something that you wanted?"

"Of course," Amelia said, not understanding his meaning.

"So why wouldn't God be inclined to do the same?"

Logan's eyes were intense and his expression so captivating that for a moment Amelia forgot to be offended. Instead she simply asked, "To what purpose? I was fourteen years old; my youngest sister was barely ten. To what purpose does a merciful God remove mothers from children?"

"Good question. Wish I had the answer."

Amelia felt instant disappointment. She'd fully expected one of those quaint Christian answers like, "God needed another angel for heaven." Or, "God had need of your mother elsewhere." Amelia knew better. Especially since she left three grieving children and a devastated husband.

"You seem taken aback," Logan said softly. "Did you expect me to tell you the mind of God?"

Amelia couldn't help but nod. "Most other Christians would have. They have their wonderful little answers and reasons for everything, and none of it ever makes sense. To me, if there were a God, He would be more logical than that. There would be a definite order and reason to things of course, a purpose."

"And you think that's missing in our world?" Logan questioned, seeming genuinely intrigued by the turn the conversation had taken.

But Amelia felt weary of it all. She was tired of seeking answers when she wasn't even sure what the questions were. She couldn't make sense of her life or of her mother's death, and therefore, to cast her frustration aside seemed the only way to keep from going insane.

"I think," she said very softly, "that the world has exactly the order we give it. No more. No less. If people are out of control, then so, too, the world."

"I agree."

"You do?"

Logan smiled. "Surprised?" Amelia nodded and he continued. "God gave mankind free will to choose Him or reject Him. A great many folks refuse Him and chaos and misery ensue. They seek their own way and call it wisdom when they settle in their minds how the universe has come together."

"But is your Christianity any different? Didn't you decide in your own way how the universe has come together?"

"No," Logan replied. "I decided to accept God's way was the only way and that put the rest of my questions at rest."

"But don't you ever worry that you might be wrong?" Amelia asked, knowing that she was very concerned with her own version of the truth. Perhaps that was why she felt herself in a constant state of longing. There was an emptiness inside her that refused to be filled up by the reasonings and logic of her own mind, yet she didn't know what to put in its place.

Logan stretched back on his pallet. "I guess if I'd come to God as an adult, I might have wondered if the Bible was true and if God was really God. But I became a Christian when was still very young and it was easy to believe what my parents told me about the Bible and faith. I can see where it would be a whole heap harder for you. You have a lifetime of pride and obstacles to overcome. Accepting that the Bible is true would mean that your life would change, and some folks aren't willing to risk what that change might entail."

He fell silent and before long, Amelia noticed that his breathing had grown deep and even. Lying back down on her own pine bed, Amelia felt more lonely and isolated than she'd ever been in her life. *What if Logan is right?* her mind questioned. She quickly pushed the thought away. But as she drifted to sleep it came back in a haunting reminder that followed her even into her dreams.

The next day, Amelia awoke before it was fully light. The night had turned cold and Amelia's teeth chattered as she dragged her blankets around her shoulders and went to throw more wood on the fire like she'd seen Logan do. The dying coals quickly ignited the dry wood and soon a cheery blaze was crackling once again. It was this and not any sound made by Amelia that caused the rest of the camp to stir.

Logan was first to sit up, rubbing his eyes and yawning. Mary and Jonas murmured good mornings to each other before Mary took herself off for a bit of privacy. Jonas didn't seem inclined to talk and Logan was already pulling out things for breakfast.

While they were all occupied, Amelia took herself off a ways in order to study the sunrise in private. At first the blackness gave way to midnight blue and then as the slightest hint of lemon coloring suggested light, it gave way to a turquoise and brightened as the sun stretched over the snow-capped peaks. *How beautiful!* She marveled at the glory of it all.

They quickly breakfasted and were on their way by seven, the sunrise permanently fixed in Amelia's mind. They made good time, passing an area Logan called "The Lava Beds." It was here that huge boulders mingled with small ones to create a strangely desolate area. They were nearing the place where Logan said they would have to picket the horses and climb, when dark clouds moved in and rain appeared imminent.

Logan immediately went to work to find them even the smallest shelter to wait out the storm. He finally found a suitable place where they would be snug under the protective ledge of a particularly wide rock shelf. Jonas and Logan picketed the horses, while Amelia and Mary carried their things to the rock. The heavens opened up, as if cued by their having found shelter, and poured down a rain of tremendous proportion. Lightning flashed around them just as Jonas and Logan came to join the women.

C-R-A-C-K! Thunder roared, causing Amelia to nearly jump out of her skin. It seemed as if they sat atop the world and the fullest impact of the storm was to be spent on them alone.

Logan grinned and eased a little closer to Amelia. Another flash of lightning caused Amelia to put her hands to her ears and press herself tighter to the wall. She felt terribly embarrassed by her childish display, noting that Mary and Jonas had their heads together talking as though nothing at all was amiss. She rallied herself in spirit and was determined to display more courage when a blinding strike of lightning hit directly in front of them with its deafening boom of thunder.

Amelia shrieked and threw herself at Logan in such a way that she feared she'd knocked the wind from him. Hearing him groan, she pulled back quickly but found his arm around her.

"Stay, if it makes you feel better. I promise, Mary and Jonas aren't going to care."

Amelia smiled weakly at Mary. "I've never been in a storm like this," she said, barely able to form audible words.

"Logan knows how they go," Mary replied, which seemed to offer Amelia approval for her actions.

Turning to Logan, Amelia temporarily forgot the storm around her and concentrated instead on the one in his eyes. Her heart pounded harder, while her breath felt as though it were caught around the lump in her throat. Licking her dry lips, she eased away and hugged her arms around her. *Better to find strength and comfort from within than to lose another portion of myself to this rugged mountain man.*

After a time the storm passed, but Logan judged by the skies that another would soon follow and the climb to the top of Long's Peak was postponed. As they descended back down the mountain, hoping to reach the heavy cover of pines before the next storm was upon them, Logan tried to treat the matter light-heartedly.

"We'll just try again later on," he said confidently. "Sooner or later, we're bound to get you to the top."

Amelia tried not to be disappointed. In truth, by this time her emotions were so topsy-turvy that she wasn't at all certain whether she cared if the trip was canceled or not. She rode sedately, saying very little except when addressed with a direct question. There was a great deal this trip had brought to mind and there was still the rest of the summer to think it through.

Chapter 12

From that day, the summer passed much more quickly than Amelia had expected. Not a moment went by when she wasn't painfully aware that soon the snows would threaten to close off access to the plains. Soon she would be headed back to England and her marriage to Sir Jeffery. She tried to push down her fear, but it rose up like a phoenix from the ashes of her heart, threatening to slay her in mind and soul.

Her joy came in spending her days with Logan. With her father and Jeffery absorbed in their hunting and her sisters busy with the Gambett girls, Amelia found herself free to work with Mary each morning and then with Logan. She had copied down nearly every specimen of vegetation in the area, and Logan had taught her how to identify animal tracks and to mark her position from the village using the elements around her. She thought it almost her imagination but swore her hearing had become better as she could make out sounds in the forested mountains that she'd never heard before. One day, when their water ran out, Logan had taught her how to listen for the sounds of water. Once she learned what it was that she was trying to hear, Amelia was amazed. The sounds had always been there, but she was just unaware of them. Before, the sounds in the air had come to her as a collective noise, but now she could separate the trickling of a mountain stream from the rustling of aspen leaves.

She had learned to depend more upon her other sense as well. Her sight and sense of smell were two things Logan said were absolutely necessary for staying alive. As they traipsed through the woods together he would often stop her and ask what certain smells were, and Amelia was quite proud to find that she was rapidly learning to identify each of these as well. Without realizing it, Amelia had spent the summer learning how to survive in the Rockies.

The bittersweetness of her circumstance, however, caught up with her one afternoon when her father sought her out.

"Amelia, we need to talk."

She looked up from where she was jotting down notes on a strange little bird that she had mistaken for a woodpecker.

"Just a moment, Father," she said, finishing her notes. "I've identified that pesky noise we've lived with these months. You know that pecking sound that comes at all hours of the day and night?" She didn't wait for him to reply. "It seems that this bird is a chipping sparrow and it chips away all the time. It actually feeds its young even into adulthood when they are fully capable of feeding themselves. Isn't that fascinating?" This time she put the pen down and looked up to find her father's serious expression.

"Quite," was all he would reply on the matter before taking a seat across from her. "Amelia, you have sorely neglected the one duty I gave you—which was to allow Sir Jeffery to pay you court. I say, I've never seen a more stubborn woman in all my life, unless of course it was your mother."

Amelia smiled. "A high compliment if ever there was one."

The earl shook his head. "I'm afraid it wasn't intended as one. See here, I know how you feel about being forced to marry, but the truth is I can't have the family coffers being depleted because of your foolishness. Why any reasonable solicitor would allow your grandmother to set out a trust to unmarried daughters is beyond me. Why it positively reeks of inappropriateness."

"It was Grandmama's money, after all, and she was only worried that her family might find themselves in situations of desperation and heartache. Grandmama had found it necessary to marry a man she didn't love, and all for financial reasons. She didn't want the same fate to befall her daughter or her granddaughters, yet now you propose to do just such a thing in order to keep the money for yourself." Amelia knew the anger in her heart was rapidly flooding over into her tone of voice.

"You have no right to speak to me thusly," the earl said rather stiffly. "I have to do what I feel is right for the benefit of the entire family, not just one member."

Amelia shook her head. "No, Father, I believe you are considering only one member—yourself." She slammed her book shut, mindless of smearing the still-damp ink. "I've tried to be orderly about this and I've tried not to bring you undue pain, but I must speak honestly here." She swallowed hard and thought of the conversation she'd overheard her father having with Jeffery the night before. Logan would chide her for eavesdropping, but this time it served to clarify the mystery behind her father's desperation to marry her to Jeffery.

"I know about your gambling debts," she began, "and the fact that you owe Sir Jeffery a great deal of money." The earl's eyes widened in surprise. "I'm not the simpleton you would give me credit for being. It wasn't hard to learn about this, nor was it difficult to learn that you had promised Jeffery land in Scotland, land, I might add, that has been in our family for generations and that must pass through the succession of marriage or death, rather than be sold."

"Furthermore, I know that Jeffery covets the land for his own purposes, some known to me and others I'm sure are unknown, but nevertheless he wants that land. So now we come to the inheritance my grandmother set in place, an inheritance that passed to my mother and made the prospects of marrying beneath our status not quite so distasteful."

The earl pounded his fists on the table. "Enough! You know very well that I loved your mother and she loved me. Ours was not a marriage for fortune and status and you know well how the name of Amhurst suffered for just such impropriety."

Amelia took a deep breath and sighed. "Yes, but I must ask if it wasn't worth it."

Lord Amhurst said nothing for a moment. His expression fell and he, too, sighed. "I could lie and say that if given the choice to do it all over again, I would marry another woman. But the truth is, I loved your mother very much and I would not trade our time together."

"So why are you trying to force such a thing upon me? If I were to inherit my share of the trust, do you believe I would leave you to suffer? How heartless you must think me."

"Nay, I never thought you heartless, but your share of the trust would never pay back what I owe Chamberlain. I'm sorry, Amelia." His resolve seemed to return. "You will have to marry Sir Jeffery."

Amelia felt as though a noose were being slipped around her neck. She rose with as much dignity as she could muster. "Your foolishness, not mine, has caused this situation. I find it completely unreasonable that I should be the one to pay for your mistakes. Let Jeffery marry one of my sisters. They both seem quite head-over-heels in love with the man."

Her father shook his head. "He wants the land that is to pass to you, Amelia. It is the Scottish estate that passes to the eldest that appeals to him."

"So I am to be sold off for the price of land and the sum of gambling debts?"

"Call it what you will," her father replied in a voice that suggested deep regret, "but avail yourself to Sir Jeffery in a proper courting manner and settle your mind on the fact that this marriage will take place."

Later that week while dressing quietly for dinner, Amelia felt a desperation building inside that couldn't be cast away with the assurance that she'd somehow work things around to her way. Jeffery had lost little time in picking up his pursuit of Amelia and as his attentions became bolder, Amelia was forced to sequester herself to her cabin for fear of what he might do next.

Penelope and Margaret were already talking of returning home and of all the things they would do. Amelia tried to remember her own earlier desires to return to England, but they'd passed from existence and now she wanted instead to remain in Estes. It was almost humorous to her that in the three months they'd spent in America, and Estes in particular, her views about the barbaric ways of the Americans had changed. She had come to look at Marry as a mother image and she cherished the time spent under her tutelage. She'd learned to cook and bake, as well as sew practical garments and quilt. Mary had also shown her how to properly clean house and wash clothes. And when time had permitted, Amelia had even taken lessons in tending the vegetable garden and livestock.

As she pulled on her gloves for dinner she looked at her hands and realized how worn and rough they'd become. Back in England her friend Sarah would be appalled at the sight of calluses upon a lady's fingers, but Amelia wore them as badges of honor. She'd earned those calluses by working at Mary's side and she was proud of what she'd accomplished.

"Oh do hurry, Amelia," Penelope whined. "We'll never be able to sit down to dinner if you don't finish getting ready."

"I, for one, refuse to wait," Margaret said, grabbing her shawl. "Come along, sister. Amelia will bring herself when she's ready. Maybe we can corner Sir Jeffery and he'll tell us more tales of his adventures in China."

"Oh yes," Penelope said, nodding her head. "That would be grand."

They left Amelia in a rush of chatter and anticipation of the night to come. She stared after them through the open door and shook her head. If only she could feel such enthusiasm for Sir Jeffery, none of this might have ever happened. The afterglow of sunset left a haunting amber color to the sky over the mountains. The chill of autumn was approaching and with it came a longing that Amelia could not explain. If only they had never come to America she would never have laid eyes on the Rocky Mountains and never have met Logan Reed.

Logan.

Her heart ached from the very thought of his name. She was hopelessly in love with him, and yet there was nothing to be done about it. Logan was as poor as a church mouse and he could never offer to pay off her father's debts the way Jeffery could. Her father owed Jeffery over seventy-thousand pounds and even with her trust, the debt would barely be half paid. It was rapidly becoming a hopeless state of circumstances.

"Well, well," Jeffery announced from the door. "I looked about for you and found you missing."

"With good reason," Amelia said rather angrily. "I wasn't yet ready to present myself at dinner."

Jeffery leered. "I could help you. . .dress."

"As you can see, I'm quite dressed and I suggest you keep your disgusting thoughts to yourself."

She moved across the room to retrieve her shawl and heard Jeffery close the cabin door. Turning around, she found that he'd already crossed the room. He took hold of her roughly and crushed her against him in a fierce embrace.

"Stop it, Jeffery!" she declared and pushed at his chest.

Jeffery only laughed and held her fast. "You mustn't put me off. We're to be man and wife after all. A kiss of passion shared between two lovers is quite acceptable."

"But you forget. I do not love you," Amelia answered, kicking Jeffery's shin as hard as she could.

He immediately released her and Amelia scurried from the room, panting for breath and close to tears. Jeffery had so frightened her with his actions that she was quite uncertain as to what she should do next. Fleeing into the darkness behind the lodge, Amelia waited until her breathing had calmed and her heart stopped racing. *What should I do? What can I do?* Her father had made it quite clear and there was no other answer. She waited several more minutes, knowing that she was keeping everyone from their meal, then with a sigh she went to face them all. Walking slowly, as if to her own execution, Amelia entered the lodge and the dining hall without the slightest desire to be among people.

"Ah, there she is now," Lord Amhurst announced. "Amelia, dear, come and join us in a toast."

Amelia looked up and found the entire party staring at her. Everyone seemed quite joyous and Jeffery stood with an expression of sheer pride on his face. They weren't apparently unhappy with her for the delay of their dinner and instead seemed extremely animated.

"What, might I ask, are we drinking a toast to?" she asked hesitantly.

The earl beamed a smile upon her. "Sir Jeffery has told us that this night you have accepted his hand in marriage." Her father raised his drink. "We are drinking to you and Sir Jeffery and a long, happy marriage."

Amelia felt the wind nearly knocked from her. She looked from her father to Jeffery and found a sneering grin on his face. His expression seemed to say, "I told you I would have my way."

"Well, do come join us," her father said, rather anxiously. "We've waited all summer for this."

Amelia found it impossible to speak. A lump formed in her throat and tears were threatening to spill from her eyes. Without concern for appearances, she turned and ran from the lodge.

Fleeing down the stairs and into the night, Amelia barely stifled a scream as she ran full-speed into Logan Reed's arms. She couldn't see his face but heard his chuckle and felt a sense of comfort in just knowing he was near.

"I'm so sorry," she said, trying to disentangle her arms from his.

"I'm not. Want to tell me what you were running from?" Amelia felt the tears trickle down her cheeks and a sob escaped her throat. Logan's voice grew more concerned. "What is it Amelia? What has happened?"

"Nothing," she said, unable to keep from crying.

He took hold of her upper arms. "You're crying, so something must be wrong."

"Just leave me alone."

His voice was low and husky. "Amelia, I care about your pain and so does God. He can help you through this, even if I can't."

She jerked away, angry at the suggestion. "If God cares so much about pain, then why does He let His children suffer? I'm going to my cabin," she declared and walked away.

Logan was quickly at her side and it wasn't until she'd opened the door to her still lighted cabin that she could see that he was smiling.

"What? Are you going to laugh at me now?"

"Not at all. It's just that I thought you didn't believe in God."

"I don't."

"Then why did you say what you did about God letting His children suffer."

"Because you are always throwing your religion and God in my face!" she declared. "You always fall back on that and always use that to settle every issue that has ever arisen between us."

"Because He is my foundation and my mainstay. God cares about your pain, but haven't you brought it on yourself? Don't you hold any responsibility for your own actions?"

"Oh, go away, Logan," she moaned in sheer misery. *Why did he have to say those things?*

With a shrug of his shoulders, Logan surprised her by turning to leave.

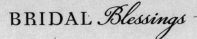
"I'm gonna pray for you Amelia. I know you're having a rough time of coming to terms with God, but just remember, He already knows what's in your heart and He knows the future He holds for you."

With that he was gone and Amelia closed the door to cry in earnest. *Why is this happening to me and what in the world am I to do about any of it?* Giving up on the world and conscious thought, Amelia stripped off her dinner clothes and pulled on a nightgown. Then, mindless of her sisters, she blew out the lamp and threw herself into bed to have a good long cry.

Chapter 13

Well, if you ask me," Penelope began, "I think it positively scandalous the way you put Sir Jeffery off."

"No one asked you," Amelia said flatly. She busied herself with quilting and tried to ignore her sisters and the Gambett girls.

"Mother says it is outrageous for you to suppose you will get a better match than Sir Jeffery," Josephine Gambett said, pushing up her glasses. They immediately slid back down her nose.

"Yes, Mother believes you are seriously jeopardizing your family's position with the Queen. After all, Sir Chamberlain's mother is a dear friend of Her Majesty," Henrietta added, not to be outdone by her sister.

Amelia felt her cheeks burn from the comeuppance of these younger girls. She thought of a hundred retorts, but bit her tongue and continued stitching.

"I think it's pure selfishness on your part," Margaret said with a little stomp of her foot. "There are other people to consider in this situation."

Amelia finally set aside her quilting and looked hard at each of the girls. "If you'll excuse me, I believe I would prefer the company of adults." With that she got up and, without any conscious plan to do so, made her way to the cabin her father shared with Mattersley. She knew he would be there cleaning his guns and in her mind she formed one last plan to plead her case.

"Father?" she said, knocking lightly upon the open door.

Mattersley shuffled across the room. His face looked pinched and his eyes were sunken. "Come in, Lady Amhurst. The earl is just now occupied with the weapons."

Amelia smiled at him. Even here in the wilds of America, Mattersley held to the strict code of English propriety. "Thank you, Mattersley." She started to walk past him then stopped and asked, "How are you feeling? You look a bit tired."

Mattersley seemed stunned by her concern. "I am well, Miss."

"You should have some time of to yourself," she said, glancing to where her father sat. "Father, don't you agree?"

"Say what?" the earl questioned, looking up.

"I believe Mattersley is working too hard and some time off would serve him well."

"Oh, well yes," her father said, genuinely seeming to consider this. "A capital idea! Mattersley, you go right ahead and take the rest of the day—"

"No," Amelia interrupted, "a day will certainly not afford him much of a rest. I suggest the rest of the week. He can stay upon the lodge. I know Mary has an extra room."

"Oh." Her father seemed quite taken aback.

"There is no need for that, sir," Mattersley said in a voice that betrayed his weariness.

"My daughter is quite right," Lord Amhurst answered, seeming to see the old man for the first time. "You've been out on nearly every hunt with us and working to keep my things in order. I can surely dress myself properly enough for the rest of the week, what?"

⌒

"Very good, sir," Mattersley replied and Amelia thought it almost sounded like a sigh of relief.

"Well, now that this matter has been resolved," she began and took the chair beside her father, "I thought we might address another."

"Do tell?" the earl replied and continued with cleaning his shotgun.

"Father, I have come to plead with you one final time to release me from this preposterous suggestion that I marry Sir Jeffery." The earl said nothing and so Amelia continued. "I cannot marry a man I do not respect, and I hold not the slightest respect for Sir Jeffery. I also cannot bring myself to consider marrying a man I do not love."

"Such modern notions do you a grave injustice, my dear," her father replied. "My mind is set and this is my final word. You will marry Chamberlain. In fact, I've arranged for us to depart Estes in three weeks. We will travel by stage from Greeley to Denver and there you will be married."

"What! How can you suggest such a thing? Why that won't even allow for a proper wedding, much less a proper English wedding," Amelia protested.

"It is of little concern. Sir Jeffery and I discussed the matter and we both believe it to be to the benefit of both parties."

"What parties? You and Jeffery? Because, I assure you it will never be to my benefit." She got to her feet, trembling from her father's declaration. "I cannot understand how my own father would sell me into such an abominable circumstance."

"And I cannot imagine that I raised a daughter to be so defiant and disobedient," the earl replied, looking at her with a stern expression of dismay. "Your mother would not be pleased in the way you've turned out. Even she would find your temperament to be unwarranted."

"Mother would understand," Amelia said softly, the anger being quickly replaced by the realization that her father could care less about her feelings. "And once, when you and she were still together, you would have understood, too."

She left the cabin and felt as though a damp, cold blanket had been thrust upon her shoulders. The weight of her father's sudden declaration was more than she'd even imagined him capable of turning out. Immediately her mind sought for some manner of refuge. *There has to be something I can do.*

She walked a ways up the mountainside and paused beside a formation of boulders and rock. Hiking up her skirt, she climbed to the top by inching her way along the crevices and hand-holds. Once she'd managed to achieve her goal, she sat down in complete dejection and surveyed the village below.

Three weeks was a very short time.

She sighed and thought of leaving Estes and knew that it was tearing at her in a way that she'd never prepared herself for. She would have to leave the clean, crisp mountain air and the beauty that she'd never grow tired of looking upon. *And for what? To return to the cold, damp English winters? To be the wife of that unbearably cruel bore?*

She felt a tear trickle down her cheek and rubbed it away with the back of her sleeve. She almost laughed at herself for the crude gesture. *In so many ways I've become one of them. How can I go back to England now?*

"I can't do it," she whispered. "I can't go back."

That left her with very few alternatives. She couldn't very well talk her father into letting her remain in America. Soon enough she would be twenty-one and her father would never allow that day to come without her being properly married to Sir Jeffery.

"I could run away," she murmured and the though suddenly seemed very possible. *Logan has taught me how to find my way around,* she reasoned. *I could hide out in the mountains until after my birthday and then Father would have no choice.* But her birthday was the twenty-third of November and by that time this entire area would be snow-packed and frightfully cold. There was no way she would survive.

"But I don't want to survive if I have to marry Jeffery."

With that declaration an entirely different thought came to mind. Taking her own life could not be ruled out as a possible alternative. She thought of Crying Rock and the Indian maid who'd bravely gone to her death rather than face the unbearable ordeal of marrying a man she abhorred. *I'm no different than that woman. My sorrow is certainly well-founded. To leave this place, this lovely, wonderful place would be sheer misery.* And yet, even as she thought it, Amelia knew it wasn't just the place—it was Logan. Marriage to any man other than Logan was simply unthinkable.

"But he doesn't feel the same way I do," she chided. "He has his God and his religion and he doesn't need a woman who would fight him with intellectual words and philosophies." *No, Logan needs a wife who would work at his side, worship at his side, raise a family at his side. Logan would expect her to believe as he did, that God not only existed but also played an intricate role in the lives of His children. And that in doing so, He gave them a Savior in Jesus Christ.*

Something her mother had once said came back to haunt her. "Only the foolish man believes there is no God, Amelia. For the Bible says, 'even the demons believe in God, and they tremble.'"

Amelia gazed out over the valley and sighed. Logan said she had but to open her eyes to the handiwork of God to realize His existence. But how could she believe in God, much less in the need to worship Him and follow all manner of rule and regulation laid out in the Bible? To what purpose was there such a belief as the need for eternal life? Wasn't it just that mortal man could not stand to believe that his important life ended in the grave? Wasn't the idea of immortality something mankind comforted itself with in lieu of facing the truth that once you died, that was all there was? After all, most religions she'd studied had some form of immortality for their believers. It was rather like a parting gift from a high-society soiree. Something to cherish for those who had the courage to play the party games.

"I do not need such comfort," she whispered and hugged her arms close. "When my life is done, it is done and there will be no marriage to Sir Jeffery and no longing for what I can never have."

Suddenly it seemed quite reasonable to put an end to her life. In fact, it was almost calming. If there was nothing else to concern herself with, why not stop now? She'd seen more of the world than most people. She'd enjoyed the pleasures of the privileged life and she'd once known the love of good parents and siblings. *So what if I never know the love of a man—never know the joys of motherhood?* She wiped the tears that were now pouring freely from her eyes.

"I will go to Jeffery and plead my case before him. I will tell him honestly that I have no desire to marry him and suggest to him a different course," she told the valley before her. She climbed down from the rock and smoothed her skirt. "If he refuses to give consideration to my desires, then the matter will be resolved for me."

She thought that there should be some kind of feeling of accomplishment in making such a decision, but there wasn't. She felt empty and void of life. "I am resigned to do this thing," she said as an encouragement to her broken spirit. "There is no other way."

Chapter 14

S ir Jeffery, I wonder if I might have a moment of your time," Amelia began one evening after dinner.

He seemed to sneer down his nose at her as though her request had somehow reduced her to a beggar. "I would be honored," he said and extended his arm for her.

Amelia, seeing all faces turned to behold her action, placed her hand upon his sleeve. "I suggest a short walk, if that would meet with your approval," she said cautiously.

"But of course, Lady Amhurst. I am your servant."

Amelia said nothing more, but allowed Jeffery to lead her amicably from the lodge.

"I must say this is a pleasant surprise. Dare I hope you're coming around to my way of thinking?"

Amelia let go of him and shook her head. "No, rather I was hoping to persuade you to my way of thinking."

"How so?"

"Sir Jeffery, I have no desire to marry you. I do not love you and I never will. I cannot make it any clearer on this point." She turned to him in the dim lamp light of the porch and hoped he would understand. "I know about your hold on Father and I know about your desire for the Scottish property." She held up her hand to wave off his question. "I overheard you two discussing the matter one evening. Therefore, I know, too, that you are not marrying me because of any great love, but rather because you want a good turn of business."

"Fair enough," Jeffery replied and leaned back against the porch railing. "But your knowing the circumstance does nothing to change my decision."

"But why not? Why not be an honorable man about this and allow Father some other means by which to settle his debt?"

"I'm open to other means. If you can put the seventy thousand pounds in my hand, I'll call the entire wedding off."

"Truly?" she asked, feeling at once hopeful.

Jeffery sneered and laughed. "But of course, you can't put that kind of money in my hands, even if you inherit, can you?"

"Perhaps not right away, but I could put over half of it in your hands."

"What? And leave yourself with no income. If you do not marry, your father is sure to exile you to that pitifully cold Scottish estate you seem so inclined to hang on to. Without funds, how do you propose to live?"

"I hope to sell my book when we return to England. Lady Bird suggested—"

"No, Amelia. I will not call of this wedding on your hopes and the suggestions of Lady Bird."

"And there is no other way to convince you?"

"None. Now stop being such a foolish child about it all. You'll have the very best of everything, I assure you. And if you're concerned about your freedom to find true love, I will even go so far as to say that as long as you are discrete about your affairs, I will be most tolerant of them."

∞

Amelia was totally aghast. "I would never consider such a thing!"

Jeffery sighed and spoke tolerantly as though dealing with a simpleton. "It is done all the time, Amelia dear. Most of nobility take lovers because they've been forced into loveless marriages. I'm simply trying to offer you what would be an acceptable arrangement in lieu of your sacrificing to a marriage of arrangement."

Noises from the front of the lodge porch told Amelia that her sisters and their friends were making their way over to the Amhurst cabin. They were giggling and talking in rapid—fire succession about some point or another. It probably amounted to nothing more than their ritual game of after—dinner whist. Amelia lowered her voice to avoid drawing attention to herself.

"I am appalled that you would suggest such a thing. Marriage is a sacred institution, not something to be flaunted about and infringed upon by numerous affairs."

"My dear, you are quite naive to believe such a thing. I had thought you to be more mature about these matters, especially in light of your disbelief in holy affairs. I thought you above all other women to be removed from such nonsense."

"Faithfulness has never been nonsense to my way of thinking."

"Ah, but it is your way of thinking that is keeping this matter unresolved. Your father made up his mind to accept my generous offer. It will benefit all people in one way or another. Yes, even you will benefit, Amelia, and if you would but stop to think about it, you would see that I speak the truth. You might even come to enjoy my company after a time, and furthermore, to find pleasure in my bed."

Amelia dismissed such notions with her coldest stare. She hoped Jeffery felt frozen to the bone from her look. "I believe we've said all there is to say," she stated and turned to leave. Jeffery did nothing to stop her.

"You'll soon see for yourself, Amelia." He called after her, then laughed in a way that suggested he was very much enjoying the entire matter.

Amelia hurried to her cabin, fighting back tears and angry retorts. She knew that there was little to be done but accept her fate. Suicide seemed her only answer and her heart grew even heavier as she considered how she might accomplish such a fate.

"I want to wear the green one," Penelope argued and pulled the gown from Margaret's hold. Both sisters looked up guiltily as Amelia entered the room to find them fighting over her gowns.

When Amelia remained fixed in her place, saying nothing of reprimand, Penelope took the opportunity to explain. "There is to be a dance tonight. They're clearing the lodge's main room and Mary is fixing refreshments. It won't be as nice as a fancy ball, but I'm positively dying to dance. And Mr. Reed said the local men will come and serve as partners."

Margaret lifted her nose in the air and said, "I do hope they bathe. Some of these Americans seem not to know what a benefit water and soap can be." Her attitude suggested she might be reconsidering her appearance at the dance, but just when Amelia figured her to be absent, Margaret's expression changed to one of pleading desperation. "You simply must let us borrow your dresses. You have so many pretty gowns that you've not even worn and we've only those old things." She waived to a small stack of discarded gowns.

"Do whatever you like," Amelia finally said in a voice of pure resignation. "You may have all of my dresses for all I care. I won't be needing them anymore."

"You're only saying that to make me feel bad," Penelope said, puffing out her chest indignantly. "Just because you are marrying Sir Jeffery in Denver and will receive a new trousseau, you think you can be cruel."

"Yes, you are very mean-spirited, Amelia," Margaret agreed. "I think I've never met a more hateful person. You'll have Sir Jeffery and his money and go to court and spend your days in all the finery and luxury money can buy. We'll still be trying to make a proper match."

"Yes," Penelope added with a sigh, "and hoping that our husbands will be as handsome and rich as Sir Jeffery." Both of them broke into tittering giggles before Penelope sobered and tightened her hold on the gown as though Amelia might change her mind. "So you needn't be so smug Amelia. You may walk around with your nose in the air for all we care."

Amelia looked at them both. She was stunned by their harshness and hurt by their comments. These were her sisters and there had been a time when they were all close and happy. She remembered joyous times when they were little and she'd played happily with them in the nursery. She loved them, even if they couldn't see that. Even if time and sorrow had made them harsh, and strained their ability to be kind. She saw hints of their mother woven in their expressions. Margaret looked like their mother more than any of them, but Penelope shared a similar mouth and nose. Amelia sighed. They should be close, close as any three people could ever be. But they thought her a snob and a spiteful, prideful person, and perhaps they were right. It seemed only to fuel the idea that the world would be a better place without her in it.

No wishing to leave them with a bitter memory of her, she offered softly, "I do apologize. I fear you have misjudged me, however. It was never my intentions to make you feel bad."

Margaret and Penelope looked at her in complete surprise. Amelia wondered if they had any idea of what she was about to do. They were so young and childish and probably concerned themselves only with what color would best highlight their eyes or hair. No doubt they prayed fervently that Amelia would allow Jeffery the freedom to dance with them and pay them the attention they so craved. *Will they mourn me when I am gone? Will anyone?*

"You don't care at all how we feel. All summer you've pranced around here like some sort of queen. Always you've had the best of everything and Father even allowed you to remain behind from the hunt when we had to drudge about this horrid country looking for sport!" Penelope declared.

"Yes, it's true!" Margaret exclaimed in agreement. "You had Jeffery's undivided attention and positively misused him. You have no heart, Amelia."

Amelia could no longer stand up under their criticism. She felt herself close to tears again and rather than allow them to see her cry, turned at the door to walk away. "You needn't worry about the matter anymore," she called over her shoulder. "I'll take myself to the Crying Rock and relieve you of your miseries."

Crossing the yard, Amelia looked heavenward. A huge milky moon shown down to light her way and a million stars sparkled against the blackness. Mother had told her that stars were the candlelights of angels.

"We can't always see the good things at hand, but we can trust them to be there."

Amelia sighed and rubbed her arms against the chill. "You were wrong, Mother. There is no good thing at hand for me."

She made her way up the mountain through the heavy undergrowth of the forest floor. She only vaguely knew the path to the Crying Rock and hoped she'd find the right way. Tears blinded her from seeing what little moonlight had managed to filter down through the trees. She'd never been one given to tears, but during these few months in America she'd cried enough for a lifetime. Now, it seemed that her lifetime should appropriately come to an end.

Her sisters' harsh comments were still ringing in her ears and her chest felt tight and constricted with guilt and anguish. *Perhaps they're right. Perhaps I am heartless and cruel. The world would be a much better place without me.*

God cares about your pain. Logan's words came back to mind so clearly that Amelia stopped in her place and listened for him to speak. The wind moaned through the trees and Amelia realized that it was nothing but her mind playing tricks on her. *There is no God,* she reminded herself, chiding herself for being foolish.

"Even if there were," she muttered, "He wouldn't care about me."

∞

Logan leaned against the stone wall of the fireplace and wondered if Amelia would join the evening fun. He'd watched her from afar and saw that her mind was overly burdened with matters that she refused to share. He'd prayed for her to find the answers she longed for.

Over in one corner, Lord Amhurst and Sir Jeffery were steeped in conversation and Logan couldn't help but watch them with a feeling of contempt. *What kind of man forces his child to marry against her will? Especially a man who represents nothing but fearful teasing from childhood and snobbish formality in adulthood.* He longed to understand better and not feel to judgmental about Amelia's father and his insistence that she wed Jeffery Chamberlain. He knew very little except for what he'd overheard and none of that gave him the full picture. He'd tried to get Amelia to talk about it, but even when he'd caught her in moments where she was less guarded about her speech, she refused to share her concerns with him.

His mind went back to the conversation he'd overheard earlier that evening between Amelia and Jeffery. He'd been coming to the lodge and rounded the back corner just in time to hear Amelia tell Chamberlain that she believed in faithfulness in marriage. Chamberlain certainly hadn't, but it didn't surprise Logan.

"Well, well, and here come some of our lovely ladies now," the earl stated loudly.

Logan looked up to find Amelia's sisters flouncing about the room in their finery. Lady Gambett and her daughters were quick to follow them into the room, but Amelia was nowhere to be found.

"I say, Penelope," Lord Amhurst began, "isn't that one of Amelia's gowns?"

Penelope whirled in the pale-green silk. "Yes, Father, it is."

"You know how particular your sister is about her gowns. It will certainly miff her to find you in it."

"She knows all about it," Penelope replied.

"Yes, Father, she does. In fact, this is her gown also and she told me I could wear it," Margaret chattered. "Although it is a bit large."

Logan smiled, seeing for himself that Margaret's girlish figure couldn't quite fill out the bodice. He could imagine Amelia growing impatient with them both and throwing the gowns in their faces. Sipping a cup of coffee, Logan tried to hide his smile and keep his thoughts to himself.

In one corner, several of the boys were tuning up their fiddles and guitars to provide the evening's music, while the earl exchanged formalities with the newly arrived Lord Gambett. They talked for several minutes while the ladies gathered around Jeffery, each vying for his compliments. Some of the local men straggled in and Logan nearly laughed at the way they each paused at the door to shine their boots on the backside of the opposite leg. Never mind their jeans might show a smudge of dirt, so long as their boots looked good. Logan almost felt sorry for them, knowing that the prim and proper English roses would hardly appreciate the effort.

"We're certain to beat the snow if we leave at the end of next week instead of waiting," Logan hear Lord Gambett say.

"What do you say, Mr. Reed? Is the snow upon us?" Lord Amhurst suddenly questioned.

"It's due, that's for sure," Logan replied. "But I think you're safe from any real accumulation. We might see a dusting here and there, but it doesn't look bad just yet. Of course, with mountain weather that could all change by morning.

The musicians were ready and awaited some kind of cue that they should begin playing. The fiddle player was already drawing his bow across the strings in what Logan knew to be an American-styled call to order. He looked around the room and, still seeing no sign of Amelia, he questioned the earl about beginning the music.

"I see Lady Amhurst is still absent, but if you would like, the boys are ready to begin playing."

The earl glanced around as though Amelia's absence was news. "I say, Penelope, where is that sister of yours? She doesn't seem to be here."

Penelope shrugged. "She left the cabin after telling us to wear whatever we wanted. She was mean-tempered and said she wouldn't be needing these gowns anymore. We presumed she said that because of her marriage to Sir Jeffery. Don't you think it was mean of her to boast that way?"

Lord Amhurst laughed, "At least she's finally coming around to our way of thinking, what?" He elbowed Jeffery and laughed.

"Indeed it would appear that way," the sneering man replied.

Logan hated his smugness and thought of his lurid suggestion that Amelia would come to enjoy his bed. Logan seethed at the thought of Amelia joining this man in marriage. He had worked all week long to figure out what he could do to resolve Amelia's situation. He couldn't understand her loyalty to a father who would be so unconcerned with her feelings, and yet he respected her honoring him with obedience. *Somehow there has to be a way to make things right for Amelia.* He though of approaching the earl and asking for Amelia's hand, but he as already certain that the man would never consider him a proper suitor, much less a proper husband.

"I congratulate you, Chamberlain, on your powers of persuasion. You must have given her a good talking to in order to convince her to marry."

"Maybe it was more than a talking to," Lady Gambett said in uncharacteristic fashion.

The girls all giggled and blushed at this. They whispered among themselves at just what such possibilities might entail, while Jeffery smiled smugly and accepted their suppositions. Logan barely held his temper and would have gladly belted the grin off Chamberlain's face had his attention not been taken in yet another startling direction.

"But did Amelia say when she might join us?" the earl asked, suddenly seeming to want to push the party forward.

"No," Penelope replied, "she said she was going off to cry on some rock. I suppose she'll be at it all night and come back with puffy red eyes."

"Then she'll be too embarrassed to come to the party," Margaret replied.

Logan felt his breath quicken and his mind repeated the words Penelope had just uttered. *"She said she was going off to cry on some rock." Did she mean Crying Rock?* He put his cup down and signaled the band to begin. He wanted no interference on exiting quickly and figured with the music as a diversion he could make his way out the back kitchen door.

He was right. Logan slipped from the room without anyone voicing so much as a "Good evening." His thoughts haunted him as he made his way to the end of the porch. He grabbed a lighted lantern as he jumped down from the steps. *She doesn't want this marriage and she knows about Crying Rock.* He mentally kicked himself for ever taking her there.

"Lord, if I've caused her to seek a way out that costs Amelia her life, I'll never forgive myself," he muttered.

Chapter 15

As if drawn there by sheer will, Amelia finally made her way to Crying Rock. She stood for a moment under the full moon and looked down at the valley below. Across the mountains the moon's reflection made it appear as though it were day. The dark, shadowy covering of pine and aspen looked like an ink smudge against the valley. The mournful sound of the wind playing in the canyons seemed to join Amelia's sobs in sympathetic chorus.

Her gown of lavender crepe de Chine did little to ward off the bit of the mountain breeze. The polonaise styling with its full skirt and looped-up draping in back gave a bit of protection, but the wind seemed to pass right through the low-cut bodice and was hardly deterred by the chiffon modesty scarf that she'd tucked into it. The finery of a Paris gown meant little to her now. *What good were such baubles when no one cared if you lived or died?*

She stepped closer to the edge and wiped her tear-stained face. *Father will be very unhappy when he learns what I've done. All of his plans will be for naught, and yet he'll still have his money and the land will pass to Penelope.* Perhaps her sister would go willingly into marriage with Sir Jeffery. Thinking of Jeffery made her stomach hurt. He was mean and crude and just standing over the dizzying drop made her remember his cruelty to her as a child.

"This thing must be done," she said to the sky and then sank to her knees in misery. *If only there were some reason to go on with life.* She simply couldn't see herself at Jeffery's side playing the innocent wife while keeping her lovers waiting in hidden rooms. Furthermore, to imagine that Jeffery would entertain himself in such a manner bothered her pride more than she could admit. If Jeffery had at least loved her, it might have been possible to go into the marriage. But he wanted nothing more than her father's money and the manipulative power to control all that she would inherit. Amelia felt sick just imagining the arrangement.

"If God did exist—" she said softly and lifted her gaze again to the panoramic view of the mountains. She thought of Logan and all that he'd share with her about God and the Bible. She thought of his faith to believe in such matters. He was totally unwavering, even when she made what she knew was a strong argument against his beliefs, Logan wouldn't argue with her about God. And it wasn't because Amelia hadn't sought to stir up a conflict now and then. Logan would merely state what he believed to be the facts and leave Amelia to sort through it herself. She remembered one conversation that had taken place several days earlier in which she had asked Logan how he could be so certain that he was right in his beliefs.

"How can you be so certain that I'm not?" he had questioned. "I'm willing to bet my life on my beliefs. Are you?"

Amelia felt a chill run through her at the memory. Was she willing to bet her life on her beliefs? Her mother's faith had been the foundation for their household. Her father had even admitted that it was one of the things that had attracted him to her in the first place.

"Mother, why did you leave us?" Amelia whispered. "Why did you have to leave me with so many questions? If God loves us as you always said He did, then why did He cruelly take you from the children who needed you? Where is God's mercy in that? Where is the love?"

The rustlings of the wind in the trees below were all that came back in reply.

"All right," she said, giving in to the tremendous longing in her soul. "If You exist, God, then why do you allow such tragedy and injustice? Why, if You are such a loving Father, do You allow Your children to experience such pain?" She paused in questioning and rubbed her arms against the mountain chill. "Why do You allow *me* to hurt so much?"

"I want to believe," she said and this time the tears came. "I want to believe." She sobbed and buried her face in her hands. "But it hurts so much and I'm so afraid that You won't be any more constant than Mother was. If I believed, would You merely go away when I needed You most, just as she did?"

A verse of Scripture from childhood from the last chapter of Matthew, came to memory. "And, lo, I am with you always, *even* unto the end of the world."

"But the world is filled with a variety of beliefs and religious nonsense," Amelia protested against the pulling of her spirit. "How can I know that this is real? How can I know that I am choosing the right path?"

Logan had said it was a matter of faith and in believing that the Bible was truly the word of God. Logan had also said that God proved himself over and over, even in the little day-to-day points of life.

"God, if You are real," Amelia said, lifting her face to the starry, moonlit sky overhead, "then You must show me in such a way that I cannot miss it in my blind foolishness."

But even if God was real He wouldn't change my plight. What tiny thread of hope had begun to weave itself through her broken heart, snapped with this sudden realization. She was still facing her father's edict that she marry a man she didn't care about. She would still find herself headed back to England within the month. And she would still lose the man she loved.

Logan came to mind with such a powerful urgency that Amelia no longer fought against it. She loved him as truly as she had ever loved anyone, and in many ways, intimate and frightening ways, she loved him more than she had ever loved anyone else. Logan was like no one else in the world. He cared to share his faith with her in such a way that it wasn't merely preaching for the sake of fulfilling his obligation to God—rather it was that his heart was so full to overflowing with love for his God and Savior that he couldn't help but share it.

Then, too, Logan was perhaps the only man who had ever treated her with respect that didn't come from a sense of noble obligation. Logan spoke his mind and refused to play into her role of "Ladyship," but he also afforded her a kindness and gentleness of spirit that only her mother had ever given her. But of course, that didn't mean he loved her and love was truly all that Amelia longed for in life.

"There is no reason to live without it," she whispered. "Oh, God, if You are real then give me a reason to live. Send me love. Real and true love. Please, let someone love me." She sobbed.

"I love you," Logan said from somewhere behind her. "Even more, God loves you, Amelia."

∞

The sound of his voice startled her so badly that Amelia hurried to her feet, tangling her skirt around her legs as she tried to straighten up. Caught off guard by Logan and by the gown's hold on her, Amelia lost her balance and fell to the ground. The impact caused a piece of the rocky ledge to give way and Amelia felt herself slipping from the safety of Crying Rock.

Digging her hands into the rock and dirt, she thought, *Not now. I can't die now!* But even as the thought crossed her mind, she was more than aware of her dangerous situation. With what she thought would surely be her last breath, she screamed Logan's name.

"Amelia!" he cried out from overhead. "I thought I'd lost you!"

She pressed her body against the cold, hard granite and for the first time in her life began praying earnestly. She barely heard Logan calling her name and refused to even lift her fact to search for him overhead.

"Amelia, you have to listen to me," Logan said again. "Can you hear me?"

"Yes." She barely breathed the word.

As he moved overhead, bits of rock and dirt pelted down on hear head causing Amelia to shreik in fear. "Don't be scared, Amelia. I'll soon have you right as rain."

She would have laughed had the predicament not been so grave. *Don't be scared?* She was long past scared. She was terrified to the point that she thought she might pass out cold and end any hope of her rescue.

"Listen to me, Amelia. I can reach your hand if you lift your arm up."

"No, I'm not moving," Amelia replied, hardly daring to breath.

"You have to do as I say or you may well be on that ledge for whatever time you have left on earth."

She said nothing for several heartbeats and then spoke in a barely audible voice. "I can't do it, Logan."

Logan seemed not to hear her. "Look up and to your right. I'm reaching down as far as I can and I can almost touch your head. All you have to do is give me your hand. I promise I won't let you go."

"I can't do it," she repeated sternly.

"Yes, you can," he told her, sounding so confident that she felt a surge of hope. "Trust me, Amelia. Have faith in me and what God can do."

Amelia felt the pounding of her heart and the fierce chill of the wind as it whipped up under her skirt from the canyon below. She wanted to believe that Logan could do what he claimed. She wanted to trust that God would honor her prayer of desperation.

Slowly, methodically, she released her grip on the rock. Her hands ached from their hold, but slowly she stretched her fingers until they were straight. She lifted her arm ever so slowly. She refused to look up, terrified that she would find the distance too far to make contact with Logan's hand. But then his hand clamped down on her wrist jarring her rigid body to her toes. Amelia had to force herself not to cry out.

"I've got you. NO just don't fight me and we'll be okay," Logan called down to her. "I'm going to pull you back up on the count of three. One. Two—"

Amelia's heart was in her throat. *If I die now there will never be any hope of reconciling myself to God.*

"Three!" Logan exclaimed and Amelia found herself being hoisted back up the rock wall. She heard her crepe de Chine skirt tear against the jagged edge and the loose dirt rolling off the ledge as Logan dragged her across it. In the time that it took to realize what had happed Amelia lay atop the ground with Logan panting heavily at her side.

He jumped up quickly and pulled her away from the edge to more stable ground. Wrapping his arms around her, he held her in a trembling embrace that told her how afraid he'd been. He sighed against her ear and Amelia thought it all more wondrous than she could take in. She relished the warmth of his body against hers and the powerful hold of his arms. *He loves me*, she thought. If only she could stay in his arms forever.

Then, without warning, she started to giggle and then to laugh and Logan pulled away to look at her quite seriously. The thoughts flooding through her mind, however, would not let her speak a word of explanation. It was almost as though the missing joy in her life had suddenly bubbled over inside.

"Amelia, are you all right?"

She nodded and continued to laugh so hard that tears came to her eyes.

"It's shock," he said authoritatively. "Come sit down."

Shaking, Amelia allowed him to lead her to a small boulder and sat willingly when he pushed her to do so. She was still laughing, however, at the very idea that she had asked God to give her a sign so clear that she could not miss the truth! What remained comical in her mind was that God could hardly have made it any clearer, and even Amelia, in her childish refusal to believe in His presence, was ready to admit her folly.

Logan sat down beside her and pulled her gently into his arms. She looked over and found his expression so fearful that it sent her into new peals of laughter.

"I'm sorry," she alternated between gasps and giggles. "It's just so, so—" Her voice fell away in uncontrollable mirth.

"Amelia, honey, you've got to calm down," Logan said softly. Her hair had come loose during her escapade up the mountain, and Logan methodically stroked it as if to calm her.

"It's just," she said, finally gaining control of her voice, "that I asked God to prove Himself to me. I asked Him for a sign that even I couldn't ignore and then He does just that, getting my full attention by gangling me over the ledge! Oh, Logan, don't you see how funny it is?"

Logan nodded and smiled. "I remember you asking Him for love, too."

This did the trick in sobering her completely. "Yes, I did." She looked deep into his eyes, unable to make out their brilliant green shading in the moonlight. "I'm glad you came."

"Me, too."

With their faces only inches apart, the kiss that followed seemed more than natural. Amelia felt Logan bury his warm fingers in her hair in order to slant her head just enough to give him free access to her mouth. She was stunned by the kiss at first, and then a flaming warmth seemed to radiate out from where their lips touched. It flowed down through her body until

Amelia wanted to shout aloud with joy.

"Amelia," Logan sighed her name as he pulled away from the kiss. "I love you, Amelia. Please tell me that you could love a barbarian."

She smiled. "I *do* love you, Logan Reed."

With this, he kissed her again, only this time less urgently and when he pulled away, Amelia could see that his eyes glistened. "I thought I'd lost you," he whispered.

"I couldn't see a reason to go on, but neither did I have the courage to put an end to my life," Amelia admitted.

"It doesn't take courage to kill yourself," Logan interjected. "That's the coward's way out."

"I was in such turmoil. I kept remembering the things my mother had taught me about God and the things you kept pushing in my face." At that she smiled and took hold of his hand. "Logan, you were right to keep after me. I've always known God existed, but I didn't want to admit it because if He existed in the power and glory people told me about, it also meant that He had the power to keep the bad things in my life from happening. But He didn't. He let Jeffery torture me as a child. He let my Mother die before I was ready to say good-bye to her and He left me to be forced into a marriage with a man I can't abide." She paused and searched Logan's face for condemnation. When she found only love reflected in his gaze, she continued.

"To believe in His existence meant I had to accept that He knew what was happening and that He stood by and let it happen. That seemed cruel and heartless to me. The God my mother had always told me of was merciful and loving. I couldn't accept that He would do such a thing or even allow someone else to do those things. Does that make any sense?"

"I think so," Logan replied. "But how about now? Those things haven't changed. And there are still horrible tragedies in life. Tragedies that won't just go away overnight."

"That's true," Amelia said thoughtfully, "but I suppose I must simply accept that fact. I don't imagine life will always make sense, but what does make sense to me is that if there is a way to deal with the bad times in peace and confidence, then that's what I want. I've watched you all summer and your peace and assurance have driven me nearly insane."

He laughed at this and hugged her close. "Your uppity, stubborn 'I'll-do-it-myself' attitude has nearly driven me to drink, so I guess we're even." He ran his hand through the blond silk and smiled. "Oh, and I always wondered what you'd look like with your hair down and now I know."

"And what exactly do you know?" she asked impishly.

"That you are the most beautiful woman in the world," Logan replied. "What little of it I've seen."

"There's no place else in the world as pretty as Estes, Logan, and no place I'd rather be."

"So what are we going to do now?" he asked softly.

Amelia smiled and pulled back far enough to look into his face. "I'm ready to lay it all out before God, Logan. I'm ready to face life and march back down the mountain and do what I'm told to do." She bit at her lower lip and looked away before adding, "At least I think I am. It won't be easy to leave you."

"Leave me? Who said anything about you leaving me? I want you to marry me, Amelia."

She shook her head. "That, Logan, is impossible. There are things you don't know about that prevent my giving in to such a dream. And believe me, that is my dream. I would love to marry you and stay here in the mountains for the rest of my life. I know it deep down inside me, just as I know that I'm ready to accept Christ as my Savior." She paused, feeling suddenly shy about her declarations. "But it is not possible for us to marry."

"With God," Logan said, reaching out to life her face, "all things are possible. The Bible says so and I believe it with all of my heart, just as I believe you will one day be Mrs. Logan Reed."

Amelia felt the tears come anew. She looked at him there in the moonlight and tried to commit to memory every line and angle. She reached out and touched the mustache that she'd so often longed to touch and found it soft, yet coarse, against her fingers. Funny, but she'd not even noticed it when he'd kissed her.

She gazed into his eyes, seeing the longing and love reflected there for her—longing and love she held in her own heart for him. *How can I explain that could never be his wife? How can I walk away from the only man I will ever love and marry another?*

As if sensing her thoughts, Logan took hold of her hand and kissed her fingers gently. "All things are possible with God," he repeated. "Not just some things, but all things."

"You don't understand, Logan. My father needs me to marry Jeffery. He owes him a great debt and Sir Chamberlain will brook no nonsense in collecting on the matter."

"Does he love you?" Logan asked quite seriously.

"No. I think that man incapable of love. But he does desire my land," she said, smiling at the irony of it all. One man wanted her heart, another her land and she was stuck in the middle with her own longing and need and no one but God knew what that might mean to her.

"Do you love him?"

"Certainly not!" she declared with a look of horror.

"I love you, Amelia," he said simply. "I love you and I want to marry you, not for land or money or noble title, but because life without you would be unbearable. I think I fell in love with you the morning after our first all-day ride. You tried so hard to keep from grimacing in pain as you got on that horse the next morning and I thought to myself, 'Here's a woman with real spirit.' Then I think I loved you even more when you went bustling around camp trying so hard to work at every job I gave you. I pushed you a bit too hard, but I got my reward. It put you in my arms."

"You asked me to choose between barbarians or twits," she murmured. And you thought I chose Jeffery."

"No, I didn't."

"But you said—" She paused, cocking her head to one side as if to better understand him.

"I said that I could see you'd made your choice. I never said you chose Sir Twit. But I could see the argument you were having with yourself over feelings that you couldn't yet come to terms with. So I gave you over to him, hoping that the misery would drive you right back to me."

"I couldn't sleep that night for the things you made me feel," she admitted.

"Me either. So you see, I'm not ready to give up and say this can't be done. I'm quite willing to fight for you and pay off your father's debt if necessary."

"You can't. It's a great deal more money than either of us could hope to raise."

"How much?" he asked flatly, with a look of disbelief on his face.

"Seventy thousand pounds."

"Done."

"Done?" she questioned. "Where in the world are you going to come up with seventy thousand pounds?"

"Well, it probably won't be pounds, but American dollars will spend just the same."

She shook her head. "Don't joke about this."

"I'm not joking."

She could see by the serious expression on his face that, indeed, he wasn't joking. "How are you going to come by seventy thousand dollars or pounds?"

"I'll take it out of the bank."

"You mean rob it?" she asked in alarm.

Logan laughed until Amelia thought he would fall off the rock on which they were sitting. "No, silly. I'll withdraw that much from my account."

"You have that much money?"

"And a good deal more," he said soberly.

"But I thought—"

"You thought because I live here in Estes and lead guided tours into the park that I was too dirt poor to go anywhere else. Isn't that right?" She nodded, feeling quite guilty for her assessment. "Well, it isn't true. I've got more money that I'll ever need thanks to a little gold mine my father and I own. The truth is, I live this way because I love it. Estes is the only place in the world I ever came to that when I first laid eyes on it, I felt like I'd come home."

"Me, too," she whispered, barely able to speak. *Did God bring me here to bring me home to Him? To Logan?* It was more than she could take in all at once. *It this how God is making Himself real in my life? To suddenly answer all my needs in one powerful stroke?*

Logan got to his knees and pulled her down with him. "First things first," he said, pulling her closer. "You said you were ready to accept Christ as your Savior, right?" Amelia nodded, forgetting everything else for a moment. "Then that is where we start our new life together," he replied and led her in a prayer of repentance.

Chapter 16

Snow blanketed the mountaintops while a light powdery dusting covered the valley below. They had left Estes days ago and Amelia had felt an apprehension that grew into genuine fear. What if Logan couldn't convince her father to release her from the engagement to Sir Jeffery? What if Jeffery, himself, refused? With each step the horses took, with every descending clip of their hooves against the dirt and rocks, Amelia felt something inside her die.

She watched both men with anxious eyes, all the while praying fervently. Her father seemed mindless of her dilemma and Jeffery only appeared smug and self-satisfied with the circumstance. Logan promised that God would provide an answer and a way to see them through, but Amelia wasn't as steady in her faith as Logan and the possibility seemed completely out of reach.

Shortly before noon, Logan stopped the party to rest the horses and to Amelia's surprise he beckoned Sir Jeffery to follow him into the forest. Appearing quite annoyed with their barbaric guide, Jeffery did as he was bid, but not without a scowl of displeasure plastered across his aristocratic face. In a short while they returned to join the party and Jeffery seemed all smiles and satisfaction. Amelia was puzzled by this turn of events, but no more so than when Jeffery heralded her father and the two men began to have a feverish discussion. From time to time her father nodded and glanced in her direction, but no one summoned her or indicated a need for her presence and so Amelia remained with her horse, seeing to it that he was properly watered.

They remounted and made their way another hour or so, weaving back and forth across the St. Vrain River before emerging from the canyon to face some six miles of flat prairie land. Longmont would be at the end of the prairie ground and Amelia felt her hope giving way. Longmont represented the place where they were to take the stage to Denver and forever leave Estes, and Logan, behind them. She shuddered, fought back tears and prayed for strength to endure whatever God decided. And all the while she felt her heart nearly breaking with desire to turn around and run back to the safety of Estes.

How could she leave?

She glanced over her shoulder to the mountains. They seemed gray in the harsher light, and the chill in the air left little doubt that winter would soon be a serious business in the area. She gripped the reins tighter and ignored the single tear that slid down her cheek.

How could she leave Logan?

She watched him lead the way across the dried-out prairie and tried to imagine sitting in her damp, drafty English manor house without him. Months ago, she wouldn't have given a single shilling to extend her trip to America by even a day, and now she knew she'd gladly trade the rest of her life to be able to marry Logan and share even a few days as his wife.

"I say," the earl called out to his companions, "this place seems worse for the passing of time."

"Indeed," Lord Gambett replied, gazing about. "Not at all pleasant. It was hot and unbearable when we departed and now we find it dusty and devoid of life."

Amelia smiled at this. Months ago, she would have agreed with Lord Gambett, but now, with the training Logan had given her, Amelia observed life everywhere. Insects, animals, autumn vegetation. It was all here; it was just a matter of where you looked.

"Whoa," she heard Logan call to the party. She glanced forward to find that everyone had halted their horses on the edge of town. "I believe you all know your way from here," Logan said sternly. "Tie up your mounts in front of the hotel and take your personal belongings with you. I'll see to the horses and gear and meet you to settle up in about half an hour. I'll also bring your trunks at that time."

Everyone nodded and urged their horses forward to the hotel. Amelia saw her father and Mattersley press forward with Penelope and Margaret in tow, but she couldn't bring herself to join them. She stared, instead, at Logan astride his horse. Logan, whose face was tanned and sported a new two-day growth of beard. Logan, whose jeans accented his well-muscled legs and whose indigo-dyed, cambric shirt hugged him in a way Amelia longed to imitate. He pulled off his hat, wiped his brow and finally noticed that she was watching him. With a grin, he replaced the hat and nudged his horse her direction.

"You having trouble following directions again, Lady Amhurst?"

She felt a lump in her throat that threatened to strangle her. "No," she barely croaked out.

His mustache twitched as he broke into a broad smile. "Faith, Amelia. Have faith."

"It's stronger when I'm with you," she replied.

"Don't put your faith in me. Remember, your strength comes from God and He will help you."

She nodded. "Okay, Logan. My faith is in God." She spoke the words aloud hoping it would help her to feel more confident. "But how are we going to—"

"Don't worry about anything. Now join up with your family and I'll see you in half an hour." He winked at her before leading his horse off in the direction of the livery.

"Don't worry—have faith," she murmured and urged her mount forward. "Easier said than done."

∽

Half an hour later, Amelia was just as nervous as when she'd left Logan. Her father seemed preoccupied with some matter, while Sir Jeffery was suddenly paying far more attention to Penelope and Margaret than he'd done throughout the entire trip. When she could stand it no longer, Amelia went to the earl and demanded to know what was going on.

"Amelia, Sir Jeffery has agreed to release you from your engagement."

Her mouth dropped. Recovering her composure she asked, "He did? But what of the money?" At this Mattersley took several steps away from the earl and pretended to be preoccupied by studying the ceiling.

Her father shrugged. "He dismissed the debt as well. I have no idea what you said to him, Amelia, but there it is."

"But I don't understand."

"It would seem that you have won this round. I. . .well. . .perhaps I was overly influenced to marry you off because of the debt." He looked at her intently. "I never meant any harm by it, Amelia. I thought you could be happy in time. I suppose now you are free to remain unmarried."

"But what of the inheritance and your concerns for the family coffers?" she asked warily.

Weariness seemed to mar his brow. "You gave your word that you'd not see us suffer and I've always known you to be a woman of truth. Having you stay on with me as your sisters marry and leave will no doubt be a comfort in my old age."

How strange, Amelia thought wondering how she might broach the subject of Logan's proposal and her own desire to remain in America. How could she explain the change in her heart when she'd been the one to protest leaving England in the first place?

"Ah, good, you're all here," Logan said, striding into the room as though he were about to lead them all in a lecture symposium.

Lord Amhurst looked up with Mattersley doing likewise, but Penelope and Margaret remained in animated conversation with Sir Jeffery. Lord and Lady Gambett stared up wearily from their chairs, while Henrietta and Josephine looked as though they might start whining at any given moment. Amelia dared to catch Logan's gaze and when he smiled warmly at her it melted away some of the fear she felt.

"Your trunks are outside," he announced, "and the stage is due in two hours. I'd suggest you take your breaks for tea and cakes before heading to Denver. There isn't much in between here and there, and you'll be mighty sorry if you don't."

"I believe this will square our account," Lord Gambett said, extending an envelope.

Logan looked the contents over and nodded. "This is mighty generous of you, Gambett." The man seemed notably embarrassed and merely nodded before muttering something about seeing to the trunks.

"And this should account for us," Lord Amhurst announced, providing a similar envelope.

Logan tucked the envelope into his pocket without even looking. "If you have a moment, I'd like to speak with you privately, Lord Amhurst."

"I dare say, time is short; speak your mind, Reed. We haven't even secured our tickets for the stage."

"They're reserved in your name, I assure you. Five tickets for Denver."

"Five? You mean six, don't you? Or did you reserve Sir Jeffery's separately?"

"No, I meant five." Logan looked at Amelia and held out his hand to her.

Amelia hesitated only a second before joining Logan. Even Penelope and Margaret gasped at the sight of their sister holding hands with their American guide. Mattersley was the only one to offer even the slightest look of approval and that came in the form of a tight-lipped smile.

"I've asked Amelia to marry me, and she said yes. Now I'm asking for your blessing, Lord Amhurst."

"Why I've never heard of such rubbish!" the earl exclaimed. "Amelia, what nonsense is this man speaking?"

"It isn't nonsense, Father." Amelia noted that her sisters had gathered closer, while Lady Gambett, seeing a major confrontation in the making, ushered her girls into the dining room. Jeffery stood by looking rather bored and indifferent. She smiled up at Logan and tried to calm her nerves. "It's all true. I would very much like to marry Logan Reed and since Sir Jeffery has kindly released me from our betrothal, I am hoping to have your blessing."

"Never! You are the daughter of an earl. You've been presented at court and have the potential to marry. . .well. . .to certainly marry better than an American!"

"But I love an American," Amelia protested. "I can do no better than to marry for love."

"I forbid it!"

"Father, I'm nearly twenty-one," Amelia reminded him. "I can marry without your consent, but I'd much rather have it."

"You marry this man and I'll cut off all inheritance and funding from you. You'll never be welcomed to set foot on my property again."

"Isn't that what Grandfather Amhurst told you when you decided to marry Mother?" Penelope and Margaret both gasped in unison and fanned themselves furiously as though they might faint.

The earl reddened at the collar and looked quite uncomfortable. "That was a different circumstance."

"Not so very different to my way of thinking." Amelia dropped her hold on Logan and gently touched her father's arm. "Father, don't you want me to know true love as you and Mother did?"

"And you love this man enough to lose your fortune?"

"She doesn't need a fortune," Logan interjected. "I have enough for the both of us." This drew everyone's attention. "Look, there doesn't need to be any pretense between any of us." Logan drew out two envelopes and handed them to the earl. "I won't take your money for the trip and you can give this back to Lord Gambett, as well. Also, he said reaching in for yet another envelope, "this is yours Chamberlain. You will find one hundred thousand dollars awaiting you at the bank in Denver."

"One hundred thousand?" Amelia questioned.

Logan smiled. "I had to make it worth his trouble." Jeffery said nothing but tucked the envelope into his pocket. Lord Amhurst stood staring at his own envelopes while Logan continued. "As I said, Amelia doesn't need the Donneswick fortune. She'll be well-cared for by me and she won't want for anything, unless of course, it's your blessing."

The earl looked positively torn and Amelia instantly felt sorry for her father. "I love him, Father," she said, tears glistening in her eyes. "You wanted me to marry before my twenty-first birthday and I'm finally agreeing to that."

"Yes, but—" he looked at her and suddenly all the harshness of the last year seemed to fade from his expression. He looked from Amelia to Logan and seemed to consider the idea as if for the first time. "I say, you truly wish to be married to him and live here, in America?"

"I truly do." She leaned over and kissed her father on the cheek, whispering in his ear, "Logan makes me happy, Papa. Please say yes."

He smiled and touched Amelia's cheek. "You will come for visits, won't you?"

"Of course we will," she replied. "So long as we're both welcomed."

He sighed. "Then you have my blessing, although I offer it up with some misgivings."

"Oh, thank you, Father. Thank you!" Amelia gave him an uncharacteristic public embrace before throwing herself into Logan's arms.

Logan hugged her tightly and happily obliged her when Amelia lifted her lips for a kiss.

"Ah, I say," the earl interrupted the passionate display, "but I don't suppose we could find a man of the cloth in this town, what?"

Logan broke the kiss and nodded. "Parson's waiting for us as we speak. I didn't figure you'd much want to leave her here without seeing her properly wed."

The earl very ceremoniously took out a pocket watch and popped open the cover. "Then I say we'd best be going about it. I have a stage to catch shortly, as you know."

Epilogue

I thought you said May around here would signal spring," Amelia said, rising slowly with a hand on her slightly swollen abdomen. She looked out the cabin window for the tenth time that morning and for the tenth time found nothing but snow to stare back at her.

"Hey," Logan said, coming up from behind her, "we didn't make such bad use of the winter." He wrapped his arms around her and felt the baby's hefty kick. "See, our son agrees."

"What he agrees with," Amelia said in her very formal English accent, "is that if his mother doesn't get out of this cabin soon, she's going to be stark raving mad."

"We could read together," Logan suggested. "We could get all cozied up under the covers for warmth, maybe throw in some heated rocks from the fireplace to keep our feet all toasty. . . ." His words trailed off as he nuzzled her neck.

"I believe we've read every book in the cabin, at least twice," she said, enjoying his closeness.

"We could play a game of cards. We could get all cozied up—"

"I know. I know," she interrupted. "Under the covers for warmth and throw in some heated rocks, but honestly Logan I'm going to throw one of those rocks through the window if we can't do something other than sit here and count snowflakes."

"Maybe, just maybe, if you can bear to be parted from me for a spell, I'll ride down to Mary's and see if she can come up here for a bit. Maybe you ladies could share quilting secrets."

"But I want to get out! I want to walk around and see something other than four walls and frosted windows. I may be with child, but that certainly doesn't mean I'm without feet on which to walk. Please, Logan."

Logan sighed and laid his chin atop her head. "If you promise to dress very warmly and to wear your highest boots, and do everything I say, then I suppose I could be persuaded to—"

"Oh, Logan, truly?" Amelia whirled around, causing Logan's head to snap back from the absence of support. "When can we go? Can we go now?

Logan laughed, rubbed his chin and gave Amelia a look that said it all.

She liked the way he was looking at her. It was a look that suggested that she alone was responsible for his happiness and if they remained snowed in the cabin for another six months, he'd still smile in just exactly the same way. He touched her cheek with his calloused fingers and smiled. "Good things take time, Lady Amhurst."

"Mrs. Reed," she corrected. "I'm happily no longer a lady of noble standing."

He grinned roguishly. "Oh, you're a lady, all right. But you're my lady now."

She smiled and felt a surge of joy bubble up inside her. "God sure had a way of getting my attention," she said, putting her hand over his.

"The stubborn, impatient ones are always the hardest," he whispered before lowering his mouth to hers.

Amelia wrapped her arms around Logan's neck and returned his kiss with great enthusiasm. She'd found the happiness that she'd never thought possible, and come September, she was going to have a baby. Logan's baby—and she was Logan's lady, and somehow that made the long winter seem not quite so unbearable.

MY VALENTINE

Dedication

Dedicated to David Brown with much thanks and gratitude for the extensive research on the Jewish faith, culture, and people. *Bist a mensh!*

Chapter 1

January, 1835

Hear, O Israel: The LORD our God is one LORD.
DEUTERONOMY 6:4

Darlene Lewy hurried to pull on warm woolen petticoats. It was a frosty January morning and living so close to the harbor waters of New York City, the Lewy house always seemed to be in a state of perpetual cold. Shivering and slipping a dark-blue work dress over her head, Darlene could hear her father in his ritual of morning prayers.

"Shema Israel, Adonai eloheinu Adonai echad," he recited the Hebrew in his heavy German accent.

Darlene embraced the words to her heart. "Hear, O Israel: The Lord our God is one Lord." She smiled. For all of her years on earth she had awakened each morning to the sound of her father's faithful prayers.

Humming to herself, Darlene sat down at her dressing table. Taking up a hairbrush, she gave her thick, curly tresses a well-needed brushing, then quickly braided and pinned it into a snug, neat bun on the top of her head. She eyed herself critically in the mirror for any escaping hairs. Dark-brown eyes stared back at her from beneath shapely black brows. She was no great beauty. At least not in the eyes of New York's very snobbish social circle. But then again, she wouldn't have been welcomed in that circle, even if she had have been ravishingly beautiful and wealthy to boot. No, the upper crust of New York would never have taken Darlene Lewy into its numbers, because Darlene was a Jewess.

Deciding she made a presentable picture, Darlene hurriedly made her bed and went to the kitchen to stoke up the fire and prepare breakfast. Her kitchen was a sorry little affair, but it served them well. Had her mother lived, perhaps they would have had a nicer house, instead of sharing the three-story building with her father's tailoring shop and sewing rooms. But, had her mother and little brother survived childbirth, fifteen years earlier, Darlene had little doubt they'd still be living in Germany instead of America.

"Neshomeleh," Abraham Lewy said, coming into the room.

Darlene could not remember a time when he had not greeted her with the precious endearment, "my little soul." "Good morning, Tateh, did you sleep well?" She gave him a kiss on his leathery cheek and pulled out a chair for him to sit on.

"It is well with me, and you?"

Darlene laughed. "I'm chilled to the bone, but not to worry. I've stoked up the fire and no doubt by the time we get downstairs to the shop, Hayyim will have the stove fires blazing and ready for the day." Hayyim, her father's assistant, was a local boy of seventeen who had pleaded to learn the tailoring business. And, since Abraham had no sons to carry on his tradition of exquisitely crafted suits, he had quickly taken Hayyim under his wing. Darlene knew that the fact Hayyim's father and mother had died in a recent cholera epidemic had much to do with her father's decision, but in truth, she saw it as an answer to prayer. Her father wasn't getting any younger, and of late he seemed quite frail and sickly.

Darlene brought porridge and bread to the table and waited while her father recited the blessing for bread before dishing up their portions.

"Baruch ata Adonai eloheinu melech ha-olem ha-motzi lechem min ha-Aretz." Praise be Thou, O Lord our God, King of the universe, Who brings forth bread from the earth. Abraham pulled off a chunk of bread while Darlene spooned cereal into their bowls.

"There will be little time for rest today. Our appointments are many and the work most extensive," he told her.

"I'll take care of all of the book work," she answered as if he didn't already know this. "I've also got Mr. Mitchell's waistcoat buttons to finish putting on. Is he coming today?"

"No, he'll come tomorrow. I told him we must have a week to finish and a week we will have."

Darlene smiled. "Eat, Tateh." The Yiddish word had never been replaced by Papa as she heard many of her neighboring friends call their fathers.

Abraham gave his attention to the food, while Darlene watched him for any telltale signs of sickness. The winter had been hard on her father and even though he'd stayed indoors except for trips to the synagogue on *Shabbes,* "Sabbath" as her American friends would say, Darlene worried that the grip or cholera or some other hideous disease would take him from her.

"You should hire another boy to help you with the work. There's no reason why you should work yourself into the ground," Darlene chided. She had taken on the role of worrier since her mother's death and even though she had been only five at the time, Abraham said she filled the role quite adequately.

"Oyb Gott vilt—If God wills," Abraham answered and continued eating. It was his standard response to subjects he didn't wish to continue discussing.

Darlene gave the hint of an unsatisfied snort before clearing her dishes to the sink and returning for her father's. He was a stubborn man, but she loved him more dearly than life itself. She tried not to notice that his hair was now completely white, as was his beard and eyebrows. She tried, too, not to see that his coat hung a little looser around his shoulders and that his complexion had grown sallow. Time was taking its toll on Abraham Lewy.

With breakfast behind them, Darlene hurried to tidy the kitchen. Her father had already gone downstairs to begin his work day and she didn't wish to lag behind and leave him alone. For reasons entirely beyond her understanding, Darlene felt compelled to watch over her father with a jealous regard. Maybe it was just concern over his winter illnesses. Maybe it was the tiniest flicker of fear down deep inside that made her question what might happen if her father died. She had no one else. Even Bubbe, her father's mother, had passed on years ago. If Abraham were to die as well, there would be no one for Darlene to turn to.

Changing her kitchen apron for the one she wore in the shop, Darlene made her way down the rickety wooden stairs. She would not allow her mind to wander into areas of morbidity. She would also say nothing to her father. He would only begin suggesting the names of local men who might make good husbands and Darlene refused to hear anything about such nonsense. She would never leave her beloved Tateh.

"Good morning," Hayyim said with a nod as Darlene passed by.

"Good morning." Her words were rather curt given the fact that her mind was still on the distasteful idea of marriage. Hayyim, three years her junior, was very much taken with her, and looked at her with such longing that it made Darlene uncomfortable. He was a child as far as she was concerned and his feelings were nothing more than a crush. She could only pray that God would forbid such a union.

She was nearly to the front counter when the door bells jingled merrily and two men entered the shop. Their warm breath puffed out against the accompanying cold air and Darlene couldn't help but shiver from the draft.

Dennison Blackwell, followed by his son Pierce, entered Lewy & Company, stomping their feet at the door. A light snow had started to fall and the evidence left itself on the doormat.

Abraham stepped forward to greet them. "Welcome," he said, his w's sounding like v's. "It is fit only for sitting by the fire, no?"

"Indeed you are right," Dennison Blackwell said, shaking off little flakes of snow from his coat lapel. "It's only just now begun to snow, but the air is cold enough to freeze you to the carriage seats."

"And your driver?" Abraham said, looking past Pierce and out the window. "Would he not want to sit in the kitchen and warm up by the stove?"

"That's kind of you, but we won't be terribly long and Jimson doesn't mind the cold. He's from the north and actually embraces this weather."

Abraham smiled. "Then God did have a purpose for such things."

Dennison laughed. "Yes, I suppose He did at that."

Darlene watched the exchange with little interest. What had captured her attention, however, was the tall, broad-shouldered form of the younger Mr. Blackwell. She stole glances at him from over the ledger counter and nearly blushed to her toes when he looked up and met her stare with a wink and a smile.

"*Oy,*" she muttered under her breath and hurried to lower her eyes back to her work.

"It seems," Dennison was saying, "that both Pierce and I will be required to attend the annual Valentine's ball."

"Ah, this is the auction where bachelors are sold to their dates, no?" Abraham said in a lowered voice that suggested the entire affair was a bit risque. "Such doings!"

"True enough. Pierce has been abroad for some time and now finds that his wardrobe could use a bit of updating. We'll start with a suit for ball and he can come back later to arrange for other things."

Pierce smiled. "My father highly praises your work. I was going to journey to London and have my suits made there, but perhaps I won't have to travel so far after all."

"Certainly you won't," Abraham said with complete confidence. "We do much better work here. You will be more than happy, I think."

Taking their outer coats, Abraham motioned them into the back room, where he and Hayyim would take measurements and suggest materials. Darlene couldn't help but watch the trio as they passed through the curtained doorway. Pierce Blackwell's dark eyes had penetrated her strong facade of indifference and it shook her to the very core of her existence. How could one man affect her in that way? Especially one Gentile man.

She busied herself with the ledger, but her curiosity was getting the better of her. Not knowing what they were talking about was most maddening. If she dusted the shelves near the back room entrance, perhaps she would be able to overhear their conversation. Taking up a dusting rag, she moved methodically through the small room.

"I suppose the easiest way to explain it," Dennison Blackwell said, "is that we, too, serve one God, but one God with three very distinctive portions."

Darlene's hand stopped dusting. *What in the world is going on?*

Dennison continued. "We Christians believe in one God, just as you of the Jewish faith believe. However, we believe from Scripture that God has made Himself available to His children in three different ways. He is God our judge, God our Savior, and God our Spiritual leader and consolation. Thus we say, God the Father, the Son, and the Holy Spirit. It's like an apple. You have the core of the fruit, where the seeds lay in wait. Next you have the sweet meat of the fruit itself and finally the tough, durable skin that covers over all. One apple, yet three parts."

Darlene nearly dropped her cloth. What kind of *mes-hugge* "crazy" talk was this? God and apples? Did the Gentiles worship fruit or was that all that existed between their ears for brains? The very idea of comparing God to an apple outraged her. She dusted furiously at the door's edge without seeing her work. Instead, she concentrated on the curtain which separated her from the men.

"Hold up your arm, Mr. Blackwell," her father said authoritatively.

"Please, call me Pierce. My father says you two have become good friends. I'd be honored to consider you the same."

"The honor is mine. Your father is a good man."

Silence seemed to hold the room captive for several minutes and Darlene found herself breathing a sigh of relief. *Good,* she thought, *Tateh won't allow for such blasphemy to continue in his shop.* She was about to turn away when her father's voice caused her to stop.

"So the misunderstanding is that we Jews believe you have taken other gods, while you are telling this old man that there is but one God and you serve Him alone?"

"Correct," Dennison answered and Darlene felt a strange sinking in her heart.

"I remember when I came to America, Reb Lemuel, our rabbi in the old country, admonished me to remember the Word of God in Deuteronomy." Abraham began to recite, " 'And it shall be, when the Lord thy God shall have brought thee into the land which he sware unto thy fathers, to Abraham, to Isaac, and to Jacob, to give thee great and goodly cities, which thou buildedst not, And houses full of all good things, which thou filledst not, and wells digged, which though diggedst not, vineyards and olive trees, which though plantedst not; when thou shalt have eaten and be full; Then beware lest thou forget the Lord, which brought thee forth out of the land of Egypt, from the house of bondage. Thou shalt fear the Lord thy God, and serve him, and shalt swear by his name. Ye shall not go after other gods, of the gods of the people which are round about you.'"

Good for Tateh, Darlene thought as Abraham's recitation ended. He would never fail to tell the truth before man and God.

"There. That should do for you," Abraham said. Darlene could hear the rattling of items and longed to know what was happening. Her father continued, "Perhaps the Scriptures speak not of New York City, but the heart of the matter is still intact, no?"

"I agree," Dennison replied. "And were our God a different one from yours, I would be inclined to agree. But honestly, Abraham, we serve the same God."

Darlene was nearly knocked to the ground by Pierce Blackwell's solid frame coming through the curtain. Gasping, she was stunned by his firm hold on her arm and the look of amusement in his eyes.

"Weren't we talking loud enough for you?" He grinned broadly and released her to stand on her own.

"Shhh," she insisted with a finger to her lips. She moved quickly from the curtain, irritated with both herself for getting caught, and Mr. Pierce Blackwell for doing the catching.

Pierce followed her back to the ledger counter. "I'm certain they would include you in the conversation if you but asked. Would you like to know more about what they were discussing?"

"Leave me be," she said and turned her attention to a column of numbers. She would try for the fourth time to figure out why the column didn't add up to match the one on the opposite page.

Pierce would not leave her be, however. In fact, he made it his particular duty to keep at her for an answer. "I'm serious. My father and your father have been discussing the Christian faith for some time now. They contrast the differences between Jews and Christians and reason together the similarities. I'd be happy to enlighten you. . . ."

"I won't hear such blasphemy!" Darlene interrupted. "I won't be *meshummad* to my people."

"Meshummad?"

"A traitor," she replied harshly. "Now, please leave me alone. I have work to do and you mustn't interrupt me again or I shall never find my mistake."

Pierce glanced down at the column of figures. "It's there in the third column. You have a six and it should be an eight."

She looked up at him with wonder written in her expression. His stern expression was softened by a gentle smile. "I don't believe you." She quickly added the numbers and realized he was right. "How did you do that? There are more than fifteen numbers there. How can you just look down at my paper and instantly see that?"

Pierce shrugged. "I've always been able to do that. I guess I'm just good with figures."

"I suppose that would be an understatement," she said, still not allowing herself to really believe him. She tore a piece of brown paper from its roll and jotted down a row of numbers. "Do it again."

Pierce looked at the paper for only a moment. "Three hundred twenty-four."

Darlene turned the paper back around and used a stubby pencil to add up the column. "Three hundred twenty-four," she muttered. She looked up at him with real admiration, momentarily forgetting that she disagreed with his theology. "I must say, that is most impressive."

Pierce gave a tight, brief bow. "So does that mean you aren't mad at me anymore?"

Darlene slammed the book shut. "I'm not mad. Now if you'll excuse me, I have work to do." She hurried across the room and made a pretense of re-rolling a bolt of discarded remnant cloth.

"Well, if we can't discuss religion," Pierce said, following her doggedly across the shop, "perhaps we could speak of something else."

"There is nothing to discuss." She finished with the bolt and took up her sewing basket. "I have work to do."

"That's the third time you've said that," he mused.

She glared at him. "It's true."

"I suppose it is, but does it preclude us having a simple conversation?"

He was so totally insistent that Darlene knew there'd be no dealing with him other than to stop running and allow the discussion. She sat down to her work table and took up needle and thread. "So talk."

Pierce leaned against the wall and crossed his arms casually. He watched her for several moments, making Darlene stick herself twice with the needle. When he said nothing, she finally began the conversation the only way she could think of. "So you are going to the annual Valentine's Ball?"

Pierce grinned. "Yes. My Aunt Eugenia insists I attend. It's for charity and she always manages to purchase my ticket, so I end up with the young woman she desires I keep company with."

Darlene shook her head. "Why not just skip the dance and invite the woman to dinner at your house?"

"My reaction exactly." Pierce laughed. "I told my aunt that fancy dress balls were of no interest to me, but she insists I owe society a debt and that this is one way to repay it."

"Sounds like a lot of nonsense to me."

"Valentine's Day or the dance?"

"Both." Darlene's reply was short and to the point. She picked up a black waistcoat and placed a button against the chalk mark her father had made.

"Have you no interest in dancing or in receiving valentines from your many admirers?"

"I suppose I don't. I'm not very familiar with either one." She stitched the button to the coat and deliberately refused to look up. She was afraid of what Pierce's expression might say. Would he disbelieve her or worse, pity her?

"Valentine's Day can be a great deal of fun. You can set up amusing limericks and post them to a friend, or you can pen something more intimate and romantic and send it to your true love."

"Oy!" At Pierce's mention of true love, Darlene had managed to ram the needle beneath her fingernail. Instantly, she put her finger in her mouth and sucked hard to dispel the pain. Tears welled in her eyes, but still she refused to lift her face.

"Are you all right?" Pierce asked.

"Yes. Yes. I'm fine." She prayed he'd drop the subject or that his father would conclude his business in the back room and both Mr. Blackwells would leave the premises. She studied her finger for a moment then took up her sewing again.

"So, do you have a true love?" he asked.

Darlene barely avoided pricking her finger again. Resigning herself to the path of least pain, she put her sewing down and shook her head. "No. I have no suitors and I've never sent valentines. I don't find myself in the circle of those who dance at fancy parties either for charity or reasons of romantic inclinations."

"Have you never received a valentine?"

Pierce asked the question in such a serious tone that Darlene had to look up. He seemed very concerned by this matter, almost as though he'd asked if she'd never had decent food to eat.

"No, we don't celebrate such nonsense. Now, if you'll please excuse me..." She fell silent at the sound of her father's voice.

Dennison and Abraham came through the curtain. "I can have both suits ready in time for the ball. You will be pleased I think, Pierce." Her father beamed a smile first at Pierce and then at her.

"I'm certain I will be, sir." He turned to Darlene once again. "It was a pleasure, Miss Lewy. I've enjoyed our conversation."

Darlene nodded and, feeling her face grow flushed, she hurried to lower her gaze back to her work. *Oy, but this day has been a trying one already!*

Chapter 2

For there is no difference between the Jew and the
Greek: for the same Lord over all is rich unto all that call upon him.
ROMANS 10:12

Pierce finished doing up the buttons of his satin waistcoat and went to the mirror. He studied the reverse reflection of his cravat as he tied it neatly into place, then gave himself a quick once-over to make certain nothing was left undone. His gleaming dark eyes only served to remind him of another pair of eyes. Just as dark and far more beautiful behind ebony lashes, Darlene Lewy's eyes were burned into his mind. She had stimulated his thoughts all day, and now as the hearth fires burned brightly for dinner, Pierce had still been unable to put the feisty woman from his mind.

He took up a fine blue frock coat and pulled it on. He adjusted the sleeves and collar, all the while wondering if Darlene would help to sew his new Valentine's suit. It was silly, he knew, to ponder such useless matters, but the lovely girl would not leave his mind, and for the first time in his twenty-six years, Pierce was rather besotted.

Hearing the chimes announce the hour, Pierce made his way to the drawing room, where he knew he'd find the rest of his family. Constance, his fifteen-year-old sister, sat rigidly proper in her powder-blue silk, while Aunt Eugenia's ever-critical gaze roamed over her from head to toe in order to point out some flaw. Dennison stood bored and indifferent at the window.

"Good evening," Pierce said, coming into the room. He walked to his Aunt Eugenia and placed an expected kiss upon each of her heavily powdered cheeks. Then, turning to his sister, he winked and stroked her cheek with his hand. "I see we're all very much gathered together."

Dennison turned and nodded with a smile. "There must be a foot of snow out there already."

Pierce shrugged and took a seat on the couch opposite Eugenia. "It's a part of winters in New York. I suppose by now we should just expect it, eh?"

"It makes paying one's obligatory visits very difficult," Eugenia declared. At forty-four she was a woman of proper elegance and grace. Her dark-brown hair showed only a hint of gray and was swept up into a high arrangement that made her appear a bit taller than her petite frame could actually boast.

"Perhaps New York society will endure your absence for one day," Pierce suggested with a smile. This made Constance suppress a giggle, but not before Eugenia delivered a scowl of displeasure at her niece.

"Young people today do not understand the obligations of being in the privileged classes. There are rules, both written and unwritten, that simply must be adhered to. It is the responsibility of your elders," she said, looking directly at Constance, "to ensure that your behavior is acceptable and proper."

Pierce rolled his eyes. Aunt Eugenia was stuffy enough for them all. Let her adhere to society's demands and leave the rest of them alone. Changing the subject, Pierce beamed a smile at his sister and asked, "And how did you fill your afternoon, Miss Constance?"

"I wrote thank-you letters," she said with a hint of boredom.

Constance was a delicate young woman. She was just starting to bloom into womanhood with her tiny figure taking on some more girlish curves. Her dark-brown curls had been childishly tied up with a bow, but nevertheless, Pierce saw the makings of great beauty.

"Well, if the lake freezes over properly, we'll go ice skating tomorrow, how about that?" Pierce offered.

Constance's face lit up with excitement, but it was quickly squelched by Eugenia's overbearing declaration. "Certainly not! Constance has been a bit pale of late. I won't have her out there in the elements, only to catch her death."

Pierce looked to his father, the only one really capable of overriding Eugenia. Dennison smiled tolerantly at his sister. "Eugenia, the girl cannot live locked away behind these walls. If she is pale, perhaps it is because her face never sees the light of day. I say let her go and have a good time. Pierce will take proper care of her."

Constance jumped up and threw her arms around her father's neck. "Oh, thank you, Papa!"

"Well, that's settled then," Pierce said with a nod to his aunt. He was growing ever weary of her mettlesome ways and the only reason he continued to endure them was that she hadn't actually caused any real harm. Not yet.

"Dinner is served," remarked a stately butler from the entry door.

"Thank you, Marcus," Eugenia declared.

Dennison came to her side and offered his arm. With a look of cool reserve, Eugenia allowed him to assist her, leaving Pierce to bring Constance.

"Oh, thank you ever so much, Pierce," Constance said, squeezing his arm. "You are a lifesaver. I should have completely perished if I'd had to spend even one more day in this house."

Pierce chuckled. "Well, we couldn't have that."

"What did you do today?" Constance asked innocently. "Did you meet anyone new? Did you have a great argument with anyone?"

"How curious you sound." He led her to her chair at the dining table. "But the answer is no, I did not argue with anyone and yes, I did meet someone new."

"Oh, do tell me everything!"

"Prayers first." Constance's enthusiasm was halted by her father's declaration.

Grace was said over the meal with a special offer of thanksgiving for their health and safety. With that put aside, dinner was served and a fine, succulent pork roast drew the attention of the Blackwell family.

"So, who did you meet?" Constance questioned, while Pierce cut into a piece of meat.

"I met Father's tailor, Abraham Lewy, and his daughter, Darlene. She's very pretty with black hair and dark eyes like yours. Oh, and they have a man who works for them, but I can't remember his name. He's only a little older than you and quite dashing."

Constance blushed. "Is Darlene my age?"

"No," Pierce replied with a glint in his eye that was not missed by his aunt. "No, she's definitely older. Probably eighteen or so."

"She's twenty," his father declared. "And quite a beauty."

"She's a Jewess," Eugenia said as though it should put an end to the entire discussion.

"That's true enough," Pierce replied, "but Father is correct. She's quite beautiful."

"What's a Jewess?" asked Constance.

"It's a woman of the Jewish faith." Dennison replied.

Eugenia sniffed indignantly. "It means she's not one of us and therefore need not be further discussed at this table."

"Will she go to the Valentine's Ball?" Constance refused to let the matter drop.

Pierce shook his head. "She's never even had a valentine sent to her. Much less danced at a party for such a celebration."

"I should very much like to go to such a dance." Constance's voice was wistful.

"You've not yet come of age," Eugenia declared. "There are the proprieties to consider and if no one else in this family holds regard for such traditions, then I must be the overseer for all." She sounded as though it might be a tremendous burden, but Pierce knew full well how much Eugenia enjoyed her dramatic role.

"You should ask Miss Lewy to the dance," Constance told her brother. "If she's especially pretty and likeable, you could probably teach her all of the right steps."

Pierce nodded and gave her a conspiratorial wink. "Or, I could just have you teach her. You dance divinely."

Dennison laughed. "Perhaps our Constance could open her own dance school right here."

"Perish the thought!" Eugenia exclaimed. "I have enough trouble trying to manage the child without you putting improper ideas in her head."

Dennison smiled at his children and waved Eugenia off. "It was nothing more than good fun, Sister. Do still your anxious mind or you'll have a fit of the vapors."

Dinner passed in relative silence after that. Eugenia's nose was clearly out of joint and Pierce had little desire to pick up the conversation again if it meant listening to some cold disdain toward Darlene and her kind.

Finally, Eugenia and Constance dismissed themselves to the music room while Pierce and Dennison remained at the table to linger over coffee.

"You seem to have a great deal on your mind."

Pierce looked at his father and nodded. "I keep thinking about the Lewys."

"One Lewy in particular, eh?"

"Perhaps Darlene did capture my attention more than Abraham, but you seemed to have him engrossed with the topic of Christianity."

Dennison pushed back a bit and sighed. "Abraham and I have been having regular talks about our religious differences."

"How did that get started?"

Dennison looked thoughtful. "His wife died in childbirth fifteen years ago."

"Just like mother?"

"Yes, it was a strange similarity. They were still in Germany and Darlene was only five. Abraham lost both his wife and their new son."

"When did they come to America?"

"Only about five years ago. Tensions seem to follow the Jewish people and for a number of reasons Abraham considered the move a wise one. I believe his choice was God-directed. He worked hard to save enough money to make the move and to set up his shop here in New York. I happened upon his work through a good friend of mine and I've taken my business to him ever since."

"How is it I've never heard you talk about them?"

Dennison smiled. "You've been a very busy man, for one thing. I can't tell you how good it is to have you back from Europe."

Pierce finished his coffee and stared thoughtfully at the cup for a moment. "I've never been at home in New York. I can't explain it. I wasn't at home in London or Paris, either. I guess I know that somewhere out there, there's a place where I will be happy, but stuck in the middle of Aunt Eugenia's social calendar isn't the place for me."

Dennison chuckled. "Nor for me, although my dear sister would believe it so. After your mother died, God rest her soul, Eugenia hounded me to death to remarry. Of course, there was Constance to consider. Such a tiny infant and hardly able to find nourishment in that weak canned milk cook gave her. Hiring a wet nurse was the only thing that saved that girl's life."

"It is a strange connection between us and the Lewys. Both mothers perished and they lost their baby as well. It must have been very hard on Darlene as well. A five-year-old would have a difficult time understanding the loss. I was eleven and struggled to understand it myself."

"Yes, but you had faith in the resurrection. You knew that your mother loved Christ as her Savior. I think the death of his wife caused Abraham to question his faith rather than find strength in it. When I first met him we discussed things of insignificant value. Darlene was much like Constance, gangly and awkward. All little girl running straight into womanhood. Oh, and very shy. She would scarcely peek her head out to see what her father was doing."

Pierce smiled, trying to image Darlene in the form of Constance. "I'll bet she was just as pretty as she is now."

Dennison looked at his son for a moment. "Don't buy yourself a heartache."

This sobered Pierce instantly. "What are you saying? Surely you don't follow Aunt Eugenia's snobbery because the Lewys are not of our social standing?"

"No, not at all. Social standing means very little if you have no one to love or be loved by. Money has never been something to offer comfort for long." Dennison leaned forward. "No, I'm speaking of the theological difference. You are a Christian, Pierce. You accepted Christ as your Savior at an early age and you've accepted the Bible as God's Holy Word. Darlene doesn't believe like you do, nor will she turn away from the faith of her fathers easily. Marrying a woman who is not of your faith is clearly a mistake. The Bible says to not be unequally yoked with nonbelievers."

"But I wasn't talking marriage," Pierce protested and looked again to his coffee cup.

"Weren't you?" Dennison looked hard at his son and finally Pierce had to meet his father's gaze. "Be reasonable, Pierce. You found yourself attracted to this young woman. Where would you take it from this point? Friendship? I find it hard to believe it would stop there, but there it must stop."

"You've worked to change Abraham's mind. Why can I not work to change Darlene's?"

"I have no problem with you desiring to share your faith with others. But I think you should seek your heart for the motivation. If this is a personal and selfish thing, you may well cause more harm than good. However, if you truly feel called of God to speak to Darlene, then by all means do so, but leave your emotions out of it."

Pierce tried to shrug off his father's concerns. "You worry too much about me. I know what's right and wrong. I won't throw off my faith or be turned away from God." He got to his feet. "I believe I'll retire for the evening. I have a good book upstairs and I'd like to spend a bit of time in it before I go to bed."

Dennison nodded. "Sleep well, and Pierce, it is good to have you home again."

Pierce smiled. "It's good to be home."

Upstairs, comfortably planted in his favorite chair, Pierce picked up his book and opened to the marked page. He was just about to begin the fifth chapter when a knock sounded on his door. By the heavy-handed sound of it, Pierce was certain he'd find Eugenia on the opposite side.

"Come in," he called, sitting up to straighten his robe.

"It's a bit early for bed, isn't it?" Eugenia asked rather haughtily.

"I thought I'd like to read for a while."

"I see. Nevertheless, I've come to express my deep concern about our dinner conversation."

"Concern?" Pierce closed the book and shook his head. "What possible concern could our dinner conversation have given you?"

Eugenia drew back her shoulders and set her expression of disdain as though it were in granite. "I simply cannot have the scandal of you being indiscreet with that Jewess."

"I beg your pardon?" Pierce felt his ire rise and struggled to keep his temper under control.

"I could clearly read your mind and the interest you held for the Lewy girl. I must forbid it, however. I cannot imagine anything more sordid than you taking up with that. . .that woman."

"Her name is Darlene and she is very pleasant to be around. And whether or not I hold any interest in her is none of your concern." Pierce got to his feet and crossed the room. "Aunt Eugenia, I love you and care a great deal about your comfort, but I am a grown man and I will no longer tolerate your interference in my life. I left this house three years ago because of such discomfort and I will not be driven from it again."

"Well! I've never heard such disrespect in all of my life. I've done nothing but see to your welfare. When my dear husband departed this earthly life, I knew it was my duty to help poor Dennison raise you children properly. If I instilled culture and social awareness in your life, then you will find yourself the better for it and not the worse."

Pierce felt the heat of her stare and refused to back down. "Since you came to me with this matter, I am going to speak freely to you. I am certain Father appreciated the companionship and assistance you offered him with Constance. As you will recall, however, I was already a grown man of twenty-three when you came into this house. I need neither your care nor grooming to make my mark upon society, because I have no such plans for myself or society. These are things of importance to you, but certainly they do not concern me."

"They concern the well-being of this family. Would you see your father's reputation ruined because you chose to marry a Jewess?"

"Why must everyone assume I mean to marry the girl? I've only just met her and I thought she was a lovely creature with a fiery spirit."

"So I'm not the only one to broach this subject, eh? Perhaps I'm not the lunatic you make me out to be." Eugenia's face held a smug regard for her nephew.

"I've never thought you to be a lunatic, Aunt Eugenia. Mettlesome and snobbish, yes, but never a lunatic."

"Well!" It seemed the only thing she could say.

Pierce continued, "I will go to your charity balls and I will allow you to parade me before your society friends. I will use the proper silver and talk the proper talk. I will dance with impeccable skill and dress strictly in fashion, but I will not be dictated to in regards to the woman I will choose as my wife. Is that clear?"

"You have to marry a woman of your standing. To marry beneath your station will do this family a discredit. Then, too, imagine the complications of marrying a pauper. You must marry a woman of means and increase the empire your father has already begun."

Pierce could take no more. He walked to the door and opened it as a signal to his aunt that the conversation was at an end. "I will marry for love, respect, admiration, and attraction, be that woman of Jewish heritage or not. I seem to recall the Word of God saying we are all the same in the eyes of the

Lord, and that whosoever shall call upon the name of the Lord will be saved. I realize the importance of marrying a woman who loves God as I do, and if that woman should turn out to be a Jewess who embraces Christianity and recognizes Christ as the true Messiah, I shan't give her social standing or bank account a single thought."

Eugenia stepped into the hall, clearly disturbed by Pierce's strong stand. "You'd do well to remember the things of importance in this world."

"I might say the same for you, Aunt. My father admonishes me to marry a woman of Christian faith, and that is clearly set in Scripture. By what means do you base your beliefs?" He closed the door without allowing her to reply and drew a deep breath. "I've only just met the girl," he muttered to himself, "yet everyone has me married to her already."

Chapter 3

And it shall be, if thou do at all forget the LORD thy God,
and walk after other gods, and serve them, and worship them,
I testify against you this day that ye shall surely perish.
DEUTERONOMY 8:19

Nearly a week after her encounter with Pierce Blackwell, Darlene felt herself getting back in the routine of her life. She could almost ignore the image of the handsome man when he appeared in her daydreams, but it was at night when he haunted her the most. And in those dreams, Darlene found that she couldn't ignore the feelings he elicited inside her. Never in her life had she given men much thought. Her father urged her to seek her heart on the matter and to find a decent man and settle down. He spoke of wanting grandchildren and such, but Darlene knew that down deep inside he was really worried about her, should something happen to him.

"Tateh," she called, gathering on her coat and warm woolen bonnet. "I'm leaving to go to Esther's."

Abraham peered up from his cutting board. "You should not go out on such a cold day."

"I'll be fine. It's just down the street. You worry too much." She smiled and held up a bundle. "We're making baby clothes for Rachel Bronstein." Her father nodded and gave her a little wave. "I'll be back in time to dish up supper. Don't work too hard."

She hurried out of the building, firmly closing the door that stated "Lewy & Co." behind her. It was a brisk February morning and the skies were a clear, pale blue overhead. The color reminded Darlene of watered silk. Not that she ever had occasion to own anything made from such material, but once she'd seen a gown made of such cloth in a store window.

The sky was a sharp contrast to the muddy mess of the streets below. Gingerly, Darlene picked her way down the street, trying her best to avoid the larger mud holes. The hem of her petticoats and skirt quickly soaked up the muck and mud, but she tried not to fret. No one at Esther's would care because their skirts would be just as messy as hers.

The noises of the street were like music to her ears. Bells ringing in the distance signaled the coming of the charcoal vendor. She'd not be needing

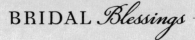

him to stop today, and so she only gave him a brief nod when he passed by.

"Fresh milk! Freeeesh milk!" another man called from his wagon. Cans of milk rattled in the wagonbed behind him and Darlene grimaced. She had never gotten used to what she deemed "city milk." It wasn't anywhere near as rich as what she'd been used to in Germany. Rumor had it that dairymen in the city were highly abusive with their animals, and that not only were the conditions unsanitary and unsavory, but the cows were also fed on a hideous variety of waste products. Vegetable peelings, whiskey distillery mesh, and ground fish bones were among the things she'd heard were used to feed New York's dairy cows. Even thinking of such a thing made her shudder.

A young boy struggled by with bundles of wood over each shoulder. "Wood, here! Wood!" Behind him another boy labored to entice a mule to bring up the wood-ladened cart.

All around her, the smells of the city and of the working class made Darlene feel a warmth and security that she couldn't explain. She thought of the people who lived in their fine brick houses on Broadway and wondered if they could possibly be as happy as she was. Did fine laces and silks make a home as full of love as she had with her father? *Certainly not,* she mused and jumped back just in time to avoid being run over by a herd of pigs as they were driven down the street.

Let the rich have their silks and laces. Her life with Tateh was sweet and they had all that they needed—the Holy One, blessed be He! But in the back of her mind Darlene remembered her father's conversation with Dennison Blackwell and then her own with Pierce. It was as though another world had suddenly collided with hers. Pierce knew what it was to live in fine luxury. He could have figures in his head with complete ease, and he was more than a little bit handsome.

Esther's tiny house came into view. It was there, tucked between a leather goods shop and a cabinetmaker, and although it was small, it served the old widow well. Trying to scrape the greater portion of mud from her boots, Darlene gave a little knock at the door.

A tiny old woman opened the door. She was dressed in black from head to toe, with nothing but a well-worn white apron to break the severity. Her gray hair was tightly wound into a bun at the back of her neck, leaving her wrinkled face to stand out in stark abandonment. "Ah, Darlene, you have come. Good. Good. I told Rachel and Dvorah you would be here."

"The streets are a mess. If you take my things, I'll leave my boots here at the door."

"Nonsense!" Esther declared. "The floor will sweep. Come inside and sit by the fire. You are nearly frozen." The old woman led her into the sitting room. "See Rachel, our *Hava* has come." *Hava* was Darlene's Hebrew name.

Rachel, looking as though she were in her eleventh month of pregnancy, struggled up from her chair and waddled over to Darlene. Bending as far over as she could to avoid her enormous stomach, Rachel kissed Darlene on each cheek and smiled.

"I was afraid you would be too busy. Hayyim told my husband the shop is near to bursting with customers."

"Yes, the rich *goyim* have come to extend their social season wardrobes. They won't have us at their parties, but they wear our suits!" Darlene said with much sarcasm.

"Who would want to go to a Gentile party, anyway?" Esther said, taking Darlene's coat. "You couldn't eat the food."

"Feh! *Kashruth* is such a bother anyway! We'd just as well be rid of it, if you ask me," a dark-headed woman said, entering behind Esther.

"Ah, but what does God say about it, Dvorah?"

Dvorah was much more worldly than the rest of the woman Darlene knew. Her father was a wealthy merchant and could trace back a family history in New York nearly one hundred years. Nevertheless, they were Jewish and no matter how liberally they acted among the Gentiles, they would never be accepted as one of them.

"I leave God's words to my father's mouth," Dvorah replied, swishing her lavender gown with great emphasis. "I'm much busier with other things." She smiled sweetly over her shoulder before picking up her sewing.

"We all know what Dvorah is busy with," Esther said in a disapproving tone. "And I tell you, it is an honest shame to watch a young woman of your upbringing chase after the men the way you do. You need to refrain yourself from acting so forward, Dvorah. Your mother, *oy vey!* What she must go through."

Dvorah shrugged, indifferent to Esther's interfering ways. Darlene saw this as a good opportunity to change the subject. "So, Rachel, how are you feeling?"

By this time Rachel had waddled back to her chair and was even now trying to get comfortable. "I'm fine. Just fine. The baby should come any day and since you've been so good to help me sew, he will have a fine assortment of clothes to wear."

"What 'he'?" Esther questioned. "So sure you are that the child is a male?"

Rachel blushed and Darlene thought she looked perfectly charming. "Shemuel says it will be a boy."

Esther grunted. "Your husband doesn't know everything."

"May God make it so," Darlene proclaimed.

The women worked companionably for several hours and when the hall clock chimed noon, Esther offered them something to eat and drink. They were gathered around the table enjoying a fine stew when Esther brought up the one subject Darlene had hoped to avoid.

"So how is it with your father?"

"He's well, thank you." She slathered fresh butter on bread still warm from Esther's oven and took a bite.

Esther narrowed her eyes and leaned forward. "I've heard it said that he's talking matters of God with the *goyim*."

How Esther managed to know every private detail of everyone's life was beyond Darlene, but she always managed to be right on top of everything. She swallowed hard. "My father has many customers and, of course, they speak on many matters."

Esther looked at Darlene with an expression of pity. "Hayyim said that there are talks of why the Christians believe we are wrong in not accepting their Messiah."

"Hayyim should honor my father's goodness to him and remain silent on matters of gossip." Darlene knew her defense was weak, but what could she say? To admit that her father's conversations concerned her would only fuel Esther's inquisitive nature.

"So has Avrom betrayed the faith of his fathers?" Esther questioned, calling Abraham by his Yiddish name.

"Never!" Darlene declared, overturning her tea cup. It was like all of her worst fears were realized in that statement. Without warning, tears welled in her eyes.

Rachel reached out a hand to pat Darlene lovingly. "There, there," she comforted, "Of course Avrom would not betray our faith."

At this Darlene choked back a sob. "He talks with Mr. Blackwell." It was all she could manage to say, and for some reason it seemed to her that it should be enough.

"It will not bode well, I tell you," Esther commented, refilling Darlene's cup.

Rachel ignored Esther. "Why are you so upset? Has your father said something that causes you to worry?"

Darlene shook her head. "No, but...well," she paused, taking time to dry her eyes. "I can't explain it. I just have this feeling that something is changing. I try to tell myself that I'm just imagining it, but I feel so frightened."

"And well you should. If Avrom turns from his faith he will perish," Esther declared.

"Oh, hush with that," Dvorah replied. "Darlene does not need to hear such talk."

"There will be plenty to hear about once word gets around," Esther said rather smugly.

"Yes, and no doubt you will help to see it on its way!" Dvorah's exasperation was apparent. "Leave her be. Come, Darlene, I'll walk you home and the air will cool your face." She got up from the table without waiting for Darlene's reply.

Esther shook her head in disapproval. "You should speak with the cantor, *Hava*."

Their congregation was too small to support a rabbi, and Ruven Singer, a good and godly man, took on the role of cantor for their group. He led the prayers on *Shabbes* and was always available to advise his people regarding God's law.

"Mr. Singer could speak with Avrom, if you're worried," Rachel offered.

Darlene nodded and drew a deep breath to steady her nerves. She accepted her coat from Dvorah, who even now was doing up the buttons on a lovely fur-trimmed cape. After enduring another suggestion or two from Esther and a sincere thank you from Rachel for the baby clothes, Darlene followed Dvorah outside.

"That old woman!" Dvorah declared. "Busybody Esther should be her name!"

This made Darlene smile. "She always seems to know exactly what everyone is up to. I don't dare make a wrong move with her only two blocks away."

Dvorah laughed. "She told me my dress was too exciting. Six inches of mud on the hem and she thinks I'm dressing too fine."

"It is lovely." Darlene had thought so from the first moment she'd laid eyes on it, but with Esther, who would dare to say such a thing?

"Thank you. Oh, look, a hack. I'd much rather be driven home than walk." She waved her handbag once and the driver brought the carriage to a stop. "Don't forget what I said." Dvorah waved from the hack and then was gone.

"I won't," Darlene muttered to no one. But already, thoughts of the luncheon conversation were racing through her mind. So much so, in fact, that as Darlene set out to cross the muddy, bottomless street, she didn't see the freight wagon bearing down on her.

Just as she looked up to catch sight of the horses' steaming nostrils, Darlene felt strong arms roughly encircle her and pull her to safety. Gazing up in stunned surprise, she nearly fainted at the serious, almost angry expression on Pierce Blackwell's face.

"Were you trying to get yourself killed?" he asked. Then without waiting for her reply he pulled her against him and asked, "Are you all right? You didn't get hurt, did you?"

"No. I mean yes." She shook her head and sighed. "I'm fine. You can let me go now." He only tightened his hold and Darlene actually found herself glad that he did. Her legs felt like limp dishrags and she wasn't at all certain that she could have walked on her own accord.

"Let's get you inside and make sure you're all right," he half-carried, half-dragged her the remaining distance to the Lewy & Co. door. Opening it, Pierce thrust her inside and immediately called for her father.

"Mr. Lewy!"

"Don't!" Darlene exclaimed, trying to wrench free from Pierce. "You'll scare him out of ten years of life."

Pierce ignored her complaint. Abraham hurried into the room with a look of concern on his face. His gaze passed first to the man who had called his name and then to the pale face of his daughter.

"What is it? What is wrong?"

"Nothing, Tateh. I'm fine." Darlene hoped that by hurrying such an explanation, her father would breathe easier.

"She was nearly killed by a freighter," Pierce replied. "I believe she was daydreaming and didn't even see him coming. There was no way the poor man could have stopped."

"I'm fine, Tateh. I'm just fine."

Abraham seemed to relax a bit. "You are certain?"

"Absolutely. I wouldn't lie to you." Darlene smiled sweetly, more than a little aware that Pierce watched her intently.

With the moment of crisis in the past, Abraham turned his gaze to Pierce. "You saved my *Havele*. You have my thanks and never ending gratitude."

Pierce looked at him with a blank expression of confusion. *"Havele?"*

"*Hava* is Hebrew. It means Eve. *Havele* is just a way of saying it a little more intimately. Perhaps you would say, Evie?"

"But I thought, I mean, I remember my father saying her name is Darlene."

"Don't talk about me as though I'm not here!" Darlene suddenly exclaimed. Gone was the fear from her encounter with the freighter. "My mother liked the name Darlene and that is what I'm called. Now please let me go."

At this, Pierce released her with a beaming smile that unnerved her. He bowed slightly, as if to dismiss the matter, but Abraham would have nothing of it.

"I have no fitting way to reward you," he began, "but I shall make for you six new suits and charge you not one penny."

"Tateh, no!" Darlene declared without thinking of how ungrateful she must sound. She knew full well the cost of six suits and while they were living comfortably at this point, there was no telling what tomorrow could bring. They shouldn't become indebted to this man.

But they were indebted. Pierce Blackwell had saved her life.

It was only then that the gravity of the situation began to sink in. With a new look of wonder and a sensation of confused feelings, Darlene lifted her face to meet Pierce's. "I'm sorry, I just mean that suits hardly seem a proper thanks."

"I completely agree," Pierce replied. "And that is why I must say no. I did not rescue your daughter for a new wardrobe. I have funds aplenty for such things. I happened to be here because I have a fitting appointment. God ordains such intercessory matters, don't you think?"

"I do, indeed," Abraham said and nodded with a smile. "I do, indeed."

His acceptance of Pierce's words only gave Darlene reason to worry anew. It was exactly these matters that had caused her to walk in front of the freighter. Certainly such thoughts could only cause more trouble. What if her father thought Pierce's God was more important and more capable of dealing with matters? What if her father gave himself over to the teachings of the Christians! Esther's words came back to haunt her. *He will perish*, Darlene thought. God would turn His face away from her beloved Tateh and he would surely die.

Chapter 4

By faith Abraham, when he was called to go out
into a place which he should after receive
for an inheritance, obeyed; and he went out,
not knowing whither he went.
HEBREWS 11:8

Pierce closed the door to Abraham's shop and hailed his driver. He could still feel the rush of blood in his ears and the pounding of his heart when he'd seen Darlene about to die. She'd nearly walked right into the path of that freighter and all with a sad, tragic look on her face. It was almost as if she were facing an executioner. Surely she hadn't intended to kill herself!

Pierce ordered his driver to take him to his commission merchants office, then relaxed back into the plush leather upholstery of the carriage. No, Darlene wouldn't kill herself. There'd be no reason for that. But perhaps there was. Pierce didn't really know her at all. He toyed with several ideas. Perhaps she'd just been rejected by a suitor? No, she'd told him there were no suitors in her life. Perhaps she'd lost the will to live? Pierce was certain she couldn't bear to be parted from her father. Then what had caused such a look of complete dejection?

His Wall Street destination was only a matter of a few blocks away, and before he could give Darlene another thought, his driver was halting alongside the curb. Pierce alighted with some reservations about the meeting to come. His man, Jordan Harper, was quite good at what he did, but Pierce had never gotten used to letting another man run his affairs. Of course, when he'd been abroad it was easy to let someone else take charge. He knew that his father would ultimately oversee anything Harper did, and therefore it honestly didn't appear to compromise matters in Pierce's mind. The only thing he'd ever disagreed on with his father had been the large quantities of western land tracts Pierce had insisted on buying. The land seemed a good risk in Pierce's mind, and it mattered little that hardly anyone had ever heard of the dilapidated Fort Dearborn or the hoped-for town of Chicago.

Climbing the stairs, Pierce pulled off his top hat and entered the brokerage offices where Harper worked. A scrawny, middle-aged man of questionable purpose met Pierce almost immediately.

"May I help you, sir?"

Pierce took off his gloves, tossed them into the top hat and handed both to the man. "Pierce Blackwell. I'm here to see Jordan Harper."

"Of course, sir. Won't you come this way?" the man questioned, almost as if waiting for an answer. At Pierce's nod, he whirled on his heels and set off in the direction of the sought-after office.

Black lettering stenciled the glassed portion of the door, declaring "Harper, Komsted, and Regan." The older man opened the door almost hesitantly and announced, "Mr. Blackwell to see Mr. Harper."

The room was rather large, but the collection of books, papers, and other things related to business seemed to crowd the area back down to size. Three desks were appointed to different corners of the room, while the fourth corner was home to four rather uncomfortable-looking chairs and a heating stove.

Jordan Harper, a man probably only a few years Pierce's senior, jumped up from his chair and motioned to Pierce. "Come in. I've been expecting you." The scrawny man took this as his cue to exit and quietly slipped from the room, taking Pierce's hat and gloves with him.

"Take off your coat. Old Komsted keeps it hot enough to roast chestnuts in here." The man was shorter than Pierce's six-foot frame, but only by inches. He ran a hand through his reddish-brown hair and grinned. "I've made quite a mess this morning, but never worry, your accounts are in much better shape than my desk."

Pierce smiled. He actually liked this man, whom he'd only met twice before. "My banker assures me I have reason to trust you, so the mess is of no difference to me."

Harper laughed. "Good enough. Ah, here it is." He pulled out a thick brown ledger book and opened it where an attached cord marked it.

Pierce settled himself in and listened as Jordan Harper laid out the status of his western properties. "You're making good profits in the blouse factory. They're up to eighty workers now and I found foreign buyers who are ready to pay handsomely for the merchandise. Oh, and that property you hold near Galena, Illinois, is absolutely filthy with lead and has netted you a great deal of money. Here are the figures for you to look over. Here," he pointed while Pierce took serious consideration of the situation, "is exactly what the buyer paid and this is what your accounts realized after the overhead costs were met."

"Most impressive," Pierce said, sitting back in his seat. "I see you've earned your keep."

Jordan smiled. "I've benefited greatly by our arrangement, Mr. Blackwell, but you don't know the half of it yet. It was impossible to catch up to you while you were abroad. It seemed every time I sent a packet to you, you'd already moved on. Several of my statements were forwarded, but eventually they'd be rerouted back to New York and, well, they're collecting dust in the files downstairs."

"I kept pretty busy," Pierce commented, "but my father trusted your work, and so I felt there was nothing for me to concern myself with. Of course, I was a little younger and more foolhardy three years ago."

Jordan laughed and added, "And a whole lot poorer."

Pierce raised a brow. "Exactly what are you implying, Mr. Harper?" There was a hint of amusement in his tone.

"I'm not implying one single thing. I want you to look here." Jordan Harper quickly flipped through several pages. "As you will see, I took those tracts of land that you purchased at the Chicago site and, in keeping with your suggestion that should prices look good, I should sell as much as two-thirds of the property, I did just that."

Pierce again leaned forward to consider the ledger. At the realization of what met his eyes, Pierce jerked his head up and faced Jordan with a tone of disbelief. "Is this some kind of joke?"

"Not at all. In fact, it's quite serious. I take it from your surprise that you haven't bothered to check on all of your accounts when you were visiting the banks?"

"No, I suppose I didn't concern myself with it," Pierce admitted. "But you're absolutely sure about this?"

"The money is in the bank, and I get at least twenty offers a week to buy the balance of your land in Chicago."

Pierce looked at the figures again. "But if I understand this correctly, and I'm certain I do, the original $100,000 investment I made has now netted me over one million dollars?"

"And that's after my commission," Jordan said with a smile.

Pierce shook his head. Who could have imagined such an inflation of land prices? "I knew it would be a valuable investment, but I figured it would be ten or twenty years before I realized it."

"Chicago is bursting at the seams. It's growing up faster than any city I've ever seen the likes of. People are taking packets across the Great Lakes and making their way to Chicago every day. The population has already grown to over three thousand. Why just yesterday I saw an advertisement offering passage from Buffalo to Chicago for twenty-five dollars. Everybody's getting rich from this little town."

"And you saved out the tracts I asked you to?"

"Absolutely! You can sell them tomorrow if you like or build your own place."

"Sounds to me," Pierce said thoughtfully, "that hotels and boarding houses would be greatly in need."

"All those people have to live somewhere, Mr. Blackwell."

Pierce smiled. "Indeed they do."

Hours later, Pierce was still thinking about Chicago. He'd picked up all the information he could find on the small town and while contemplating what his next move should be, wondered if his next move might ought not to be himself.

He left the papers on his bed and went to stand by the window, where heavy green velvet curtains kept out the world. Pulling them back, Pierce thought seriously about leaving all that he knew in New York. It had been easy enough to go abroad. European cities were well-founded and filled with elegance, grace, and fine things. But Chicago was in the middle of nowhere. It hadn't been but three years since the Indian wars had kept the area in an uproar. There was no main road to travel over in order to get to the town, and even packets to Chicago were priced out of the range of the average citizen. Perhaps Pierce could invest in a mode of transportation that would bring that price down. New railroads were springing up everywhere and canals were proposed for the purpose of connecting Lake Michigan to the Mississippi River. It was easy to see that this was a land of opportunity. But could he leave all the comforts of home and travel west?

A light snow was falling again, and with it came images of the young woman he'd held so close earlier in the day. He liked the way Darlene fit against him. He liked the wide-eyed innocence and the look of wonder that washed over her face when he refused to release her. He liked the smell of her hair, the tone of her voice, even the flash of anger in her dark eyes. He let the curtain fall into place and sighed. If he went west, there would be no Darlene to go with him. At least here he could see her fairly often on the pretense of embellishing his wardrobe. But a man could own only so many suits of clothing.

He sat down again on the bed and looked at the papers before him. Then without knowing why, he thought of Valentine's Day and the dance. Darlene had declared herself unfamiliar with both, and this had truly surprised Pierce. A thought came to mind and he toyed with it for several minutes before deciding to go ahead with it. He grinned to think of Darlene receiving her first valentine. What would she think of him? Perhaps he could leave it unsigned, but of course, she'd know it was from him.

Deciding it didn't matter, Pierce jumped up and threw on his frock coat. Valentine's Day was a week from Saturday, so there was plenty of time, but Pierce wanted to have just the right card made.

Chapter 5

Wherefore the children of Israel shall keep the sabbath. . .
It is a sign between me and the children of Israel
for ever: for in six days the LORD made heaven and earth,
and on the seventh day he rested, and was refreshed.
Exodus 31:16,17

Darlene worked furiously over the cuffs of Pierce Blackwell's long-tailed frock coat. It would soon be dark and the Sabbath would be upon them. There was never to be any work on *Shabbes*, for God himself had declared it a day of rest and demanded that His people honor and keep that day for Him.

Esther sat companionably, for once not making her usually busybody statements, but instead helping to put buttons on the satin waistcoat that Pierce would wear the following night. Such deadlines made it necessary for Darlene and Abraham to elicit additional help, and the fact that Valentine's Day came on a Saturday made it absolutely necessary to have everything done as early on Friday as possible.

Shabbes began on Friday evening when it was dark enough for the first stars to be seen in the sky. By that time, all work would have to be completed and put aside. No work was to be done, not even the lighting of fires on such cold, bitter mornings as February in New York could deliver. For this purpose, Abraham paid a *Shabbes goy*, a Gentile boy to come and light fires and lamps. Darlene knew that many families could not afford to pay someone to come in, and for them she felt sorry. They were strictly dependent upon the goodness of neighbors and sometimes they went through *Shabbes* without a warm fire to ward off the cold.

Finishing the cuff, Darlene held up the coat and smiled. She knew Pierce would be handsome in the black, redingote-styled frock coat. The tapering of the jacket from broad shoulders to narrow waist only made her smile broaden. Pierce would need no corset to keep his figure until control. Of this she was certain.

"Such a look," Esther remarked, staring at Darlene from her work.

Darlene laughed. "I was only trying to imagine what it might be like to dance at a party where men dress so regally."

"*Oy vey!* You should put aside such thoughts. Next, you'll be considering marriage to some rich *goy*, if you could find one who'd have you."

Darlene felt her cheeks flush and instantly dropped the coat back to her lap and threaded her needle. She prayed that Esther wouldn't notice her embarrassment, because just such thoughts had already gone through her mind.

"So, you do think of such things!" Esther showed clear disgust by Darlene's breech of etiquette. "*Bist blint*—are you blind? Such things will only lead you to heartache."

Darlene waved her off. "I'm not blind and I'm not headed to heartache or anything else. I simply wondered what it might be like to own fine things and not be looked down upon by the people in the city. Is that so bad?"

Esther studied her closely for a moment. "There is talk, *Havele*. Talk that should make your father take notice. The cantor knows that Avrom's faith is weakening."

"Never! It's not true!" Darlene shouted the words, not meaning to make such an obvious protest.

"If he turns from God, he will be a traitor to our people. No one will speak to him again. No one of Hebrew faith will do business with him. If that happens, *Havele*, you will come and live with me." She said it as though Darlene would have no choice in the matter.

"I will not leave Tateh. Such talk!" She got up from her work and excused herself to tend to Sabbath preparations upstairs. Hurrying up the rickety backstairs, Darlene couldn't help but be upset by Esther's words. It was true enough that her father would be considered *meshummad*—a traitor—if he accepted the Christian religion of Dennison and Pierce Blackwell. But surely that could not happen. They were God's chosen people, the children of Israel. Surely her father could not disregard this fact.

She finished putting together the *schalet*, a slow-cooking stew that would simmer all night long and be ready to eat for the Sabbath. This would enable her to keep from breaking the day of rest by preparing meals. Turning from this, Darlene set about completing preparations for their evening Sabbath meal. This was always a very elegant dinner with her mother's finest Bavarian china and a delicate lace tablecloth to cover the simple kitchen table.

Setting the table, she hummed to herself and tried to dispel her fears. Surely things weren't as bad as Esther implied. The small roast in the oven gave off a succulent, inviting smell when Darlene peered inside. It would be done in plenty of time for their meal and it was a favorite of her father's. Perhaps this would put him in a good frame of mind and give him cause to remember his faith. Perhaps a perfect *Shabbes* meal would focus his heart back on the teachings of his fathers.

Filling a pot with water and potatoes, Darlene left it to cook on the stove and hurried back to finish the Blackwell suit. Hayyim was to deliver the suits before Sabbath began, and with this thought, Darlene silently wished she could go along to see where Pierce lived. No doubt it was a beautiful brick house with several stories and lovely lace curtains at each and every window. With a sigh, she pushed such incriminating thoughts from her mind and joined Esther.

"It is finished," Esther announced. "I must get home now and make certain things are ready."

"Thank you so much for helping me. Did Tateh pay you already?"

"Yes, I am well rewarded," Esther said, pulling on her heavy coat. Darlene went to help her, but she would have nothing to do with it. "I may be an old woman, but I can still put on my coat."

Good, Darlene thought. *She has already forgotten our conversation and now she will return home and leave me to my dreams.* But it was not to be. Without warning, Esther turned at the door and admonished Darlene.

"You should spend *Shabbes* in prayer and seek God's heart instead of that of the rich *goyim.*"

And you should mind your own business, Darlene thought silently, while outwardly nodding. She did nothing but present herself as the most repentant of chastised children. With head lowered and hands folded, Darlene's appearance put Esther at ease enough to take her leave.

"Gut Shabbos, Hava."

"Good Sabbath to you, Esther."

With Esther gone, Darlene breathed a sigh of relief and called to Hayyim. "The Blackwell suits are finished. You can take them now." She let her fingers linger on Pierce's coat for just a moment before Hayyim took it.

"Darlene, you look very pretty today," Hayyim said, lingering as if he had all the time in the world.

Darlene felt sorry for him. She knew he was terribly taken with her, but her heart couldn't lie and encourage the infatuation. "Thank you, Hayyim. You'd better hurry if you're to get home in time for Sabbath."

Hayyim nodded sadly. Darlene watched him take up the rest of the clothes in a rather dejected manner. Better she make herself clear with him now, than to lead him on and give him reason to hope for a future with her.

Just as she was about to got upstairs and finish with the meal, a knock sounded at the back door. Wondering if Esther had forgotten something, Darlene glanced quickly about the room, then went to open the door.

Five children ranging in age from four to twelve stood barefooted and ragged in the muddy snow. These were her "regulars," as Darlene called them.

Destitute children who came routinely on Friday afternoon to beg for food and clothes.

"Ah, I thought perhaps you had forgotten me," she said with a smile. "Come in, come in. Warm yourselves by the fire." She motioned them forward and they hurried to the stove, hands outstretched and faces smiling.

Darlene stuck her head out the door and noted that two older youths, probably in their middle teens, waited not far down the alleyway. She smiled and motioned for them to join in, but they shook their heads and went back to their conversation. They only watched over the little ones. Darlene knew they were probably older siblings who realized the younger children could persuade better charity from sympathetic adults, without being expected to work in return.

She closed the door to the cold and turned to meet the sallow faces and hopeful eyes of the little ones. "I have a surprise for you. I hope you like sweets."

The children nodded with smiling, dirt-ladened faces.

"Good. You wait here and I'll be right back." Darlene hurried into the next room, where she had saved them a collection of things all week long.

Nebekhs—the poor things! They had nothing, and no one but each other. Their parents were most likely involved in corrupt things that took them away from wherever they called home. If they had parents. Some were orphans who roamed the streets only protected by the various street rowdies who had taken residence in the area. The hoodlums taught them to steal and to beg and in return, they provided some semblance of a family.

Gathering up armloads of remnant cloth and a small brown bag of sweets, Darlene went back to the children. "I think you'll like this," she said, putting the cloth down and holding out the bag. "There's plenty inside for everyone, even your friends outside."

One little girl, barely wrapped in a tattered coat, reached her hand in first and pulled out a peppermint stick. "Ohhh!" she said, her eyes big as saucers. This was all the encouragement that the others needed. They hurriedly thrust hands inside the sack and came up with sticks of their own.

"Now, here are some nice pieces of cloth that can be made into clothes. And I have a small sack of bread and several jars of jam." Darlene went to retrieve these articles and returned to find five very satisfied children devouring their peppermint.

"Can you carry it all or should I call for your friends?"

"Ain't no friends. Them's my brothers Willy and Sam," one little boy replied.

"Well," Darlene said, opening the door, "would you like for them to come and help?"

"No, ma'am," the oldest boy of the group announced. He had the remains of a black eye still showing against his pale white face. "We can carry it." And this they did. The children each took responsibility for some article with the youngest delegated to carrying the candy sack.

"I'll see you next week," Darlene said and waved to the elusive Willy and Sam. They didn't wave back, but Darlene knew they saw her generosity. How sad they were trudging off in the filthy snow. Little feet making barefoot tracks. Silent reminders of the children's plight. Darlene wanted to cry whenever she saw them. No matter what she did for them it was never enough. Scraps of material and sweets wouldn't provide a roof over their heads and warmth when the night winds blew fierce. *How could God allow such things?* she wondered. How could she?

Without willing it to be there, the image of Pierce Blackwell filled her mind. She wondered if the Blackwells in all their finery and luxury ever considered the poor. The Valentine's ball Pierce and his father would attend was purported to be for charity. Would children like these know the benefits of such a gala event or would the rich simply line their pockets, pay their revelry expenses and advertise for yet another charity ball?

The children had passed from view now and only their footprints in the snow remained to show that they'd ever been there at all. Noting the fading light, Darlene rushed to close the door and get back to her work. There was still so much to do in order to be idle on the Sabbath.

An hour later, Darlene breathed a sigh of relief and brought two braided *Hallah* loaves to the table. Stowing images of the ragged children and Pierce Blackwell away from her mind, Darlene set her thoughts to those of her *Shabbes* duties. She could hear her father puttering in his bedroom and had a keen sense that in spite of her worries, all was well. Taking down long, white candles in ornate silver holders, Darlene placed them on the table and went to the stove. In a small container beside the stove, long slivered pieces of kindling were the perfect means for lighting the *Shabbes* candles. Darlene came to the table with one of these and after lighting the candles, blew out the stick. Then with a circular wave of her hands as if pulling in the scent from the candles, she covered her eyes and recited the ritual prayer.

"*Baruch ata Adonai, eloheinu melech ha-olam, ahser kiddeshanu bemitzvotav, vetsivianu le'hadlik ner shel Shabbos*—Blessed art thou, Oh Lord, who sanctifies us by His commandments, and commands us to light the Sabbath lights."

Chapter 6

Wherefore by their fruits ye shall know them.
MATTHEW 7:20

Pierce lightly fingered the edge of a starfish shell and waited for his name to be called. He hated with all of his being the very fact that he was seated in the City Hotel ballroom, waiting to be auctioned off to the highest bidder. What would happen if Aunt Eugenia failed to top the bidding and buy him out of harm's way? Then again, what if Aunt Eugenia's way was one and the same?

The City Hotel's ballroom had been transformed into a lush underwater world. Heavy blue nets hung overhead to give the illusion of being underwater with a greedy fisherman hovering dangerously overhead. Many considered it pure genius to compare catching an eligible bachelor to amassing a good catch of fish, but Pierce wasn't among their numbers. He was literally checking his pocket watch every fifteen minutes and remained completely bored by the entire event.

"And bachelor number twelve is Pierce Blackwell. Mr. Blackwell, please come forward."

Pierce sighed, adjusted his new coat, and went up to the raised platform where he would be auctioned to the highest bidder. Putting on his most dazzling smile, Pierce pretended to be caught up in the evening's amusements.

"Pierce is with us after a three-year absence in Europe, and the ladies here tonight are no doubt in the best of luck to be a part of this gathering. As you can see, Mr. Blackwell would make an admirable suitor for any eligible young woman." Giggles sounded from the ladies in the audience.

"The bidding will open at one hundred dollars," the speaker began.

A portly matron in the front waved her fan and started the game. Pierce remained fixed with the facade of congeniality plastered on his face. He nodded to each woman with a brilliant smile that he was certain wouldn't betray his anguish.

"The bid is at eight hundred dollars." The crowd ooohed and ahhhed. The heavy-set woman holding the eight hundred dollar bid blushed profusely and fanned herself continuously.

"One thousand dollars," Eugenia Blackwell Morgan announced and a

160

hush fell across the room. She stepped forward in a heavy gown of burgundy brocade. Multiple strands of pearls encircled her throat and in her hand she held an elaborate ivory fan. She cut a handsome figure and appeared to know it full well. Pierce personally knew many men who would love to pay her court—if she was a less intimidating woman.

"The bid has been raised to one thousand dollars. Do I hear one thousand, one hundred?" Silence remained and there was not one movement among the bidding women. Pierce wondered if by prior arrangement, Eugenia had forbid any of them to outbid her.

"Then the bid is concluded at one thousand dollars." Applause filled the air and Pierce bowed low as he knew he was expected to do.

Stepping down from the platform, he went to his aunt and bowed low once again. "Madam," he said in a most formal tone.

"Oh, bother with you," Eugenia said, and swatted him with her fan. "Come along."

Pierce offered his arm and Eugenia took it without a word. Although it was proper for a gentleman to lead a lady, Eugenia clearly made their way through the crowd to the table she had reserved to be her own. Sitting there waiting was an incredibly beautiful young woman. Her thick dark hair reminded Pierce of Darlene, but that was where the similarities ended. The haughty smile, sharply arched brows, and icy-blue eyes of the woman clearly drove the image of Darlene from his mind.

"Pierce, this is Amanda Ralston. She is the only daughter of Benjamin Ralston."

Pierce bowed before the woman and received her curt little nod. "Your servant," he said and looked to his aunt for some clue as to how the game was to be played.

"No doubt you are familiar with her father's name and their family," Eugenia said with pale, tight lips. "I will leave you two to discuss matters of importance and to dance the night away."

Inwardly, Pierce groaned. Outwardly, he extended his arm. "Would you care for some refreshment? The bidding will no doubt continue for some time."

With a coy, seductive smile, Amanda put her gloved hand on Pierce's arm. "Perhaps later. Why don't you join me and tell me about your time in Europe?"

He took the chair opposite her. "What would you like to know?" He was evasive by nature and with this woman he felt even more of a need to maintain his privacy.

"You were away a very long time. Did you perhaps lose your heart to some young Parisian woman?"

Pierce's expression didn't change. "No, I simply had no reason to return to America."

"No reason? There's a fortune to be made in this country and men like you are the ones to do the making."

Well, thought Pierce, *she certainly has no trouble putting her thoughts into words.* "America did fine in my absence."

She laughed a light, stilted laugh. "Mr. Blackwell, you do amaze me. This is a time of great adventure in America. A great deal of money is changing hands. Don't you want to be a part of that?"

"Money changes from my hand all the time," he replied smugly.

"Well, the more important thing is that it returns ten-fold," she fairly purred.

Pierce thought of his land deals in Chicago and wondered if she'd swoon should he be as vulgar as to mention figures. She was clearly a woman looking out for her best interest and as far as Pierce was concerned, her interests were far removed from his.

"I find this conversation rather dull for a party," Pierce finally spoke. "Surely a young woman of your caliber would rather discuss dances and debuts rather than banking ledgers."

Amanda lifted her chin slightly in order to stare down her slender, well-shaped nose. "My father believes the banking system is doomed to fail. What say you to that, Mr. Blackwell?"

Pierce looked at her thoughtfully. She was incredibly beautiful. Maybe too much so. Her emerald-green gown was a bit risque for her age, at least by Pierce's standards. Should Constance ever show up in such a gown, he'd be persuaded to throw a wrap about her shoulders. Amanda seemed fully comfortable, if not motivated by, the daring low decolletage of the gown. Her creamy-white shoulders glowed in the candlelight, while the ecru lacing of her gown urged his gaze to travel lower. Pierce refused to give in to the temptation and pulled his thoughts away from Amanda. Music was beginning at the far end of the ballroom. No doubt the auction was completed and now the dance could start again.

"Would you care to dance?" Pierce asked politely.

"I suppose it would be expected," Amanda replied.

With the grace of a cat, Pierce was at her side. He helped her from the chair and led her across the room to where other couples were already enjoying the strains of a waltz. Pierce was not entirely certain he wished to waltz with Amanda. It was such a daring dance of holding one's partner close and facing each other for a time of constant consideration. But, he'd been the one to open his mouth and bring her this far. He supposed there was little to do but carry through.

He whirled her into the circling dancers and tried not to think about the way dancing seemed to further expose her figure to his eyes. Didn't she realize how blatantly obvious her assets were being admired by every man in the room?

"Perhaps," he said a bit uncomfortably, "this gown was not intended for such dancing."

Amanda looked at him with complete bewilderment. "Why, whatever do you mean, Mr. Blackwell?"

Pierce coughed, more from nervous energy than the need to clear his throat. "It's just that the cut of your gown seems, well, a bit brief."

Amanda's laughter rang out in a melodious tinkling sound. "Why, Mr. Blackwell, that is the idea."

Pierce felt his face grow flushed. There was no dealing politely with this woman. "Miss Ralston, I am not in the habit of keeping company with women whose sole purpose in designing a gown is that they should overexpose themselves to the world."

"My father says that beautiful things should be admired," she replied curtly. "Do you not think I'm beautiful?"

Pierce wanted to say no, but that would be a lie. "Yes, your countenance is lovely. Your spirit would raise some questions, however."

"My, and what is that supposed to mean? Spirit? Why you sound as though you were some sort of stuffy reverend from the downtown cathedrals."

Pierce turned her a bit too quickly, but he held her fast and she easily recovered the step. "I am a man of God, but not in the sense you suppose. I am of the Christian faith and I believe in women keeping themselves discreetly covered in public."

"Ah, but what about in private?" She tripped and fell against him. Only then did Pierce realize it was deliberate. "Oh my, have I compromised you, Mr. Blackwell?" she asked with a hint of a giggle.

Pierce could stand no more. He set her back at arm's length and admonished her. "If you cannot contain your enthusiasm for the dance, madam, perhaps I should lead you from the floor."

"Remember, you're mine for the evening. Charity and such, you know." She was amused with his discomfort and it registered clearly on her face and in her voice.

Without warning, Pierce pulled her rudely from the circle of dancers. "It seems I've winded myself," he said with a look that challenged her to suggest

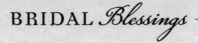

otherwise. "I'll take you back to our table."

She said nothing as he escorted her back and only after she had been seated did Pierce excuse himself to bring back refreshments. "I won't be a moment," he promised and left her very clearly alone.

Rage coursed through him. She was no better than the women of the night, only she wore expensive satin and jewels. He would throttle Constance if she ever dared to toy with men in such a fashion. Taking up two glasses of punch, Pierce tried to steady his nerves before returning to the table. Without thought he downed both cups before realizing what he'd done. Smiling sheepishly, he put one cup down, offered his for a refill, and picked up another for Amanda.

He walked slowly back to the table. Maybe too slowly for by the time he'd returned there had gathered a number of seemingly unattached young men. He wondered silently if he could just slip away unnoticed, but Amanda hailed him in her bold and open fashion.

"Oh, Pierce, darling," she announced, "I thought I'd simply perish before you returned. You gentlemen will excuse me now, won't you?" She batted her eyes coyly at the group and smiled as though promising each of them something more than she could deliver.

The men graciously but regretfully took their leave, and Pierce was finally able to place the cup of punch on the table at her fingertips. "It was good of them to keep watch over you in case you expired before I returned," he said sarcastically and took his seat.

"Why, Pierce Blackwell, you're jealous." She laughed and took a long sip of her punch.

Pierce couldn't decide the path of least resistance and so said nothing. This only added fuel to Amanda's imagination. "Mrs. Morgan told me that your father is quite anxious to settle you down with a wife. I must say, I was honored to be singled out for such consideration. You know my father has made himself a tidy sum of money, nothing compared to your father, of course." She stopped for a moment, took another sip of punch, and continued, "But together, we would clearly stand as one of New York's wealthiest couples."

"I'm not going to live in New York," Pierce finally announced.

"Oh, well, Paris then? Or perhaps Boston?"

Pierce shook his head. "Chicago." He couldn't help but get satisfaction from the expression of disappointment on her face.

"Chicago? My, but where in the world in that?"

"It's a little town in Illinois. It sits on Lake Michigan."

"And why would you ever plan to live there?" She was obviously filled with horror at such a thought.

Pierce smiled. "Because this is a time of great adventure in America." He used her own words against her, but she didn't seem phased by his strategy.

"Yes, of course, but moving to such a place would be complete foolishness for one of your social standing. Such moves as those are justified by the poorer classes who seek to set up a new life for themselves."

"But I seek such a life for myself. I've grown quite weary of the life I've known here in New York."

Amanda was aghast. "But I could never agree to marry you unless we lived in New York City."

"I never asked you to," Pierce said smugly. "Perhaps my aunt presumed too much. Perhaps she led you to believe a falsehood about me, but I assure you I am no more interested in marrying you than you are in marrying me. Now, I suggest that I deliver you back to your father's protection and end this farce."

Amanda's face betrayed her anger. "No one treats me like this. I am a Ralston!"

"That you are, madam, and if left up to me, that you would remain."

The gasp she made was not very ladylike and certainly louder than polite society would have accepted, had the room been quiet enough in which to hear it. Pierce merely got to his feet, offered his arm once again, and waited for her to make up her mind.

"I haven't all night, Miss Ralston. Come, we'll tell your father that something has prevented my staying out the evening. No harm should be done, as it was Blackwell money that secured me as your companion this evening." With that, Pierce nearly dragged her to her feet.

It was a stunned and openly hostile Amanda that Pierce delivered to the care of her mother. Mrs. Ralston was ever so sorry to learn that Pierce was suddenly called away. Pierce begged their forgiveness, then hurried from the gathering before Aunt Eugenia could spot him and force him to stay.

Outside the hotel, Pierce quickly found his driver and urged him to spare no time in exiting the scene. Cold and uncomfortable in the emptiness of his carriage, Pierce had thoughts for only one thing. One woman. Darlene.

For the first time that evening, he smiled. He thought of how he'd arranged for his valentine to be delivered that afternoon and wondered what Darlene thought of the impulsive and rather brazen gesture. Suddenly he felt warmer. Just the thought of her made him push aside the discomforts of the night. There would be much to answer for tomorrow. His aunt would be unforgiving for his rude escape. But he was much more concerned with how Darlene would react to his card.

His father's warning words came back to haunt him and Pierce was suddenly filled with an uneasiness born of knowing the truth. Darlene was not of his faith and she would reject everything about his Christian beliefs, just as he would reject her disbelief in Christ. Unless God somehow persuaded Darlene to open her heart to the truth of who Jesus really was, further consideration of her could only lead to heartache. But Pierce knew that in many ways it was too late. He was rapidly losing his heart to Darlene, and the thought of rejecting his feelings for her was more than he wanted to deal with.

"She's a good woman, Lord," he prayed aloud in the privacy of the carriage. "She's responsible and considerate, and she loves her father and respects his wishes. She's beautiful, although I don't think she knows it, and I admire her greatly. Surely there's some place for her in my life. Surely there is some way to share with her the Gospel of Christ." But even as Pierce prayed, he knew his words were born out of self-desire.

Chapter 7

And he shall be for a sanctuary; but for a stone of
stumbling and for a rock of offence to both the houses of Israel,
for a gin and for a snare to the inhabitants of Jerusalem.
Isaiah 8:14

Darlene looked apprehensively at the envelope in her hands. It had arrived during the Sabbath and because she knew it was nothing in regards to keeping the day holy, she had put it aside until Sabbath had concluded. Now, however, there was no putting off her curiosity. With breakfast concluded and her father already occupied with something in his room, Darlene sat down to the kitchen table and opened the envelope.

The card slid out quite easily and caused Darlene to gasp. It was cream colored with gold-foil trim and a lace-edged red heart in the center. The words, *My Valentine*, topped the card, while at the bottom tiny Cupids held a scroll with a more personal limerick.

My heart I do give and display,
For this, our first Valentine's Day.
Let me say from the start, I will never
*   depart,*
My heart from yours never will stray.

Darlene stared at the card for several moments before turning it over. There was no other word, no signature, nothing at all to indicate who had sent it. But Darlene was already certain who had sent it. There was only one possible person. Pierce Blackwell!

After the initial shock wore off, Darlene began to smile. She fingered the lacy heart and wondered if Pierce had ordered this especially made for her. Perhaps it was a standard card he sent to all women, for surely there must be many fine ladies of his acquaintance. A twinge of grief struck her. Perhaps he had sent this as a way of laughing at her. Maybe it was his only means of making sport of her ignorance. She frowned and looked at the card with a more serious eye.

Hearing her father come from his bedroom, Darlene quickly put the card back into its envelope and tucked it in her apron pocket. Glancing up, Darlene was startled to find that Abraham was not dressed in his shop clothes, but in his best suit with hat in hand.

"Tateh?" she questioned. "You are going out?"

Abraham seemed a bit hesitant to discuss the matter. "I am."

Darlene shook her head. "But I don't understand. Is there something we need? Some errand I can help you with?"

"No." He placed his hat on the table and smiled. "I should talk to you about the matter, but it was not my wish to cause you grief."

"What grief?" Now she was getting worried.

Abraham took a seat beside his daughter and reached out to take her hand in his. "I'm going to the Christian church today with Dennison Blackwell and his family."

"What!" Darlene jumped up from her seat, snatching her hand away.

Abraham lowered his head and it was then that Darlene noticed his head was bare. The *yarmulke* that he had religiously worn all of his life, was absent. This was more serious than she'd imagined.

"Tateh, I don't understand." Her voice betrayed her concern.

"I know."

His simple statement was not enough. Darlene came back to the table and sat down. She was stunned beyond words, yet words were the only way to explain her father's decision. He looked so sad, so old, and for the first time Darlene considered that he might die soon. Now he wanted to change religions? After a lifetime of serving God in the faith of his ancestors?

"Why don't you explain and I'll try to be quiet," she suggested.

Abraham looked up at her. His aged face held an expression of sheer anguish. "I've wanted to explain for some time. I know there are rumors among our friends. I know you have had to deal with many questions."

It was true enough. Yesterday, after going to the synagogue with her father, Darlene had found herself surrounded by friends and neighbors, all wanting to know what was going on with her father. Still, she'd not expected such an open showing of defiance. There was no way she could hide the fact that Abraham Lewy was going to the *goy's* church.

When she said nothing, Abraham continued. "There are many questions in my mind about the Christian faith. The Israelites are the chosen people of God, but Dennison showed me scripture in the Bible that makes it hard to deny that Jesus was truly Messiah."

"The Christian Bible is not the Torah," she protested.

"True, but the Scriptures Dennison shared are from Isaiah and those Scriptures are a part of our Bible, as well."

"This is so confusing," Darlene said, feeling as though the wind was being sucked from her lungs. "Are you saying to me that you believe their Jesus is the Messiah we seek?"

"I'm saying that I see the possibilities for such a thing."

Very calmly, Darlene took a deep breath. "How? How can this be? You told me as a child that Jesus was merely a man. You told me the disciples who followed him took his body from the tomb and hid it away in order to support their lies of His resurrection." Her voice raised and the stress of the situation was evident. "You told me the *goyim* served three Gods not one, and now you tell me that Isaiah's words have caused you to see the possibilities of the Christian faith being right and the Jewish faith being wrong?" She felt as though she might start to cry at any moment.

"*Neshomeleh,* do not fret so. You must understand that I do not consider this matter lightly. I am seeking to know the truth."

"But if Jesus is the Messiah, who needs Him? Still our people suffer, for hundreds of years they suffer. Even now, we are misfits, and less than human in the eyes of some.

"If Jesus is Messiah, where is His Kingdom? Where is our deliverance?" Darlene knew the words sounded bitter, but she didn't care.

Abraham patted her tightly gripped hands. "I only seek the truth. My love for you is such that I would not seek to put your soul in eternal jeopardy. If there is even the slightest possibility that I am wrong, then I wish to learn the right and teach it to my children before my days are finished.

"You see the *mezuzah*?" Abraham looked up to the small ornate box that graced the side of the kitchen door. "Within that box are precious words from Deuteronomy. We kiss our hands and touch the *mezuzah* as a representation of our love and obedience to God's commands."

Darlene looked to the box with its silver scrolling and tiny window. They'd brought this particular mezuzah with them from Germany, and she knew full well it had come from her mother's family. Others were nailed to the wall beside other doors, but this one was very special. The ritual of the *mezuzah* was as automatic and commonplace as breathing. She touched it reflexively whenever she entered the room and because it was so routine, she seldom reflected on the parchment words held within.

"On that paper God speaks, saying, 'And these words, which I command thee this day, shall be in thine heart. And thou shalt teach them diligently unto thy children, and shalt talk of them when thou sittest in thine house, and when thou walkest by the way, and when thou liest down, and when thou risest up.' God has commanded me to train you, Darlene. I cannot fail you by ignoring the truth. Should my choices have been wrong, should I be too blind to see, it would be a tragedy. Would you not rather know the truth?"

"But how can you be certain that the truth isn't what you already believe it to be?" she questioned softly.

Abraham gave a heavy sigh. "Because my heart is troubled. There is an emptiness inside that won't be filled. I used to think it was because of your mother's death. I reasoned that she was such an important part of my life, that the void would quite naturally remain until I died. But with time, I realized it was more than this. I felt a yearning that I could not explain away. When Dennison Blackwell began to speak to me of his faith, a little fire ignited inside, and I thought, 'Ah, maybe this is my answer.'"

"But Tateh, how can you be sure? You can't give up your faith and embrace the Christian religion without absolute certainty. How will you find that?"

"Because I don't have to give up my faith in order to embrace Christianity. That is the one thing I continue to come back to. Of course, the Jews believe differently about Messiah, but they still believe in Messiah. To acknowledge that Jesus of Christian salvation is also Messiah seems not so difficult a thing."

Darlene was floored by this and longed to ask her father a million questions, but just then a knock sounded loudly on the door downstairs.

"That will be Dennison," Abraham said, getting to his feet. He took up his hat and placed his arm on Darlene's shoulder. "Do not grieve or be afraid. God will direct." He paused for a moment. "You could come with me?"

"No!" she exclaimed, then put her hand to her mouth to keep from saying the multitude of things that had suddenly rushed to her mind. Tears flowed from her eyes and a sob broke from her throat when Abraham bent to kiss the top of her head.

He left her, touching the *mezuzah* faithfully, but this time it impacted Darlene in a way she couldn't explain. Suddenly her world seemed completely turned upside down. This Jesus of Christian faith seemed to be at the center of all of her problems. How could she ever be reconciled to her father's new search for truth, when all of her life the truth seemed to be clear? Now her father would have her question whether their beliefs were accurately perceived.

Her father's absence made the silence of the house and shop unbearable. Darlene had no idea when he might return and all she could do was busy herself with the handwork he'd given her. Hayyim was hard at work in the cutting room when she came to take up her workbasket. He looked up and smiled, but quickly lost his expression of joy and rushed to her side.

"You've been crying. *Vos iz mit dir?*"

She tried to shake her head, but couldn't. "Nothing's the matter. I'm all right."

"No, you're not. You look like something truly awful has happened. Here," he led her to a chair, "sit down and tell me what's wrong."

All Darlene could remember was that Hayyim had shared information from the shop with Esther. Of course, Esther was an old woman, butting in wherever she could in order to learn whatever there was to learn. Still, Hayyim should have been more discriminating.

"I'm fine," she insisted. "There's much to be done and Tateh won't be back for several hours. He has a meeting with Mr. Blackwell."

"On a Sunday? I thought that rich *goy* went to synagogue, I mean church, on Sunday."

Darlene shrugged. "It is no concern of mine. . .or yours." She narrowed her eyes at Hayyim. "You mustn't talk about my father to other people. There are those who say you gossip like an old woman and I won't have it, do you understand? My father is a good man and I won't have people look down upon him because of loose, idle palaver."

Hayyim looked genuinely sorry for his indiscretion. "Esther has a way of getting it out of you," he said by way of explanation. "I didn't even realize I was talking until I was well into it. I meant no harm."

Darlene pitied him and for a moment she thought he might cry. "I know well Esther's way. Just guard your mouth in the future."

"You know I would never hurt you, Darlene. You know that I would like to speak to your father about us."

"There is no 'us,' Hayyim. I do not wish to marry you and I will not leave Tateh."

"I would never ask you to leave him. I would work here as your husband and make a good life for you and your father. I would care for him in his old age and he would never have to work again."

Darlene smiled because she knew Hayyim was most serious in his devotion. She shook her head. "I could not take you for a husband, Hayyim."

"Because I am poor?" He sounded the question so pathetically.

Darlene touched her hand to his arm. "No, because I do not love you, nor would I ever come to love you."

She left him at that, knowing that he would not want her to see him cry or show weakness. He was still a child in some ways, and although being orphaned by his parents and losing his brothers all to cholera had grown him up, Hayyim was not the strong, intelligent man she would hope to call husband.

A fleeting image of Pierce Blackwell came to mind and Darlene reached into her pocket for the valentine he'd sent. She pulled it from the envelope and for a moment, remembering that Pierce's father was the cause for her heavy heart, thought to throw it in the fire. But she couldn't destroy it. For reasons quite beyond her ability to understand, Darlene put her work aside and went quietly to her bedroom. Going to her clothes chest, she gently lay aside her nightgowns and put the envelope safely away. Replacing the gowns, she felt a strange tugging at her heart. Pierce might be a Gentile, but he was considerate and intelligent and very handsome. It was difficult not to be persuaded by such strong visual enticements.

Going back downstairs, Darlene picked up her sewing and began her work. There was much to consider. Her father's words still haunted her and the questions in her mind would not be put aside. Perhaps she would go later and speak with Mr. Singer. Without a rabbi to consult, perhaps Mr. Singer could advise her. But to do so would betray her father's actions and bring about harsh reprisals. Still, to say nothing and have no knowledge of what she should do could only cause more grief. Perhaps if she knew more, she could persuade her father to give up this foolish notion of accepting Christianity as being truth. Otherwise, this issue of Jesus as Messiah was going to be quite a barrier to overcome.

Chapter 8

I know that ye are Abraham's seed; but ye seek to kill me,
because my word hath no place in you.
JOHN 8:37

Darlene walked bitterly into spring with a heaviness of heart that would not be dispelled. She listened to her father's words and knew him to be quite excited about the things he was learning. There were phrases he spoke, words that meant something different than they'd ever meant before. Salvation. Redemption. The Holy Spirit. All of these frightened Darlene to the very core of her being.

Now, with less than a week before Passover, Darlene didn't know whether to make preparations for a *seder* meal, or to just plan to spend Passover with Esther. By now, everyone knew that her father was a man torn between two religious views. He went faithfully to the synagogue on Friday evening and Saturday, but on Sunday he went to the Christian church with Dennison Blackwell. He was rapidly viewed as being both crazy and a traitor, and neither representation did him justice as far as Darlene was concerned.

The ringing of the shop doorbells caused Darlene to jump. Nervous these days from a constant barrage of Esther's questions, Darlene had decided that every visitor could possibly represent some form of gossip or challenge related to her father. This time, her assessment couldn't have been more accurate. With a look of pure disdain, Reuven Singer filled the doorway. He wore a broad-rimmed black hat, with a heavy black overcoat that fell to the floor. His long gray beard trailed down from thick, stern lips and one glance into his pale-blue eyes caused Darlene to shiver.

"Good morning, Mr. Singer. Tateh is out, but I expect him back soon."

"I know full well that your father is out. I know, too, where he has gone. He's at the church of his Christian friends, no?"

"It's true," Darlene admitted. She felt sick to her stomach and wished she could sit down. "You're welcome to wait for him upstairs. Come, I'll make tea."

"No. Perhaps it is better we talk."

Darlene glanced around her. Hayyim was on the third floor moving bolts of cloth. She knew he'd be busy for some time and would present no interruption for the cantor. "We can sit in here or go in the back."

"The back, then."

She nodded and led the way. Her hands were shaking so violently that she wondered if the cantor was aware of her fear. She offered him the more comfortable of two stuffed chairs and when he had taken his seat, she joined him. Barely sitting on the edge of her chair, Darlene leaned forward, smoothed her skirt of pale-blue wool, and waited for Mr. Singer to speak.

"Miss Lewy, it is believed by many that your father has fallen away from the teachings of his fathers. I cannot say how much this grieves and angers me, nor can I stress enough the dangers you face."

Darlene swallowed hard. What should she say? To admit to everything she knew might well see her father ostracized by his own people. Deciding it was better to remain silent and appear the obedient child, Darlene did nothing but look at her folded hands.

"Avrom has feet in two worlds. It cannot remain so. He is a Jew or he is a traitor to his people."

Darlene could not bear to hear him malign her father. Squaring her shoulders, Darlene looked him in the eye. "Mr. Singer, may I ask you a question?"

The old cantor seemed taken aback by her sudden boldness. He nodded, his gray beard bobbing up and down with the motion.

"I've heard it said," she hesitated. She wasn't a scholarly woman and all of the things she was about to say had come straight from her father's mouth. She could only hope to accurately translate the things she'd been told. "I've heard it said," she began again, "that the words of Isaiah make clear the coming of Messiah. The Christians believe Isaiah speaks of Jesus, but we believe it speaks of Israel. Is this true?"

The cantor eyed her quite sternly for a moment. "It is true."

"The Christians also believe that Jesus is not only Messiah, but that He offers salvation to anyone who comes to Him."

"And what salvation would this be?" the cantor questioned. "Would it be salvation from the persecution our people have faced from their kind? Would it restore Israel and Jerusalem back to our people? Salvation from what, I ask?" The deep, resonant voice clearly bore irritation.

"Well. . ." Darlene was now sorry to have brought up the subject. So much of what her father had shared regarding the Christians seemed reasonable, but confusing. "I thought it to mean salvation from death."

"You are of God's chosen people, Miss Lewy. By reason of that you are already saved."

"But the Christians believe. . . ."

"Feh! I care not for what the *goyim* believe. You are responsible for three things. *Tefillah*—prayer. *Teshuvah*—repentance. And *tsedakah*—righteousness. If you do what is right in God's eyes, make your prayers, and turn away from your sins, God will look favorably upon you. The only salvation we seek is for Israel. Why do you suppose we say, 'Next year in Jerusalem'? We mourn the destruction and loss of our beloved homeland. We long with fervency to return. Messiah will rebuild Jerusalem and the Holy Temple and restore his people to their land. The Turks now control it. Would you have me believe that the Christian Jesus came to earth but was unable to establish such restoration?"

"I don't know," she answered honestly. "I suppose that is why I ask."

The cantor seemed to soften a bit. "It might be better if you were to leave this place. Esther has already told me there is room for you in her home. She would happily take you in and keep you."

"Leave my father? How could this be in keeping with the scriptures to honor him?" Darlene was devastated by the suggestion.

"He is a traitor to his people if he believes that Jesus is Messiah. He will be forsaken and there will be no fellowship with him. He will become as one dead to us and you will be as one orphaned."

Darlene couldn't help but shudder. She thought of the tiny, homeless children who frequented her doorstep. Would she be reduced to begging scraps of food and clothing from the friends and neighbors who would deem her father unfit—*apostate*—dead? She shuddered again. "I could not leave Tateh. He isn't well and he might die. He needs me to care for him."

The old man's harsh demeanor returned. "He will surely perish if he turns from God. As will you. Will you become *meshummad*—traitor to your faith and people? Will you trample under foot the traditions of your ancestors and break the heart of your dear, departed mother? If you follow your father into such betrayal, you will leave us no option but to declare you dead, as well."

Darlene felt shaken and unsure of herself. "I. . .I'm not. . ."

The cantor got to his feet. "Christians have sought to destroy us. They treat us as less than human and disregard us, malign us, and even kill our people, all in the name of Christianity. Can you find acceptability in such a faith?" He didn't wait for an answer, but strode proudly from the room.

Darlene sat silently for several moments. She could feel her heart racing and perspiration forming on her brow. Why did such things have to be so consuming? The ringing of the bells caught her attention, and Darlene thought perhaps Mr. Singer had returned. Jumping to her feet, she was surprised to find her father standing in the door. A quick glance at the clock on the wall showed her that more time had passed than she'd been aware of.

"Tateh, you're back!"

Abraham smiled broadly. "That I am and I have news to tell you. Come upstairs and we'll sit together."

Darlene followed her father, wondering what in the world he had to tell her. His countenance was peaceful and his smile seemed to say that all was well, but in her heart Darlene feared that this talk would forever change their lives.

"Let me check on your dinner," she said, barely hearing her own words. She opened the oven to reveal a thick-breasted chicken roasting golden brown. Poking a fork into the center of it, she was satisfied to watch the succulent juices slide down the sides and into the pan.

"Come, dinner will wait," Abraham stated firmly.

Darlene closed the oven and took her place at the table. It was always here that they shared important matters. It was at a similar table in Germany that her father had told her of her mother and brother's death. It was at that same table he had announced their departure for America. What could he possibly wish to share with her now?

"What is it, Tateh?"

Abraham smiled. "I have invited the Blackwells to share Passover with us."

Passover? Her heart gave a sudden lurch. If Tateh was considering Passover, perhaps things weren't as bad as she supposed. But to invite the Blackwells to their *seder* was a shock.

"You've asked them here? For our *seder*?"

"Yes. The message this morning at their church was all about Easter and the last supper of Jesus Christ. The last supper was a celebration of Passover. Pierce said that he wondered what that Passover feast might have been like, and I told him he should come see for himself."

"And they accepted?"

"Dennison and Pierce did. Mrs. Morgan, Dennison's widowed sister, declined interest. I don't think she much cares for our kind." His words were given in a rather sorrowful manner. "Of course, she also takes a strong stand where Dennison's youngest child is concerned and refused for both herself and Constance Blackwell."

"I see." Darlene felt a lump form in her throat. "Well, I suppose I have preparations to see to."

"You are unhappy with this?" Abraham looked at her so tenderly that Darlene couldn't distance herself from him.

"No, not really." She considered telling him about the cantor, but decided against it. "I'm just surprised that they would want to come."

Abraham chuckled. "I think Pierce would make any excuse to come. He seems most anxious to see you again. He always asks about you and wonders how it is that you are ever away when he comes for fittings."

Darlene blushed, feeling her cheeks grow very hot. She thought no one had noticed her purposeful absences. "I suppose it is because I have much to do."

Abraham laughed even more at her feeble attempt to disguise the truth. "Daughter, you are not so very good at telling falsehoods. I've seen the way your face lights up when I speak of him. Perhaps you have a place in your heart for him?"

"No!" Darlene declared a bit too enthusiastically. "He's not of our faith and besides, I would never leave you."

"You will one day. It is important for a woman to marry and I will see you safely settled into a marriage of love and security before I die. So, if you think you can prolong my life on earth by simply refusing to marry, think again."

Darlene saw the glint of amusement in his eyes. She loved this man more than any other human being. Falling to her knees, she threw her arms around his waist and with her head on his lap began to cry. "I love you, Tateh, please do not jest about your death. I'm afraid when I think of you dying and leaving me behind. I think of how much it hurt to lose my mother and I can't bear the thought of your passing."

Abraham stroked her hair and tried to reassure her. "That is why the truth is important to me, Darlene. I want to be absolutely sure of my eternity. Does that sound like a foolish old man who is afraid to die?"

"Of course not!" she declared, raising her gaze to meet her father's eyes.

"Well, it's the truth. I am a foolish old man and I'm afraid to die. Dennison Blackwell isn't afraid to end his life on earth because he has great confidence in what will happen to him after his earthly life is completed."

"And you don't have such faith in your beliefs?" She dried her eyes with the back of her sleeve and waited for his answer.

He gently touched her cheek with his aged fingers. "If I could say yes, I would and put your mind forever at ease. But I cannot say yes."

"I'm afraid, Tateh."

"I know." He smiled sympathetically. "I suppose it would do little good to tell you not to be afraid."

"Very little good," she said with a hint of a smile on her lips. She got to her feet and Abraham stood too, wrapping her in his arms.

"You will make for the Blackwells a fine *seder*?" he questioned softly.

"Of course, Tateh. It will be the very best."

"Good. Now, I must go to work and earn for us the money for such a feast."

Darlene let him go without another word. She made her way to her bedroom and closed the door quietly behind her. Standing there in the stark, simple room, Darlene couldn't help but wonder where the future would take them. Surely if her father converted to Christianity, they'd find it impossible to remain in the neighborhood. Mr. Singer had already made it clear that they would be cut off from the community and called dead.

Drawing a deep breath, Darlene went to her bed and sat down. *No matter what happens*, she thought, *no matter where I am led, I will not forsake my father. I will not be blinded by the prejudice and stupidity of my own people.* She saw her reflection in the dresser mirror and tried hard to smile. Her eyes were still red-rimmed from crying and her face rather ashen from the shocks of the day, but deep inside, Darlene knew that her spirit thrived and that her heart was complete and whole. She would not be defeated by these things. She had trusted her father all of her life. To deny his ability to look out for her very best interests now would be to subject all of his ways to speculative guesses.

Dropping her gaze, Darlene caught sight of the chest where Pierce's valentine lay hidden away. She'd never spoken to him of the matter. In fact, her father was quite right to mention her disappearances when Pierce was scheduled to arrive in the shop. She felt nervous and jittery inside whenever she thought about Pierce Blackwell. There was no future with him, but he stirred her imagination in a way that could be quite maddening. With very little thought, she went to the chest and retrieved the pristine card.

She traced the letters *My Valentine* and wondered if Pierce had ever given it a single thought after having it delivered to her. He must think her terribly rude to have never thanked him for his thoughtfulness. And she truly believed that the act had been inspired by thoughtfulness and not because Pierce wanted to mock her inexperience with the day.

And now they were coming for Passover.

Pierce and his father would arrive to share her favorite celebration. Would they mock her faith, or would they understand and cherish it as she did? She thought of the recited words of the Passover dinner. The questions that were always asked and the responses that were always given. "What makes this night different?" she whispered and replaced the valentine in the chest. And indeed, she couldn't help but know that this night would be most different from all the others she had known.

Chapter 9

And it shall come to pass, when your children shall say unto you,
What mean ye by this service? That ye shall say, It is the sacrifice of the
LORD's passover, who passed over the houses of the children of Israel in
Egypt, when he smote the Egyptians, and delivered our houses.
And the people bowed the head and worshipped.
EXODUS 12:26–27

Darlene had worked diligently to rid the house and shop of any crumb of leaven. She swept the place from the top floor down and burned every bit until she was satisfied that the house was clean. This was in keeping with the teachings of her Jewish faith, and it made her proud to be such an important part of Passover. She remembered asking her bubbe why they had to eat unleavened bread and why the house had to be kept so clean of crumbs. Bubbe had told her the story of Israel's deliverance out of Egypt and it came to be a story she remembered well, for it was retold with every Passover celebration.

"When our people were in Egypt," Bubbe had said, "they were slaves to the Pharaoh. They suffered great miseries and God took pity upon them and sent out Moses to appeal to Pharaoh to let God's people go. But of course, Pharaoh was a stubborn man and he endured many plagues and sufferings upon his own people before finally agreeing to let the Israelites go free. The last of these great plagues was the most horrible of all. God told Moses he would take the life of every firstborn in the land of Egypt. Our people smeared blood over the doors and windows and the destroyer passed over, seeing this as a symbol of obedience unto God. Then, they had to rise up with haste to make the great journey to freedom. There was no time for the bread to rise and so they ate unleavened bread. Thus Passover became the Feast of Unleavened Bread."

Darlene still shuddered to think of such a monumental judgment upon the land. She remembered the verses Bubbe had quoted. "For I will pass through the land of Egypt this night, and will smite all the firstborn in the land of Egypt, both man and beast; and against all the gods of Egypt I will execute judgment: I am the Lord."

Darlene felt a deep sense of awe in that statement. It was such a moving reminder. "I am the Lord." *Baruch Ha-Shem,* she thought. *Blessed is the Name.*

With her mind focused on the preparations for Passover, Darlene forgot about the Blackwells. Instead, she wondered if her father would participate with the same enthusiasm he had once held for the ceremony. Surely he still felt the same about the deliverance of God's people from bondage. Freedom was a most cherished thing in the Lewy household and Darlene knew full well that her father didn't take such matters lightly. But perhaps the Christians in their faith were not so concerned with such things. What if the Blackwells had convinced her father that such freedom and remembrances were unimportant?

This was her first conscious thoughts of Pierce and his father. She grew nervous trying to imagine them at the *seder* table. Would they wear *yarmulkes?* Would they recite the prayers? Would they scoff and laugh at the faith of her people?

Somehow, Darlene couldn't imagine Pierce or his father being so cruel, but she reminded herself that she really didn't know either one all that well. Putting aside her worries, Darlene began to think about Pierce. She'd caught a glimpse of him leaving the shop one day and couldn't help but notice the way her heart beat faster at the very sight of him. Why did he have to affect her in such a way? Why could she not forget his smiling face and warm brown eyes? Sometimes it hurt so much to imagine what life with Pierce might be like. She knew what it felt like to be held securely in his arms. Would he hold her in that same possessive way if they were married? Would his smile be as sweet and his manners as gentle if she were his wife?

"No!" she exclaimed, putting her hands to her head as if to squeeze out such thoughts. It was sheer madness to imagine such things. Pierce was a Christian and she was a Jew. There was no possibility of the two coming together as one.

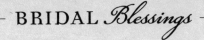

The Blackwell carriage drew up to the shop of Abraham Lewy. Pierce felt the anticipation of seeing Darlene mount within him and he found himself anxious to push the evening forward. If his father sensed this, he said nothing. In fact, little talk had been exchanged between them because two hours earlier, Pierce had announced his desire to move to Chicago. Dennison hadn't taken the news very well. A number of protests to such an idea were easily put forth, but Pierce had answers for all of his father's concerns. Hadn't they been his own concerns when first the thought of such a trip had come to mind? How will you live? How will you travel there? How will you survive in the wilds of Illinois? They were legitimate questions and Pierce couldn't pretend that he had all of the answers.

Seeing his father's brooding face, Pierce offered him a word of consolation. "Don't fret about this that hasn't come to pass. I promise I won't make any rash decisions, and I will discuss everything with you first."

"Discuss, but not necessarily heed my advise," Dennison muttered.

Pierce realized that nothing he said would offer comfort and gave up. He sprang from the carriage and, without waiting for his father, went to knock on the shop door. Closed for Passover, the window shade on the door had been pulled and even the shop windows were shaded for privacy. As his father came to stand beside him, Pierce couldn't help but feel the racing of his heart and wondered if his father would make some comment about the inappropriateness of Pierce's interest in Darlene. But before any word could be exchanged, Abraham Lewy opened the door and smiled.

"Ah, you have come. *Shalom*."

"*Shalom*, my friend," Dennison replied. "And my thanks for this invitation to your home and celebration."

It was a most somber occasion, and yet Pierce could hardly contain himself. He knew that just up those wooden stairs, Darlene would be scurrying around to make everything perfect for the occasion. He wanted to see her more than anything, and all other thoughts were wasted on him.

"Come, my Darlene has already made ready our table," Abraham said. "Oh, and here." He pulled out two *yarmulkes* and handed them to Dennison and Pierce. "You will not mind wearing a headcovering for prayer, will you?"

"Of course not," Dennison announced and promptly placed the *yarmulke* on his head.

Pierce held the small black piece for a moment and smiled. "My pleasure," he announced, putting it into place. All he could think of was that this might in some way bring about Darlene's approval. He certainly didn't believe it necessary for prayer, but he knew it was something she would expect.

They made their way up the stairs, slowly following Abraham's aged form. Pierce felt the *yarmulke* slip off his head just in time to replace it. Dennison was having no better luck. As they entered the dining area, Pierce saw Abraham touch his hand to his lips and then touch a small metal box at the inside of the door. He pondered this for a moment, wondering what the box represented, but then Darlene appeared, and he thought of nothing else for a very long time.

She was lovely, just as he'd remembered her. She wore a beautiful gown of amber satin and lace, and her hair had been left down to cascade in curls below her shoulders. Her response was friendly and open, but Pierce saw a light in her eyes when she met his gaze and it caused a surge of energy

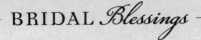

to flow through him.

"Good evening, my dear," Dennison said first. "Thank you for the invitation to share such an important celebration with you." The *yarmulke* slid off his head and onto the floor. Dennison laughed and bent over to pick it up, just as Pierce's did the same.

Everyone laughed, but it was Abraham who spoke. "For you, Darlene could fetch some hat pins?"

They all laughed again and Pierce and Dennison replaced the *yarmulkes.*

Then it was Pierce who spoke. He tried to steady his nerves and keep his voice even. "Darlene, it's wonderful to see you again. I see you've managed to avoid the freighters."

She blushed as he knew she would at the reminder of their last meeting. "Good evening, Mr. Blackwell," she said rather shyly.

"Nonsense, my name is Pierce. You must use it and give me the honor of addressing you by your given name."

Darlene looked hesitantly at her father and Dennison Blackwell before nodding. "Very well, Pierce."

She hurried away after that and Pierce wished that he could follow her. "Do you need help with anything?" he called after her.

"No. Everything is ready."

She was only a few feet away, but space seemed to represent an unbreakable wall to Pierce. Her rejection of his help left him with nothing to do but listen to the conversation of his father and Abraham, and to make an occasional comment when asked for one.

"Come," Abraham said, "we'll begin our *seder*."

Pierce took in every detail of the setting. A beautiful lacy cloth lay over the table and two lighted candles, in intricate silver holders, were placed atop this. There was also a strange tray of some sort with six circular indentions. Each indention held some food article, but none held the same appeal as the delicious aroma of whatever Darlene had in the oven. Pulling out a chair, Pierce saw that there was a cushion on it. Gazing around he noted a cushion at the back of every chair. Perhaps the Lewys feared that their guests would expect luxury.

Darlene took her seat opposite Pierce, looking up for a moment to meet his gaze. He smiled, hoping that it would both charm and relax her. She seemed tense in his presence and he wondered if perhaps she would have rather he not share her Passover *seder*.

Abraham began the opening prayer and from there the ceremony seemed to pass in a blur of fascination for Pierce. It was all so different from anything he'd ever known, yet there was also an air of familiarity. Had he not been taught from the Bible about Moses and the slavery of Israel? Yet for Darlene and Abraham, there seemed an appreciation for this remembrance that Pierce had no understanding of. He had known an easy life. He had known a life of privilege. Thinking this, Abraham's next words caught Pierce's attention and seared a place in his heart.

"We speak this evening of other tyrants and other tyrannies as well. We speak of the tyranny of poverty and the tyranny of privation, of the tyranny of wealth and the tyranny of war, of the tyranny of power and the tyranny of despair, of the tyranny of disease and the tyranny of time, of the tyranny of ignorance and the tyranny of color. To all these tyrannies do we address ourselves this evening. Passover brands them all as abominations in the sight of God."

Abominations in the sight of God? Pierce could only wonder at the meaning for surely God had no problem with wealth and prosperity. Unless, of course, it led to greed and cruelty. He thought of Amanda Ralston. The tyranny of ignorance and color gave him thoughts of Eugenia and her fierce dislike of the Jews in their city. All the things named as tyrannies were the very essences of those things that separated one people from another.

The ceremony continued and Pierce was surprised when Darlene got up and retrieved a pitcher of water, a bowl, and a towel. Abraham noted his confusion and smiled.

"It is recorded in the *Talmud*, the hands should be washed before dipping food."

Pierce watched as Darlene placed the bowl at her father's side. He held his hands over the bowl and she poured a small amount of water from the pitcher. Abraham rubbed his hands together and accepted a towel from Darlene on which to dry them. This process was repeated for Dennison, and finally for Pierce. He sensed her anxiety and nervousness. Without looking up, he held his hands as he'd seen the others do and when she handed him the towel, their fingers touched for just a moment. He heard her draw in her breath quickly and kept his face lowered. Such a sobering ceremony deserved his respect, but he really felt like smiling because he was growing ever more certain that Darlene felt something powerful for him.

After washing her own hands, Darlene retook her place and the *seder* continued. There was a passing of raw parsley, which was used to dip in salt water, and Abraham directed them all in the recitation of the blessing, first in Hebrew and then in English.

"Praised be Thou, O Lord our God, King of the universe, Who created the fruit of the earth."

There were more prayers and the breaking of the unleavened bread, or *matza* as Abraham called it, and Pierce was completely mesmerized by the process of this ceremony. There were symbolic reasons for everything and he suddenly found that he wanted to understand it all at once.

Without warning, Darlene spoke in a soft, but clear voice that reminded Pierce of a little girl. "Why is this night different from all other nights?"

He wondered if this was part of the ceremony or just a reflective thought because of his presence at her *seder*. He didn't have long to wait before realizing that this was yet another portion of recitations. Abraham spoke out in his deep, authoritative voice.

"In what way do you find this night different?"

"In four ways," Darlene answered, "do I find it different."

"What is the first difference?"

Pierce paid close attention as Darlene replied. "It differs in that on all other nights we eat bread or *matza*, while on this night we eat only *matza*."

"And what is the second difference?

"It differs in that on all other nights we eat vegetables and herbs of all kinds, while on this night we must eat bitter herbs."

Abraham nodded. "And what is the third difference between this night and all other nights?"

"It differs in that on all other nights we do not dip vegetables even once, while on this night we dip them twice."

"And what is the fourth difference?"

"It differs in that on all other nights we eat in an upright or a reclining position, while on this night we recline at the table."

Pierce began to realize the purpose for the cushion at his back. There was so much that he was unaware of and he felt like an outsider intruding on something very precious.

"The four differences," Abraham concluded, "that you have called to our attention are important and significant. They are reminders that freedom and liberty are cherished values not to be taken for granted."

The words touched Pierce as Abraham continued to explain. "To appreciate what it means to be free, we must be reminded of how it feels to be enslaved."

Pierce felt a chill run up his spine. He took his freedom for granted. He took his wealth and the privileges he enjoyed for granted. He didn't know what it was to be enslaved, with the possible exception of the way Darlene had enslaved his heart.

Abraham continued with a recitation of the enslavement of the Israelites under the Egyptian taskmasters. He stressed the importance of retelling the story of deliverance lest any man forget God's blessings and the importance of freedom. There were other stories and a remembrance of the ten plagues God had brought upon Egypt when Pharaoh would not let the children of Israel go.

Then came another phase of the *seder* and Abraham raised a bone that lay upon the *seder* tray. This was symbolic of the *paschal* lamb that was eaten on Passover eve when the Temple stood in Jerusalem. "What does this bone remind us, and what does it teach us?" Abraham questioned and then continued. "It reminds us of the tenth plague in Egypt, when all the firstborn of the Egyptians were struck down. It reminds us of the salvation of the Israelites whose homes were spared. For *Pesach* means more than *paschal* lamb; it has another meaning. It means, 'He skipped over.' The Lord skipped over the houses of those whose doorposts bore the blood of the lamb." Abraham lowered the bone and said very seriously, "The willingness to sacrifice is the prelude to freedom."

Pierce felt a trembling in his body and clearly knew the hand of God was upon him. Perhaps he was in more bondage than he knew. He wondered if he had a heart for sacrifice and whether he could give up all that he loved, for the sake of freedom in God.

Abraham then raised the *matza*. "This *matza* that we eat reminds us of the haste with which the Israelites fled from Egypt. The dough that they were baking on the hot rocks of the Egyptian fields was removed before it could leaven, and so it remained flat."

He lowered this and picked up the *maror*, bitter herbs represented here by horseradish. "The bitter herbs symbolize the bitter lot of the Israelites who were enslaved in Egypt. *Pesach, matza,* and *maror* are the symbolic expressions that represent freedom in all ages. Today we might say they symbolize sacrifice, preparedness, and hope. These are necessary elements in the fight for freedom."

Pierce's thoughts were turned inward as the *seder* concluded. He barely heard the words while going through the motions of the ceremony. His heart and conscience were pricked with the meanings and representation of the things he did. When he'd agreed to come to the *seder*, Pierce had thought nothing of how it might affect him. He'd only thought of Darlene and how she might affect him. But now, in the humble quiet of their home, Pierce's mind ran in a multitude of directions. To have freedom from the greed and prejudice of New York society, he would have to sacrifice his comfort. To go forward in a positive and clearly mapped-out manner would require preparation. And, to serve God more directly and in a completely life-changing way would require hope. Hope in that which he could not see, but was certain existed.

The *seder* meal was completed and the symbols cleared away by Abraham, while Darlene brought out a most extensive feast. Pierce watched her intently, wondering quietly to himself whether she'd ever consider leaving New York as his wife.

As they sat around the table enjoying a huge beef roast, Pierce was surprised when Abraham spoke. "Your celebration of Easter seems to share something with our Passover."

"It shares a great deal," Dennison replied. "We remember that Jesus ate the Passover *seder* with His disciples before going to His death on the cross. This time of year reminds us, too, of freedom. We Christians have freedom from eternal death because of Christ's sacrifice on the cross. He prepared a way for us to be reconciled with God, and because of this we have hope that He will come again for us."

Darlene's expression seemed to change from indifference to revelation. She said nothing, but Pierce saw the change and wondered if God had somehow stirred her heart to understanding.

"And," Pierce added quickly, hoping that his words would reach her, "the blood that Christ shed for us is like that of the lambs' blood sprinkled over the doorposts of the Israelites, although more precious because it was the sacrifice of God's son rather than that of a simple beast. But both represent the shedding of blood in exchange for death passing us by. Christ died that we might not have to."

Darlene looked at him for a moment, and in those few precious seconds, Pierce believed that God had finally made Himself known to her. Perhaps there would be no instantaneous revelation. Perhaps it would be years before she would understand what had happened. However long it took, Pierce knew that seeds had been planted and he was confident that God could harvest Darlene's heart for His own.

Chapter 10

But God commendeth his love toward us, in that,
while we were yet sinners, Christ died for us.
ROMANS 5:8

After sharing Passover with the Blackwells, Darlene knew that she'd never be the same. It was impossible to stop thinking about the words Dennison and Pierce had shared. Also, it was impossible to not remember the joy in Father's face and the certainty in which he shared his heart on the matters of Christianity and Judaism. And, alas, it was also impossible to forget Pierce Blackwell. His gentle smiles pervaded her thoughts. His searching eyes and questioning expressions made her realize that he wanted to know more about her. But why? Why was Pierce paying her so much attention? In the months that had passed since that *seder* dinner, he had come by for visits, brought candy and trinkets (always for both herself and her father), and he seemed completely determined to better know her mind on certain issues.

What did she think of westward expansion? What did she know about the new railroads? What had she read about the western territories and states? Did she like to travel? Would she ever consider leaving New York City?

Oy vey! But the man was annoying!

That night had not only given her reason to consider her heart and soul, but had also changed forever her relationship with her father. Abraham now openly attended church with the Blackwells and more frequently was absent from the synagogue. This made Darlene depressed and discouraged, but even more so, she found herself consumed by a deep, unfillable void. Why did Tateh have to embrace Christianity and turn away from the Hebrew faith? He hadn't announced the rejection of Judaism, so Darlene tried to keep hoping that her father was merely studying the *goy's* faith with a scholarly interest. But deep down inside, she knew it wasn't true.

In his bedroom, Darlene could hear her father at prayer. He would wear his *tallis,* the fringed prayer shawl of black and white. He would also have his *tefilin,* leather boxes, strapped to his forehead and left arm. Inside these boxes were the Scriptures of Exodus thirteen, verses one through ten, dealing

with the remembrance of God bringing the Hebrew children out of bondage and commanding them to keep God's laws. On his head would be his
yarmulke and from his mouth would come the familiar prayers she'd heard all
of her life. These were the markings of his Jewish faith. Why then would he
lay them aside in a few moments, eat breakfast with her, and go to the *goy's*
church with the Blackwells?

Tears came to her eyes and she wiped at them angrily with the back of
her sleeve. It wasn't right that her father should leave her so confused and
alone. Why must she struggle through this thing? Why should there be such
despair in her heart?

She brought bread and porridge to the table and set it down beside a
huge bowl of fruit. She loved the summer months when fruits and vegetables
could be had fresh. Fetching a pitcher of cream, Darlene tried to rally her
heart to gladness. They had plenty and were well and safe. Her father's health
had even revived a bit with the warmth of summer. Surely God was good
and His protection was upon them, in spite of her father's search to better
understand Christianity.

"Good morning, *Neshomeleh*," Abraham said, coming into the kitchen.
He reached a hand to his lips and touched the *mezuzah* as he always had.

Darlene smiled and came to greet her father with a hug. "Good morning, Tateh. Did you sleep well?"

"Yes, very well." His smile warmed her heart, just as his kiss upon her
forehead put her at ease. "And you?"

"It is well with me, also."

They ate in companionable silence, but when Abraham had finished, he
eyed Darlene quite seriously and said, "I have a favor to ask of you."

Darlene put down the dish she was clearing and asked, "What is it?"

"Sit."

She did as she was asked, but in her mind whirled a thousand possibilities. What was it that he would ask of her that required she sit down? "What
do you want of me, Tateh?"

"Come with me today. Come to the Blackwell's church and be at my
side. It is important to me and I only ask because it would mean a great deal."

"But why now? Why is it suddenly so important to you?" Darlene felt
fear constrict her chest. It was difficult to breathe.

Abraham smiled lovingly and put his hand upon her arm. "Because today, I will accept Jesus into my heart."

"What!" She jumped up from the table. "You can't be serious!"

"Darlene, I have never been more serious. These long months I have
searched for answers to questions that have eluded me all of my life. The

knowledge given to me through the *Tanakh* and the New Testament has answered those questions."

"New Testament?"

Abraham smiled tolerantly. "It's the story of Jesus and His followers. It tells how believers in Christ should act and live. It filled my longing and took away my emptiness."

Darlene thought of her own longing and the emptiness that haunted her. She swallowed hard and sat back down in a rather defeated manner. "Then you are no longer of the faith. What of your friends and the shop? You will become as dead to them."

"Most likely," Abraham agreed. "But then, they haven't exactly been very friendly these last months anyway. I make a good living from people who are not Jewish, so the shop should not suffer overmuch."

"But Hayyim will leave us. How will you manage to work without help?"

"I'll advertise for a Christian. There must be plenty of Christian young men who would take up the job of tailoring."

Finally Darlene had to ask the one remaining question. "What of me? What of us? The cantor says I should leave you and live with Esther. He says you are a traitor and that should you reject your faith, I must leave or face the possibility of becoming a traitor as well."

Abraham shook his head. "There is nothing between us that must cause us to part. Come with me today and I believe you will come to understand my choice. In time, you may well come to make that choice for yourself and when you do, I want to be at your side."

Darlene stared at the table rather than meet her father's joyous expression. How could she be so sad when he was obviously so happy? How could she, who had listened to the words and advice of her father for all of her life, now reject his words because they seemed rash and contradictory to everything he had taught her?

"Please come with me today."

His pleading was more than she could bear. In that moment Darlene knew that should she be forever branded a traitor, she would still go with her father wherever he asked her to go. "I'll come with you," she whispered in a voice that barely contained her grief.

Abraham leaned over and kissed her on the head. "Thank you, my little soul. You are all that is left to me on this earth."

∽

Darlene was still thinking about his words when the Blackwells' carriage arrived and Dennison Blackwell stepped down to greet them. Darlene had put on her best gown, a pale-blue muslin with huge gigot sleeves and lace trimming around the neck. It was a simple dress, yet it was her finest. In her mind she had imagined Pierce taking her by the arm to lead her into his church, and it was then that she wanted to look her very best.

"Good morning, Abraham, Darlene," Dennison said in greeting. "Have you ever known a more perfect day?"

"It is very lovely," Abraham said, then took hold of Darlene's arm. "My daughter will come with us today. Is there room in your carriage?" He looked up at the open landau where Eugenia and Constance Blackwell sat on one side, while Pierce occupied the other.

Dennison was at first quite surprised, but quickly enough a broad smile crossed his face. "There is plenty of room and you are very welcome to come with us, my dear."

Darlene felt her heart give a lurch when Pierce stood up and held out a hand to assist her up. "We're very glad to have you join us," he announced, while Eugenia gave her a harsh look of disdain. "You may sit here with Constance and my Aunt Eugenia."

Darlene put her gloved hand in his and allowed him to help her into the carriage. Eugenia looked away, while Constance smiled most congenially and made room for Darlene to sit in the middle. Abraham took his place between Pierce and Dennison and without further fanfare, they were on their way.

Immediately, Darlene was painfully aware of the contrast to her best gown and the Blackwell women's Sunday best. Constance wore a beautiful gown of pink watered silk. The trimmings alone were worth more than Darlene's entire dress. Tiny seed pearls decorated the neckline and heavy flounces of lace trimmed the sleeves and skirt. Her hair had been delicately arranged in a pile of curls and atop this was a smart-looking little hat complete with feathers and ribbons. A dainty pink parasol was over one shoulder to shade her from the sun and around her throat lay a strand of pearls, all perfectly white and equally sized.

Eugenia, of course, was attired even more regally in mauve-colored satin. Darlene tried not to feel out of place, but it was obvious to anyone who looked at her that she felt completely beneath the standing of her companions.

Dennison introduced her to his sister and daughter, but only Constance had anything to say. "It's so nice to have you with us."

"Indeed it is," Pierce said with great enthusiasm.

⟨⟩

The church service was unlike anything Darlene had ever known. The women and men sat together for one thing, and somehow Pierce had managed to have her seated between himself and Constance. She was very aware of his presence. The smell of his cologne wafted through her head like a delicate reminder of her dreams. She couldn't suppress the fantasies that came to her mind and while they joined in to sing and share a hymnal, Darlene wondered what it might be like to marry Pierce and do this every Sunday.

What am I thinking? She admonished herself for such thoughts, while in the next moment her heart betrayed her again. To be the wife of Pierce Blackwell would mean every manner of comfort and luxury. It would mean having gowns of silk and satin. It would mean never having to worry about whether enough suits were made to pay the rent and grocer. She stole a side glance at Pierce. He caught her eye and winked, continuing the hymn in his deep baritone voice. Marriage to such a man would also mean love. Of this she had no doubt. Pierce Blackwell would make a most attentive husband.

The minister began his sermon by praying a blessing upon the congregation. Darlene watched for a moment, then bowed her head and listened to his words.

"Heavenly Father, we ask your blessing upon this congregation. We seek Your will. We seek to know You better. We ask that You would open our hearts to the truth, that we might serve You more completely. Amen."

Well, Darlene thought, *that wasn't so bad.* She relaxed a bit. Maybe this wasn't going to be such an ordeal, after all.

The minister, a short, older man, seemed not that different from the cantor. He wore a simple black suit and while he had no beard, his mutton-chop sideburns were full and gave the appearance of at least a partial beard.

"It is good to come into the house of the Lord," he began. His words were of love and of a deep joy he found in God. Darlene couldn't help but be drawn to his happiness.

"God's love is evident to us in many ways," the minister continued. "God watches us with the guarded jealousy of a Father to His child. You fathers in the congregation would not allow a thief to sneak into your homes and steal your children from under your watchful eye, and neither does God allow Satan to sneak in and steal their hearts and souls.

"Just as you provide for your children, so God provides for us, His children. If your child was lost, you would seek him. If he was cold, you would warm him. If your son or daughter was hungry, you would give your last crumb of bread to feed them. So it is with God. He longs to give us good things and to care for us in His abundance." Darlene was mesmerized.

"God wills that none should be lost. He gave us His Son Jesus Christ as a gift of love. Seeing that we were hopelessly lost, separated by a huge cavern of sin and despair, God sent his Son Jesus, to reconcile us to the Father. Is there anyone here who would not try to rescue your child from a burning house? Would any of you stand idly by and watch your children drown? Of course not. And neither would God stand by and watch us sink into the hopeless mire of sin and death, without offering us rescue.

"But what if you reached out a rope to your drowning child and they refused to take it? What if you tore open a passage in the burning house, but your child refused to come forward? So it is with God, who extends to us salvation through Jesus Christ, only to have us refuse to accept His gift." Darlene felt as though the minister was speaking to her alone. She'd never heard such words before. No wonder her father found himself confused. No wonder he questioned his faith.

"Will you be such a child?" the minister asked. "When God has offered you a perfectly good way back to Him, will you reject it? Will you throw off the lifeline God has given you in His Son? Will you die without knowing Christ as your Savior?"

Darlene could hardly bear the now-serious expression on the minister's face. He seemed to look right at her and, inside her gloves, Darlene could feel perspiration form on her hands. She wanted to get up from her seat and flee from the building, but she couldn't move. Should the building have caught fire and burned down around her, Darlene knew that it would have been impossible to leave.

The minister spoke a short time more, then directed those who would receive Christ to step forward and publicly declare their repentance. Her mouth dropped when Abraham stood. She had known he would do this, but somehow watching it all happen, she didn't know what to think. A kind of despair and trepidation washed over her. It was as if in that moment she knew a wall had been put in place to forever separate her from her beloved Tateh. A wall that she could only remove if she accepted Christ for herself.

As if sensing her fears, Pierce put her hand over hers and gave it a squeeze. This gesture touched Darlene in a way she couldn't explain. It was as if he knew her heart, and that somehow made it better. *Does he understand my loss?* she wondered.

Hearing a confession of faith from the man who had nurtured her so protectively, Darlene felt all at once as though he'd become a stranger to her. And yet, was it this that disturbed her most? Or was it the words of the minister? Words that made more sense than she would have liked to admit?

∽

The ride back home was spent in animated conversation between Dennison and Abraham, and Pierce and Constance. Eugenia remained stubbornly silent, while Darlene felt her mind travel in a million directions. All of which brought her continuously back to the dazzling smile and penetrating brown eyes of Pierce Blackwell.

"I'm glad you took time from the shop to accompany us today," Pierce told her.

"Do you work in your father's shop?" Constance asked in complete surprise.

Darlene nodded. "Yes. I do sewing for him."

"How marvelous. Tell me all about it," Constance insisted.

Eugenia harrumphed in obvious disgust and with that simple gesture, Darlene saw all her girlish dreams of marriage to Pierce fade. Of course, there had never been any real possibility of a lowly Jewess marrying a rich Christian socialite, but she had felt at least comforted by the possibility.

"My father is a tailor, as you know. We make suits and shirts, just about anything a man could possibly need for dressing."

"And they do it very well," Pierce added. "I have never owned such fine clothes."

"And you work with your father? Did you help with my brother's suit?" Constance asked, completely fascinated by this.

Darlene eyed the rich-green frock coat and nodded. Pierce's gaze met hers and his lips curled automatically into a smile. "I didn't know that," he said, running his hand down the sleeve of his coat. "It only makes it all the more special."

Darlene felt her face grow hot. It made it special to her as well. She could remember running her hand down the fabric and wondering what Pierce would look like when it was completed. She had sewed the buttons onto the front with a strange sort of reverence, imagining as she worked how Pierce's fingers might touch them later.

"How wonderful to do something so unique!" Constance declared.

"It is hardly unique to do a servant's labor," Eugenia finally said. With these words came a silence in the carriage and a sinking in Darlene's heart.

Dennison frowned and Eugenia, seeming to sense that her opinion would meet with his disapproval, fell silent again. The damage was done, however. Darlene grew sullen and quiet, while Pierce looked away as if disgusted by the reminder of her station in life. There would never be a bridge between their worlds and the sooner Darlene accepted that, the happier she would be. But even forcing thoughts of Pierce from her mind did nothing to dispel the stirring memory of the minister's words that morning. Nor would it displace the image of her father going forward into acceptance of Jesus as Messiah. There was no going back now. There would be no chance of changing her father's mind about Christianity. But what worried Darlene more was that she wasn't sure she still wanted to change his mind.

Chapter 11

But the wisdom that is from above is first pure, then peaceable,
gentle, and easy to be intreated, full of mercy and good fruits,
without partiality, and without hypocrisy.
JAMES 3:17

Pierce listened with bored indifference to Amanda Ralston's description of the new art museum her father had arranged to be built. The truth of the matter was, he was bored with the entire party. Amanda's party. Amanda and all her shallow, haughty friends.

The only reason he'd even come was that Eugenia had insisted on the matter until there was simply no peace in the house and even his father had asked him to do it as a favor to him. So it was because of this, Pierce found himself the center of Amanda's possessive attention.

"Darling, you haven't had any champagne," Amanda said with a coy batting of her eyes.

"I don't drink champagne and you know that full well." He tried not to frown at her. No sense having anyone believe them to be fighting.

Amanda pouted. "But then how shall we toast our evening?"

Pierce looked at her and shrugged. "I have nothing to toast, my dear. Why don't you go find someone who does?"

Amanda refused to be dealt with so harshly. "I had this gown made especially with you in mind. Don't you think it's lovely?" She held up her glass and whirled in a circle. The heavy gold brocade rippled in movement.

"It looks very warm," he said noncommittally. "I'm certain it will ward off the autumn chill."

Amanda was clearly losing patience with him. "Pierce, this gown cost over sixty dollars. The least you could do is lie about it, even if you don't like it."

"I see no reason to lie about it, and the gown is quite perfect for you. Sixty dollars seems a bit much. I know a great tailor, if your seamstress insists on robbing you."

"Oh, bother with you," she said, stomping her foot. "You are simply no fun at all."

"I didn't come here to have fun. I came because you and my aunt decided it should be so. There would have been no rest in my house if I'd refused."

"But Pierce," she said in a low seductive whisper, "didn't you want to see me? Don't you enjoy keeping company with me?"

Pierce looked at her in hard indifference. "I'd rather be mucking out stables."

"That's hideous!" She raised her arm as if to slap him, then thought better of it and stormed off. Pierce saw her exchange her half-empty glass for a full one before moving out of the room.

The rest of the evening passed in bits of conversation with one group and then another. Pierce, finally relieved of Amanda's annoying presence, found a moment in which to discuss westward expansion with several other men.

"It seems to me that we must settle this nation of ours or lose it," a broad-shouldered man with red hair was saying. "There's plenty who would take it from us. I say we move off the Indians and pay people to settle out west. Give them the land for free, although not too much land. Just enough to spark an interest."

"How would you move them all there?" asked an elderly gentleman. "There's not a decent road in this country. Even the civilized towns suffer for want of better roadways."

"True enough," said Pierce. "Perhaps the government could develop it. There's surely enough money in the U.S. coffers to plow a few roads."

The redheaded man nodded. "Even so, it would take months, years, to make decent roads. We need people in the West now!"

His enthusiasm gave fuel to the spark already within Pierce's heart. "I've allowed myself some investments in Chicago. I've given strong thought to the possibilities of life there." This caused his companions to stare open-mouthed at him.

"You don't mean to include yourself in such a thing?" the older man questioned.

"Why certainly, I do." Pierce couldn't figure out why they should so adamantly declare the need for people in the West, yet find it unreasonable that he would consider such a thing.

"No, no. That would never do. You would have to deal with all manner of corruption and lowlife."

Pierce eyed the old man with a raised brow. "And I don't have to here? New York City is worse than ten western cities put together. Greed runs so rampant in this town that a man would sell his own soul if it promised a high enough return."

The redheaded man laughed at this. "Well, buying your soul out of hock seems a great deal easier than uprooting yourself and leaving the comforts of home behind. Monetary investments are one thing. Flesh and blood is quite another."

Pierce smiled. "I couldn't agree with you more. It is exactly for those reasons that I consider the possibilities of such a move."

It was then that Amanda chose to reappear. "What move are you talking about, darling?" She placed her hand possessively on Pierce's arm.

"It seems your friend would like to move out amongst the savages." The older man chuckled while the redheaded man continued. "I can just picture you at his side, Amanda dear. Dirt floors dusting the hems of your expensive gowns, six children grabbing at your skirts."

Amanda's laughter filled the air. "Oh, certainly Mr. Blackwell is making sport of the subject. He has too much here in the city to ever go too far. Isn't that true, darling?"

Pierce shook his head. "No, actually I'm quite seriously considering the move. Perhaps when spring comes and the weather allows for long-distance travel, I will resettle myself in Chicago."

"You can't be serious, Pierce." Her facade of genteel refinement vanished.

"I've only been telling you of my interest for months now."

Amanda waited until the other gentlemen had considerably moved away. She pulled Pierce along with her to a balcony off the main room and turned, prepared for a fight.

"Pierce, this is ridiculous. Your aunt assures me that it is your father's wish you marry and produce heirs. Now, while I have no desire to find myself in such a confining predicament, I would see fit to participate at least once in such a matter."

Pierce laughed. "Are you talking about giving life to a child, or suffering through a party for fewer than sixteen people?"

"This is a matter of grave importance; I won't stand your insults."

"Indeed it is a matter of grave importance." Pierce almost felt sorry for the young woman. She was clearly in a rage of her own creation. Her face was flushed and her eyes blazed with a fire all their own. She would have been pretty had she not been so conniving and self-centered. "Please hear me, Amanda. I have no desire to marry you. Not now. Not ever. I am not in love with you, which is the most important thing I believe a marriage should have. Without a mutual love and respect for each other, marriage would be nothing more than a sham of convenience. That kind of thing is not for me."

Amanda seemed to calm a bit. "Marriage is more than emotional entanglements, Pierce, and you know it as well as you know your bank account. To marry my fortune to yours would ensure our future. It would set forever our place in society. Imagine the possibilities, Pierce."

"I have, and they do not appeal to me."

"You aren't that stupid," she said, the caustic tone returning. "You are too smart to throw away your future. You've worked hard to set it into place."

"You are exactly right," Pierce replied.

She smiled with a seductiveness that ordinarily would have been charming. "I knew you'd see it my way."

"Oh, but I don't. I merely said you were right about my being too smart to throw away my future. I'm not about to sit around in houses that look fit only to be mausoleums, stuck in the middle of a city that's driven by greed and avarice and married to a woman who concerns herself only with parties and the value of her possessions." He turned to leave, but Amanda reached out to hold him.

"If you leave, I'll see you ruined!"

"Do what you will, Amanda, but do it without me."

He strode from the room without so much as a backward glance. He heard the sounds of the party behind him, the tinkling of glass, the faint strains of the stringed quartet, the laughter of shallow-minded associations. It was all a facade. There was absolutely nothing real or of value here for him.

He hailed a hack and gave the driver his address. Chicago loomed in his mind like an unattainable prize. Somehow, he would make his way west. Somehow, he would leave New York behind.

Darlene. The name came unbidden to his mind. Could he leave her as well? Could he walk away from a woman he was now certain he loved? He couldn't suggest marriage, not with their religious differences. He couldn't take her away from her father, and even if he suggested Abraham accompany them west, Pierce didn't know if the old man was well enough to do so.

Chicago would mean leaving Darlene. Chicago would mean throwing off every matter of security ever known to him and going into the unknown alone. Could he do it? Could he leave the comforts of life as he knew it, and forge into the wilds of Illinois?

The hack pulled up to the red brick house and stopped. After paying the driver, Pierce made his way inside and found the house quiet. Grateful for this blessing, he made his way to the library. Tossing his frock and waist coat aside, Pierce undid his cravat and eased into a plush leather chair. On the small table beside him, a copy of the newspaper caught his eye.

Picking it up, he scanned the pages for anything of interest. "Irish Riots on the Wabash and Erie Canal," titled one article. Another announced the cause of some shipping disaster. He looked for something related to Chicago or travel west and found only one tiny article related to the suggested building of a railroad from New York State to the rapidly growing towns of

Cincinnati and Chicago. It was such a small article and told with such a negative slant that Pierce was certain no one would paid it much mind.

He folded the paper, tossed it aside, and stretched out his long legs. *Dear God,* he began to pray, *what is it that I should do? I have no peace here. No happiness within my soul. I am as out of place as a fish taken from water. Society bids me be greedy when I would be generous, and tells me to have nothing to do with those who are beneath my status, when I would take all mankind to my heart.* He sighed. *Oh, God, please show me the way. Give me peace about the direction I should take. Give me a clear path to follow. Amen.*

"Whatever are you doing in here?" Eugenia questioned from the door. "I heard a carriage and couldn't imagine what you were doing home so early."

"I left because the party was not to my liking," he answered simply.

Eugenia frowned. "But what of Amanda? Surely she compensated you where the party was lacking."

"She was the one lacking the most," Pierce replied.

Eugenia looked behind her before entering the room and closing the door. "Pierce, you and I need to talk."

"We've talked aplenty as far as I'm concerned. Just leave it be." Exhaustion registered in his voice.

"I don't wish to cause you further grief, but you must understand," Eugenia began, "it is very important to your father that you settle down and marry. Amanda Ralston is everything you could ever hope to find in a wife. She'll be congenial. She'll run your home efficiently and she'll never interfere in your business. She's been groomed for just such a job since she was old enough to walk. Amanda knows her place and she'll benefit you in many ways."

"But I don't love her. I could never love her."

Eugenia grimaced. "Who could you love? That little Jew?"

Pierce narrowed his eyes. "Don't think to bring Darlene into this matter."

"Why shouldn't I? She clearly is a part of this matter. You fancy yourself in love with her, and I say forget it. She is not of your kind."

"And which kind would that be? The greedy kind? The selfish kind? Oh, wait, I know, maybe it's the kind who look down on others because they are different." Pierce got to his feet. "I'm glad she's not of those kind. But what you tend to forget because you're so mired in it yourself, is that I'm not of that kind either!"

"You are better than she is!" Eugenia said, blocking his escape by throwing herself between him and the door.

"No," he said, shaking his head. "I'm not. I'm not better than Darlene. I'm different in some ways, I'll give you that much. But I am not better. The Bible says that we should love one another, even as God loves us. Do you suppose God loves Darlene less because she's of Hebrew lineage? Jesus, Himself, is of such lineage! What if God loved me less because I'm not?"

"You cannot marry a Jew. Even by your own standards and beliefs you cannot do such a thing. You'd forever link yourself to a woman who would never believe as you do. Think of the irreparable harm you could do yourself."

Pierce picked up his coats and with little trouble, maneuvered Eugenia out of his way. "I'm finished discussing this. If you ever bring up the subject again, I will leave this house for good."

"I'm only trying to be wise about this, Pierce."

He realized that she truly believed this. Turning, he said, "Man's wisdom and God's are often two very different things. I've tried it man's way. Now I seek God's."

Chapter 12

The preparations of the heart in man,
and the answer of the tongue, is from the LORD.
PROVERBS 16:1

So who are the flowers from?" Abraham asked his daughter.

Darlene stood holding a newly arrived bouquet of roses and the blush on her cheeks felt as warm a red as the flowers. "They're from Pierce Blackwell. He's coming this afternoon to. . .well. . .see me."

Abraham smiled and nodded. "That's good. I think he likes you."

"For whatever good that could ever do him," Darlene muttered and took the flowers upstairs to put on the kitchen table. Then, without thinking consciously of what she was doing, she hurried into her bedroom and changed her clothes.

Wearing a simple gown of green cotton and ivory ruching, Darlene tried to steady her nerves as she sewed a silk lining into a frock coat. Pierce had sent her flowers before, but never roses and never such a large bouquet. She felt a surge of anxiety and drew a deep breath. *I mustn't let him see me so jittery,* she thought. *I don't want him to think I'm drawing unmerited conclusions in this matter.* But she was. She was already imagining all of the most wonderful things that Pierce could come and tell her. Furthermore, she imagined how she might respond to just such things.

Even though Darlene knew and anticipated Pierce's arrival, it was still a surprise when he bounded through the door. He was dressed in a stylish brown suit that her father had made. His waistcoat of amber and orange might have appeared too loud on another man, but it seemed just right on Pierce.

"Hello," he said with a dashing smile and deep bow. "You look very pretty today."

Darlene put aside her sewing. "Thank you." She didn't know what else to say, so she folded her hands and said nothing more.

"You received my note, I presume."

"Oh, yes." She nodded, then remembered the roses. "The flowers are simply beautiful. I've put them upstairs. I was afraid down here someone might knock them over." She was also afraid that if Esther saw them she'd immediately begin questioning Darlene for all the facts.

"I thought you might enjoy them. I was passing a shop and saw them in the window. With winter coming on, I thought they might perk up the place a bit."

"They brighten the kitchen considerably."

The silence seemed heavy between them and Pierce searched for another topic. "And your father, is he well?"

"Yes. Well, he has a cold, but I'm hoping it won't be anything serious."

"Good."

"What of your family?" Darlene asked, raising her eyes to look upward.

"They are well. Constance had a birthday last week. She's sixteen now and feels very grown up."

"I remember sixteen quite well," Darlene replied. "I didn't feel very grown up at all. Of course we'd not been long in this country. I was struggling to improve my English and to make a good home for Tateh."

"I wish I could have known you then," Pierce said in a soft, almost inaudible tone.

Just then Abraham returned from an errand. His arms were full of brown paper-wrapped packages, and Pierce and Darlene hurried forward to take the burden from him.

"Tateh, you shouldn't have carried all of this yourself. I could have gone back and brought it home."

"Nonsense." He waved away her concern. "I'm an old man, but I'm still good for some things, no? Ah, Pierce, good day to you. I heard you were coming this afternoon."

"Yes," Pierce replied, putting the packages where Darlene motioned. "I would like very much to take Darlene for a walk. Would that be acceptable to you?"

Abraham smiled and struggled out of his coat. "It would be very acceptable. She works too hard now that Hayyim is gone."

"And you haven't found another assistant to help with the work, I take it?"

"No, but God will provide. He always has." Abraham's words would normally have comforted Darlene, but since all of the changes in her father's life, she was never certain whether she should take hope in such things.

"Of course He will. If I learn of anyone who might be adequate help, I'll advise them to come to you." Pierce then turned to Darlene. "Would you mind walking with me? It's a bit chilly, but otherwise very nice."

"I'll get my shawl," she replied. Now curiosity was taking over her fears. She had never known Pierce not to discuss every single matter of interest in front of her father. What was it that he wanted to say to her in private? And if it wasn't a matter of discussing something with her, then why was he suggesting the walk? For a fleeting moment she hesitated. What if Esther saw her? *Oy!* What mutterings and innuendos she'd have to answer to then!

She pulled a cream-colored shawl around her shoulders. She'd only finished knitting it two days earlier, and this was her first real opportunity to show it off. Pulling a bonnet over her dark-brown hair, Darlene hurried to join Pierce. If Esther saw her, she'd just deal with it later.

"I'm ready," she announced. "Tateh, are you sure you can spare me?"

"Be gone with you already," Abraham said with a chuckle. "You can do Pierce more good than me."

And then they were outside and walking amicably down the street. When Pierce offered his arm, she hesitantly took it. Outside in the public eye it would mean dealing with more than just Esther. What would any of her friends say if they saw her walking with the *goy?* She squared her shoulders. It didn't matter. They'd all turned their backs on her father and she wasn't going to concern herself with what they thought. Oh, they were nice enough to her face and Esther still invited her over from time to time, but she knew they were all talking about her behind her back. And, she figured the only real reason Esther still called on her was for the simple purpose of gathering information.

"You don't seem to be listening to me."

Darlene looked up with an apologetic smile. "I do tend to get caught up in my thoughts."

"Yes, I know. That's why I suggested walking with you. I'll keep an eye for the freight wagons while you daydream. But it comes with a price."

"Oh?"

"Yes." He nodded and added, "You must tell me what those dreams are about."

She shook her head. "They weren't really daydreams. I was actually thinking of the old neighborhood and how much it has changed."

"Has the neighborhood changed, or have you changed?"

"Some of both," she admitted. They walked past a fishmonger's cart and the heady scent of fish and other seafood assailed her nose. "Some things never change," she said, wrinkling her nose.

Pierce laughed and pulled her a little closer. "But change can be good, don't you think?"

"Is that why you've come to talk to me today?" *There, she thought. I've just come right out with it and I don't have to wonder any more what he's up to.*

Pierce wasn't phased by her boldness. "Yes," he answered simply.

"So what change is it that you wish to discuss?"

"I'm leaving New York."

The words hit her like boulders. "Leaving? Where are you going?" She tried hard to sound distant and unconcerned.

"Chicago. It's a fairly new town in Illinois. It's quite far to the west and there's great opportunity to be found there."

"I see." She focused on the ground.

"Darlene, I wondered if you and your father might consider moving there also. I mean, I know what your father has experienced here in the neighborhood. He's told my father about some of the ugly letters. . ."

"What letters?" Darlene interrupted. "I've heard nothing of letters."

Pierce looked genuinely embarrassed. "I'm sorry. I presumed that you knew."

"Tell me everything," she demanded, and halted in the middle of the street as they crossed. "I have to know what has been said."

"Surely you know already," he pulled at her arm, but she held her place. "Come now, Darlene. I will share what I know, but not in the middle of the roadway."

She allowed him to take her along and waited silently, although impatiently, for him to tell her the truth.

"Apparently there have been some threats," Pierce said as delicately as he could. "I believe the letters are harmless enough, but they probably bear consideration. I know the shop has been vandalized twice."

"But that was probably only street urchins," she said, even now wondering about the truth of the matter.

"Your father thinks perhaps it is more than that." Pierce pulled her into an alleyway and stopped. "You must know that he doesn't wish to worry you, but, Darlene, I do fear for both of you. I know the ugliness of those who cannot accept what is different from what they know. Your Jewish friends can be just as prejudiced as my Christian friends."

She nodded, knowing that it was true. She could remember well the haughty stares of neighbors when her father stopped going to the synagogue. It was as if the Lewy family simply ceased to exist. Oh, they tried to be kind to her whenever she was alone, but ridicule followed even her. Especially when people asked her why she didn't leave Avrom and go to live with Esther.

"Chicago could be a new start for you both. I have property there and would be happy to set up a new shop for you. It could be as big as you like and I'm certain we could entice someone to sign on as an assistant to your father."

Darlene felt a single moment of excitement, then shook her head. "Tateh would never leave."

"Well, well. What have we here?"

"Looks like rich folk to me."

Pierce thrust Darlene behind him as he turned to face a group of filthy street rowdies. "What do you want?"

"Money, same as you uppity dandies," one of the taller boys said, coming a step closer.

"And jewels," another boy said. "Give us your lady's jewels."

There were five of them, with another two watching the street at the end of the alley. One of the boys produced a club and began whacking it in his hands. "Let's have it," he said in a low, menacing tone.

Pierce moved a step back, pinning Darlene in place against the brick wall behind her. "I think we can work this out with no need of violence. Let the lady go and you may have my wallet."

"We'll have your wallet and the lady if we want," the boy replied.

Darlene peered around Pierce's shoulder. They couldn't be much more than teenagers, certainly not men. She was about to say something, but just then one of the five pointed at her.

"Wait a minute, Willy. That's the lady that helps us from the tailor shop. We can't rob her."

Pierce relaxed enough for Darlene to slip out from behind him. "I know your little brother. You must be Sam."

The boy nodded, looking rather sheepish. "Come on, guys. These are good folk."

The gang backed off and ran down the alley, signaling to their conspirators as they passed by. Pierce started to go after them, but Darlene reached out and took hold of him.

"Please let them go. They're only trying to survive. They wouldn't have hurt us."

"It didn't look that way to me," Pierce said angrily. "Scum and lowlife! That's all they're good for. The filth and despair of this neighborhood are all they know. Probably all they care to know. The lower classes always breed this kind of criminal element. Something should be done to clean up this neighborhood and rid it of the vermin."

"But Pierce," she said in a calm, soothing tone, "I am this neighborhood. My friends and family all live here. If you condemn them all because of the actions of a few, then you must surely condemn me as well."

This sobered him and he pulled her quickly back onto the main street before something else could happen. "I didn't mean it that way and you know it. I have only the highest admiration for you."

"But there are many in your circle of friends who believe we are nothing

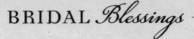
but Jewish scum. The Christ-killers. That's what they call us."

"But they can't blame you or your people for what a few. . ." he fell silent.

Darlene smiled, knowing that his words were about to match hers. "People can be cruel without even knowing it. We came to this country for many reasons. One of the most inspiring was the growing hatred of Jews in my native home of Germany. That hatred started innocently enough with whispered insults and indifference. Gradually the name calling and assaults on our homes resulted in our being unable to live in certain areas and work at certain jobs. Can you imagine allowing such hatred to dictate the laws of the land?"

"How can you not hate them in return?" Pierce asked.

"I don't know. I suppose it is like Tateh says, 'To hate another requires that you keep the ugliness of their deed written on your heart so that you might hold it up to remember them by.'"

"Your father is very wise. Perhaps that is why his heart was so open to the Word of God regarding Jesus."

Darlene nodded. "It may well be." She felt the familiar stirrings and knew that, more than anything else, she would like for Pierce to better explain Jesus to her. "I wonder if you would tell me a bit about your Jesus."

If Pierce was surprised by her words, he didn't say so. "Jesus came as a baby to this world. You know of the Christmas celebration?" Darlene nodded. "We celebrate His birth and give gifts to each other in honor of the day. In truth, Jesus came to a lowly Jewish couple, a carpenter and his wife. Joseph and Mary. He was a gift from God to the world. He came among men, because God wanted to draw all men to Him. He wanted to give man a path to forgiveness and eternal life. Jesus said in John fourteen, 'I am the way, the truth, and the life: no man cometh unto the Father, but by me.' So you see, we believe that by accepting Jesus as Messiah and repenting of our sins, we accept the way to God and eternal life."

They were back to the shop by now, but Darlene wished they could walk on forever. She found her heart clinging to every single word Pierce said. Could it be true? Could Jesus really be the Messiah her people looked for? Had they simply missed the signs or had they willingly ignored them?

"And you believe all of this, without any doubt at all?" she asked softly, looking up to find Pierce's tender expression.

"Without any doubts or fears," he whispered, taking her small hands in his own.

"But what makes you so certain?" She felt a tingle of excitement shoot up her arm and goosebumps form on her skin.

"He makes me certain," Pierce replied. "He makes me certain deep within my soul."

Chapter 13

And she shall bring forth a son, and thou shalt call his name JESUS:
for he shall save his people from their sins.
Matthew 1:21

They stood by the shop door for what seemed a long time before Darlene finally turned the handle and went inside. Pierce followed her, but paused just inside the door.

"Think about what I said," he told her.

Darlene couldn't help but think of all the things he'd said. Things about leaving New York, wanting her and her father to go to Chicago, and that Jesus loved her. "I will," she promised. And then without warning, he gave her one more thing to think about.

Taking her face in his hands, he placed a very light kiss upon her lips. "I love you," he whispered. Darlene opened her eyes in a flash of confusion and wonder. She stared up at him, not really believing she'd heard the words accurately.

As if reading her mind, he repeated them. "I love you. I think I always have."

Before she could say a single word, he turned and left the shop, gently closing the door between them. To Darlene it was a moment she would always remember. Pierce Blackwell loved her and had kissed her as a token of his affections. Touching her hand to her lips, she could scarcely breathe. *He loves me?* It wasn't mere infatuation on her part? She thought of the hundreds of daydreams she'd had about him. Dreams of marriage and love, romance, and a future as Pierce Blackwell's wife.

"Darlene, is that you?" her father called from upstairs.

"Yes, Tateh." She could barely say the words. Her voice seemed incapable of working properly and her legs felt like leaden weights.

"Are you all right? Is Pierce still with you?"

"No. I mean, yes I'm all right, but Pierce has gone home." At least, she presumed he'd gone home.

She forced her legs to work and pulled the bonnet from her head as she made her way upstairs. She thought about Pierce and his words about Jesus. *Tateh believes in Jesus,* she thought. *Pierce believes in Jesus. Why should I not believe in Him just because all of my life I've been taught one way?*

At the top of the stairs she paused. The only person in the entire world who could help her now was her father. "Tateh," she called, coming into the kitchen, where he sat eating a bowl of soup. "I need to talk to you."

Abraham put down his spoon and motioned her to take a chair. "Is something wrong? You look as though you bear the weight of the world."

Darlene put aside her bonnet and shawl and sat down. "Tateh, there are things I want to know about."

"What things?"

She took a deep breath. "Pierce told me that Jesus came to make people a way back to God. He said Jesus said that He was the way and that no one could get to God except by going through Jesus."

"That is true."

"But our people do not believe in Jesus as Messiah. They don't believe that they need someone to make a way for them to God." She paused, reflecting on a lifetime of training. "They believe each man is responsible for his own sin, so therefore how could Jesus take on the responsibility for all mankind and settle the matter for even those people yet to come?"

Abraham smiled. "Because God loves us, He showed mercy. He gave Jesus as a means to demonstrate his love. Not only for the people of His own time, but for the future generations. He was born purposefully to save His people, and Darlene, we are His people, even before the Gentiles."

"But our people rejected him as Messiah. They saw Him die and presumed that He couldn't possibly be what they expected."

"Not only that, but Jesus made a great many people, especially those who were high Jewish authorities, very uncomfortable. His way would bring change and people often resent change."

Darlene thought instantly of Pierce and his words about change being good. "But if Jesus was the Messiah we looked for, why have our people suffered so? Are we being punished for rejecting Him? Is God reckoning with us for something we didn't understand?"

"Who can know God's mind?" Abraham said with a shrug. "I suppose I look at the world and our place within the bounds of mankind and I say, 'There are many problems here.' Not only the Jews suffer. Think about history. Even the Christian church has had its bloody times. The world has seen plagues and sufferings throughout. Even here in America the plight of the slave is evidence of injustice. They were taken from their homes and forced away from families and loved ones in order to work for people they didn't know. Many people are hurting and suffering. I don't think God has forgotten us. Remember the sufferings of Job?"

"Yes, but how can God continue to let such things go on? Can't He see what is happening?"

Abraham shrugged. "I think He keeps better watch than you imagine. It's a matter of trusting, Darlene. We have to have faith just as the children of Israel had faith that God would lead them through the desert."

"Yes, but God allowed them to wander for forty years," she added.

"But was that because of God's indifference or their sin?"

Darlene nodded. "I guess I see what you're saying. We often suffer our lots in life because of our own disobedience. By our own hand we create the miseries of the world, is that right?"

"I believe so," Abraham replied.

"Then the Jewish rejection of Jesus could well have something to do with our people's miseries. Not because God is angry that we rejected the Messiah, but because we continue in blindness to seek another way."

"Perhaps."

Darlene looked at her father and in her heart she felt the birth of something very precious. It was a trust in God that she'd never before known. "Tateh, is Jesus the Messiah?"

Abraham smiled. "He is."

"And you are certain? There is no room for doubt in your heart?"

"None."

"That's what Pierce said."

"And what did you think of that?"

Darlene sat back and breathed a deep breath. What did she think of it? Wasn't that part of the reason she was seeking out her father's advice? "He seemed very confident. I suppose I envy that confidence. When I am with my friends, I feel there is an emptiness that no one can explain. When I was little, I thought like you, that it had to do with Mother's death. When I got older, my women friends told me that I was simply yearning for a husband and family. But Tateh, I don't believe that's what I'm looking for.

"There are many women in our community who are married with many children of their own, and yet, I know there is a void within them as well. I've talked to Rachel and Dvorah and even Esther and all of them have known this emptiness. Esther says she fills it with work and other things."

"Mostly gossip and sticking her nose where it doesn't belong, no?" Abraham said with a smile.

"It's true Esther is an old busybody, but perhaps she is one because she is empty and lonely inside. Who knows?" Darlene replied with a shrug.

"God knows and He sees all."

"I do believe that." She thought of Pierce's certainty and of her father's unwavering faith. "And you believe that the Messiah has already come and that He is Jesus. You believe that the Christians are right and that we Jews are wrong."

"I believe that Jesus came to save all people. I believe the faith of my fathers is valid and important, but falls short of a complete understanding of God's love and mercy. You must understand, Darlene, I do not throw away my Jewish heritage to take up one of Christianity. I am a Jew, but I also believe in Jesus."

Darlene shook her head. "I don't see how this can be so. I've been taught since I can first remember that you cannot be both Jewish and Christian. I've been taught that Jesus is not the Messiah we seek, for if Jesus was Messiah why did He not set up his Messianic Kingdom and restore Jerusalem? I so want to believe what you say is true, but a lifetime of beliefs stand between me and Jesus."

Abraham took hold of her hand and patted it lightly. "God will make a way through the desert. Just as He made a way for the Israelites so long ago. You mustn't be afraid to let God show you the way, however. Pray and trust Him, and let Him show you the truth."

"But how will I know that it is the truth, Tateh?" She searched his face, knowing that her expression must surely register the pleading of her soul.

"You will know," he said smiling. "You will know because God will give you peace of heart and mind."

⊚

In the warmth of his bed, Pierce awoke in the middle of the night with only one thought He had to pray for Darlene! He felt the call so urgently that it wouldn't let him be

"Dear God, what has happened? What is it that I should pray about?" He struggled with the covers of his bed and went to the fireplace to rekindle the flames.

The fire caught and grew, bringing with it a warm-orange glow to the room. Sitting cross-legged in front of the hearth, Pierce reached up to the nightstand and took down his Bible. He read for several minutes, but again the urgency to pray was upon him. He buried his face in his hands, struggling against the image of Darlene's innocent expression after his kiss.

"Father," he began in earnest. "I love Darlene, but I know Your Word tells me not to be unequally yoked with unbelievers. I can't help loving her, though. She is a special part of my life and I've already told You that I will walk away and go to Chicago without her, if that's what You want me to do."

Utter misery took hold of him and it felt as though a part of his heart was being ripped in two. When had she become so important to him? When had he lost his heart so completely to her? There had to be a way to bridge the distance. There had to be an answer he was not seeing. *I love her, and I want her to be my wife!* But even as he acknowledged this truth, God's Spirit overshadowed it with the Word. What fellowship could light have with darkness?

"But God, she's not evil. She's faithful to serve You in her own way."

The words seemed to echo in his mind. "Her own way." Not God's way.

This did nothing to lay aside the need to pray and so Pierce tried to refocus his thoughts and pray just for the woman he loved. "Darlene needs to know You, Father. She needs to know that You love her and she needs to accept Jesus into her heart. Please dispel her fears and let her mind be open to the truth. Give her peace, dear God. Let her come unto You and know the joy and contentment of being reconciled."

Assurance flooded Pierce's soul. This was good and right and exactly what he needed to do. Until the wee hours of the morning, Pierce continued to pray for Darlene and her father. It was as if a spiritual battle was raging somewhere and Darlene's soul was the prize. Pierce was not about to let go of her, and he knew that God would not let go of her either. Feeling a stillness within, Pierce collapsed into bed just as the horizon brought the first signs of morning light.

"I love her, God," he whispered, "but I give her to You."

Chapter 14

*For we know in part, and we prophesy in part. But when that which
is perfect is come, then that which is in part shall be done away.*
1 Corinthians 13:9–10

December came in with bitter cold and strong winter winds. Darlene found it impossible to keep the house warm, and in spite of her efforts, Abraham grew weaker. When he finally succumbed to his illness and remained in bed, Darlene knew that her worst fears were coming true. Somewhere, deep down inside, she knew that her father was dying.

She tried to busy herself so as not to think about such morbid things. She took what few orders she could get for suits and cut them herself, relying on the briefest of measurements lest she cross over the line of propriety by measuring the men herself. She was up before the light of day and still working long into the hours of the night. Cutting patterns out of heavy wool, stitching through thick layers until her fingers bled, and constantly worrying about her father. And through it all, her heart reflected on the words of her father and of Pierce. She thought of God's love and the hope that was found in the belief that Messiah would one day come and properly restore all things. If only Messiah would come now.

Every week when Sabbath came, she would light the candles and ask the blessing, but her heart sought something more. Her soul yearned to understand in fullness the mystery that eluded her. Sometimes when her father slept, she would creep in to sit by his side, and as she sat there she would pray for understanding. Once, she even picked up his Yiddish New Testament, a gift from Dennison Blackwell. Thumbing through the pages, she found a most intriguing passage in a section marked, "The First Letter of Paul the Apostle to the Corinthians." Chapter thirteen was all about love. The writer said, in his own way, that even if he were really good and had the best of intentions and kept the faith, but didn't have love, it was all for nothing.

Verse twelve caught her attention and stayed with her throughout the days that followed. "For now we see through a glass, darkly; but then face to face: now I know in part; but then shall I know even as also I am known." That's how she felt. Like she was seeing God and the world through a dark, smudgy glass. There were parts that seemed glorious and too wondrous to speak of. Like Messiah and God's ability to forgive. There were also parts that seemed clouded and vaguely open to understanding. Like eternity and Messiah's coming and whether her people had been wrong to reject Jesus.

Sitting as close to the kitchen stove as possible, Darlene worked at her sewing and allowed her thoughts to drift to Pierce. She hadn't seen him in weeks and she couldn't help but wonder if he'd already left for Chicago. He'd said that he loved her, but apparently there was nothing more he could say or do, for he'd never written or come back to say more. Perhaps it was just as well. They lived in two very different worlds.

Darlene tried to imagine him at home. No doubt the comfort of his wealth kept him from too seriously considering his love for a Jewess. Still, he had asked her to come west with him. He'd promised to help her and Tateh. A shop in Chicago! She tried to envision it. Pierce had said it could be as large as she liked. How wonderful it would be to plan out such a thing. She would make all the rooms on the ground floor so that her father wouldn't have to trudge up and down the stairs. She'd put their rooms at the very back and make it so that the shop could be completely closed away from the living quarters. And they'd have huge fireplaces and stoves to keep the building warm.

A loud knock sounded on the downstairs door, causing Darlene to nearly drop her scissors. She put aside her sewing and hurried down the stairs. *What if it's Pierce?* she wondered and smoothed back her hair with one hand while adjusting her shawl with the other.

She peered through the window shade and was surprised to find Esther standing on the other side. "Esther, it's freezing outside; you shouldn't have come out!" she chided.

"It was colder in the old country. I can bear a little cold," she said, hurrying through the door nevertheless. She held out a covered pot. "It's soup for your father. I've heard it said he is ill."

Darlene took the pot. "Yes, he is. He's bedridden and I'm afraid it will be a long, slow recovery. The doctor says he's sick with consumption."

"Feh!" Esther spat out in disgust. "He is sick because he has angered God!"

"How can you say such things?" Darlene asked angrily. "Did my father not provide for you when you had nothing?"

"It is true enough, but he had not forsaken the faith of his ancestors then. Now he has and God is punishing him for his waywardness. Mark my words, Darlene, you will fall into corruption and be lost as well. Don't think I haven't heard that you keep company with the *goyim*. You will be forever lost if you turn from God."

"I'm certain that is true," Darlene replied. "But neither I nor my father have done that." She paused and some of the anger left her. "Esther, have you never wondered about Messiah?"

"What's to wonder? Messiah will come one day and that will be that. Of course, we should live so long!" The wind picked up and played at the edges of their skirts.

Darlene shivered and she knew that Esther must be cold. "Do you want to come upstairs and talk?"

"No," Esther replied. "Rachel and Dvorah are helping me to make a quilt for Mrs. Meyer."

"And you didn't ask me to help?" Darlene tried not to show how hurt she was. She would no doubt have begged off anyway.

"It is better you decide your loyalties first. There's been a great deal of talk about you and Avrom. You should set yourselves right with God and seek His forgiveness. Then we will talk again."

"But my heart is right with God," Darlene protested. "I've done nothing wrong."

"You are the daughter of your father. Avrom's house is in danger because his heart is corrupt with *goyishe* reasonings. You must convince him to repent and then perhaps God will heal him of his afflictions. Don't forget about the sins of the fathers being revisited upon the children."

"And just what are you saying by that?"

Esther's forehead, already wrinkled with age, furrowed as she raised her snowy-white brows. "Only that you are close to corruption by staying here."

Darlene felt her temper dangerously close to exploding. Exhaustion was making her bold and unfearing. "Tateh has God's wisdom and a peace of soul that I have yet to find in our congregation. We say that Messiah will come and make all things right, and I'm telling you that Messiah may well have already come to try."

Esther put her hands to her ears. "I'll not listen to anymore. You're a *meschuggene* just like your father! Better you should leave him now!"

"No, I won't desert him like everyone else. It was good of you to bring him soup. I will bring you back the pot later tonight."

Esther seemed to have nothing more to say and quickly left the shop. Darlene took the soup upstairs, poured it into her own pot, then put it on the stove to keep warm. She went to check on her father and found him awake and seemingly better.

"Tateh, Esther has brought you some soup. Would you like some now?"

"No, just come and sit with me," he said in a weak voice. "I would tell you some things before it's too late."

"Shh, Tateh! Don't say such things."

Abraham tried to sit up, but he was too weak. Falling back against his pillow, he reached out a hand to Darlene. "Please hear me," he said, breaking into a fit of coughing.

She took his hand and sat down on the edge of his bed. He looked so very old and fragile now. Once her Tateh had been a pillar of strength and she looked to him for the courage she lacked. Now, she wished with all of her heart that something could be done to help him. But the doctor said there was nothing to be done. Nothing could help rid him of the consumption that seemed to ravage his lungs.

Darlene waited in silence, not moving so much as a muscle lest she cause him to cough even harder. He struggled for breath and finally the spell subsided. "I'm going to a better place," he said softly. "You must promise me that you will not be afraid."

Darlene knew better than to argue with him. "I promise," she said, wondering if she could really keep her word.

"And another promise," he whispered.

"What is it, Tateh?"

"Promise me that you will think about Jesus. I don't want to die knowing that you might forever be lost."

Tears came to her eyes as she hugged his hand to her face. "I can't bear for you to talk about death. I can't bear to think of life without you."

"Jesus is the true Messiah. I want very much for you to know that. Don't be afraid of the world and the things that would hide the truth from you." He began coughing anew and this time when the attack subsided, there was blood at the corners of his lips.

"I want to know that Jesus is truly the Messiah," she said. Tears fell upon his hand as she kissed it. "I don't want you to leave me."

"We'll never be parted again if you accept Jesus as your Atonement," he said in a voice filled with as much longing as Darlene felt in her heart.

"What must I do?"

Abraham's eyes seemed to spark with life for a brief moment. "You must only ask Him into your heart. Ask His forgiveness for your sins, and He will give it to you!"

Darlene thought of this for a moment. A peace filled her and she knew in an instant that it was the right thing to do. There was no image of Pierce or her dying father, or the ugliness of her friends and neighbors; there was only this growing sensation that this was the answer she had sought all along. Jesus would fill the void in her heart and take away her loneliness.

"Then let it be so," she whispered. "I want Jesus to be my Savior."

"*Baruch Ha-Shem,*" Abraham gasped and closed his eyes. "Blessed be The Name."

Darlene saw the expression of satisfaction that crossed her father's face. It was as if a mighty struggle had ceased to exist. Was this all that had kept him alive? Was this so important that he couldn't rest until he knew Darlene believed in Jesus?

Outside the wind howled fiercely and Darlene remembered that she needed to return Esther's pot. "Tateh, I must go to Esther's and take back her soup pot. I won't be gone but a minute."

"Wait until tomorrow," he said in a barely audible whisper.

"I think it might well snow before then and I'd rather not have to go out in it. I'll only be a few minutes and besides, no one will bother me. Ever since that day when Pierce and I were accosted by the rowdies, I've had the assurance of Willy and Sam that we'd be safe. They even keep an eye on the building in case anyone wants to vandalize it. I think they're the reason our so-called friends haven't broken any more windows in the shop."

Abraham drew a ragged breath and opened his eyes. "Then God go with you."

She leaned down and kissed his cold, dry forehead. "And with you."

Pausing at the door, Darlene kissed her hand and touched the *mezuzah.* The action was performed as a reminder of how she should always love God's Word and keep it in her heart. In that moment, it became more than an empty habit. In that moment, Darlene was filled with a sense of longing to know all of God's Words for His people. She glanced back at her father and felt a warmth of love for him and the Messiah she had finally come to recognize.

"Jesus." She whispered the name and smiled.

Chapter 15

And the world passeth away, and the lust thereof:
but he that doeth the will of God abideth for ever.
1 JOHN 2:17

Pierce sat with his shirt sleeves rolled up and his collar unbuttoned—a sure sign that he was hard at private work. Within the confines of his room, he couldn't help but wonder if he'd miss New York when the time came to leave. When in Europe, home had been all that he could think of. But then thoughts of Eugenia's demanding ways, his father's constant absences, and Constance being torn between the two adults she loved most in the world would dissolve any real homesickness. Perhaps it would be the same when he moved west to Chicago.

He looked at the latest letter he'd received from Chicago. He'd hired a well-respected contractor and was already the proud owner of a hotel. Well, at least the frame and foundation were in place. The five-story building was, as the letter put it, enclosed enough to allow indoor work during the harsh winter months. There would, of course, be a great deal of interior work to be done. Pierce remembered the blueprints with pride. The hotel would stand five stories high and have one hundred twenty rooms available for weary travelers. Located close to where packets of travelers were deposited off of Lake Michigan, Pierce knew his hotel would be the perfect moneymaker. And, with more than enough room to expand, Pierce had little doubt he could enlarge his establishment to house more than two and maybe even three hundred people.

Leaning back in his chair, Pierce tried to imagine the finished product. Brick with brass fixtures would make a regal first impression. Especially to that tired soul who longed for nothing more than a decent bed and perhaps a bath. There were also plans for a hotel restaurant, and Pierce had felt a tremendous sense of satisfaction when he'd managed to secure one of the finest New York chefs for his hotel. It had cost him triple what it would have cost to hire a less-experienced man, but Chef Louis de Maurier was considered a master of cuisine and Pierce knew his presence would only improve the hotel's reputation.

Of course, the fine imported oak and mahogany furniture he planned to ship would be a tremendous help as well. Each hotel room would be supplied with the very best. Oak beds with finely crafted mattresses. The best linens and fixtures money could buy would also draw the better-paying customer. He thought of how there would be many people who couldn't afford such luxury and immediately thoughts of a lower-priced, less-formal hotel began to formulate in his mind. He could build a quality hotel and supply it with articles that were sturdy and durable, but not quite as fine. Each room could have several beds and this way poorer folks could share expenses with several other people. He could charge by the bed, instead of by the room. *Chicago was going to be a real challenge,* he thought, and scratched out several of his ideas onto paper.

Then, as always happened during his daydreams, Pierce's mind conjured images of Darlene. He'd purposefully left her alone after suggesting she and her father come west. More importantly, he'd left her to consider that he loved her. He hadn't intended to tell her that, but there was a desperation in him that hoped such words just might turn the tide. If she knew how he felt, perhaps she would encourage her father to consider the trip to Chicago. And already, Pierce was prepared for just such a decision. He'd managed to locate a doctor whose desire it was to relocate to Chicago. For passage and meals, the man had agreed to travel with Pierce and act as private physician to Abraham Lewy. This way, Pierce was certain that Darlene could find no objections to the idea of going west.

He frowned as he thought of the stories he'd been told by his father. Stories of how Darlene's friends had turned away from the Lewy family. Stories of how Darlene was forced to sew what few orders she could obtain by herself. He tried not to think of her shoulders bent and weary from the tasks she bore. He tried, too, not to think of her face marred with worry over the health of her father, which Dennison had already told him had been considerably compromised by the cold winter weather.

I love her, Lord, he prayed. *I love her and want her to be my wife, but I won't go against You on this. If You would only turn her heart toward You and open her eyes to the need for salvation, I would happily take her as my wife and love her with all of my heart.*

"Pierce? Are you in there, Son?" Dennison Blackwell questioned.

"Yes, come in." Pierce yawned and straightened up.

Dennison opened the door. "I wondered if you would join me for coffee in the library. There are some things I think we should discuss."

"Things? Such as?"

"Such as Chicago and your insistence to cast away the world you know for the wilds of the West and what you do not know."

Dennison seemed so genuinely upset that Pierce instantly got to his feet. "I would be happy to put your mind at rest."

He followed his father down the hall and into the library, which stood at the top of the main staircase. Dennison closed the door and motioned Pierce to take a seat, while he himself began to pace.

"I know you're a grown man and have every right to the future of your choosing, but I cannot say that this idea of yours doesn't bother me. Chicago is hundreds of miles away and travel is precarious at best." He held up his hand lest Pierce offer any objections. "Yes, I know the Erie Canal is making travel to the Great Lakes much easier. I've even managed to obtain information on a variety of wagon trains and stagelines that go west."

"You've left out the possibility of taking a sailing vessel to New Orleans and then going up the Mississippi and across Illinois," Pierce said with a grin. "Oh, Father, you really shouldn't be so worried. I know this is where God is directing me to go. There's so much to be done and men of my standing, with the capital to back them, can not only make a huge fortune, but also benefit the masses who also are dreaming of a new start. Chicago has nearly four thousand residents and it is projected that by 1840 there will be twice that many people."

"That's all well and good, but. . ."

"Father, why don't you come west with me? We could build an empire! I still own a great deal of land in Chicago and we could develop it together."

Dennison smiled sadly at this. "I thought we were doing that here in New York."

"But I can't bear the snobbery of this town much longer. The prejudices are enough to drive me mad."

"And you think Chicago will be without its own form of prejudice?"

Pierce knew his father had a point. "I'm sure they do have prejudice, but they aren't formed around the tight little society that New York has made for itself. I've never known another town, with the exception of Boston, that holds its lofty council above all others and looks down its nose at those considered beneath it."

"Then you haven't looked very close," Dennison said with a smile. For some reason this seemed to put him at ease and he took a chair across from Pierce and poured a cup of steaming black coffee. "I've traveled to some of the same places you have. London. Paris. Munich. They all have their 'tight little societies' as you put it. You know as well as I do how laws have been passed in Germany to discriminate against the Jews. Some towns are even forbidden for them to live in, and others are denying them the right to own property and businesses. I'm telling you, Pierce, there is no place in this world that is without its own form of prejudice."

Pierce poured his own coffee and sighed. "I know you're right. It just seems a shame to watch people so divide themselves. Their greeds and lusts take over and they give little consideration for those who suffer."

"It was no different in Jesus' time. You must understand, Pierce, there will always be those who suffer injustices. All you can do is your very best to see that you aren't a part of it and that you render aid where you can."

"But don't you understand? That's what I'm trying to do now. In leaving New York, I leave behind their ways and their snobbery. I say to them, in essence, enough is enough and I will no longer be party to your corruption. And I am already prepared to render aid. I found a Jewish doctor who is a new Christian. He desires to go west and I have offered to pay his passage to Chicago in turn for his acting as private physician to Abraham Lewy."

"Abraham? He has agreed to go with you to Chicago?"

"No, but I'm certain that once I speak to him of the benefits he will want to go."

"And if he doesn't?"

Pierce shrugged and pushed back thick brown hair that had fallen onto his forehead. "I don't know. I guess I kind of figured if I made him an attractive offer, he'd naturally want to come along."

"And Darlene? Was she a part of the attractive offer?"

Pierce grinned. "Well, of course Darlene is included. I mentioned to her the idea and told her I'd help her father establish a new shop and home."

"And what did she say?" Dennison eyed his son quite seriously.

This question took some of the wind out of Pierce's sails. "She didn't think he'd want to go."

"I thought as much. You see, Abraham and I have often discussed the matter of moving west. Many of the Jews who came here over the last ten years have done so only with westward expansion in mind. They aren't comfortable in the large eastern cities, where people are cruel with hate and prejudice. They are more inclined to migrate west and form their own towns and societies. Abraham considered such a thing, but he was sure that his age was against him. Thinking he was too old, he settled here and found friends he could trust."

"But I want very much for them to know peace and to be accepted into the community. Now that Abraham is a Christian, surely people will take him in and treat him respectfully."

"They will always be Jewish by blood. They look like Jews, they sound like Jews, and they have Jewish names. People are going to know. Whether they worship in a synagogue or a church, people are going to think of them as Jews. And, you're forgetting one very important thing. Darlene is still of the Jewish faith."

"But it is my prayer that she'll come to know Christ."

"But until she does, Pierce, she is still very much separated from you in her beliefs. You have fallen in love with this woman, I know that. But I'm telling you that marriage to one such as her can only spell disaster for you both."

Pierce only frowned and sipped at the hot liquid in his cup. He felt the familiar resentment of wanting something that he knew he couldn't have.

"If you were to marry her without her having accepted Christ, who would perform the ceremony? A rabbi? A minister? Then, too, would you attend a church or a synagogue and when would you actually honor the Sabbath? On Saturday or Sunday? What happens, even if you both amicably decide to worship God your own way, when children come along? Will you raise them as Christians or as Jews? Can't you see, Pierce, there is no peace in a divided house. You cannot walk both paths and remain true to either one. You are a Christian. Your foundation for living is in the salvation you know in Christ. You base your beliefs on the Christian Bible and you know that the teachings there are absolute truth. To marry Darlene would be to cast off all that you know as right."

"But Darlene is only one small issue. Even men in the Bible married women of other cultures and nations."

"That's true. But Ahab married Jezebel when she was still an idolatress and it was a disaster. Samson fell in love with Delilah and it led him into tragedy."

"But what of Ruth the Moabitess?"

"Yes, she accepted the Jewish faith and culture and so became acceptable for Boaz to marry. Do you see Darlene giving up her faith and culture for you?"

Pierce put down the cup and shook his head. "I wouldn't want her to do it for me. I want her to know Jesus for herself. I want her to be saved because God has opened her eyes to the truth."

Dennison nodded. "I'm glad to hear you say that, because if she changes faiths for you, and not because God has so moved her heart, it will never take root and grow in her heart."

"I know," Pierce replied, and indeed he did know it full well. Wasn't it the same thing that had given his heart hours of frustration and grief? Wasn't it the very burden he had laid at his Savior's feet, begging for hope and a satisfactory solution?

"Are you completely certain that God is leading you to Chicago?"

Dennison's question hit a spot deep in Pierce's heart. "Yes. I feel certain."

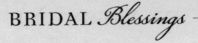

"How do you know for sure that it is right?"

Pierce sighed. "Because I have such peace about going. Even," he paused, "when I count what I must leave behind, I know that it is the right thing to do."

"And if those things left behind include Darlene Lewy?"

"I told God I'd leave her, too." Pierce looked up, his eyes filling strangely with tears. "Don't think it's easy for me to say these things. Don't think it's easy for me to leave you and Constance, either. But I know that I have to do it. I know this is right. I've prayed and considered the matter and always the answer is, 'Yes, go to Chicago.' I can't forsake what I know is God's will for my life."

"Nor would I ask you to," Dennison said, leaning forward to place his hand over his son's. "It won't be easy to let you go again, but if you are this convinced that God is leading you, then I must have peace in it and trust Him to know the way that is best. It won't be easy for me, either. It will be lonely here without you, and there will be a void that only you can fill. But, alas, children do grow up and find their own way. I'm gratified to know that you seek God's counsel. It makes me confident that I have done right by you."

"Of that you may be certain," Pierce replied, putting his hand in his father's. He squeezed it gently.

Outside, the wind died down a bit and as it did the sound of distant bells could be heard clanging out in the night. Fire was a common thing in New York and the fire departments were the best in the world. Each station had its own signals and this was clearly a signal for their own neighborhood.

Pierce jumped up and ran to the window, wondering if he could see where the fire might be. An eerie sensation ran through him and the hairs on the back of his neck stood up. Inky blackness shrouded the town and even the bit of moon overhead did nothing to light the darkness. His heart began to race faster with each clang of the bell.

"I can't see anything!" he declared.

"Perhaps Mack knows," Dennison suggested.

Three of the Blackwells' coachmen, including Mack, were volunteers with the neighborhood fire department, so Pierce lit out of the room on a dead run, hoping to hear some bit of news. For reasons beyond his understanding, he couldn't shake off the sensation that something was terribly wrong. It was more than the simple signal of the fire. Fires were commonplace things. Poorly built clapboard buildings and careless vagrants were well-known reasons for fires, not to mention those finer houses that went up when lamps were knocked over or fireplaces were left unattended. It was more than this and he had to know what it was that drove him to concern.

"Where's the fire?" he shouted, passing through the kitchen into the breezeway.

"Don't know," the cook answered in her brusque manner. "Nobody tells me anything."

Pierce felt the stinging cold bite at him through the thin material of his shirt. He went to the stable, refusing to turn back for a coat. "Where's the fire?" he asked again, this time to one of his remaining groomsmen.

"Lower end. Business district. They're calling out extra help because the Old Slip is up in flames and their department's hoses and pumps are frozen solid."

"The Old Slip? Are you certain?" Pierce's heart pounded in anticipation of the answer. Darlene and Abraham were less than two blocks up from the harbor and well within the Old Slip district.

"Aye, I'm certain. We had a rider come through afore the bells even sounded. Charlie and Mack grabbed up their gear and took off just as the signal came through. It's going to be a bad one."

"What about Ralph?" Pierce questioned, referring to the third Blackwell volunteer.

"He's in bed with a blow to the head. That new bay we bought got a bit out of control."

"Saddle my horse," Pierce said, ignoring the news about the injured man. "No, wait, a carriage! Get the landau ready and I'll drive it myself!" The groomsman stared at him in stunned silence. "Get to it, man! I'm going for my coat and I want it ready when I return. Oh, and throw in a stack of blankets."

Darlene! It was all he could think of. *Darlene and Abraham are in danger!*

He raced up the stairs, taking them two at a time. His father's concerned expression did nothing to slow him down. "It's the Old Slip," he called over his shoulder. "It's bad."

Nothing more needed to be said. Pierce knew that his father would understand his need to go. Dangers notwithstanding, Pierce had to find a way to get Darlene and Abraham to safety. His father would expect no less.

In his room he grabbed his frock coat and heavy woolen outer coat. Forgetting his top hat, he barely remembered to take his gloves and muffler.

"Bring them back here," his father said as he passed him in the hall.

"I will," Pierce replied and hurried off into the night. He had to find them. He had to save them. *Dear God, please don't let me be too late!*

Chapter 16

When thou passest through the waters, I will be with thee; and through
the rivers, they shall not overflow thee: when thou walkest through the fire,
thou shalt not be burned; neither shall the flame kindle upon thee.
Isaiah 43:2

After placing a kiss upon her sleeping father's forehead, Darlene secured her bonnet and did up the buttons of her coat. She felt a new peace and excitement that she couldn't put into words. She had accepted Jesus into her heart and the wonder of it consumed her. She felt giddy, almost like laughing out loud. What was it Pierce had told her? Something about having great joy in knowing a personal relationship with God. Was that why she felt so wonderful?

Grabbing up Esther's newly washed pot, Darlene hummed to herself, nearly skipping down the stairs. She felt so good! Her father had been very pleased with her choice and while she knew that pleasing him was important, it wasn't the reason she'd accepted Jesus as Messiah. No, God had done a work in her heart and she had come to Him in the full belief that there was more to life than laws and traditions.

She pulled the door to the shop closed and sniffed the air. There was a faint scent of wood smoke on the breeze, but on a night as cold as this, it wasn't unusual for the air to hang heavy with the smoke of coal and wood. She snuggled her face into the fur collar of her coat and hurried down the street to Esther's. She was already determined to share her new faith with Esther, even knowing that the old woman would call her a traitor and crazy. For reasons beyond what Darlene could understand, however, she knew that she had to try to make Esther see what Christianity was all about. It wasn't leaving the Jewish faith behind. It was fulfilling it in the Messiah they had always known would come.

In the distance she could hear the clang of the fire bells. *How sad,* she thought, *that someone would suffer through the cold of the night while fire consumed their home or shop.* She instantly asked God to put out the blaze and keep the unknown folks from harm. New York seemed always to suffer with fires and Darlene couldn't help but wonder if Pierce's Chicago would be any different.

Pierce! The very thought of Pierce Blackwell caused her to tremble. Always before she'd been hesitant to dream of the words he'd told her. "I love you," he'd said and Darlene had pushed them aside knowing that a Jew could never marry a Christian. *But now we share faith in Christ,* she thought, and a smile broke across her painfully cold face. Just as quickly as it had come, however, it faded. *I'm still poor and unworthy of his social standing. Nothing can change that.*

She knocked on the door of Esther's tiny house and waited for some reply. After several minutes of stomping her boots to keep her feet from freezing, Darlene was happy to see the old woman peek from behind her curtained window.

"Hava!" Esther exclaimed, opening the door, "You should not have come out. The pot could wait until tomorrow."

"I know," Darlene said, coming into the house. She waited for Esther to close the door and take the pot before continuing. "I wanted to talk to you for a moment. I wanted to apologize for my attitude earlier."

Esther had just returned from her kitchen and the look upon her face was one of surprise. "You have changed your mind? You will live with me now?"

Darlene shook her head. "No, I didn't change my mind about that. Look," she hesitated, knowing that her words would not be well received. "I know you've worried about Tateh ever since he accepted the Christian Jesus as Messiah, but Esther, there are things you do not know. Things that I myself do not know, but am trying hard to understand. Tateh told me that Jesus didn't come to cancel out the laws of Moses, but to fulfill them. He said if we do the things Jesus commanded, we will still be keeping the laws."

"Feh!" Esther said indignantly. "Jesus commanded! What right does He have to command anything?"

"Because He's Messiah. He's God's Son and God sent Him into the world to save us from our sins!"

"Oy vey!" Esther said and pulled at her hair. "You haven't allowed such talk to fill your head, have you?"

Darlene smiled. "No, it's filled my heart. Oh, Esther, you must listen to me." She reached out and held the old woman's hand. "I know how hard this is for you. It was hard for me as well. I listened to the things Tateh said, I worried about his standing in the community and whether or not his friends would desert him, but God's peace is upon him. You don't understand and I'm not very good at explaining it. Tateh is very sick, but he's not afraid. God has given him great peace through Jesus. And He's given me the same peace."

Esther's face registered understanding. "Get out of my house. You and your father are dead to me from this moment on." She jerked her hand away and opened the door.

Darlene moved to the door, but turned back. "Please, Esther. We've been good friends all these years."

Her pleading fell on deaf ears. It was just as it might have been months ago had someone tried to talk to her about Jesus. No, that wasn't true. Because the words Pierce and her father had shared caused Darlene to think and ponder them over and over. She had been angry about them and rejected them as truth, but she always listened and later reflected. All she could do was hope that Esther would do likewise.

"I'll go, but I'll also pray for you."

The clang of fire bells suddenly grew louder and from somewhere in the darkness came shouts and screaming. Darlene looked up and even Esther came outside to see what might be the problem. Gazing up one way, Darlene saw nothing but the occasional glow of lamplight shining through the windows and a street lamp here and there. Turning, however, to look down the street from where she'd only come moments before, Darlene cried out, putting her hand to her mouth at the sight of bright orange and yellow flames. The wharves were on fire!

"Tateh!" Darlene rushed down the street, mindless of Esther's cries that she not go. Her father would be in danger and far too weak to move even if he was aware of the fire. She ran as fast as her legs would carry her, but the cold had made her stiff and with each step her feet felt like a million pins and needles were pricking them.

She was appalled to see the flames grow brighter. The fire was less than a half block from her shop. The heat was already warming her and thick black smoke was choking out her breath. A crowd had started to gather on the street and Darlene was startled when a policeman grabbed her.

"There, there. You can't be going in!" he declared.

"I have to. My father is in there." She pointed to the building, now only a block away.

"You can't go in. Leave the rescues to the fire department. Besides, I'm sure your papa will have seen the fire by now and made his way out."

"No, you don't understand. He's very sick." She wrenched away from him, but saw he wasn't about to let her pass. Just then a group of rowdies could be seen down the block breaking out the glass window of a shop and stealing what they could take.

The policeman called out for them to halt, and the distraction was enough to allow Darlene time to slip down the alley and make her way to the back door of the shop. Thick smoke poured down the alleyway as though it were being sucked through the narrow channels by some unseen force. Darlene buried her face in the fur of her collar and felt her way along the buildings. Stumbling over trash and other abandoned articles, Darlene finally reached the shop and turned the handle. The door didn't budge. It was locked!

"Of course it's locked," she muttered. She pushed up against it, but it refused to give. She ran at it, thrusting her shoulder against the door, but while it bowed ever-so-slightly, it wouldn't give in and only managed to cause Darlene a great deal of pain. She would have to gain entrance by going through the front, but how?

The smoke was most caustic now and she began to cough. Her eyes were burning fiercely and she knew there was no time to waste. She would go back to the front and if anyone tried to stop her, she would fight them any way she could.

Retracing her steps, Darlene found that the crowd had grown larger and that the policeman was now moving them even further up the street. He had been joined by three other members of his profession and no one seemed to notice Darlene as she slipped through the shadows and into the shop.

Panting, she slammed the door shut behind her. Inside, the smoke was not as bad, and with the light of the flames growing ever brighter, Darlene didn't even need a lamp to make her way up the stairs.

Still coughing, she choked out her father's name and hurried up the steps. She thought to grab some of their most precious articles and instantly reached up to take the *mezuzah* from the kitchen door. She tucked this into her coat pocket and for some reason thought of Pierce's valentine. She ran to her room, but just then a tremendous boom rattled the very floorboards beneath her feet. It sounded like a building collapsing, and instantly Darlene forgot about gathering up anything else and went to get her father. She had already formed a plan in her mind. She would help him from the bed and once they were downstairs and outside she would call those ever-efficient policemen and get them to help her carry her father to safety.

"Tateh!" she exclaimed, hurrying into the room. "Tateh, there's a fire. It's got the entire Old Slip in flames. Come, we must hurry!" She pulled back the covers and went to get her father's coat.

Abraham remained silent and still. Darlene shook him hard. "Tateh, wake up."

And then, without waiting for any sign that he had heard her, Darlene suddenly knew that he was gone. "No!" she screamed into the smoky night air. "No!" She threw herself across his body and cradled him against her. "Don't die. Please don't die."

But it was too late. Abraham Lewy was dead.

The sound of bells and firemen mingled with breaking glass and the shouts of desperate people. There was no time for mourning, and though Darlene felt as though a part of her heart died with her father, self-preservation took over and she suddenly knew that she must hurry or perish in the fire.

Unable to consider leaving her father to be consumed by the flames, Darlene pulled his cover to the floor, then rolled his body off the bed and onto the cover. It wasn't an easy process, for even though her father had lost a great deal of weight, Darlene wasn't very big.

"Oh God," she prayed aloud, choking against the thickening smoke. "God, help me please. I believe You have watched over me this far. I believe you have taken Tateh to Your care, but I don't want to leave him here. Please help me!"

She struggled against the weight of her father and placed him in such a way that she could pull him along on the cover. How she would ever make it down the stairs without losing control of the body, she had no idea. But she was determined to try.

Pausing at the landing to draw her breath, Darlene screamed when hands reached out to close around her arm.

"It's me, Darlene."

"Pierce?"

"Yes, come on. I've got to get you to safety. Where's your father?"

"He's dead," she said, so matter-of-factly that it sounded unreal in her ears.

"Dead?"

"Yes, he's here on the floor. I have him on his cover and I was taking him out of the building." Her mind seemed unable to accept that Pierce had come. "Are you really here?" she asked suddenly.

Pierce laughed, but it was a very short, nervous laugh. "Yes, I'm really here. Now come on." He reached down and hoisted Abraham to his shoulder. "The building next door is already in flames. We'll have to hurry or we'll never get out in time." He coughed and gasped for air and this seemed to open Darlene's senses to the gravity of their situation.

"Hurry," she called over her shoulder, making her way down the stairs. She had just reached the bottom when the east wall of the shop burst into flames. It lit up the smoky room and instantly ate up the dry wood of the shelves.

"We'll have to go out the back way!" she yelled above the roar of the fire. Pierce nodded, and pushed her forward.

"Hurry up," he said. "Hurry or we'll die!"

Darlene pushed through the putrid smoke as if trying to cut a way through to the back room. There was no way to see in the smoke now, and suddenly she grew frightened wondering if Pierce was still behind her. There was no breath to be wasted on words, however, and all she could do was pray that God would allow them both to find their way.

Flailing her arms before her, Darlene finally hit the wall of the back room and then the door. She fumbled with the latch and slid back the lock. Pulling the door open only brought in more smoke and by now her head was growing light from the lack of oxygen. She felt dizzy and wondered if she could possibly make it another step. Slumping against the door frame, she was startled when Pierce pushed her through. He seemed to have the strength of ten men as he pulled her along the alleyway.

Hazy images filtered through Darlene's confusion. She knew they were in danger, but now, gasping for each breath, she couldn't imagine that anything mattered as much as fresh air. She wondered where they were going. Her mind played tricks on her and she became convinced that if she could just rest for a few moments, all would be well.

They had reached the front of the building and now the entire shop was in flames. Darlene still felt Pierce's iron-clad grip on her wrist, but her legs were growing leaden. She turned to see the walls of her home collapse and knew that the end of her world had come.

"My valentine!" she cried, suddenly trying to jerk away from Pierce.

"What?"

The air was only marginally better here, but Darlene felt her senses revitalized. "My valentine, the one you gave me!"

"I'll buy you a hundred others. You can't go back now; the place is completely destroyed." He pulled her along and made his way down the block to where he had hidden his buggy. *Thank you, God,* he offered in silent prayer. His one consuming worry had been that someone would find the landau and steal it for their own transportation.

Putting Abraham in the back, Pierce grabbed up several blankets and pulled Darlene to the driver's seat with him. He tucked blankets around them and then urged the nervous horses forward.

They made their way down the alley and side streets until they'd reached Wall Street. From here they could see the bright flames and eerie glow in the night sky, but the air was clean and only marginally scented with smoke.

"I don't even know if Esther made it out," Darlene suddenly murmured.

"But you're safe." Pierce put his arm around her shoulder and pulled her close. "I was so afraid I'd lose you."

Darlene looked up at him. The landau lantern swung lightly in the breeze, making a play of sending out shadowy light to fall back and forth across their faces. "My father is dead." She said it as though Pierce could possibly have forgotten.

"I know," he answered. "I'm so very sorry, Darlene." He pulled her closer and wrapped his arms around her very tightly.

Crowds of people were lining the streets and as some went running to help with the fire, others were struggling to carry possessions to safety.

"The fire's comin' this-a-way!" a man yelled out and encouraged people to flee.

"Nothing will be left," Darlene said softly. She lay her face against the coarse wool of Pierce's coat. "I have nothing now."

"You have me," he whispered. "You've always had me."

Chapter 17

*Wherefore he saith, Awake thou that sleepest,
and arise from the dead, and Christ shall give thee light.*
EPHESIANS 5:14

Darlene's first waking moment was filled with panic. She had no idea where she was and the thought filled her with a consuming urgency. Sitting up abruptly, she looked around the room and found nothing that she could recognize. Early dawn light filtered through the gossamer-like curtains and gave the room only a hint of the day to come.

Flowered wallpaper lined the walls and a very soft mauve carpet touched her feet when Darlene got off the bed. She hurried to the window and was greeted with the stark reality of a cold winter's day. The neighborhood, an avenue lined with leafless trees and shrubs, was elegant even in this setting. Black wrought-iron fencing hemmed in the yard, and beyond this Darlene could make out the brick street.

Then the memories of the night before flooded back into her mind. The fire. Her father's death. Pierce. She sank to her knees on the carpeted floor and wept. Everything was gone. All lost in the fire. Her father had died, succumbing to consumption, and now she was truly alone. She wrapped her arms around her and felt the soft folds of the nightgown. *It isn't even my gown,* she thought. The only thing left to her in the world were the clothes she'd worn out of the fire. And Pierce.

The last came as a tiny ember of thought. Pierce had said that she would always have him. But even that seemed lost and unlikely. How could he ever take her to be his wife? Especially now that she had nothing to offer him in the way of a dowry. The shop had burned to the ground, no doubt, and with it went every possible material article she could ever have offered a husband.

She cried even harder at this loss. Burying her face in her hands, she pulled her knees to her chest and thought of what she was going to do. It was all too much. She would have to bury her father, but even the idea of this caused her more misery than she could deal with. Who would perform the service? Her father was a Christian and would require a Christian burial, but she had no idea what that entailed. Who would prepare the body? The *hevra qaddish,* Jewish men from her community, would have normally prepared her father for burial and *Kaddish* would have been recited. Would anyone recite *Kaddish* over Abraham now? Would he have wanted them to? She was so confused.

Drying her eyes against the lacy edge of her sleeve, Darlene tried to remember if her father had ever made mention of such things.

Just then a light knock sounded upon the bedroom door. Getting to her feet, Darlene scrambled into the bed and pulled the covers high. "Come in," she called out and was surprised when Dennison Blackwell appeared.

"Are you up for a visitor?" he questioned.

She nodded, not really feeling like company, but knowing that this man had been her father's best friend in the world seemed to be reason enough to endure his visit.

He was dressed in a simple shirt and trousers. On his feet were slippers and a warm robe was tied loosely over his clothes to ward off the morning chill. "Forgive me for such an early visit, but I heard you crying and I felt compelled to come to offer you whatever comfort I could."

Darlene felt tears anew come to her eyes. "I tried very hard to be quiet," she said, snuffing back the tears.

"My dear, there is no need for that. Should you desire to cry down the very walls around you, you would be perfectly in your rights." He brought the vanity chair to her bedside and sat down wearily. "I am so very sorry about your father. He was my dearest friend and I will always feel the loss of his passing."

"He held you in very high regard," she replied, feeling the need to comfort him.

"And you?" Dennison said. "Are you going to be all right? Did you suffer any injuries during the fire?"

"I'm well," she said, feeling it was almost a lie. "I'm devastated by Tateh's death, but the fire did not harm me." *Other than to take everything I hold dear,* she thought silently.

"I thank God for that. When Pierce left here last night, all I could do was drop to my knees and pray. I feared for his safety, for yours and your father's, and I grieved for those I knew would be destroyed by the fire."

"I was so shocked when Pierce showed up that I could scarcely comprehend that he was really there. The smoke made my mind confused and incapable of clear thought and there was no way I could have carried Tateh to safety." She paused here, wiping away an escaping tear. "I couldn't let him be burned up in the flames. I knew he was already dead and I knew that he would be in Heaven with God." Dennison eyed her strangely for a moment, but she hurried on before he could speak. "I even knew that I would see him again, because he told me we would all be joined together in Heaven. But the pain of losing him and then the idea of leaving him to the fire, was just too much. I hope you don't think me terribly addle-brained."

"Not at all," Dennison murmured. His mind was clearly absorbed and this concerned Darlene.

"I don't know how to ask you this," she struggled for words. "I mean. . . well you see. . ."

"What is it, child?" he said, suddenly appearing not at all preoccupied. He reached out to pat her reassuringly. "You have only to name your request."

"It's my father's burial. You see, I have no idea what should take place, and I have no money. Everything was lost in the fire."

Dennison smiled. "You have nothing to worry about. I will see to everything and I insist on paying for the funeral myself. This will be one thing I can do in Abraham's memory and honor. I will see to it all." He paused, his face sobering. "But tell me, my dear, will you be grieved by the Christian service? Should I also plan for some type of service in your Jewish faith?"

Darlene shook her head. "I'm no longer of that faith. At least not like I was. Tateh said that Jesus is the fulfillment of our Jewish faith, but I'm still very new at this."

"Are you saying that you've accepted Jesus as your Savior?"

"Yes. Last night, before Tateh died. We talked and I felt such a peace. I know my friends would say that losing Tateh and everything I had on earth is my just punishment for forsaking the faith of my fathers, but I don't believe that. I don't know why, but I still have a peace inside that the fire didn't consume. Does that make sense?"

Dennison's face seemed filled with light. "It makes wonderful sense. I'm so very pleased to hear about your acceptance of Christ. Oh, Darlene, how happy your father must have been. He could die in blessed assurance of seeing you again in Heaven. It must have given him a great deal of peace."

"Yes, I believe it gave him the peace to die. At first, I was angry and very sad, but I lay here thinking last night that Tateh wouldn't want me to grieve. He would want me to trust God and not be angry that God took him from me."

"That's very wise coming from one so young."

Darlene swallowed hard and tried to smile. "I can't repay you for what you've done. At least, not yet. I don't know where I'll go or what I'll do. My Jewish friends will have nothing to do with me now that they know I believe in Jesus as Messiah."

"You've told them already?"

"I told Esther last night and that's as good as telling them all." This did make her smile and Dennison couldn't help but grin in a way that reminded her of Pierce. "They'll believe me to be a traitor and so I'll be an outcast."

"It won't be easy to face such a thing."

"Oh, I don't think I'll go back," Darlene said in a thoughtful way. "I don't know what I'll do just yet, but the old neighborhood is behind me now. I'm sure there's very little left after the fire, anyway."

"Well, that much is true. They're still trying to put out the flames. I'm afraid it burned all the way up to Wall Street and consumed most everything in its path."

Darlene nodded. "Somehow, I thought it would be that way." She squared her shoulders. "But God will provide, right?"

"Of course!" Dennison said and patted her hand again. "He already has. You are welcome to stay here for as long as you like. We've plenty of room and I know Pierce will be very happy to have your company here."

Darlene felt her cheeks grow warm. "I'm very thankful he came to us last night."

"As am I. Does he know about your new faith?"

Darlene shook her head. "No. There was no time to speak of such things and all I could really think about was Tateh being dead."

"He's going to be delighted," Dennison said with a huge smile. "I think it will be an answer to his many prayers concerning you."

"Concerning me?"

"You sound surprised. Surely you know he has deep feelings for you."

Her face grew even hotter. How could she explain that Pierce's feelings couldn't possibly be as strong as her own? Then, too, how could she speak to this man, his father, of the love she felt for his son? The Blackwells were rich and quite esteemed in society; surely Dennison Blackwell would not want to hear of her love.

"I see I've embarrassed you. Not to worry, I won't say another word. But you should tell Pierce of your acceptance of Jesus at the first possible moment. It will probably answer a great many questions for you." With these mystic words he rose to his feet. "I will leave you to rest. You are not to get up from that bed for at least two days. Doctor's orders."

"What doctor?" Darlene questioned in confusion.

Dennison shrugged. "Doctor Blackwell," he said with a laugh. "A poor excuse for a physician if ever there was one, but nevertheless, I insist. I may not be a doctor, but I know that you've endured far too much for your own good. Two days of bed rest and pampering and you'll feel like a new person."

"Mr. Blackwell?"

"Yes?"

"Thank you for being so kind. You and Pierce have both been so generous. I know that my father came to an understanding of Jesus through you."

"You are most welcome, my dear."

"Would you extend my thanks to Pierce? Tell him that his prayers were answered."

Dennison looked confused. "You want me to tell him that you have found Jesus for yourself? Don't you want to wait and tell him yourself?"

"I think he will take great peace of mind from it and since he's partially responsible, I think he should know as soon as possible. Do you mind?" she asked, suddenly concerned that she'd expected too much.

"Not at all," he said in a fatherly way that implied great pride. "It shall be my honor."

He left her with that, and Darlene relaxed back against the pillows. Her heart felt much lighter for the sharing of her concerns. Mr. Blackwell said that she could remain in his home for as long as she liked. This gave her great comfort, and that he would tell Pierce that Darlene was now a Christian. She yawned and snuggled down into the warmth of the bed. She tried to imagine Pierce's reaction, but before she could consider anything else, her eyelids grew very heavy and finally closed in sleep.

∞

Several hours later, Darlene awoke to the sound of someone puttering around her room. Groggily opening her eyes and forcing herself to sit up, she found a young woman in a starched white apron and high-collared black work dress standing at the foot of her bed.

"Good morning, ma'am. I'm Bridgett. I've brought your breakfast. Mr. Blackwell said to remind you that you're not to set foot out of the bed, except for the hot bath I'm to draw for you after you eat."

A hot bath? Darlene thought. But Tateh had only died the night before! Did these *goyim* have no sense of propriety? How could she indulge in such comforts during the mourning period? Then it suddenly hit her. Perhaps bathing in such circumstances was a Christian tradition. *Oy vey!* but there was so much to learn.

Darlene smiled weakly. Bridgett's immaculately ordered red hair caused her to smooth back her own tangled curls. "I'm a frightful mess," she declared.

Bridgett made no comment, but instead brought Darlene breakfast on a lovely white wicker bed tray. Poached eggs, toast and jam, and three strips of bacon were neatly arranged on a delicately patterned china plate. Beside this was an ornate set of silverware, a linen napkin, and a steaming cup of tea.

"Thank you," she said, but the girl only bobbed a curtsey and took herself off through a side door.

Darlene looked at the breakfast and almost laughed out loud at the bacon. *Oy vey!* but what would Esther say? She wondered how it was with Christians and how she would ever learn the right and wrong thing to do. Were there things that Christians didn't eat? Studying the plate a moment longer, Darlene decided against the bacon.

The toast and jam were safe enough and it was this that she immediately began to eat on. Gone was the headache of the night before and the only reminder was the heavy smell of smoke on her body and in her hair.

When the maid returned, Darlene had finished her tea and toast and set the tray aside.

"The bath is in here, ma'am."

Darlene stared after Bridgett and finally followed her. She found herself in a charmingly arranged room. A huge tub of steaming water awaited her and beside it was a tray with a variety of bath salts and scented soaps. On the other side stood a lovely vanity with so many lotions and powders that Darlene couldn't imagine ever using them all.

"I'll take your gown, ma'am," Bridgett said, obviously waiting for Darlene to disrobe.

Feeling rather self-conscious, both because of the stranger and the finery around her, Darlene hesitated. Thinking of the *mikveh*, the ritual bath used by Jewish women for cleansing before marriage, and after childbirth or menstruation, Darlene no longer felt shy. The *mikveh* required that her body be inspected before immersion and therefore it was far more personal. Bridgett merely wanted to take the gown away and leave her to privacy of her bath.

"Do your people bathe during times of mourning?" Darlene asked hesitantly.

Bridgett's expression contorted. "My people?"

Darlene twisted her hands anxiously and rephrased her question. "Do Christians take baths. . .well, that is to say. . .is it all right to take a bath after a loved one has died?"

Bridgett looked at her strangely for a moment. "They take a bath whenever it suits them. Cleanliness is next to godliness or so my mother says."

Darlene nodded, feeling torn between old traditions and new. Well, she'd put aside the bacon, so perhaps accepting the bath wasn't too bad. After all, Bridgett said it was perfectly acceptable. Slipping out of the gown, she handed it to the maid and stepped into the tub.

Darlene sank into the hot water with a grateful smile on her face. She let the water come over her shoulders and finally dipped her head below and enjoyed the sensation of warmth. She was at peace and her heart, though heavy for the passing of her father, was not worried. She allowed her mind to think of Abraham and of the happiness he'd had in knowing that she'd found Jesus. It was the most important decision she could ever make, he'd told her once. And now she knew for herself that it was.

After her bath, Bridgett reappeared with a fresh gown of soft-pink lawn and a robe to match. After helping Darlene dress, Bridgett took her to a chair beside the fireplace and proceeded to dry her long wet hair. Darlene had never known such care and thoroughly enjoyed the pampering. It wasn't long before Bridgett had the long, tangled mess dry and brushed to a shining, orderly fashion. They agreed to leave it down before Bridgett led Darlene back to bed, where fresh linens and covers replaced the smoke-scented ones from the night before.

She'd barely gotten back into bed when the door was flung open and Eugenia Blackwell swept into the room.

"That's enough, Bridgett. You may go," she said in her haughty, superior way.

Bridgett bobbed again and hurried from the room, taking Darlene's towels with her. Eugenia frowned at her for a moment, leaving Darlene to feel rather intimidated. She thought perhaps she should say something, but couldn't imagine what it might be.

"Well, I see you have composed yourself," Eugenia said, staring down at Darlene.

"Yes, you've all been very kind to help me." *There,* thought Darlene. *I've said something complimentary and surely she'll realize I only mean to be a congenial guest.*

"Yes, of course. But then, what else could we do? It wasn't as if we had a choice."

Darlene frowned. "Mr. Blackwell assured me it was no trouble."

"But he would say that, my dear. That's how it is done in proper society."

Darlene cringed inside at the coldness in her voice. It was clearly evident that Eugenia did not share her brother's hospitality toward Darlene.

"May I be frank with you?" Eugenia suddenly asked.

This surprised Darlene, who thought Eugenia had done quite a complete job of that up till now, without seeking anything closely resembling permission. "Of course," she finally managed to say.

Eugenia took up the chair vacated earlier by her brother. Sitting across from Darlene, she maintained her rigid, austere posture and frowned. "You must understand that what I am about to say should remain strictly confidential." Darlene nodded and Eugenia continued. "I am, of course, quite sorry to learn of your father's death. However, your presence in this house creates a bit of a problem for us. I find my nephew easily confused by you and because of this he has begun to question the things that should matter most in his life."

"I don't know what you're talking about," Darlene said in complete confusion.

"But I'm sure you do," she replied rather snidely. "Pierce fancies himself in love with you. Whether or not he's mentioned this to you is of little concern to me. Eventually he will come to his senses and you will be forgotten. Pierce will marry Amanda Ralston, a woman chosen for him by his father and myself. Amanda is of a proper New York family and can offer Pierce much by their marriage." Darlene felt as though Eugenia had actually struck her a blow. "You, my dear, simply cannot be so heartless as to want Pierce to give up the things that make him happiest."

"Certainly not."

Eugenia smiled rather stiffly. "I'm glad to hear you say it. Therefore, you will understand when I say, also, that you cannot remain in this house. Pierce will continue to be confused by you and I'm afraid that if you remain, his father will have no other choice but to cut him off entirely. This would be a grave tragedy."

"But, I thought, well. . ." Darlene fell silent. She wasn't about to try to explain her thoughts to Eugenia Blackwell Morgan. The woman obviously could not care less that her words had pierced Darlene through to the soul.

"The kindest thing you can do is to leave as soon as possible. Don't make a scene and don't even say goodbye. I will give you assistance in reaching whatever destination you like."

"But I have no one now and Mr. Blackwell is arranging my father's funeral. I certainly can't just walk away from that."

"I suppose you are right," Eugenia said, as if only considering this for the first time. "After the funeral then. I will come to you and supply you with the proper funds. You can take yourself to a hotel until you find somewhere to board permanently." She got to her feet, acting as though the matter was entirely resolved. "You can only mean disaster to Pierce, and if you care at all about his well-being, you will go as soon as possible and give him nothing more to dwell on."

Darlene wanted to scream at her to mind her own business, but frankly the shock of Eugenia's forward nature was more than enough to silence her. She was still staring at the chair Eugenia had just vacated when a loud knock on her bedroom door signaled yet another visitor.

"Come in."

Pierce burst through the door with a huge smile on his face. "Father just told me your news. Darlene, I'm overwhelmed." He paused for a moment as though stricken by her appearance. "You are so beautiful!" he declared.

Darlene tried to smile, but Eugenia's words came back to haunt her. Perhaps she was bad for Pierce and perhaps her love for him would spell disaster if left unchecked.

Pierce crossed the room and took hold of her hands. Raising each one to his lips he kissed first one and then the other. "I'm very happy that you've accepted Jesus as your Savior. I can't begin to tell you how I've prayed for this very thing."

"I know," she whispered. "I remember you said you would pray for me to know the truth. Before Tateh died, he helped me see that truth for myself."

Pierce pulled up the chair so that it touched the side of the bed. "I can't tell you how sorry I am that he's gone. I wanted so much for you and your father to come west with me. I even secured a physician to travel with us. He's a man of your own people who also believes in Jesus."

The idea that Pierce would do this for her father deeply touched Darlene. "How very kind."

"I suppose I had my motives," he grinned. "I wanted to leave no stone unturned, so to speak. I wanted there to be no arguments, nothing that would stand in the way of your coming along. Now that he's dead, I realize you will feel his loss very profoundly, but I know, too, that you need to make decisions about your own future. A future I hope will include me."

Darlene lowered her face and looked at her hands. Eugenia's cold eyes and haughty stare seemed to be all that she could think of.

"I know this is a bit overwhelming, and I won't say another word on the matter until after the funeral. I just want you to have heart and be assured that you needn't worry for tomorrow." He leaned over and surprised her by kissing her gently on the cheek. "I still love you."

He left without expecting any reply and Darlene could feel her cheek burning where his lips had touched it. *He loves me, but I'm no good for him.* She fell back against the pillows and at once wished more than ever that her father could be there to advise her. *Pray,* an inner voice seemed to whisper. *Pray to your Heavenly Father and He will advise you.* This thought gave her peace. Perhaps God would show her what to do.

Chapter 18

And the LORD God said, It is not good that the man should be alone;
I will make him an help meet for him.
GENESIS 2:18

Darlene reflected on her father's funeral in the silence of her bedroom. The Christian funeral had been quiet and simple and very comforting. The minister had spoken of a day when all things would be passed away and the resurrection of those in Christ Jesus would take place. She tried to imagine what a reunion it would be and how very happy her father would be to see her again, and how he wouldn't be sad or sick.

She looked down at her sober gray gown. Eugenia had insisted that black would be more appropriate, but this was a dress borrowed from Constance and Darlene didn't want anyone to go to the expense of dying it black and making it unusable to the young girl again.

"Borrowed clothes and somebody else's room," she muttered to the walls, "that's all I have left." Well, that wasn't entirely true. Dennison had told her of a small insurance policy that her father had taken on the shop. It seemed that the policy was protection against fires and would allow, in cases of complete destruction, a small amount of money for rebuilding. He had promised to see to the situation in a few days and to take care of all the necessary paperwork. Darlene was relieved, even if it only amounted to several hundred dollars. It would give her enough money to take care of herself for a while and it would allow her more freedom to decide her future.

She went to the window and stared out on the false spring day. For all appearances it would seem spring was just around the corner, but she knew better. They all did. Sometimes fair weather came in the middle of winter, just like this. It would lull you into a false sense of security and then render you helpless in a blizzard or ice storm. Maybe that's what she was allowing to happen to her in regards to the insurance money. Was she being lulled into a false sense of security by placing her values in monetary needs? Tateh had said, "God will provide." And of course, He always did. So why should she fret so now, and seek all manner of solutions, all of which had nothing to do with God?

"Oh God," she whispered the prayer, "I'm afraid and I don't know very much about how to follow Jesus. I need help and I don't know where else to turn, but to You. You've always been there and Tateh said You were the same God of my childhood, that You are now of my adulthood. Tateh said You would never fail and never desert me and that I could come to You with all of my hopes and fears and You would take care of my needs." She saw the empty branches of the trees rustle slightly in the breeze. "I need You, God. I need to know what I must do and where I should go. I love Pierce so much, but I know that his aunt is right. I can never be the wife he needs. Please help me."

She felt so torn apart. Tateh was gone and Pierce soon would be. She had no idea where to go or what to do, and she wanted so much to please God and be brave.

"I'll never be good enough," she said with a sigh, and then the words of the minister came to mind. At Abraham's funeral, he had said that no one was saved because they were good enough. He said they were saved by grace and that one need only have faith in that grace in order to find their way to God.

"I can have faith," she whispered and the words gave her heart strength. "I can have faith. I might have no answers and very little money, but faith is the one thing I can surely dig up from within." She smiled and knew that if Tateh were here, he'd be quite pleased with her.

The door to her room opened abruptly and Darlene knew without turning around that it would be Eugenia. She was the only one bold enough to simply enter the room without knocking.

"I see you haven't yet changed back into your own clothes," Eugenia announced. "Well, I suppose there is still time."

Darlene looked at her, but said nothing.

"I've brought you enough money to keep yourself in decent style until you can find a job or other friends to take you in." Eugenia tossed a small cloth bag onto the bed.

"I don't want your money, Mrs. Morgan."

"Nonsense. You will take it and I will have the carriage ready to take you wherever you might instruct him to go. I think it would be best if you were to make your departure before the evening meal. Any delay you make will only create further problems."

"But Mr. Blackwell is handling my affairs and..."

"You are no good for this family and even worse for Pierce."

"I would disagree with you, Madam," Pierce said, entering the open door without warning. "I believe quite the contrary. Miss Lewy is excellent for me and I intend to see that she never gets away from me. Now, stop interfering and leave us to talk."

Eugenia was stunned by his comeuppance. "How dare you speak to me like that?"

Pierce put a protective arm around Darlene's shoulders. "You've stuck your nose into my business one too many times, Aunt. Father and I have already discussed Darlene's future and I have great plans for her."

"But this is nonsense," Eugenia stated firmly. "You must marry a woman of means and one with a social bearing that matches your own. You cannot dally with this little Jewess and expect your future to know anything but heartache. I have already spoken with Amanda and she assures me that she'll take you back, no questions asked."

"As I said earlier," Pierce replied, his voice rather cold and unemotional, "you are interfering where no one wants you and I won't tolerate your attitude toward Darlene any longer. Either see your way fit to treat her with respect, or leave." He dropped his hold on Darlene and stepped forward as if to create a barrier between Darlene and his aunt.

"Well!" Eugenia declared and left without another word.

Pierce turned. "It seems I am ever saving you from runaway freighters or burning buildings or destructive old women," he said with a smile. "I'm sorry for Eugenia's attitude. I promise you that she doesn't speak for me or for my family."

Darlene sobered a bit. "She's right though. I don't fit into your world."

Pierce laughed. "So what? I don't fit into my world. I despise the rhetoric and snobbery. I've long planned to leave it, as you well know. There's only been one thing stopping me."

"What?"

"You," he said softly.

Darlene looked up into his face and felt her protests melt away. His dark eyes seemed to drink her in and his face beckoned her touch. Denying herself no longer, Darlene reached a hand to his cheek and found his hand quickly covering hers to hold it in place.

"I love you," he said.

Darlene knew her moment of truth had come. She lowered her gaze. "I love you," she whispered in a barely audible tone.

"What was that?" He lifted her chin with his free hand. His eyes sparkled with amusement. "I couldn't quite hear you."

"I love you," she stated quite frankly. "Although I've tried not to."

"But why?" He sounded almost hurt.

Darlene shook her head. "Right now, I can't think of one reason."

"I'm serious. If there's something I should know. . ."

She put her finger to his lips and felt a current of excitement coarse through her. "I thought you should marry someone of your own standing. I can never serve proper teas in proper parlors and I will never be accepted by your society friends. To them a Jew is a Jew is a Jew, whether he believes in Jesus or not."

Pierce pulled her tightly into his arms. "I'm not marrying my society friends, nor do I care one whit what they think. God knows our hearts, Darlene. He has brought us together and brought you to an understanding of His Son Jesus. Do you suppose He would desert us now?"

Darlene melted against him, feeling such a strange sensation of emotion. She truly did love him, but she loved him enough that she couldn't bear the thought of saddling him with an improper wife. "But what of Chicago?"

"What of it? I plan to go there and build us a new life. I will build you the finest house ever seen that far west and people will come from miles around and say, 'Look what that man did out of love for his wife!'"

"Oh, Pierce, be serious."

"I am. I want to spend the rest of my life showing you just how serious I am," he said in a low, husky tone that put goosebumps on Darlene's arms. "I want you for my wife. I've wanted it since last year when I came for my Valentine's suit. Remember?"

"I couldn't forget. I lost my valentine in the fire," she said sadly. "It was quite precious to me because I knew, even though you'd not signed it, that it was from you."

"Marry me," Pierce whispered against her ear. He kissed her lightly upon her hair, then her cheek, and finally her lips. Hovering there, he whispered again. "Marry me and be my valentine forever."

"But. . ."

He silenced her with his lips in a passionate kiss and when he pulled away, Darlene smiled. "I suppose I should give in on your ability to kiss alone, but I won't." Pierce frowned and she continued. "You must consider that people in Chicago might well not like you being married to a Jewess. You have to think about this because it might well ruin your reputation and end your prosperity. *Di libe iz zis —nor zi iz gut mit broyt.*"

"And what's that supposed to mean?"

"Love is sweet—but it's better with bread. In other words, love won't put bread on the table and it won't fill your belly when you're hungry. If people in Chicago should act harshly toward you because of me, it won't matter how much we love each other."

"Nonsense," Pierce said, holding her close. "You will be Mrs. Pierce Blackwell and your beauty and graciousness will win them all over. Now, stop putting me off and say yes."

Darlene grinned and nodded with a sigh. "Yes." It seemed so right and in her heart she knew that God had answered the prayer she'd pleaded only moments before.

Epilogue

Darlene flushed at the passionate kiss Pierce placed upon her lips. The minister cleared his throat and both Dennison and Constance Blackwell could be heard to chuckle. When he pulled away, Darlene shook her head and smiled.

"I present the happy couple, Mr. and Mrs. Pierce Blackwell," the minister announced.

"Oh, Pierce!" Constance said, coming to hug her big brother. "I'm so happy for you! How wonderful to get married on Valentine's Day!"

"He only did that so he could avoid going to the bachelor ball again," Dennison teased then added, "My dear, you are a radiant bride. Welcome to our family." He kissed her lightly on the cheek and hugged her gently.

"Thank you," Darlene whispered. "Thank you for everything."

Eugenia Blackwell Morgan's absence from the wedding did nothing to spoil the fun. The house staff laid out a wonderful wedding breakfast and everyone gorged themselves until they could hold no more. Pierce had worried that Darlene would regret such a small wedding, but she assured him over and over that it was only important that he be there, whether the rest of the world showed up or not.

When evening came and the couple made their way to the privacy of their first bedroom as man and wife, Darlene felt an uneasy nervous flutter in her stomach and trembled when Pierce lifted her to carry her across the threshold.

"I love you," he said, gently putting her down again. "I will always love only you."

Darlene's nerves instantly settled. She stared up into the face of her husband and smiled. "And I love you and so long as I live, you'll be my only valentine."

"That reminds me," Pierce said. He went to the large bureau and pulled open a drawer. Fishing out an envelope, he brought it to her and grinned. "Happy Valentine's Day."

"But I didn't get you anything," she protested.

He nuzzled her neck with a kiss. "I'm sure we'll work that out."

She blushed, feeling her face grow hot. Concentrating on opening the card, she found it to be an identical replica of the one she'd lost in the fire. But this time it was signed as well.

"To Darlene, my darling wife, with all my love, Pierce," she read and tears came instantly to her eyes. She looked up at him and saw the tenderness in his expression and knew that God had done a wonderful thing in her life. Stepping into his arms once again, she thought of the future and the hope that lay before them. It was good to know that they would face it together. It was good to know they'd have God to guide their way.

"Thank you for my Valentine," she said, pulling away. "I'll cherish it always." She turned to place it on the bureau, but Pierce reached out and pulled her back with a deep, mischievous laugh.

"I'm not letting you get away," he said. Then, grinning in a roguish manner, he pulled loose the ribbon from her hair and whispered, "Now, about my Valentine..."

Tracie Peterson, bestselling, award-winning author of over ninety fiction titles and three non-fiction books, lives and writes in Belgrade, Montana. As a Christian, wife, mother, writer, editor, and speaker (in that order), Tracie finds her slate quite full.

Published in magazines and Sunday school take home papers, as well as a columnist for a Christian newspaper, Tracie now focuses her attention on novels. After signing her first contract with Barbour Publishing in 1992, her novel, *A Place To Belong*, appeared in 1993 and the rest is history. She has over twenty-six titles with Heartsong Presents' book club (many of which have been repackaged) and stories in six separate anthologies from Barbour. From Bethany House Publishing, Tracie has multiple historical three-book series as well as many stand-alone contemporary women's fiction stories and two non-fiction titles. Other titles include two historical series co-written with Judith Pella, one historical series co-written with James Scott Bell, and multiple historical series co-written with Judith Miller.

Voted favorite author for 1995, 1996, and 1997 by the Heartsong Presents' readership, and awarded Affaire de Coeur's Inspirational Romance of the Year 1994, Romantic Times 2007 Career Achievement, American Christian Fiction Writers Lifetime Achievement 2011 and other awards, Tracie enjoys the pleasure of spinning stories for readers and thanks God for the imagination He's given. She desires that the books would Entertain, Educate, and Encourage—Tracie's three E's.

"I find myself blessed to be able to work at a job I love. I get to travel, study history, spin yarns, spend time with my family and hopefully glorify God. I can't imagine a more perfect arrangement."

Tracie was the managing editor of Heartsong Presents for Barbour Publishing for over three years and helped with acquisitions prior to that. She co-founded the American Christian Fiction Writer's organization in 2000 and continues to work with new authors, teaching at a variety of conferences, giving workshops on inspirational romance, historical research, and anything else that offers assistance to fellow writers. She often speaks at women's retreats and church functions. Her website is www.traciepeterson.com

HOPEFUL
Hearts

**Two Historical Romances
of Following Dreams to Love**

by Diann Hunt